Former boxer  Oliver's life is a mess. What was precious to him is dead, and he can sink no lower. Or can he? He will find out when, to avoid being destitute, a friend wants him to commit a robbery.

Ray Oliver becomes a lawyer, forsaking a promising boxing career and his mentor, Vinnie Sardi. He becomes an attorney at a prestigious law firm. Ray is falsely accused of mishandling a client's money. His job is in jeopardy. At a gambling casino, drunk, he argues with and punches a patron. The patron presses assault charges and sues. Criminal prosecution and disbarment are strong possibilities. Ray is contacted by his friend Sardi whom offers him an opportunity to make money. It involves a robbery. Ray, destitute and without alternatives, considers the offer.

After inviting the police officers inside, Stephens said, "What can I do for you?"

"Well, actually a couple of things," Kearse said...and almost as an afterthought, "that picture on the TV...is that your wife and kids?

"Yeah, my son's eight and my daughter is ten."
"Nice looking kids...in school now?"

"Yeah, they won't be home for a couple of hours. Why?"

"Ah, just idle curiosity...your wife...out shopping? Mine makes it an afternoon ritual...almost every day. I suppose she's

believes she's helping the economy, but on a policeman's salary...hey..." and he gave a kind of hopeless smile.

Stevens nodded, "Yeah, a little food shopping and pick up the kids. She just left. She'd probably liked to have met you. You're the first officers that have ever been to our house."

"Well, what we have to do won't take long...ya know, your wife looks like a pretty hot number. Any good in bed?

"Wha...what? What do you mean? Stevens jumped to his feet, apparently recovered in full. "There's something wrong here..." and then the realization, *"you're not cops."* But it was too late. They had jumped up and were at his sides.

They grabbed him by his arms, shook him like a stuffed toy, and manhandled him into the kitchen. Kearse grabbed Stevens by the left elbow and plunged his hand down the disposal, holding it there. Partlow reached over and put his finger on the switch.

"Devilishly Clever, a compelling story of intrigue."—**Dr. Scott Friedman D.O., Lake Orion, MI**

"In just a few pages, I found the story like the teasers for the breaking news at six. Something one doesn't want to miss."—**Richard G. Gurley, Detroit Police Sergeant (Retired), Ann Arbor, MI**

"Characters are real and intriguing, seems you witness their actions rather than reading about them."—**Michael Neymanowski, Chief of Police (Retired), Oxford, MI**

OLIVER TWISTED AND TURNED

JAMES JAY THOMAS

Moonshine Cove Publishing, LLC
Abbeville, South Carolina U.S.A.
Copyright © 2019 by James Thomas

This book is a work of fiction. Names, characters, places and incidents are products of the author's imagination or are used fictitiously. Any resemblance to actual events, locales or persons, living or dead, is entirely coincidental.

ISBN: 978-1-945181-63-4
Library of Congress PCN: 2019906434

All rights reserved. No part of this book may be reproduced in whole or in part without written permission from the publisher except by reviewers who may quote brief excerpts in connection with a review in a newspaper, magazine or electronic publication; nor may any part of this book be reproduced, stored in a retrieval system or transmitted in any form or by any means electronic, mechanical, photocopying, recording or any other means, without written permission from the publisher.

Front cover images public domain; cover and interior design by Moonshine Cove staff.

Acknowledgment

My wife Barbara for her proof reading and selflessly relinquishing personal time that we otherwise would have shared while this book was a work in progress.

My daughter, Jen , for her expertise in constructing my website and offering much needed advice.

To publisher Gene D. Robinson of Moonshine Cove Publishing, LLC for his patience and guidance throughout the editing of this book, and ultimately its publication.

To Barbara Anne, my wonderful wife of forty-two happy years and mother of three. You are my world.

About the Author

"Greetings," the letter began. And, thus in May of 1963, the author was informed that the U.S. Army needed him. It was a two-year need, but he opted for an eight-month school which extended his initial draft for another year. Crypto machine repair training took place in steel screened, locked, caged rooms behind secured walls at Ft. Monmouth, NJ. Afterward, a year in Viet Nam, and then a year in Germany. He took a European discharge and roamed Western Europe, Morocco, Denmark, and the UK before returning to his parents' home in Detroit with fifty-five cents in his pocket.

In 1967, he joined the Detroit police department: Salary, $7,424/year. Two months after graduating from the police academy, the Detroit riots began.

Married in 1977. He had a Corvette; divorced the Corvette in 1979—no room for groceries, or a baby seat.

Father of three, grandfather of four. He and his wife live in Oxford, MI, on a hilltop surrounded by an acre of grass and pines. Interests: writing, reading, gardening, and target shooting.

His website is: www.jamesjaythomas.com

Once you get rid of integrity the rest is a piece of cake.

—Larry Hagman

Oliver Twisted And Turned

Chapter 1

Vince Sardi was born Luigi DeSantis in a small village outside of Sienna, Italy. No father; his mother died giving birth. He came to America at age 16, barely able to speak English without making people smile, or outright laugh at his mangled pronunciations and inflections. He was sponsored by his uncle and aunt and adopted their last name, but their idea of family life soon proved too structured for him. The only asset he had to sell was labor. And, at age 16, the construction industry was eager to gobble up a young, eager, cash only, worker and he jumped into it wholeheartedly. English proficiency wasn't entirely necessary, anticipation of what was needed was, and Luigi was quick to pick up on what was needed. It was work, money, a chance to practice English, and maybe put together enough to move out from his uncle's house.

His first real American life's lesson came on payday. He stuffed the small wad of cash deep in his front pocket. The sun felt great on his back as he walked down the street, and with the money in his pocket he felt like a millionaire. The lesson came soon afterward. It was taught to him in an alley by two street thugs who had watched the workers leaving the construction company gate. They knew when payday was, and they picked what seemed to be the weakest among those leaving. As he neared an alley, they grabbed him. He was frightened, beaten senseless and robbed.

Luigi hated himself for being so powerless. A few days later Luigi discovered the Kronk gym. He wandered inside, took in the rank smell, and watched the sparring and workouts. He saw a man yelling instructions at two guys slugging it out in a ring. Luigi approached and stood, respectfully, at his side without saying anything and waited for his chance. A couple of minutes later the sparring session was over. The man took notice of him and said, "What'd'ya want."

Luigi, put up his fists and circled them in the air." "You show…?"

The trainer looked at the short, skinny kid with the black eyes and roughly abraded cheeks and said, "If the other guy doesn't look like that, then, yeah, you need some training." The English was pretty much wasted on Luigi. But the man nodded his head. That was it, just the one nod.

Costa?" Luigi jutted his chin out as he asked, simultaneously gesturing with his hands, palms upward.

Greely looked at him closely. The kid's clothes were seconds…maybe thirds. The instep of his left shoe, at the sole, was open slightly and he could see his naked foot; he was pitiful. He noted the boy hardly spoke English, guessed that he didn't have any money; and his couple of words and hand gestures proclaimed Italian. Greely felt sorry for him. He cobbled his best street Italian together and said, even working in what he believed to be an Italian lilt, "Primo, no costa. Luego…" and held his hand horizontally, palm down, and rotated it at the wrist in a wagging motion, as he was used to seeing Italians do, giving at the same time a slight shrug of his shoulders. Then he recalled that "luego" was probably Mexican Spanish for "later," but thought it was close enough. Luigi made the translation and nodded his head.

Greely, the trainer, always had time to cultivate a newcomer. There was no cost to him, except maybe some of his time. Perhaps, this kid could be the next world champion. Not very likely, but there was always the possibility; and then the money would flow. Greely crooked his finger at Luigi and led him to a locker room. He rummaged around in an old laundry bag and brought out a pair of trunks and socks, and he tossed him an old pair of gym shoes from a donation box.

Luigi put them on and came out. He looked a little comical because the shoes and trunks were too large. Greely held up a "wait- a-minute" finger and soon came back with a short length of rope. He tied it around the boy's waist and that was that; he couldn't do anything about the shoes. He led Luigi to a heavy bag and demonstrated what he should do. The other boys in the gym looked briefly, some smiled, but went back to their workouts. Luigi began pounding the bag. A minute later Greely grabbed his arms gently and showed him how to stand and roll his body to drive his punch into the bag, to move his feet with each punch, and simultaneously bring up the opposing hand to protect his jaw. Guiding his punches, he said: left, left, right, right. Slow at first, Luigi picked up on it and was excited when the bag began to move. He was deliberate and as he began to understand and feel the rhythm, he struck harder and harder. Greely took notice. For a newbie, the kid had power and showed spirit. His trainer's mind focused on the boy's moves. He was thinking, too early to tell, but maybe….

Luigi, thereafter, never missed a day. He trained hard and showed well in exhibition matches. His was a murderous instinct, fired by the memory of being unable to defend himself, being cowardly, and having the shit kicked out of him in the alley. He hated himself for being so spineless. His fury was awesome to behold. An opponent that showed fear enraged him, and he seemed to always provoke fear. His opponents buckled before his fierce, almost insane beating. Within two years he was a Golden Gloves contender.

His ring name—Vincent Sardi—stuck. A co-worker in the construction trade told him that Luigi was a crappy name anyway. After a while, he was just known as Vincent Sardi, usually just Vinnie, and he wore the name like a championship belt. It wasn't Vincenzo, Vinci….or, more especially, Luigi…it was a real American name. Vincent in Italian meant victor or conqueror. He thought it perfect.

Young Vincent Sardi, however, much to Greely's great disappointment, had no intention of becoming a professional boxer. He learned to box in order to defend himself and now felt confident and fearless. His focus was money and had been for some time. He wanted money now, not sometime down the hard road of boxing.

When the opportunity came to partner with a co-worker in a business of their own, they left their jobs. Vincent Sardi's English, improved greatly, and he was European hungry in the land of opportunity. The money in the home building business was better than boxing and less injurious. Three years later he bought out his partner and renamed the business the Sardi Construction Company.

Vincent discovered early on that non-taxed dollars were better than taxed dollars. He always had an eye open for a quick buck and was by any estimate cautious as a street hooker. The money in construction was always time and materials, but always allowed room for padding in addition to his cost. Sardi's magical billing practices provided a good income. The money was good, but he always felt more was better.

Sardi took side bets on almost any boxing event. He bought and sold a variety of expensive construction equipment and tools—paperwork wasn't a prerequisite, and his income tax returns were always fictional wonders.

But in addition to these side enterprises, Sardi's fascination with the ring was indelible. He visited Greely and looked over the boxing talent whenever he could. When Greely died, with equally mixed emotions of sentiment and interest, Sardi picked up Greely's torch and took his place as a trainer. Greely had been desperate to make his mark, as a matter of pride and a meaningful life, as having trained a world champion. Sardi was no different.

Vincent Sardi had no time for a family. His sole interests were making money, running the Sardi construction company and managing boxing talent, in that order. As he got older, however, he couldn't dispel a growing, inexplicable nostalgic interest in returning to Italy and living out his life in comfort. He was getting tired of waiting for his pot of gold to show up. In his mind, Italy was beckoning, louder each year. Italian women, Italian food, and Italian wine, and he would have them all. Sardi traveled to the old country every two years. He had friends and some distant family there. Each trip, he deposited a goodly sum of money in a different Italian bank.

His shirttail relatives and friends believed he had a good pension, but none thought he was rich. And that is exactly the way he wanted it. Through the years he put together a considerable nest egg, and felt he was almost ready to go. He needed only one final, big score of dollars.

It was a warm June day, when Ray Oliver showed up and interrupted those day dreams. At first, all he wanted was to work out. Sardi watched him and not long afterward asked him to spar.

Ray was quick, strong, showed magical anticipation, and had a killer instinct; he wanted to win. That was championship material…could this Oliver be *his* world champion? He befriended Oliver, gave him a job at his construction company, and took great personal interest in his training.

For three years, Ray built homes for the Sardi construction company, fought matches at every opportunity, studied hard, and saved his money. Every penny he had earned had been earmarked—some for his mother, a minimum for his living expenses, and the rest for schooling. He was demonstrably bright enough to earn a full-boat college scholarship. Somewhere between his sophomore and junior years, he came to believe that being a lawyer would satisfy all that he desired. He worked hard and graduated with a BA and a GPA high enough to be accepted by a law school. His mother died before he graduated. He mourned her passing and missed her, but was thankful for the inheritance. It would help see him through school. He was now twenty-two, recently accepted into the University of Michigan law school, and it was time to say goodbye to Vincent, the Sardi Construction Company, and boxing.

Sardi made one last emotional pitch to Ray to not abandon his future in the ring, including a last ditch, "all I have done for you" speech. Ray, for maybe the hundredth time, said he was grateful, but boxing wasn't the road he wanted. Ray was resolute and it was no longer a point for discussion. Sardi had failed to turn him, and that afternoon Sardi's world championship dream was over. Ultimately, they wished each other the best of luck, shook hands, and Ray walked out the door.

Chapter 2

Ray Oliver really wasn't a boxer, but his father had been one before he became a cop. When Ray was fourteen, his dad used to take him out into the backyard and teach him—at least that's what he called it. Ray hated these "lessons." His father was a mean bastard and delighted in punching Ray. However, he always showed Ray how he had set him up and then slipped past his guard; little comfort that. A bloody nose or bloused eye engendered more fear and hate than love. But the day his father quit the police force and deserted him and his mother, he told Ray that he had taught him everything he knew about boxing and that Ray shouldn't be afraid of anyone—and he shook his hand. That was the first time he ever complimented Ray, and the handshake was like some rite of passage. Ray watched him go, unaware that he would never return. He was the only man Ray was ever fearful of and he never saw him again.

The gym stunk more from sweat than Lysol. The lights could have been brighter, the lockers cleaner. It was a hole in the wall gym in the basement of an old school, in a dump of a neighborhood. It was down, but not out; it still maintained a reputation for turning out champion prizefighters. And that was the attraction, an avenue to wealth and fame. The official title of each hopeful was "amateur" but Ray thought apprentice sounded better. The amateurs were apprentices learning a trade. Ray believed the trades were good money, and you ended up with a pension. In boxing you had a better chance at ending up broke with a damaged face and brain. He had no desire to become a pro boxer. But he didn't have a tradesman's mindset either. He didn't want to exchange his life for a pension. He wanted a profession. He wanted to be powerful, wear a suit, make a lot of money and be respected. Just how he was going to accomplish those goals was uncertain, but with those goals in mind, he fought matches—for him it as easy as a whore turning tricks.

The ringsiders were there…not like the hooting and yelling crowds watching a Las Vegas fight, but a great many fewer and for the most part silent except for an occasional, exasperated comment born of frustration and a missed opportunity. They were a mix of managers, trainers, ex-boxers, franchise owners and a couple of curious on-lookers who came in off the street to watch a fight for free. All ringsiders but more so, present were those whose opinions mattered, the judges whom knew the craft and business first hand—the fighters called them talent scouts and indeed they were. Each boxing stable wanted world champions; each fighter would be scrutinized for the talent and will that it takes to win a title bout. This fight was a boxing match to showcase those talents. To Ray Oliver, however, it was just another fight. He had no illusion or desire to become a champion. For DeJuan Bowens it was a chance to be recognized.

Ray and DeJuan entered the ring and were announced. The loud sounding of their own names in the small arena sent a small shiver of pride down their spines. They stood less than twenty feet apart; the adrenaline coursing through their bodies and their senses sharply focused. Man vs. man; man vs. beast—the primitive visceral impact was identical.

Both fighters were 22 and evenly matched physically. It was Ray's twenty-first fight; DeJuan's sixth. At the bell, they squared off and began their dance. The soft scrapping of their feet on the canvass was punctuated by grunts and slaps as they planted their feet, threw and landed punches. DeJuan's was quick and strong but he needed more experience and lacked disciplined technique. Every time he got ready to fire off a left jab, he'd drop his right glove slightly before launching into the punch. Ray picked up on it half way through the first round—a slight feint, a pull back and drop of his right, and then the jab almost simultaneously, but not quite. He was set to crank one into DeJuan's face but the bell sounded too soon and they took their corners. Another bell and they came out like tigers. The opportunity came a moment later. Ray anticipated the punch, slipped it and countered with a stunning right hook to his head. DeJuan's face scrunched and his head seemed to bounce off his right shoulder. Ray followed it up with a left to the stomach and a powerful right cross to the chin that rolled DeJuan's eyes and buckled his knees. DeJuan, dazed, hit the canvass and stayed down for the count.

Most boxers, the pros anyway, would make some comments about how bravely their opponent fought and that they presented a worthy fight. Ray always thought that was part of the show; they didn't really feel that way. They won by a combination of skill and luck, and winning was all that mattered. What fighter ever felt bad about winning, or his beaten opponent? But there was no televised interview. Just as well because Ray felt nothing. The boy on the canvass didn't inspire him to utter any noble sportsman-like statements. Ray had kicked his ass and was glad of it.

Ray didn't want to become a professional boxer, he just wanted to make a couple of extra bucks to get through school. In the locker room Vincent Sardi slipped him his usual fifty dollars. Amateurs weren't supposed to be paid, but Sardi always said it wasn't pay, it was a "trainer's fee"—a tip for delivering an education. And, once again, he tried to talk Ray into becoming part of their fight team. And once again, Ray declined. Sardi was a part owner of the gym and had a great interest in its promotion through champion fighters. Both Ray, early on, and DeJuan had been two of their selections. But Ray didn't want that kind of life for himself. DeJuan? Sure he lost, and badly, but like Ray he had the heart and strength an owner valued and he was hungry with ambition. Sardi pitted Ray against DeJuan because DeJuan was a smart-ass and had a hard time listening to his trainer. DeJuan had the qualities of a champion, he just didn't have the correct attitude—that was Ray's job. It was DeJuan's first loss.

Chapter 3

It was one of the last warm fall days and the warmth of the late afternoon sun radiated from the marble walls of the main building of the University of Michigan law school. Ray sat on the portico of the law library, his back against the wall; the heat felt good. His thoughts, free flowing like light winds...University of Michigan Law school...ranked 8th nationally...pretty good, Ray...you're doing well. He now had direction and life was good...but as Lisa Marnen passed by he thought that life, no matter how good, could always be better.

He smiled, she smiled...and with that encouragement he left the warm bricks and walked along with her.

"I see that you've got some accounting books...so, an accountant? Auditor? Where are you going with your studies?"

"Presently, to the Bus Ad Building for a class." She cocked her head and looked at his armload of books. "Hmmm, law, eh? Well, where are you going...civil, criminal, a judgeship, or perhaps maybe even Attorney General?"

"Well, why would I settle for less than the presidency? he said, and laughed.

Lisa would be a good accountant, because she looked at him and in a flash noted his clean good looks, curly black hair, blue eyes, white perfect teeth, and scruffy shoes...and presumed a net worth of nothing more than the ordinary. If he had money, he would have better shoes.

"I will become an important accountant and work in my father's company until I cannot be promoted further, and then I will become the Comptroller General of the United States and will then work alongside of yourself, Mr. President."

"Ah, such a grand future you have planned. But that's a couple of years away. How about something a little less ambitions and more timely, like coffee at the Bodega this evening. Six o'clock good for you?" It was kind of soon to breach that subject but the Business Administration building was only two blocks from the law library and they were almost at its entrance. Ray thought that she had sized him up and would either meet him or not. Besides, he thought, the conversation kind of inspired him to directness.

Lisa rolled the possibilities through her mind and quickly concluded a harmless interlude would save her from a dreadful unpacking job. It wasn't as if she were picking out a boyfriend or husband. He was just a nice guy with a certain strength about him that had a sexy appeal.

"You buying the coffee?"

"Usually I'd split the cost but I'll buy the first round."

"Ha, that's no bargain if you're thinking of two coffees…I still have to pay. How about you buy two this time, and you buy two the next time."

Roy grinned at the suggestion. "Okay, you're on. By the way, what's your name?"

"Lisa…Lisa Marnen."

"Morning? As in the start of a day?"

"Almost, but its spelled M-a-r-n-e-n."

"Yours?"

"Roy Oliver" adding in mock condescension, "O-l-i-v-e-r" and watched how she'd take it.

She let it pass and said, "Well, Mr. Oliver we have just met, but you have determined my name, what I will become, and have secured a meeting for later on this evening. I think you are aggressive, capable, and will make a splendid lawyer."

"I believe your concern for spending will greatly enable your career as a Comptroller General. We will have this country working like clockwork."

"Well, I'm here and none too soon—class in five minutes."

"Study hard, I'm going to need a great Comptroller General. Six o'clock, right?

Lisa nodded and walked up the steps. Ray hoped she'd turn and smile at him before disappearing inside. She didn't. But she did look at him unobserved through the glass.

Chapter 4

The Bodega was just another college town greasy spoon at the edge of the campus. It was retro fifties, not that it had been remodeled to look that way, but rather that it just hadn't changed since the day the doors opened for business. Often professors graduated and stayed. Later, they became grey haired professors who came to eat and reminisce, remembering their freshman year at the college and how they scraped their coins together to afford a meal. Outside of the prices, the menu was pretty much the same. The restaurant had undergone several name changes, but the names were just new frames on an old picture.

Ray found a table and anchored it. The place started crowding up. New arrivals began looking at his table covetously. Lisa arrived late, but Ray overlooked it and made no mention of it. Neither did she.

"Hi, lawyer."

"Hi, accountant. What's a girl like you doing in a nice place like this?" he said.

"I thought you wanted to impress, so you invited me here? You bring other girls here too?

"Nope. Just a select few."

"I'm honored."

"You are. I had this table reserved for us. The food is standard fare, really not too bad, and their coffee is most excellent. I drink mine black, no sugar, you?"

"Black? God how working class. Make mine with cream and sugar—heavy on each."

Ray bowed his head slightly and said, "My how remarkably upper class of you, milady." and ordered. A couple of minutes later, two cups were banged down on the table, a spoon sticking out of hers, no saucers. In a high-class restaurant, cream; at the Bodega, milk. Both the sugar and "cream" had been added by the waitress behind the counter. The coffee's delivery was very much an unvoiced challenge: if you don't like it, tough; don't drink it. People lingered over coffee. If they didn't order food there wasn't much of a tip, and they occupied a space an eater could have. The waitress wouldn't mind if they were insulted and hoped they'd leave soon.

Lisa rolled her eyes, "Nice service, are they closing soon?"

"No, she must just be having a bad day. You ever work as a waitress?"

"I'd die first." Lisa practically curled her lips when she said that. Roy wondered how she managed to work in a half-smile through the curled lips at the same time.

He leaned toward her and said in a confidential tone, "Well, don't hold back, just tell me how you honestly feel."

She gave him a squint eyed, long look and said, "Did you ever have a desire to be a janitor?"

Ray, shut his eyes for a second, took a deep breath and let it out slowly. "Desire, no. But necessity, yes. I janitored at a restaurant for about ten months and learned some valuable lessons. For example, the regulars. There were a couple of lawyers who frequented the bar at lunch time, and often came back for dinner in the evening. Sometimes, I had to get them to move a bit to clean up a spill, or pick up some trash...and it was a most amazing thing. They would move slightly so that I could do my job, but they never looked at me...it was as if I was an invisible force. Most of the other customers would nod, maybe say hi, move and even say thanks. With the lawyers it was like pulling your hand out of the water, they just flowed back to their original position uninterrupted in their conversation. And, another thing, they were cheap. You think that having a responsible, dignified job—and the money that goes with it—you'd think they'd be a bit generous to the waitresses. Well, they weren't. Sometimes they'd just walk out without leaving a tip and I mean both at lunch and dinner. If they stiffed a waitress in the afternoon, you'd think they'd be embarrassed to return in the evening but they weren't."

"Ah, I see...so that's why you decided to become a lawyer?"

"Well, I might try to right some wrongs. After I thought about it I wondered if they brought that same attitude to the court room. If it was criminal law, did they have the same disdainful attitude toward their clients…how could they ever mount an aggressive, vigorous defense for someone, whom to their lofty minds, was waitress or janitor class, or less. They would go through the motions for the money, but they couldn't invest their heart in a case. If you don't love what you're doing how can you ever be successful? To them, low-lifes were invisible, they didn't matter. But the law does matter. And it doesn't depend on who the players are. The law needs to be applied and upheld. That's what keeps society together."

"Hey, Don Quixote, your ambitions are more along the lines of a public defender rather than a corporate lawyer. How are you ever going to make any real money?"

"Real money? Like an accountant might make?" He instantly regretted the remark.

"Working at my father's factory, I might have a shot at it. And, if and when the time came and I took over then I would probably be in the best position to know what's going on. I am an accountant; I'm working on an MBA."

"Jesus! You're anticipating your inheritance?"

"You make it seem so cold."

"Well?"

Lisa clucked her tongue, paused, and said, "Actually my father does not own a factory or anything close. I'm actually very rich and don't have to work. I'm just a little paranoid about security and need to make sure that I have something to fall back on if I lose my fortune." And with a hint of a smile, she drilled him with her eyes and began to enunciate her words slowly like she was talking to a child, "I kind of just say things like that for shock value. I would like to have a decent job, one that doesn't require waiting on tables."

"Okay, okay, I was just trying to make a point about being professional. I think if you're short in your social responsibilities, you'll carry that over into your work."

"Social responsibilities? What, being nice to a waitresses? Let me guess...do you also endorse the ideas of 'giving back to the community' and 'from each according to his ability, to each according to his needs?' "

"Wow, what a jump! Hey, I'm a diehard capitalist. I believe in profit. In fact a whole lot of profit is a good thing."

"Yeah, me too, that's why I'm working on the MBA—more money."

The conversation was a mild bantering, but it did have some serious undertones. Ray wished that it had been lighter, but on reflection he knew he had led the charge. They finished their coffee in sips between more comfortable exchanges. Neither opted for a second cup, but readily agreed to a walk. Ray paid for the coffee and put a buck down for the tip.

Lisa glanced at it and said, "I don't know why but a dollar bill is so much better than four quarters. What do you think?"

Ray thought that she had just given him a shot, but he couldn't figure it out and said what most men would have: "Uhuh" and walked her toward the door. He'd figure it out later.

The sun was going down and the breeze was mild, but cooler. They walked through the fallen, dried leaves which skittered along the sidewalk before them, creating a dry rustling sound. The car traffic had died down and the bikes had taken over. Ray was intent in his conversation and more than once Lisa had to grab him by the arm and pull him aside to avoid a bicyclist. After another close one, she kept her hold and they walked arm in arm breathing in deeply the evening air and enjoying each other.

They wandered up Tappen Street, past the Business School, the Law Quad, and turned onto S. University. It was getting dark quickly.

"Where's home?" asked Ray.

"I share an apartment with another girl. It's about ten miles from here and I make the drive every day. Not too bad, but it beats the dorms. How about you?"

"I live on campus—at the Lawyers Club."

"That must cost a bundle."

"Yeah, and I really couldn't afford it if weren't for my scholarship and grant money—and I got lucky, I picked up an internship with Wentworth, Solomon &Hughes in Detroit the first year. I've worked for them every summer since I started law school. They like me and work me about 70 hours a week. When I get back to my apartment I literally fall into bed, get up in the morning and do it all over again. I usually don't have a weekend to myself."

"Sounds brutal."

"It's tough, but it pays well and I think they're going bring me into the fold and make me an offer when I pass the bar. I've got one more year here. I love the work. It still strikes me as odd that I'm getting paid a lot for something that I love to do."

Self-confidence and determination surrounded Ray like an aura. Lisa liked the potential and her mind was grinding at the possibilities. The MBA was good, but a hotshot lawyer husband was better.

"Ray, it's been a great time but it's getting late and I have an exam tomorrow. My car's parked in the parking deck, next block. I need to go."

Ray nodded. Lisa led the way, and they walked to the four floored see thru structure and trudged up to the second level. The concrete perpetually smelled damp and looked wet. Now, at night, with the low wattage lights, it just looked dark and with most of the cars gone, creepy. Her car was parked near the staircase. It was a red Mercedes C class—a baby Benz. Ray, couldn't even guess if its cost was low or high end. It just looked sleek and expensive. And incompatible with her age and job.

"Nice car…how'd you ever come by that?" Immediately, he gave himself a mental kick --what a totally tactless question--why did he say that?

"My father bought it for me as a graduation gift."

"Some gift. It's beautiful."

"Well, it was nice of him and he can afford it. He owns a factory you know."

"I thought you said that he didn't own one."

Lisa opened the door, slipped inside, and lowered the window. The car purred to life. Its engine sounded smooth. Ray imagined that its engine may have been tuned by mechanics wearing tuxedos.

She leaned her head out of the window, smiled widely, and said, "I lied." Her tongue flicked, working the word, sending it to his eyes in sight and ears as well in sound. It was sexy.

"I'll see you Monday." she said. Not a question, but a statement.

"How will I get in touch with you?"

"Same as before, I have a 4:30 class. See you then."

And with that she flicked on the lights and drove off. Ray could hear her tires squeal slightly on the down ramp. He clumped down the stairs and walked back to the dorm. Lisa overpowered most of his thoughts and he'd have to shake that before he could settle down to his homework.

For mid-week the dorm was quiet and Ray was thankful for that. Sometimes on the weekend it could be a bit rowdy. Ray disapproved slightly, thinking that law students should be better self-disciplined.

Ray hadn't met any girl like this one. She asked questions that may or may not have answers—he couldn't always tell. She'd make conflicting statements and rebut them without flinching, she was warm but occasionally aloof and sometimes almost analytical. More than once Ray felt as though he was being measured. Since they were new to each other, he deferred judgment. She was going to take some time to figure out. She was a puzzle and that bit of mystery intrigued him. Besides, she had some great curves.

Chapter 5

Lisa drove campus speed until she left the student pedestrians and buildings, and then let it out, the wind whipping through the windows and carrying the loud music away. She stopped briefly at a Subway sandwich shop, picked up a sub, and ten minutes later she was at Arbor Landings, a neat, rambling residential complex on the outskirts of the university. It was a professional, working couples residential complex and few students stayed there because even if they partnered they couldn't afford the rent.

Lisa unlocked the door to the apartment, pushed the door shut, and threw the keys on the counter, which unfortunately continued in their momentum and slid off the other side and onto the floor.

"Damn."

"What's damn? said her roommate, stepping out of the bathroom and toweling off. My car didn't pick up a dent did it?

"No, Mike, the car's ok. The keys just hit the floor. The "damn" part is that the classes are getting longer. There's always some idiot that wants to ask questions at the last minute. And, of course, our instructor is always obliging and that cut into my library time. It got late and I was hungry to begin with so I grabbed a sub in town. I brought you one, did you eat already?"

"Yeah. I was a little frustrated I guess. Frank from work came over and we went to Mario's. We gorged on meatballs and spaghetti, and drank two bottles of Chianti. Good stuff!"

"Frustrated, hey? So, how does that translate?"

"Well, number one, Mycroft Purcell Inc., is on a new tear. 'Let's double our business by the end of the year' is the new mantra. The new exec is trying to prove his position. I think he believes he can double profit by doubling the contracts—sounds logical, but it isn't going to work. They are also on an austerity kick.

Lisa, watching the toweling operation, jutted her jaw a tad and said, "Austerity, that's not a good word. What's going to happen?"

Mike toweled while he spoke, immodest as always; his penis waved in the air as he vigorously rubbed the towel over his shoulders. Lisa glanced at it. It really wasn't too big and it was uncircumcised—she didn't really like either feature but they came with the package.

"So far, they've cut a few managers, consolidated operations, and sliced commissions to the floor people by fifty percent—they're going to pay them every other month, and they're cutting wages by ten percent across the board. I'm thinking there'll be some intense competition at first, but as the fat level dwindles, most of the floor agents will lay down on the job. Their production numbers will be pretty much the same and no one can point out another as a hindrance, and since they're necessary they'll probably not be cut. I mean who wants to work harder for less? And the company will experience a temporary rise in its cash reserves from the wage and job cuts so overall, at first it will look like a good strategy."

Lisa didn't hear much of what Mike said after the word 'cut.'

"Across the board? Does that mean you too?"

"No. I'm in an unusual position…which brings me to the number two point. I don't really know if there is a best way of bringing this up, but it's something I can't avoid, yet it might just be a blessing in disguise. Outside of the president and CEO, there are only two of us in the company that know all of its operations. The other guy, Dan, is on medical leave. That leaves me."

"And…?" Lisa said, stretching the three-letter word out until it sounded like a seven letter word.

"They're sending me to Seattle for an indeterminate time. I'm going to run the Seattle office…I'll have complete discretion over hiring, firing, buying and selling, and making contracts. I will be the number one guy…and if it works out, the job will probably be permanent. It's a step up and, for starters, it's almost fifty percent more than I'm making now. The downside is Seattle isn't making a profit. So, it'll be a test to see if I can turn it around."

"Mike, I think it's great that they think so much of you but what about us?" Lisa said that with a straight face and even managed a touch of concern in her voice. She wasn't really worried about the "us" part as much as she was thinking about the unvoiced "me" part."

"Well, I just heard about it this afternoon and I'm still turning it around. I wanted to talk to you first. I'm thinking that once I'm established you can come out and we'll get an apartment. Life will be good…and if I'm successful maybe we can make our "arrangement" a bit more permanent."

Mike, mostly dry, turned and headed to the bedroom to get dressed, throwing the wet towel on the carpeting next to the bed. Lisa hated that; he never seemed to remember.

She dreaded where the conversation might be headed. Mike, of course, was talking about marriage again. He was in love. She must have told him at least twice in the last year, as tactfully as she could, that it was too soon in their relationship to be even thinking about marriage. Actually. she was totally opposed to the idea.

Mike came out wearing PJ's. The top was unbuttoned and his belly stuck out a bit, but the way he ate it was just a matter of time before it hung over the top. He had missed handsome, but he had a pleasant face. He was jovial, pleasant, and would do anything for Lisa. He was 28, semi-successful and had potential. But as far as Lisa was concerned, he couldn't see past the tip of his nose.

He poured two wines and sat on the couch, placing the glasses on the coffee table, slopping some wine onto the coasters.

"Lisa, I'm not going to pressure you any more about marriage, but just in case you gave it some extra thought I want you to know I'm here for you. I know you want to finish school and you should do that. I've leased this apartment for a year and you can stay here; I'll pick up the utilities. If things don't work out for me, at least I'll have a place to come back to. I'm thinking that I should know what's going on inside of three months…you'll probably be out of school by then."

"You've been more than good to me. And I know in my heart that marriage is something that I should consider. Maybe being apart for a while might give us both some breathing room. It'll be good for you and me. Since we've moved in together, I've never really been alone. Three months is a long time, but what we've put together between ourselves will certainly stand a test."

"I've never lived with anyone except for my roomies in college. I do love you and would be happy to stay with you for the rest of my life. Before you, I felt alone…now, every time I come home, you're there. You are the highpoint of my day, my life."

"I swear… oh, I don't know…I'm going to miss you." She moved forward, put her arms around him, and softly asked, "When do you have to be in Seattle?"

Mike breathed out heavily, "Oh, yeah, number three, I've got to be there Saturday afternoon. The office booked me on Delta, early Saturday morning. I'm going to work through the weekend to get ready for Monday. The main office has already recalled the current CEO."

"Mike, this is Thursday evening. Why so soon? It's going to be awfully awkward for me without you."

Mike's heart pitter-patted after those words. "I'm going to get a corporate car and a little larger expense account. So, I'm going to leave you the Mercedes and--half humorously looked upward as if in prayer—please don't dent it. And, I'm going to leave you some cash. Between the expense account and the demands of the job, I won't be needing much of anything. You'll be just fine…and we can always call each other and you can hit me on-line."

Lisa, finished her wine and said, "I'm ready for bed." Mike, who had a head start on the wine at Mario's, heard the message in her voice, gulped his wine down, and gave her a long kiss and a tender squeeze on her breasts. They disappeared into the bedroom and Lisa jumped his bones good. One thing about Lisa and that is she loved sex…even though Mike wasn't too well equipped, he tried hard to make up the difference in enthusiasm and she appreciated that. They had a re-run in the morning, and thrashed around so lustily Friday night they broke a nightstand lamp.

Saturday morning, 5:30 a.m. and Mike was pretty much shot. Fortunately, he packed his bags Friday afternoon so all he needed was a quick shower, his laptop and a travel kit. They arrived at Detroit Metro just before seven; his flight was as at eight thirty.

Lisa dropped him off at the McNamara Terminal. Cars were standing two aside from the curb and a cop was busy waving them on. Mike saw a tight open space and squeezed in. A porter helped him quickly to get his bags out of the trunk. A Mercedes meant a good tip.

Mike leaned into the car and they kissed good bye. Despite Lisa's calculating her life without him earlier, she was honestly going to miss him and said so again. He turned and waved at her from the door. She waved back just before the cop began waving at her.

The Mercedes hugged the curves as she exited the airport complex and merged with Saturday's early morning traffic on the I-94. The cars were moving at moderate speed but Lisa found the right lane and dogged it, occasionally glancing at the sun rising in her rear view mirror. She was in no hurry to get back to the apartment. On the weekend she and Mike would have a leisurely morning, sometimes going out for breakfast, sometimes cooking in. Mike loved to cook and she loved his cooking. Now, the routine was broken and this morning would be particularly quiet…even uncomfortable.

Lisa didn't have any real cooking skills beyond the basics. They had groceries at home, but three months was going to be a long time and she thought she better get used to shopping for necessities; usually Mike did it. She pulled into Trader Joe's market and loaded her basket with stores and comfort foods she could deal with and several bottles of wine, a kind of comfort food in its own right. The drive home was uneventful. She wrestled the bags through the apartment door and onto the counter and began to put the groceries away. It wasn't even 9:30 a.m. She was right, the apartment was eerily quiet and even turning up the music didn't dispel the gnawing feeling of being alone.

Chapter 6

Lisa needed to busy herself by putting the apartment in order. She collected and piled clothing into the washer and did the dishes. Taking a break, she flumped onto the couch. Her school books were on the coffee table in front of her and she stared at them—a job she would like to have avoided, but it had to be done. She flicked on her computer and was about to open the "BB"—a text on marketing which was a bitch of a book and which earned it the "Blue Bastard" name among the students—probably had been named decades ago. And then a thought…cash, Mike said he left some cash…she moved quickly to the cupboard and there in the soup tureen where they kept their rainy-day stash of cash, was a large assortment of bills. She began counting, eventually tallying up…nineteen, twenty, twenty one—twenty-one hundred dollars. "Okay Mike! Thank you!" she said aloud as she clutched the bills in both hands. "Yep, three months, I can make it on that." Not a world of splendor, but for a student on a college campus with her bills taken care of, oh, yeah, she would do all right.

Lisa, with a major concern taken care of, buried herself in her studies. She had a double load, two classes, and had to be ready for both on Monday. Three hours later, brain swimming with figures, she slammed the book covers together and logged out on her computer—enough statistical theory for one session. Outside, the sun was shining and the blue sky framed a scattering of white clouds making them appear as if they were settings in a ring. She walked pool side, past the commons, the club house and down to the road, twice, before returning to the apartment. She glanced at her cell phone, and had a sudden thought of her classmate, Karen.

"Karen, hi, this is Lisa. Glad I caught you. What're you doing now?"

"Lisa. Good to hear your voice. Doing? Well, I'm doing what you should probably be doing. I'm up to my ears in statistical analysis and thinking that Monday is going to come too soon. This marketing stuff is difficult."

"Yeah, that's for sure. I've been working at it since early this morning and I'm still adrift. Want to get together and look it over?"

"Good, you're on…except we really have to buckle down and not get sidetracked in general stuff. We actually have to try to understand this crap."

"Cool. I'll be over in ten." Lisa ended the call and headed for the car.

Karen and her boyfriend owned a one family, two story, nine room house located in the Old West Side of Ann Arbor—an historic section where preservation of the buildings was an imperative, as well as membership in the association. Outside of the historical value, those considerations led to a steady increase in value for the homes as well and the owners gladly complied with the requirements. Karen, like Lisa, was working on her MBA and her boyfriend, Brad, was in the last year of Med School. They planned on marrying after graduation.

Lisa dumped her books and notes on Karen's front room table. "My head is about to burst."

Karen opened her eyes wide and nodded, saying, "Yeah, mine too. I'm thinking that maybe we might go back and forth on the questions and answers…quiz ourselves and maybe some of it will stick. How about a coffee or a Coke?"

"Great…hey, I forgot to eat breakfast, you have a roll or anything?"

"Yeah, there's a couple of slices of pizza in the fridge, okay with you"

"Perfect." Lisa covered them with a napkin and zapped them in the micro. "Wanna bite?"

"No, got enough. Last night, Brad and I killed off a huge salad and pretty much all of the pizza—that's all that's left. I snacked this morning."

While Lisa snapped a cap on a can of Coke and munched on the pizza, Karen showed Lisa her notes and asked if she had missed anything. Lisa flipped through her notebook and indicated a few pages.

"You know that class is so boring, I dozed off somewhere in the middle of his charts. My head snapped up in the middle of some point he was making. By then he was lecturing in front of the class; the charts were leaning against the wall. I knew I missed some stuff, but I didn't know I missed that much. Glad you came over, I'd been screwed for sure."

For the next two hours they poured over their notes and quizzed each other. Brad came home in the interim, showered, ate, and returned for evening classes. Lisa reflected momentarily that in a while Brad would be home for the night, and Karen would have somebody. When she went home, there would be nobody. She shook the thought from her head.

It was almost late afternoon, when Lisa and Karen quit for the day. Karen clicked open the music folder on her computer, selected Eagles, Cold Play, Kenny Wayne Shepherd and Owl City, and clicked Play all. They kicked back and closed their eyes, letting the music wash over them and move their minds elsewhere.

They were both asleep when the phone rang. The music had long since ceased.

" Karen...Brad...I'm finished for the night...some of the guys are talking about a party later on. Interested?"

"Uhhh, I don't know...." She said, shaking the nap's grip on her awareness. "Party...I got a lot of stuff to do."

"Yes, but I saw that you were on it early this morning and probably with Lisa throughout most of the afternoon. We need a break in routine...what'd'ya say? Party?" Brad conveyed encouragement and assent in his words, imbuing each with a sense of fun.

"Gee, uhhh, Lisa's still here. What time?"

"Heck, she's welcome to come. It'll be great. I'll bet she could use a break too."

"Just a minute…Lisa…"

"Well?"

The thought of the empty apartment flashed through Lisa's head and two seconds later she agreed.

"But I'm not dressed."

Karen talked to Brad for a moment and then let Lisa know that it was kind of a come as you are party, no special occasion—it was a last-minute inspiration for a Saturday night get together. A bunch of guys and girls, a couple cases of beer and some wine, chips and dip…about 9 p.m. What could be simpler, repeating the motivations intoned by Brad.

"Brad, where's it at?"

"Uhhh, I was coming to that…it's uhh, going to be at our house."

"What? Damn, Bradley! How can you do that? You let those guys talk you into partying at our house! The house is a mess. We're not ready for company. It can't be done."

"Yeah, uh, I was thinking about that and so maybe Lisa and you could make it right in a short time?"

Her voice increased an octave, "So, that's why you invited Lisa? So she could help clean?"

"Hey, not so loud…can she hear?

"Heck yeah she can hear, she ought to. That's pretty sneaky."

"Oh, come on…it'll be fun. We haven't had a party in months."

Karen initially hesitated, but eventually relented and said, "Bradley, you owe me big time…and don't expect me to clean up tomorrow."

"Sweet, I love you. I'll be in about eight thirty and the rest will trickle in afterward."

"Hmm, the rest… exactly how many people are 'the rest?'"

"Actually, I'm not really sure… there's only about twenty guys in the class and half of them probably can't make it…and maybe half of them might bring a girl…so, I don't know, maybe 15 or twenty or so."

By ten o'clock the party was in full swing. The thirty or so people that were there arrived in a party mood. They were an odd assortment of young doctors and other professionals discussing classes, business, drinking probably one more than they should, dancing, laughing and were for the most part like most any other group of party goers. Except this group would be making millions of dollars annually in a few years. Just before midnight, they had to make a beer and wine trip. They all pitched in for pizza and subs, and called in the order. Robert Lawrence, a neuro-surgeon in the making, volunteered to make the trip. He and other un-partnered hopefuls had been hovering around Lisa. Robert asked her if she'd like to accompany him—he needed help with the pizza and subs. Lisa figured he could have handled it by himself, but liked the approach and smiled a yes—she needed some fresh air anyway.

Robert was a tall thin guy with a deep and pleasant voice which reminded her of a radio announcer's. He engaged her several times through the evening and she found him to be humorous and interesting. Most of the other students were interested in themselves and where they were going in their careers. Robert did that to a certain degree, but he seemed more interested in her. She was complimented and felt comfortably good in his presence.

He drove a double black Cadillac short body with leather seats. It said style, comfort, and elegance—things which interested Lisa. They picked up the food, returned to the party and parked across the street.

It was dark and the music coming from the house was louder than anyone inside would guess.

Robert turned toward her, putting his hand gently on her shoulder and said, "Lisa, I like you." It was an undramatic, simple thing to say, but nonetheless, Lisa's heart took a little skip. He continued, "I'd like to see you again. What are your thoughts?"

Lisa truly didn't expect such a direct approach. She guessed that he liked her enough to ask to see her again, but didn't think it'd come about so abruptly. It reminded her of Ray Oliver.

Lisa's life was getting complicated.

"Well, Robert, I'm flattered. But I'm seeing someone and I don't think that'll work out too well."

He said, "Yeah, I can see where your friend would be concerned," and laughed gently. "But sometimes things don't always work out. And if that were to happen, you'd be without a boyfriend, and I'd be a distant memory. Can I have your phone number just in case. I promise I won't pester you, but I'll call faithfully once a week, every Monday evening. My conversation will be cheerful and uplifting, and you will be elated. And, I will listen to your life's story for as long as you want to talk."

Lisa believed every word that he said and was moved by what she perceived as sincerity. His deep voice gently commanding and resonating with some indefinable thing inside of her psyche, and within a short few seconds it was done—she gave him her cell number.

Robert and Lisa lugged the boxes of food into the house. They were barely missed, and only brought to mind when people saw others walking through the house munching on subs and slices of pizza.

At two in the morning, the first couples began to leave. By 3:00 a.m., the party was officially over. Lisa crashed on the couch for the rest of the night. Brad and Karen had thrown a successful party. They went to bed and snuggled, Brad slipped his arm under hers and found her breasts, thinking of getting things going. Ten seconds later they were both snoring.

Chapter 7

Morning came at the usual time but for some it seemed early. It was a grey dawn when Lisa's eyes opened and she began to recall the previous day. Mike was gone and wouldn't be back for months. Not good. Then there was Ray—promising, but an unknown quantity. And, now there was Robert who …she heard cups being rattled in the kitchen. Karen was pouring herself a cup of coffee.

Sounding sleepy, Lisa said, "Hey" from the couch. Karen got a second cup, poured another coffee, and asked, "Milk?" Lisa pursed her lips, letting an "oh" sound escape. "Got any cream?" Karen shook her head, "Nope, you get milk here." Lisa nodded, "Ok, milk and sugar it is then. Thanks." She pushed her fingers of clumped hair back behind her ears and padded barefooted across the cool tile to the kitchenette. Both sat at the counter cradling the hot coffee, staring at it and saying nothing. Brad was still in bed.

Lisa felt grungy after 24 hours in the same wrinkled and sweaty clothes. She needed to brush her teeth, a shower, and fresh clothes. A couple of yawns later, they said their goodbyes. Karen was thankful Lisa didn't want to stay longer. The coffee made the early morning better but she needed more sleep. Karen crawled in next to Brad and was asleep before Lisa drove past the guard shack.

Lisa rolled down the road as the sun began to rise over the tree tops and bling her rearview mirror. Relieved to get back to the apartment, she showered until the hot water cooled…but even that felt good.

Sunday morning meant that the apartment complex would be quiet until about one o'clock. If it was warm, a group of people would be stretched out on blankets or in the white plastic chairs around the pool, healing, from a late Saturday night party. It would be quiet. The 'Q's would crank up around 4:00 in the afternoon and there would be the smell of burgers and hot dogs in the air. There would be some music and drinking, but it would be subdued and wouldn't last. Monday morning was always a hurdle.

For most of the day Lisa thumbed through the "BB," thinking with almost every turn of a page that the book's nickname was well deserved. The information was nod-your-head boring. She polished off Mike's sub sandwich in the afternoon and found some pizza in the back of the fridge about the time the barbecue crowd and poolside people called it quits. It was almost dark when the phone rang. It was Mike and his voice was filled with excitement.

"Lisa. wow, I'm so happy to hear your voice. I know it's only been a little while, but I've really missed you."

"Same here. I gotta tell you that this apartment is so quiet and the bed is really different—I don't like sleeping alone." *At least, that part was truthful.* "Last night I finished off a bottle of wine and spent the night on the couch."

"Ouch, I know what you mean. I got in late afternoon on Saturday, and worked till about 3:00 a.m. No wine, but I slept on the couch in the woman's room and was at it again early Sunday morning. What a job...this place is really screwed up, but depending on what kind of feedback I get from the staff tomorrow, I'm thinking it has a lot of potential for profit. It just needs some aggressive management and some cost cutting measures...kind of like what's going on when I left. There's a lot more to it, but I didn't call to tell you all of that stuff. I really just wanted to hear your voice."

"That's sweet, Mike. I've studied my head off this weekend. Other than that, pretty boring. I miss talking with you in the evenings."

They talked for an hour, each genuinely glad to have someone familiar to talk with. Mike wrapped up the call by telling her that he could see where the company would need another accountant probably by the next quarter when the accounts began to pick up. He floated the job offer past her and prayed she'd be excited about the prospect. And she was...now all that Mike had to do was to invent a position...so much for cost cutting, but this was different he told himself.

Lisa was truly flattered by the job offer. But it also meant being close to Mike…not that she didn't care for him, but it was like an invisible rope. In her heart Lisa knew that what she planned for her life was not the same as Mike, and that was the root of the problem with their relationship. She did not want to be tied down. She had worked hard. She wanted a career and fully realized that she preferred being single and self-sufficient. On the other hand, there was always an exception…say, for instance, some guy who could accommodate her idea of a career, happened to be a guy who was amazingly handsome and exceptionally rich, and a good lover. The family thing, she thought, could be worked out if he was insistent…maybe an adoption and a nanny; that would probably take care of the family part. Or, if that wouldn't work, maybe in time, a divorce and a large moneyed settlement would take care of the single and self-sufficient aspect. It could go either way. However, it was too early to make heavy decisions like that…at the moment all she needed was the bottle of Merlot and some soft music. Lisa was on her third glass of Merlot when the phone rang again.

"Hello?"

"Hi, it's Monday and I'm calling as promised. Sorry about it being late, but your phone was busy earlier." Lisa recognized the voice immediately.

"Robert. I didn't think you'd remember me." He knew she was smiling. "Yeah, this has been a busy phone night. I've got a massive test in the morning and Karen and I've been comparing notes again."

"Yeah, I've got an important and heavy load in the morning too. I remember I said I'd listen to your life's story but it's late for both of us. I'd like to take a rain check on that offer and cash it in over dinner on Saturday—I'll pick you up around six o'clock, dress casual. Good for you?"

"That was pretty quick…I'll have to check my calendar and see if I have the evening free." Lisa was thinking as fast as the Merlot would allow. A short time at the party, a short time in the car…she couldn't deny that his words moved her…how much better did she want to know him?

"C'mon…nothing fancy. A nice dinner, two glasses of wine, and we could get to know each other better. I think you'll like me. I know I like you."

And there it was again, that smooth, entreating voice hugging her towards him, smoothing the way, making it easy for her to say yes. A moment later, she said softly, "Yes, that evening is open." A few minutes later, Robert wrote her address down and they said goodnight.

Lisa slid under the covers and puffed up the pillow behind her head; the bed did seem a lot larger. Her thoughts drifted—a boyfriend out of town, and she's flirting with two guys—where's the sense in that? Was it good luck to have guys interested, or bad? She woke at 3 a.m., turned off the light, and returned to a fitful sleep.

Chapter 8

Her morning class dealt with financial forensics—fraud detection and criminal investigation. It was important information, but the professor droned on in a monotone that invited inattention; it was difficult to stay awake. Later, in the library, she picked out a few books on forensics, primarily asset recovery—the point where her eyelids had begun to droop. The books could fill in what she missed, especially the one written by the professor.

The sun was bright and, in her eyes, but she saw Ray Oliver soaking in the sunshine, leaning against the law library wall. Just like when they first met.

"Hi, right on time. I just knew you wouldn't disappoint me." Ray said.

"Yep, reliable, that's me. On the other hand, I had to take this route and you were obviously lying in wait for me. Thank you for waiting."

"Okay, I'm weak. I've been wanting to see you since we said goodnight. There, I said it. I finished class a half-hour ago…like my tan?"

"Glorious, it is. And what do you have planned for us this evening?"

"You'll be out of class by five. We'll both be hungry. I was thinking the Red Hawk for a burger and then the State for a movie—it's a classic, *Harold and Maude*. Afterward we'll find a cozy bar somewhere and …."

"Okay, I'm sold. Meet you here after class." She turned and Ray watched her bound up the steps. This time she waved at him before the door closed. Ray likened the quickness of her acceptance to almost ripping an item out of his hands. He wasn't particularly into omens, but he interpreted that as a good sign.

For him, the beginning of a week always started with a review of case studies, and the introduction of an unstudied Supreme Court decision. He knew he should strap himself in a library chair and finish the memory work, but he had made good progress earlier. Truly, at the moment, the only pro and con decisions he was interested in centered on Lisa.

The air was crisp and refreshing. He felt elated. As ever, when he had something of importance on his mind, he went for a walk—the more to think about, the longer the walk; now was the time for a long walk. It had been less than two days, yet she seemed to dominate his thoughts…which were inescapable, Lisa was a welcome difference in his life and he wanted her close to him. An hour later, he arrived at the Bus Ad building as the students flowed out the door and down the steps. Lisa approached, smiled, and split her pile of books between them, saying "thanks" as though he suggested that he shoulder half the load; Ray took them dutifully. They walked and talked; both were eager for more of each other. Could any Monday late afternoon have ever been better?

Standing in front of the bar and looking up they saw large gold letters on a blue background spelling out Red Hawk, flanked by two additional signs, smaller versions spelling bar, and grill. The signs were evenly distributed over the width of the business. The colors represented yellow maize and Azure blue, the never fully agreed upon official colors of the University of Michigan. It didn't really matter unless you were a student, and maybe not even then. To most, the letters were just gold on a Ford blue background.

What the Red Hawk lacked in width, it made up for in length. The place was brightly lit. Ray and Lisa took a booth on the left. The bare brick walls supported a beamed ceiling and in places a light-colored paneling featuring an intricate maze pattern. The bar was long and impressive, a light-colored wooden construct with a huge, spotless mirror surrounded by an ornate frame. The waiter brought them a couple of beers. They were so engrossed in their conversation that they didn't notice the lack of further service. When they looked up, because their glasses were empty, the place was full and Ray had to almost yell to get the waiter's attention. He finally ambled over—Ray refigured the amount of tip he was going to get.

They ordered half-pound burgers on onion rolls, a side of beer battered onion rings, and a couple of the Hawk's micro-brews, Bell's Amber Ale. Both were hungry and although the order was large, they managed to finish. Their conversation was light and amusing and midway through the second beer Ray reached over and held her hand. Lisa liked that and wondered, for an instant, if it was something that Robert would have done.

Lisa's loyalties confused her, when she was with someone, she seldom thought of anyone else—even if she had made love to the other person the night before. There was not the slightest tugging at her heart or conscious. She would force those thoughts from her mind, almost with a shiver as a strain of the song "Love the One You're With," an old Crosby, Stills and Nash song, would briefly fire through her brain.

Ray couldn't quell his curiosity. He didn't want it to sound like an interrogation, but he wanted to know all about her.

"Where're you from?" he asked.

"Before I came here, I used to live in Rock Springs, Wyoming."

"Used to live? As in I was born there, or I lived there for a year or two?"

"Well, actually, have you ever seen those movies where a baby is left on someone's doorstep?"

"Yeah" he said, now dreading the answer.

"Well, in a way, in one sense that was me. My mother put me up for adoption before I was born. The people that adopted me had been orphans themselves; they became my mom and dad. I never saw my real mother; she never tried to get in touch with me. I don't even have a picture of her. I have no idea as to whom my father was…they were never married.

So, I suffer no pains of longing for her when you get right down to it, she was something that never existed for me. When I was ten, we were in a car wreck. My dad and mom died instantly; I was in the hospital for a couple of months with assorted broken bones. My parents didn't have any sisters or brothers and so I didn't have any blood relative to take me. No one they knew wanted another kid, besides I was crippled up and needed medical care. I was put into a foster home and waited to be adopted. And after a year or so, another one, and then another one. No one took me...that's just the way it was."

"I... I, uh, am sorry...I didn't mean to pry."

"No, nothing to it. I'm reconciled to who I am and where I came from. It was a terrible childhood, but look at me now," she flashed a triumphant smile and an uplifting of her arms like Rocky. "I'm a fully grown, independent woman, and have like most people, a couple of ugly regrets; and I'm working on a second college degree. I am successful and intend to conquer this world."

Ray mentally kicked himself, again...he seemed to have developed a talent for opening wounds and sometimes for waggling his finger in them, as well.

Lisa was wound up, probably the beer Ray surmised.

"So, you asked from where? Well, it started out in Rock Springs, WY and after my parents died, and the foster homes, I eventually ended up in a local orphanage. After a couple of years, I just "aged-out".

"Aged out? What's that?"

"Ha, that means I became eighteen years old. When that happens, you're out on your own."

"They just release you...no help from any one?"

"Yep, that the way it is. No love or loyalty from anyone. You get a handshake, and then it's out the door. I got a job as a waitress in a crappy restaurant and saved all I could from my wages and tips. I ate there for free and slept in the back with the cockroaches—the owners were ok with that. I suppose I was a cheap burglar alarm or something. I swore I would never work as a waitress again.

Anyway, after that I worked as office help in an insurance firm, went to night school at the local college, transferred to and graduated from the local university, and then got hired as an accountant at Deloitte—a big name in the field. And here I am. An additional degree, and more bucks on the horizon. Okay, so that's my life's story—what's yours?"

Lisa eyes had been focused on the beer she had been swirling slowly in her glass while she talked. Now she set the beer down and looked at Ray.

Ray hesitated. He had thought his childhood had been unfair. How those inequities paled in comparison to Lisa's life. It was his turn to swirl beer.

Ray told her about his dad who liked to give him hurtful boxing lessons and how he deserted Ray and his mother. How he labored long hours in construction and boxed to scrape enough money together to keep the house and buy food. Ray was too tough for the kids at school so they never taunted him to his face. But he knew they talked about him—no father, his mother—occasionally their family's cleaning lady. Ray never wore the in-clothes or popular gym shoes—Pumas, Adidas, Nikes? —out of the question. As a young teen, the only couple of shirts and jeans he had been proud of were those his mother bought for him at the Salvation Army resale store. He told her of his mother's death, his successes in college and in particular, law school. He dreamed of becoming someone successful and respected, with enough money to never have to live in poverty… and how dread of that lived always in the back of his mind.

The unraveling of their stories and the hopes and fears that sprung from those terrible beginnings literally bonded them together. Their intensely private inner needs for comforting and consolation slowly became a selfless desire to provide the same for the other. Their conversation was far ranging, from the intimate to the most bizarre and hilarious. A couple more beers were delivered to their table and drunk. They had lost all awareness of time and were startled when the waiter asked if they wanted "last call," the Red Hawk was closing.

The street lights cast their shadows onto the sidewalk where they blended and separated as Ray and Lisa occasionally bounced into each other, once almost dropping their books. They weren't drunk, but they had a happy buzz on and meandered down State, joyful and oblivious to all except a general perception of the brightly colored neon lights in the storefront businesses.

Ray thought one more bar stop would complete the night; Lisa agreed. The Old Town was open till two a.m. and they headed toward it. At Liberty, Lisa stopped on the corner and pointed, "Hey…look at the State Theatre…its dark, show closed." That, to their semi-inebriated minds, seemed so funny they got weak-kneed from laughter and had to hold on to each other to keep from falling. They had totally forgotten *Harold and Maude*.

The Old Town had a nice crowd…not too noisy. They found a booth, ordered a couple of beers and resumed where they left off. Somewhere in the midst of their conversation, Ray began wondering how he was going to get her alone. He couldn't even have guessed, but he was a late comer to the idea. Lisa's mind was already working on it. She wanted him.

"My roomie will be home tonight, but maybe you'd like to stop by for a drink…maybe the day after tomorrow. Wednesday evening okay with you?"

Ray nodded his head, "Sure, Wednesday's good for me too." As far as he was concerned, any day of the week was good for him. Warm, lusty thoughts pounded at him like waves on a shore.

Lisa scribbled her phone number on the table napkin and gave it to Ray. "You'll need a ride, call me." Ray didn't trust his pocket, he put it in his wallet. It was midnight and they had pretty much talked themselves out. Both had things to do in the morning, so it was time to pay up and go. Outside the door, they grabbed the handrail and took the four deep steps to the sidewalk.

Ray walked her to her car. Lisa drove him to the Lawyers Club and dropped him off, but not before he leaned across the seat, placed a warm hand on her cheek, drawing her to him and kissed her passionately. Lisa returned the kiss with as much passion. They were both breathing a little deeper than normal as Ray said good night through the open window.

Chapter 9

Robert Lawrence was excited about his Saturday date with Lisa. Having reserved a table at Wheeler's, an elegant restaurant, he anticipated a couple of drinks afterward and, hopefully, by the end of the evening she would like him at least half as much as he already liked her.

He knocked on her door exactly on time. The door swung open and Lisa, smiling, paused a moment before saying anything. She gave Robert a moment to take her in... his eyes and expression would be far better than any mirror's reflection. Robert didn't disappoint her. He was awestruck by Lisa's appearance. She wore a clinging, low cut emerald green dress, which complimented her every curve. Her blond hair was curled and shoulder length, a bright red lipstick colored her most perfect lips, gold hoop earrings, and for the first time he noticed her eyes were green. For a few seconds Robert's world stopped, but he managed a smile and asked if her sister was at home as though he disbelieved that the woman before him was Lisa.

"Ready?" she said, and without waiting for a reply, stepped out, draped a sweater over her shoulder and locked the door. Robert was most definitely ready.

Wheeler's, for Lisa, was a major change from the campus restaurants. The tuxed maître' d, checked Robert's reservation, "Ah, yes, Dr. Lawrence." This way please, and led them to a secluded table in the Spoke room. Lisa admired the elegant chandeliers, linen table clothes and napkins, and sets of crystalline glasses. The plates were china and flanked by bright, spotless silverware.

They were seated and the wine captain appeared. It was startling in that it was more like he had materialized rather than approached the table. Robert ordered two glasses of Prosecco.

"Do you have a preference?"

"Yes, I'd like the Canelia Prosecco."

"Excellent choice, sir. I'll be back in a minute." and he vanished just as quietly as he had appeared.

Robert had to smile as he summed up the waiter's response "Excellent choice, eh? You know I could have said Pepsi Cola or milk and he'd have said, 'Excellent choice'. I love it."

Lisa ignored his remark. She tilted her head toward him slightly, opened her eyes wide, and said, "Doctor Lawrence?" stressing the title.

"Oh, yeah, that...." he said in amusement, although he would rather have had that gone unnoticed. "Well, I'm almost a doctor and I find that if there is even a squeak of a request or perk, they'll sometimes bend a bit because of that. In particular, I wanted the Spoke room; sometimes it's already booked. I just wanted to make sure. The title works most of the time, except once, in my first year of med school, there was a real Dr. Lawrence that showed up after I was seated. It could have been embarrassing, but it turned out to be my father. We all moved to a larger table and I was forgiven.

Lisa laughed out loud, "Caught, eh?"

"Yeah, by my own father. And you'd think that that might die down after a while, but it didn't. It happened a couple of years ago, but I think there isn't a friend or colleague of my father's that doesn't know the story."

"Your father has a sense of humor. What're your parents like?"

"My father graduated from Harvard med school, and eventually became the head oncologist at Northwestern Hospital in Chicago, and also taught at Chicago University. Several years later, he took a parallel position at Beaumont Hospital in Grosse Pointe here in Michigan. My mom has a degree in English, and busies herself with charity work, and is devoted to, and an officer in her club—the Park Crest Women's League. I don't have any brothers and sisters, so when I went off to school their focal point changed. Each pursues their own interests, but they seem comfortable with each other—probably waiting for grandkids so they can spoil them. Robert squirmed inside a bit, thinking that maybe his commercial may have been a little too neon.

"Sounds like they're pretty much fulfilled; not much in the way of challenges left. Do you like a life that's planned, or do you like its uncertainty?"

Robert answered thoughtfully, "I really don't know. All of my schooling has been programmed...pretty much like yours. When I leave academia, I would like to celebrate by taking six months and hiking all over Europe. That would be filled with uncertainty, especially since I don't speak any foreign language. Want to come with me?"

A thought of herself hiking through the mountains, drinking wine from a bota, crunching into hard breads and eating goat cheese by the handful crossed her mind.

"Hmm, no thanks. Sore feet, rain, sleeping under overpasses and an occasional youth hostel isn't my idea of freedom. Nope, not for me. I much prefer a life of comfort...maybe a series of stays at European resorts—three months ought to do it, followed by a Mediterranean cruise, gambling casinos, and some night life, dancing, and watching the sun rise from the cruise ship's rail. Then maybe a flight to Brazil, Rio De Janeiro in particular, for more of the same."

"Why Rio?"

"No particular reason, I just like the sound of the name—hey, this is my fantasy and I can indulge my desires without restriction."

"You know, you're right. My version of escape was a little lame...I should practice my fantasies. I think I could get used to yours really quick. I hereby designate you as director of fantasies. I will knock on your door often."

They finished their drinks. Lisa watched Robert place his glass exactly in the center of his napkin.

"Why'd you do that?"

"What?"

"You're glass. You practically measured its distance from each corner of the napkin."

"Hmm...an unconscious act. I never noticed. Probably some deep psychological disorder...I think that Charles Manson used to do the same. Yours is pretty much in the napkin's corner...what do you suppose that means?"

"Statistically, I suppose it means that I had an equal chance to duplicate your placement, but due to some motor-control error it ended up in the corner."

"Ha, then you admit the goal was the center."

"Not at all, the goal was the other corner."

John, the waiter, politely intervened, taking charge of the empty glasses and asking, "Another drink or would you prefer to order?"

Robert nodded at Lisa as if to say "Eat?" and she pronounced an enthusiastic, "Yes." Robert told him they would like to eat and added, "We'd like a bottle of Perrier Jouet—I had it last time I was here; it's a great tasting Champagne."

"Ah, yes...an excellent choice, sir." He presented the menus and he was gone, leaving Robert and Lisa delighted at his consistency.

"You sound like a Wheeler's regular...come here often?"

"A couple of times a year. When my parents came in from Chicago, years ago, this is where they stayed. I joined them and we ate here. In the summer the pool is open. It's a nice get away for me."

"And for me...thanks for bringing me here. I'm hungry, what's good?"

"Their prime rib and roast duck are excellent, same for their rack of lamb and chicken piccata. Close your eyes and point your finger anywhere on the menu, you can't go wrong."

The waiter brought the Champagne in an ice bucket wrapped in a linen towel. Lisa ordered prime rib, au jus, and the baked French onion soup; Robert, the rack of lamb and a shrimp cocktail, and two sides each. John thanked them for their order, and left. Like all good waiters, John simply remembered the order; he would later translate their order onto the bill.

Robert poured the Champagne and toasted Lisa: "A happy moment, may it be repeated often." They clinked their glasses and sipped the Champagne. An otherwise romantic moment, but the bubbles tickled and made Lisa sneeze; a few driblets of Champagne rolled from her nostrils, but were quickly collected by her napkin.

"God! I'm so sorry," said Lisa through the napkin, genuinely embarrassed. "I certainly hope that this isn't the part that will be repeated often."

Robert tried not to laugh, but it was funny and a short burst of almost suppressed laughter escaped from him.

"You know, you and my mother share the same "Champagne reaction." She still does it from time to time. He was still laughing.

Lisa forced a smile. Behind that smile was a rush of almost paralyzing thoughts: S*hit! I share that with your mother? how freaking wonderful can that be…can't hardly wait to compare notes…Jesus Christ Robert, what a dumbass thing to say…*and facetiously… *what woman doesn't want to be like her date's mother, even in little ways? Shit! Shit! Shit! calm down Lisa, calm down, it's just a little thing, he probably didn't mean it to sound so…so….* She took a deep breath and let it out slowly.

Robert rekindled the conversation, soon making the mishap vanish and smoothing any misgivings Lisa might have had into nothingness. As he spoke, the candle's flames reflected in his eyes, giving them a sparkling appearance. His dark wavy hair and mellow voice were extras. She was already leaning. In her heart she knew that all he had to do was keep playing his music and she would dance for him.

"Be careful of the onion soup, the crock is very hot." John's voice intoned, as he skillfully set the crocks down before them and unknowingly put Lisa's thoughts of intimacy on hold—and Robert's thoughts of Lisa as well. Although Robert was carrying the conversation, there was not a moment when his deeper thoughts had not raced ahead as to what might be.

Robert dipped a shrimp into the sauce and voiced his satisfaction. He looked up to see Lisa's eyes shut, holding an empty spoon, savoring her first taste of the soup. "That is the most wonderful flavor…it's absolutely great. "Here," she said, filling the spoon, "take a taste." Robert leaned forward, tasted, and agreed…he liked the soup, but he had imagined the taste of her lips on the spoon as well.

The appetizers were followed by two superb entrées. The dinner was slow paced and their conversation a delight for each. The meals were faultless; neither Lisa nor Robert had room for dessert. Robert signaled the waiter, checked the bill and paid with a credit card. On the way out, Robert pressed some cash into John's hand. Lisa saw the move, and liked the personal touch.

There's a bar in this place, and several steps away is the Hub—they have a live band and dancing. What'd'ya think…up for some dancing?"

"Yes! I haven't been dancing in at least forever."

The band was almost done with their first set. Lisa and Robert grabbed a table and ordered drinks. A half hour later, the band was back and beating out an up-tempo tune. Robert grabbed Lisa by the hand and led her onto the crowded dance floor. Lisa's moves were smooth and sensual, her dress moved up and down her legs and Robert darted glances at her body as she turned. She didn't have to look; she knew he was watching and she loved it. The heavy rhythm of the music was hypnotic, they moved together almost enraptured. The colored lights played across the lively crowd, and the collective cry was for more and louder as the evening wore on. Lisa and Robert kept the pace for three or four tunes at a time, before they hit the table for a pause. And then, so soon it seemed, it was last call and last dance. Robert held Lisa especially close, occasionally pressing his chest into her breasts, and bending down to kiss her neck as they swayed to the soft music. Lisa shivered with the delight of his soft kissing and held him tightly to her.

It was closing in on two a.m. when Robert drove past the guard shack at Arbor Landings. He parked in front of her apartment, moved close, and kissed her. Robert's heart was pounding, he couldn't get enough of her. She responded with as much interest, but stopped him when his hand slid up to her breast.

Although her breathing quickened, she managed to whisper, "Hey, first date, you know?"

"Yeah, but God, you're wonderful. I want you."

Lisa came close to giving it up it there and then…there was a huge difference in wanting someone and needing someone. Most guys didn't know the difference. It was so much better to be wanted than just needed. He was still playing the right music, she just wondered if he knew the difference in tunes…nonetheless, this just wasn't the time.

"Hey, slow down, not so fast. I might like you enough…but you have to give me some time to think. I truly had a wonderful time tonight and I do like to be with you…but I did tell you I was dating someone else. Why don't you call me tomorrow?"

"What's the matter with tonight, how about a coffee?" Robert said with a slight pleading in his voice which made him slightly embarrassed, but it thrilled Lisa. This guy, this Robert Lawrence, begging…was somehow pleasing to her.

"You see the light in the front window…well, that mean's my roomie's boyfriend is with her. I don't know when they came in; they could be in bed, or watching a movie. I'm thinking this is not the best time to invite you in."

Robert, crestfallen, saw the wisdom in not pushing too hard and backed down. "Great, then we'll talk again tomorrow," and leaned forward for another kiss. This time Lisa moved forward, moved a hand to the back of his neck, and kissed him hard on the lips, slipping her tongue once, quickly, past his lips and out again. Robert, surprised, moved his head back. Before he could say anything, she had stepped from the car and shut the door. "Talk to you tomorrow, thanks for the wonderful night; see you." In ten steps she was at the apartment door and inside. Lisa's departure had been done so quickly and gracefully that Robert's "g'night" were framed on his lips, but remained unspoken. He was still reliving the moment as he turned onto the main road.

Lisa locked and latched the door behind her, turned on the kitchen light and unplugged the front table light from the automatic timer. It was time for a shower and some sleep. She made another mental note to round up all of Mike's things in the morning and get them out of sight.

Chapter 10

Sunday morning and ten o'clock...Lisa, eyes still shut, took in the morning sounds and stretched out under the sheet, pushing it down the bed, feeling it softly brushing over her breasts. Lisa cupped them in both hands, and lightly pinched both nipples, thinking to herself, *Robert almost got you girls last night...maybe next time.* Her mind floated, remembering the night's wonderful time. Eventually, her thoughts turned to the day's demands. She reluctantly resigned herself to getting up, cleaning, and studying...the usual Sunday morning routine...except when Mike was around. He would've pinched her nipples for her and they would have rolled in bed for an hour. Lisa sat on the edge of the bed and prepared for the day. The first goal for this morning was to stash Mike's stuff and the second bedroom was just the place. By default, it seemed to have already become the room of odds and ends...ski stuff, a computer table and desk top, filing cabinet, piles of books and a closet half-full of assorted clothing. The only rule was keep the door shut.

After her morning coffee, she began to load Mike's stuff into the room. The half-filled closet became fully stuffed; his personal items were piled in a corner. His extra shaving equipment, aftershaves and colognes, robe, shoes and sandals were stashed in a heap in another corner. Eventually, the bedroom Mike and she had shared was transformed into the Lisa room, while the other became the Mike museum.

Mike had been good to her and she knew she shouldn't be treating him this way, but she also knew what she wanted and Mike wouldn't be around for months...and didn't her needs matter? Practically speaking, she rationalized, there wasn't any other solution. If it wasn't unusual for a man to have a couple of girlfriends, why shouldn't it be the same for a woman? She saw Mike as a boyfriend because of her lack of commitment to him. The morality and fairness of what she was doing were just hazy issues to her at best. She wasn't a bad person, just self-centered and a little remorseless, but in a gentle kind of way...maybe partially remorseless would be a better description.

Having relocated Mike from their bedroom, she called his cell, maybe to expiate any leftover feelings she hadn't quite quenched. She wasn't sure, but it was better to call him than to wait for his call later.

"Hey, Lisa! Good to hear you, thanks for calling...what time is it there?"

"Almost eleven thirty."

"Yeah, a little after eight here. Hey, I tried to text you last night, but there wasn't any response and..."

"Yeah, I know. I got your text off the cell last night but it was so late. I went out with a couple of girls from school and we had a good time; we closed up the bar. Sorry I missed you. So, how's life in Seattle?"

"The business is doing better, and I'm getting applause from the home company for my restructuring plan, so in that sense things are doing well. But for me, personally, without you, it's one of the loneliest times in my life. I have an idea. Ready? Do you think you can get away for a weekend; it's only a five-hour flight from Detroit Metro. If you leave Friday, you can be back in time for class Monday afternoon. It'd make a real difference to me, to us, if you could come. What'd ya think...or, it'll work the same for me. I could fly there for the weekend...I've got things pretty much under control here, a weekender wouldn't hurt."

Lisa who could usually conjure up an answer was dumbstruck. This was not a good idea.

"What a great idea," she said as convincingly as possible. "Let's pick a weekend. I've never been to Seattle." She needed time to think. She didn't want to fly out to Seattle but she couldn't very well have Mike come home either and accidentally bump into Ray or Robert. Mike was easily explainable to both, they knew she had a boyfriend, but Mike would be blown away if he even suspected the truth.

"Super. Any weekend will be just great."

Lisa closed her eyes and plunged. "Next weekend would probably be the best. I'll pick up the tickets tomorrow." So how bad was this really? She liked Mike and would have a good time with him, and she had never been to Seattle. In retrospect, it really wasn't a terrible thing at all. She would get away from the campus and it'd also give her urges for both Ray and Robert a chance to cool down. Slowly, Lisa, slowly she repeated to herself…take things slowly.

"Lisa, you've made me the happiest guy on the planet. I love you."

Lisa, past the initial shock, talked freely and happily with Mike. All was well again. They talked until, like most people, they just ran out of more things to say.

"Ok, so call and give me a time you'll be getting in and I'll be there."

"Ok, call you later. Bye." Her "bye" overran Mike's "love you." No matter, Mike was elated and didn't notice.

Lisa had one morning class on Friday and it ended at 9:30. She booked a noon flight and called Mike. Afterward, she called Robert and asked if he could drive her to the airport. She hated airport parking, even the shuttle service from the offsite parking lots. If Robert was willing, why not? Robert's classes were in the late afternoon. He jumped at the chance and offered to pick her up on Monday evening, as well.

"Robert, you're a life saver. Thank you so very much." She returned his kiss.

"I'm sorry to hear about your aunt. My condolences to the rest of the family."

The porter took her suitcase, she waved at Robert, and followed the porter into the terminal. Lisa touched down at the Seattle-Tacoma International a little after two, Seattle time. Mike was waiting. He drove straight to his apartment, a luxury condo on top of a high-rise overlooking Elliot bay. It was beautiful and the view was spectacular. Twenty minutes later they were in bed.

The weekend went faster than either had expected. It was a swirl of walks, sites, and wonderful dining. Breakfast along the riverfront and later, a most excellent lunch at Fresh Bistro. Mike was using the company expense account. He wasn't sure how he was going to reconcile the expenses, but he had made some great savings moves already and he hadn't spent any personal money for the week he had been there. He believed his expenses would be approved. Mike was visiting places he had only read about, so the tour of Seattle was as new to him as it was to Lisa. Both were as excited as tourists, as indeed, they were. Everything was new and they were eager for more, more pleasurable distractions, and more time to enjoy them. But time was a problem.

For Lisa to get back on time she had to leave early. Their very late and last evening dinner was by room service at the hotel. It was a mixture of both happy and sad feelings. Hours later, Mike would have to take her to the airport; she had a 3:30 a.m. flight.

The Sea-Tac airport traffic was minimal and a curbside space was readily available. A porter was opening her door an instant later. Each said their last goodbye and shared a long, kiss while the porter stood politely at the rear of the car. Then with a wave, Lisa was gone. Mike felt a sense of loneliness already beginning to creep in; Lisa, less so; whatever departure sadness she experienced was displaced with the memory of a great weekend. She'd call Mike later that evening.

Chapter 11

Robert greeted her as she came out of the gate and walked with her to the lower level to retrieve her suitcase. About fifteen minutes later, the luggage began dumping out on the carrousel. Hers, a yellow piece with a red sticker was easy to spot and soon they were in his car, on the highway and headed for the university…both had mid-morning classes.

Lisa related some of her trip's details—how the funeral was quick, sparsely attended, and that her Great Aunt Lisa, her namesake, was eighty-one. There wasn't really much more to tell, other than she had seen some relatives that she hadn't seen in many years and the weather had been mostly cloudy. Robert was polite and listened as though he was interested.

He dropped her off near the Bus Admin building. After classes, they picked up a pizza and drove to Lisa's apartment. Robert hoped her roommate wouldn't be there.

The apartment was stuffy and needed airing out. Lisa opened the drapes, pushed the slider back and cranked out the windows. The shears billowed in and out and the air change was immediately noticeable. Robert sat in the kitchenette while Lisa popped a couple of Cokes and poured them into glasses, something she thought Robert would appreciate. Similarly, and for the same reason, the pizza was dished rather than grabbed out of the box. Despite the niceties, each ate like wolves, downing the first pieces as though they had been starving.

"You wouldn't think this place would get so…uh, airless, with your roommate being here."

"Yeah, but she often stays with her boyfriend and goes off on trips with him on the weekend. He likes to camp out and go climbing, sometimes he just cranks up his motorcycle and off they go."

"She a student?"

"Nope, she's a regular working girl, 9 to 5 usually…unless she's busy on a project."

"What's she do?"

"Don't really know her that well. I just answered an ad for a roommate and it worked out. I've never asked her what she does, except I know that she works for her father…he owns a manufacturing company—some sort of an automotive supplier, I guess."

"That might work out good for you…having a friend that's into a company with family connections."

"Yeah, that's a possibility, but Deloit's paying the freight and they expect me to return. The way it works is that if I don't come back, then I'll have to reimburse them their expenses, which are considerable. I'm also thinking that if I would jump ship, they wouldn't be inclined to come up with a good recommendation for me. In this business, it bodes well if you can show a record of fidelity. In about three months, when I finish school, all this," she waved her hand around the apartment, "will disappear like Cinderella's horse drawn coach. I'm going to have to have a place to go and Deloit is it as far as I can see at the moment. They're a good company, they pay well, and I have a future with them."

"So, there's no visiting European spas, or flying down to Rio?"

"Ha! Yeah, it's fun to imagine escape, but if it ever happens it'll have to be later on in my life. At the moment, establishing myself really matters and that's my focus. How about you…off to hike Europe?"

"I'm afraid the same applies to me. In the real world, I'll have to get going on my residency immediately or it'll have a hugely negative impact on becoming a full-fledged doctor."

"How's that?"

After three years of internship and residency, I can begin to start my career, so I won't even hit my stride until about four years from now, and that's providing I don't get into a sub-specialty—a fellowship—which will cost me a couple more years to complete. But the tradeoff is that when I finally finish, I'll be a doctor for the rest of my life, earn an excellent income, and live happily ever after. The end."

"And I thought accounting was a long haul…are you sure you want to do this to yourself?"

"My father did it. I can do it."

"So, he's the standard then?

"Yeah, he set the mark and I have to jump higher if I can. Both dad and mom are achievers; they expect it."

"How does Robert Lawrence feel about it?"

"I know they want the best for me, and I can see how my father's life turned out. Even if I don't surpass him, the profession will still lead to a comfortable and fulfilled life. Do I like medicine? That's the question that's more to the point. And the answer is yes, I love what I'm doing and where I'm headed."

Lisa well understood the answer. "When I was younger, I used to read books on getting rich…you know, mail order businesses, raising chinchillas and the like, and they all lead to some fabulous fortune. But there was always one chapter missing in each book, and that is the one that dealt with 'I love my work.' If I were ever to give work success seminars that is where I would start and eventually end: If you want to be successful, you have to love your work otherwise your work will become a humdrum drudgery."

Lisa took a bottle of red out of the wine rack and two glasses from the cabinet. She handed Robert a corkscrew and asked him to pour while she closed up…evening had arrived and the room was becoming cool.

Robert's hopes for a little "alone" time with Lisa began to rise, but were scuttled a minute later.

"Robert, I've got a lot of homework to do and I'm beat from the trip. I thought we might have a glass of wine and call it an evening. I gotta call my boyfriend in a while, and I'm thinking my roommate Kathy will be back around ten…she always comes in late on a Monday. I'm gonna hit the bed, sleep like the dead, and be up early tomorrow morning and bury my nose in the books until noon, at least."

Robert, ever considerate, said he understood. He could see she was dead tired. True, he had a heavy study schedule as well, but he would gladly forego all of it and pay the penalty for a night with Lisa.

Robert's lips tasted of wine and the long, lingering kiss Lisa gave him as he left. He was ready for more of each. A thought popped into his mind: why didn't Lisa's boyfriend drive her to the airport? But it was dismissed as quickly…obviously Lisa thought she'd rather be with him…a good sign for the home team. He smiled inwardly. While Robert thought of Lisa, Lisa was stretching out on the couch with another wine. She was asleep after the first sip. Robert slipped out of the front door and silently locked it behind himself.

Chapter 12

Morning came and car doors banged shut as people left for work. Muffled bangs for sure, but enough background noise to wake Lisa. Half asleep, she poured the wine back into the bottle, spilling most of it onto the outside of the bottle which ran down and puddled in the sink. She blasted it with the sink wand and looked forward to her own shower. But first…Lisa searched her suitcase for her cosmetic bag. Not there. *Whoa, now that's going to be a problem.* She searched her carry-on bag, and it wasn't there either. *Crap!* Last she remembered she had used it in Mike's bathroom.

She needed to talk to Mike, but it was barely eight o'clock. That would mean around five o'clock in Seattle. She'd shower and wait. In the interim, she'd study.

Ten o'clock. She dialed Mike's cell. He was up, but in conference with two employees. He told her he'd call back as soon as he could. An hour later, Lisa's studying was frustrated by two recurrent thoughts—maybe Mike forgot; perhaps she should call him again. The phone rang, it was Mike.

"Hey, what's up?"

"Well, I wanted to thank you for the wonderful weekend."

And that was true, and within several minutes of mutual remembrance, she worked in her pressing problem.

"Mike, this morning, in your bathroom, did you see my cosmetic bag."

He knew the question even before she asked it. Here it was—the moment of truth…the perfect time for the lie. He made up the conference excuse earlier because he buckled. He was ready to talk with her now, but he still had an unsettling thought that she might be able to detect deceit in the sound of his voice.

"Well, it's important. Can you send it to me…today…? I really need it as soon as possible."

"Heck, I thought you were pretty enough. You don't really need lipstick and eye shadow and all that stuff."

"Thanks. But it's not that "stuff" I need. My birth control pills are in the bag. I need them."

"Well, then, come and get 'em." Mike said in a deeper voice, trying to sound sexy and failing, "but, you don't have to worry, I'm here and you're there…."

"Uhh, Mike, it doesn't work that way. I've got to keep those little gems in my body on a daily basis. Even if I start them up again, it'll take a couple of weeks. Even if I come to see you again, we won't be able to fool around." That part, she hoped, would make an impression on Mike.

"Uhuh, yeah…that would be different. Okay, I'll get it to you as soon as possible…I'll tuck the entire bag into the mail this afternoon."

"Thanks Mike, I really appreciate that."

"Uh, hey, couldn't you just go to the local pharmacy and pick some up?"

"Yeah, if I were home in Minnesota, where my doctor's office is…I could have him write another script. No problem. But I'm here in Ann Arbor, and it won't work that way; he'd want to see me. That's why I got an extended script so I had extras just in case."

"Ah, yeah, I get it. Okay, I'll make sure it's in the mail."

They exchanged small talk for a little while longer and then said their goodbyes. Lisa felt relieved and went back to her studying, the only thing that bothered her was that she could picture the bag both in Mike's bathroom, and also in her suitcase. She was almost positive that she packed it, but she had done sillier things and dismissed the thought.

Chapter 13

Mike Trescott was a conventional man, reared by middle-class God-fearing parents, in a small town. He was typically "old school" in his thinking and practically apolitical in his view of government. His philosophy was simple; despite the tides of political difference, there would always be those in charge that would care for and protect the country; criminals would always be caught and punished; and hard work would be rewarded. His values, the ones that hit him hardest, were those that dealt with morality, honesty, and fairness. It was exactly those provincial values that were now racking his conscious with guilt.

Mike was breathing hard and his palms became sweaty, even his knees were a bit shaky. He had taken a very bold and deceitful step, and he had also lied to Lisa and guilt was giving him a pounding—those two things he would never have done to her…ever. His thoughts ran wild, maybe he was insane…maybe he should call Lisa and tell her…and then the thought hit him…*everything* he had done? No! She would hate him…but, no harm done, maybe she would forgive him. Maybe she would be convinced how much he loved her. His mind was in a turmoil. He would do anything for her…and, in fact did, much to his present discomfort. His rationalization raced to plug the holes in his scheme, but ultimately left him little comfort.

Mike felt like a thief, but he was desperate to have Lisa and, inspired, had devised a plan which began long before he left for Seattle. Lisa did pack her makeup bag in her suitcase, but he removed and hid it.

He knew Lisa wouldn't commit to a marriage soon enough for him…in fact, many of his sleepless nights revolved around her not wanting to marry him at all. She always had a way of putting off those discussions, even to the point of argument. So, he simply stopped pushing her. And that's when it happened.

Somewhere in the depths of his mind a coal of a thought began to glow, a devious thought. Mike convinced himself that he could bring about a marriage if he was clever enough. His conventional thinking led him to believe that if Lisa became pregnant, she would marry him. Happened all the time…did he not remember Mary Beth Perkins back in high school, less than ten years ago…she and Earl Hutchins got married. Same thing happened with Flourine Walker and Bud Haskins and a few more whose names had already faded from his memory. But those marriages happened. If Mike asked Lisa to quit taking the pills, he knew she would refuse. There had to be a better way.

Mike researched birth control for a week back in Ann Arbor. He learned that the pills were around 99.9% effective. So, what did that mean? What was a tenth of a baby? Ah, statistics again. It meant that one woman in a thousand, even though on the pill, could still become pregnant. Mike practically memorized the information on birth control pill usage and their cautionary advisements. The one that particularly caught his eye was "keep from freezing;" if frozen, their effectiveness was unreliable. So, before he knew about Seattle, he wrapped her three packets in a towel with dry ice, and put them in the deep freezer for a couple of days. He sabotaged her entire supply. There was absolutely no evidence of tampering, and he believed that the pills were now ineffectual. The pack she was using would run out in a short time, sooner if she didn't have the ones in Seattle.

So, thought Mike, what's the chance of being struck by lightning, the odds against winning a four-digit daily lottery ticket were one in a ten thousand, the odds against winning a huge lottery were astronomical…but, it does happen. And that's how he'd present it to Lisa. She'd have to buy it…she has three packs of pills, even if she examined the remainder of her pills long after she discovered she was pregnant, they'd be still intact. She would never know. *Yep, Mike, you just might get away with it.*

He had not anticipated being sent to Seattle, but that interruption would present only a small problem. She had a little less than two weeks to go on her present pack when he left. He figured he could get with her soon after. To his mind, since Lisa was a little like a rabbit in her desire, it probably wouldn't be too difficult to make her pregnant. And if not sooner, they no doubt later, but it was going to happen.

Chapter 14

It was late afternoon Wednesday when Ray Oliver picked out Lisa in the crowd of students and waved. Lisa hurried to his side and gave him a hug. They walked along arm in arm, not talking, just absorbing the last warmth of the day. Lisa's time with Mike was now barely a background thought.

"Missed you. How'd the weekend go?" Ray asked.

It was a simple but expected question, and Lisa was prepared for it. She wanted an additional inside glimpse of Mr. Oliver that she didn't already have. She was going to give him a little pin prick to see how he'd react.

"Great. Mike and I went to the Stratford Shakespearian Festival, saw Dangerous Liaisons—a great play, and then Niagara Falls. We did some touristy things, had a great time, and came home. I crammed Sunday night and was in good shape for Monday. How about you?"

Ray was shocked that she could be so straightforward...it was so bold and matter of fact...what a shit thing to say to him.

"Mike? Let me guess, he's your boyfriend?"

"Yeah, didn't I mention that before?"

"The boyfriend part, yeah, just didn't know his name."

Ray tried to keep his composure, but he was pissed; greatly pissed, jealously pissed. A below the belt punch would have been preferable to the way she made him feel. *So that's why she hadn't returned his calls...she was out of town...with "Mike".* They turned a corner. Ray stared at the sidewalk and leaves as they crunched underfoot. Lisa was talking, but whatever else she was saying was lost on Ray. He couldn't slow the angry thoughts...*she was out of town for the weekend...obviously she spent a couple of nights with her boyfriend. Damn! He wanted her and she was sleeping with another guy, what the hell is that all about*...but, his lawyer's training rose to the occasion and prevailed. He separated the issues and reasoned that, intellectually anyway, Mike was her boyfriend, not Ray Oliver. That was something he had to work out and getting angry was not going to help. He forced himself to calmness, and tried to carry his end of the conversation as though she hadn't landed a punch. Inside, he was seething.

Lisa knew exactly what was going on in Ray's mind; she intended it. The power of a casual wounding was exciting, even arousing. For a while, Ray's conversation rambled. He was trying to sound casual, but it was an effort and his voice had an occasional odd tone to it. She felt like she had kicked a puppy. *How could Ray be so weak? C'mon Ray, slay the dragon, come and get me.*

Ray had wobbled temporarily but recovered. He never met Mike, but instinctively knew he was an asshole.

"Lisa, I want to see you some evening…tonight, tomorrow, the next…I don't care, I want to see and be with you." There, he said it. And was disgusted with himself for spilling his guts.

"You don't know what you're getting yourself into. Mike's a tough guy, and he really likes me. There's going to be trouble."

"I can take care of myself. What I'm hearing you say is that Mike "likes" you, and you're warning me…so, you must have some feeling for me for you to say that. Here's a question for you, how much do you "like" Mike?"

"I've been with him for a long while. First in Minnesota and now here."

"That's no answer. Do you love him?"

Lisa looked away briefly and reflected on her real-life relationship with Mike. It was a question she always avoided. *Do I love Mike?* With Ray asking, it sounded like a conscious demanding to be recognized. And, she supposed, it was time to acknowledge something she always knew. The answer was heartfelt and sad. Her eyes focused on some trees and the view dimmed as she spoke the words softly, "No. I don't."

In a flash, Ray let his jealous anger leap out in a loud, accusatory voice, "Well, then why are you sleeping with him? You went away for a couple of nights…you didn't sleep in separate beds, did you?" He was immediately sorry for having said that. *How stupid could he be…what was wrong with him?*

Lisa, startled, flashed a hot, angry look at him and retorted in an equally hot-tempered voice, "What I do and who I do it with, and why, isn't really any of your business. Who the hell do you think you are?"

And that was a ball that hung, mid-air, and squarely in his court. He had no answer.

Lisa jerked her arm away from his and marched off. Ray yelled, "I'm sorry…please wait," and lastly and even more lamely, "can I at least call?" It was pathetic. She said nothing but lengthened her stride. Lisa, however, wasn't angry or hurt. Stalking off was a required affect; Ray needed a slap. Her mindset was actually more philosophical. *Why do men always assume an ownership as if a woman were a 'thing' or worse, needing permission to do something?* She hated that. What she wanted to know, Ray had shown her. It didn't make him a bad guy, only ordinary. He was, unfortunately, no different than any other guy she had known. What had she wanted? A Ray that would dismiss Mike as unimportant, that he, Ray, could love her like no other man on earth, that he was confident that if she tasted him, she would not want another. A man strong enough to lead a willful Lisa?

Later, when Ray rethought the incident for about the twentieth time, he was still at a loss to understand it. It went from a "great to see you" to a disaster within a few minutes. If he could have just ignored her story of the weekend with Mike, it would all have gone better. But how could he? In the end, he thought what had to be said was said, but he knew he overstepped his bounds. Mike was an asshole; maybe Lisa was one too. And yeah, him too.

Chapter 15

"Mike, it's been three days since we talked. Did you send the package?

"I'm sorry. I got busy and forgot, but I sent it yesterday. He lied."

"Did you post it in the morning or evening?"

"Late afternoon."

"Express delivery?"

"No, didn't think of it."

"Mike...I really needed that. If it doesn't come today, I'm going to have to start another pack of pills. I can't trust the mail to come on time. Ah, forget it...I'll just do that—start another pack. At any rate, I'll be happy to get my personal things when it does come...can't even recall what I have in the bag—lipsticks, eyeshadow, maybe even some dental floss...just stuff...okay, Mike, sorry for sounding so—"

"That's all right, I'm sorry for being so slow. It'll all work out. When you coming back to Seattle? Soon, I hope."

"Not for a while, we're headed into mid-terms and I'm swamped. Had a great time though, and I'd like to do it again. I'll let you know when I've got a window."

Moments later they hung up. Mike was both elated and tense as waves of what he had done flashed through his mind. He had been busy at his calendar counting the days she'd already missed and now, she was into the placebos he created. Soon Lisa, soon, he thought.

And Lisa did exactly as Mike predicted. In the morning she removed a birth control pill pack from the drawer, removed one, downed it, and felt as secure as always.

Chapter 16

Lisa was sorry for what she had done to Ray. She guessed at how he'd react, but she needed to know for sure. Was she angry at him for yelling at her…no, that was part of her scenario and his reaction was almost as if he were following the script, although she wished that he hadn't. Yeah, he was hurt and pissed off but that was okay. She knew he wouldn't stay that way. She needed a rest. She'd let both Ray and Robert chill for a week. She was tired and her studies needed attention.

For the next week Lisa fielded calls from all three. It was fun for the first two days. Robert stuck to the Monday's calling, but snuck one in on Friday; Mike called a couple of times that week, but they ran out of conversation soon enough. Ray called several times and sounded a bit sheepish on the answering machine. She answered twice and accepted his apology the second time it was given.

By the end of the week, Lisa was in the mood for some company. Was it to be a couple of glasses of wine and goodnight, or was it to be an overnighter? Was it going to be Ray or Robert? Both were hungry, so was Lisa. Lisa enjoyed weighing the options and ultimately picked Robert. He was the one that was going to get lucky—maybe—she'd see how it went after the wine.

"S-s-sure, I can," he stammered and repeated, "dinner at seven." He was there exactly at seven o'clock—having to drive around the complex for five minutes so that his arrival was perfect.

He smiled at Lisa as the door opened. He wore a dark jacket, white shirt, and tan pants. He looked like a fashion magazine model. Lisa felt a sudden flush of excitement—the evening was decided, just then, in the doorway, without the wine.

Robert tried to keep his eyes level with hers, but her low-cut sweater made them drop. He leveled his gaze again, but once more his eyes wandered to her cleavage. She enjoyed his momentary conflict, and asked him in.

"Have a seat," she called to him over her shoulder as she walked toward the kitchen. "Cornish hens, baked potatoes and asparagus in an hour if everything cooperates. If not, we'll just have to wait it out...I'm kind of new at this. I've got a Chablis on ice in the meantime—give me a minute."

Lisa brought the drinks and sat next to him on the couch, her short skirt growing shorter as she crossed her legs and leaned toward him. Robert welded his gaze to her face. She was beautiful and compelling. Their conversation continued as if unbroken from their first date. But all the while an undercurrent of lusty thoughts coursed through Robert's mind. He wanted to pull her close, kiss her, touch her and feel her nakedness next to his.

Dinner went well. Lisa was pleased with herself, and Robert was generous in his compliments. They cleaned the plates and stacked the dishes in the sink. Lisa insisted that they soak overnight and she'd get them in the morning.

She punched in a play list of easy listening on her computer and the speakers began a mix of mellow music. The blinds had been rolled shut and candles lit. Conversation was minimal; they both knew what was going to happen next. She slid her arm across the back of the couch and around his neck as he leaned forward to kiss her. Lisa, her lips near his ear, whispered that her roommate wouldn't be back until tomorrow evening. That was all the green light Robert needed.

The kissing and fondling became more intense. Robert wasn't shy; certainly, Lisa wasn't. Their clothes practically slid off. Robert's hands moved slowly over her body, sometimes held and moved by her own hands, pressing his hands harder onto her breasts or between her legs. Lisa swung her leg over and straddled him. She moved a breast to his mouth and held his head tightly to it. Robert worked the nipple with his tongue and Lisa felt a small shiver of delight; and then again on the other breast, and back again. She spread her thighs and moved downward, brushing his stiffness with her hairs, wetting it, her body inviting him inside. Lisa slid down his entire length, swallowing him whole and holding him there, rocking her hips. Robert met each movement with his own thrusting and pushing. He couldn't stop if he tried, his hands clutched her backside and pulled her hard to him as an "uhh" sound escaped his mouth and his mind went blank. She felt it, an empathetic rush that made her insides tingle. Yet, she wasn't even half way to where she wanted to be. She waited for Robert's eyes to open.

"The bed's more comfortable. I'll get a blanket; we'll finish the wine and lay down together. Just a minute." Lisa eased herself off of him and stepped into the bedroom. Robert laid there, his pelvis at the edge of the couch, his head resting mid-cushion, his penis pointing at the ceiling, and his thoughts swirling with excitement.

Lisa returned and they wrapped themselves in the blanket, snuggled, fondled, and drank wine. In bed, it was a romp that lasted until just before dawn.

The mid-morning sunlight brightened the blinds and sneaked around their edges, giving the apartment a soft golden glow. Quiet was just beginning to give way to the usual Saturday morning sounds—a couple of car door slams from the Starbuck's latte people, some wheeling sounds from kids on bikes and skates, and distant muffled engine sounds from the complex crews' grass mowers and weed trimmers. But none of the sounds were annoying enough to interfere with a good morning frolicking. By noon, the lawnmowers were busy on her front lawn. Robert and Lisa showered, dressed, and were working on coffees while finishing the dishes.

"So, when do I see you again?" Robert asked.

"You mean on a date, or naked?"

"C'mon…just, you know, to be together…."

"Don't know. A lot depends on what our schedules and whether or not my roommate is here."

"We could always get a room somewhere."

"Your idea of a date? Lisa teased, but followed up with, "Sounds nice. Maybe. This was only our second date. I'm not sorry this happened, but I'm thinking it would probably be a good thing to slow down a bit and give it some thought. I need some time to think, don't you? There's more to this than just sex."

"I'm happy just being with you…if you're thinking it's just sex, then let's just see each other and hold off for a while." '*Just sex,*' he couldn't believe that he had just said that. In truth, he was excited to be with her, but sex was certainly a co-equal. Robert had a hard time separating the two ideas. And 's*low down*'… that was the furthest thing from his present thoughts. Robert had become a randy billy goat, his brains were in his other head; he thought he had actually seduced her.

They ate breakfast just outside of town and spent the rest of the afternoon wandering around Frankenmuth, a half-hour's ride away. Later, Robert introduced her to Birch Run's Tony's I-75 restaurant whose meals were so large they each carried away their next day's dinner as leftovers. Dinners there were more of an event than a meal. No one in the collective memory of Tony's patronage ever left there wanting more.

It wasn't quite evening when Robert parked in front of Lisa's apartment. He hoped that she'd invite him in, but she wound it up by giving him a lingering kiss and thanking him for the day, adding 'the evening too.' The goodnight was plain enough and the compliment made it go down smoothly.

Chapter 17

Sunday was Lisa's. Karen Bartelli told her Brad was out playing golf and that lunch was a great idea. Fifteen minutes later, Lisa honked once and Karen bounded out of her house. Café Zola's was only half full, and they grabbed a seat by the window. Crêpes and coffee were the order of the day.

"Lisa, this is so good. Classes are such a weary chore. It's good to get away. I called you last weekend, but you were out. Sorry I missed you, but it's good to see that you have a life outside of just school. And now, look, a whole Sunday free. What's been happening in your life?"

"Well, for one, it's been going faster than I expected. Mike's in Seattle and won't be back for a couple of months...probably about the same time I'm finishing up here. I don't mind telling you that I've been a little lonely."

"Lonely, hey...not the way Robert tells it."

"Robert! What do you mean?"

"He's been seeing you, hasn't he?"

"Yeah...but that's kind of private. How do you know about it?"

"I know about it because guys are idiots. Brad and Robert share a couple of classes and he told Brad he's dating you."

"Damn."

"Hey, not so bad...for you, anyway, not so good for Mike."

"Hey, Karen...it's not like I'm falling in love with him. I just need to be with someone and he seemed interested. He's a likeable guy, that's all."

"Hey, okay with me. Are you sleeping with him?"

"Karen! That's a hell of a question to ask."

Karen laughed. "I just wanted to know if he's any good in bed."

"Great, I'll tell Brad that."

"Nope. Don't do that…it was just idle curiosity."

"Oh, I see…is Brad any good?"

Karen almost spluttered her coffee. "Yeah, actually he's pretty good. I think I'm going to keep him."

This time Lisa laughed.

"What's Mike doing in Seattle?"

Lisa recounted the whole story and how Mike is re-inventing the company, and how much the home office loves it.

"He's successful and that's the problem."

"What, with success? How can that be a problem?"

"Well, Mike has now established himself and his future is clear and assured. So, he wants to get married. We've been together for so long, it seems that it would be a natural thing to do. He loves me," and haltingly, she added, "I wish I could love him back…and that's the problem."

Karen pursed her lips and stared at the tablecloth and then looked up into Lisa's eyes.

"Lisa that's serious. Haven't you ever discussed this before?"

"Yeah, he's brought it up so often it's become a sore spot. I've tried to tell him, but when I get close to the answer, his voice starts to quiver and he looks away—I know he's got tears in his eyes. It breaks my heart and I just can't tell him."

"So, when will you tell him?"

"Don't know…I've been avoiding it. I thought when I'm done with school would probably be the time. When I tell him I'm returning to Minnesota, and why, he'll know for sure. I've tried to tell him several times in the past, but he's such a great guy. He's going to take it really hard."

"Well, you've got a problem…how does Robert fit in?"

"Robert. Yeah, Robert…he's a great guy too and he has a great future ahead of him. Do I like him? Yeah, I like him…but we dated only twice. I don't know where we're going."

"Do you like him better than Mike?"

"Karen, that's a real crap question."

"Maybe it's not such a bad question, maybe the answer is just uncomfortable."

"At this point, I don't have any answers."

"Well, for what it's worth, Brad tells me that Robert is absolutely in love with you and that you are all he talks about."

"C'mon Karen, I've got enough of a burden, don't tell me anymore. Please."

"Okay, enough said. I don't know Mike well enough to say anything one way or the other, but—and last comment—Robert is not only good looking, but he comes from a wealthy family—I don't mean just rich. His parents are well off, but their "nest egg" is what was left to his mother, from her parents. Ever hear of Goodyear Tire and Rubber? Well, she's a Preston, a granddaughter of the guy that bought the Goodyear' company and made it the big name it is today. Robert's dad married well, and if it wasn't for her money, he'd probably never made it through med school. Okay, that's it. I'll shut up…but he's a real catch."

"Jesus Christ! How do you know all this?"

"Brad."

"So, Robert just talks and talks about his personal life?"

"No…well, yes…no…sometime. All of this came out one time when Brad and Robert were pretty much drunk and swapping stories. Actually, when Brad came home, he was totally blitzed and told me…but, I'm guessing that he probably didn't remember much of it the next day. Anyway, he never brought it up again."

"Well, thanks for the background, but I'm really not interested in getting married."

"With a guy like Robert, you'd be set for life."

"Uhh, do I hear another commercial?"

"Sorry, it slipped out. No, more…honest."

"Karen, what are we doing?" We're both working are tails off to get a degree…for what? It was extremely difficult for me to get through college and I'm real proud of finishing. And, it was difficult to appear outstanding in a stable of workers doing the same job…to have my company see my potential. I'm being trained for advancement. I plan on using my degree—do you?"

"Not to beat a dead horse, but with the last name of Lawrence you won't need a job or career."

"Okay. Let me put it this way, after you marry Brad do you plan on working in your field?"

"Maybe for a time, but then I'll make a couple of beautiful babies and wait for my husband to come home. That's good enough for me."

"Seems like a waste…why school at all?"

"You think a doctor wants a waitress for a wife or someone who has credentials. Think what happens when you meet the parents—'Hi, mom and dad, this is Karen; she's a barmaid at Clancy's.' Even if you're not introduced that way, you know the parents will get around to doing a net worth on you. You better have something going for yourself."

"But all this time in school…all this work?"

"I met Brad by going to school, and yeah…that was worth it all."

"Didn't you have any other interests…guys?"

"Yeah. A veterinarian and a dentist."

Lisa smiled, "Which was the better lover?"

"The veterinarian, but Brad's going to be a neurosurgeon." said Karen without hesitation, and smiled like she had delivered a trump card.

"Ah, Karen…I envy you. You know what you wanted and you got it. Me? Well, I'm not sure exactly what I want. At the moment I'm just bumbling and hoping to stumble on it. I hope I find it, and when we get to middle age you and I will get together, have a glass of Champagne and reminisce."

"Hey, were you actually a bar maid at Clancy's?"

"Nope, I made that up. Actually, it was a crappy little bar named Fat Jack's and it was only for a short time. I was twenty-one, but it didn't take me too long to figure out the clientele didn't have much in the way of ambition except to get me into their bedroom. It was a poor menu, so I went back to school and the choices just got better and better."

They finished their third cup of coffee, paid the bill, and stepped out into the crisp, fall afternoon. It was a delicious, intoxicating, and runaway kind of afternoon that neither wanted to end. Inspired, they drove over to the Nichols Arboretum and walked the trails, meandering through the fields and forest, sometimes off the official paths, indulging themselves in a sense of unrestricted freedom. They walked, and talked as though they were newly met friends of long ago. Neither had paid any attention to the time, until Karen glanced at her watch and said something about Brad and dinner and the spell was broken. They headed back to the car and to Karen's home. Karen home to Brad, and Lisa home to…well, just home.

Lisa turned her cell phone on and saw that she had backed up messages from Mike, Robert, and Ray…and two others, one from a credit card company and another from someone selling magazine subscriptions. The afternoon had been invigorating and obligation free. *Why disturb that wonderful feeling with a return call to anyone? Let them hang in there. Lisa's not taking calls today.* She kicked off her shoes, cranked up the speakers and stretched out on the couch, comfortable and content, mindless of time and decisions.

Chapter 18

Lisa expected to see Ray waiting for her either going to or leaving class, and was mildly surprised when she didn't. He sounded anxious enough on the phone. She hadn't given a second thought to their little tiff and was disappointed when he didn't show. Lisa's recent dalliance with Robert was good and warmed her thoughts...but for Lisa it was also like starting a fire. Loyalty was never a problem with her when she was in the mood. Ray was handsome and she liked how he reacted to her. She was surprised when she got to her car and saw Ray leaning against a fender, holding a bunch of flowers.

"I guessed that you'd be here about now."

"Nice flowers. A gift from an admirer or did you buy them for yourself...or are both cases correct?"

Ray was still humble. "I don't have too much to admire in myself lately. I just wanted to say I'm sorry again. This is a peace offering." Then in a little stronger voice tinged with an attempt to humor, "I'm shy and if I gave them to you in front of a bunch of your classmates, I'd probably have a nosebleed."

"So, you chose the parking deck...Ray, you're so romantic."

"Thank you. I'm inspired," and grinned lopsidedly.

"Okay, so you were a little less than gracious...we've already covered that. I'm okay and you should be too. Let it go...I have. The flowers are beautiful. I have a couple vases of artificial ones, but I haven't had any real flowers in months. These are beautiful."

Lisa was in a cheerful mood, maybe even a bit capricious, and added, "C'mon over and we'll find a vase for them."

The words, "C'mon over...." echoed inside Ray's head. Had he heard right? She was still smiling; he must have. For Ray, it was an epiphany, and he immediately felt an intensely pleasing redemption.

He was in the passenger seat and buckled up as Lisa began easing herself behind the wheel.

"First, we need something to eat. I'm a bit of a fast food junkie. Pizza, Subs, Kentucky fried, Mickey D's, you name it and I'll like it. How about you, fast foods good?"

"Sure. Grew up on them, and haven't changed. K of C sounds good to me. Let's grab a bucket and a couple of sides and gorge."

A Kentucky Fried Chicken sign popped up within a couple of blocks and fifteen minutes later they were at the apartment. Lisa's cell phone rang as she went through the doorway; she punched it off immediately.

"Wine?"

"Nope. I gotta have a Coke. Sometimes a root beer, but usually a Coke. I think it was Aristotle that said, 'Coke is the handmaiden of fried chicken,' and I believe him."

"Yeah, and he probably said that in English as well. But I agree, a cold Coke is required," and she snapped the caps on two cans and set out some plates. Ray opted for a can. Lisa slid a straw into her coke and took a long drink. It had been a long day for both of them and they worked their words in between bites of chicken and forks of coleslaw, right down to the last four pieces of chicken—the drumsticks, and a partial container of macaroni and cheese.

Lisa looked into the bucket. "You ever notice the drumsticks are always the last—unless there's some kids around and they're told the drumsticks are special, they have their own handles...that way the parents get the better pieces. Grownups are crafty."

"Ya know, you're right," Ray said offhand, "my dad told me about the handles and I always went for them. I think I was about thirteen before I discovered thighs and breasts." Ray's observation was innocent, but when Lisa gave him a wry look, he understood and his cheeks took on a pink tone; he truly hadn't meant anything more. Lisa thought his blushing was sweet and told him so. Ray's color darkened another degree.

She threw him a lifeline, "You have a late class?"

"Nope, all done for the day. But like everyone, were headed into mid-terms and it's a lot of review. Doing 'okay' on a test, for a lawyer is about the same as failure. Whether it's contract law, trial procedure, or any tenet of law, okay just isn't good enough...so, the mantra is review, review, review...and then review some more. The law grads that are marginal often barf when they take the bar."

Ray tried to sound insightful, but his mind raced with bothersome thoughts. *Dumb, Ray, dumb...why do you keep saying dumb things...legs, breasts, god what's next...Lisa is making me crazy; I don't even know what I'm saying half the time. Straighten up...get a grip. God, she's beautiful. I want her.*

"Ray, I think I'm ready for that wine now. You?"

"Oh, yeah, that'd be great." *Maybe a gallon or two might straighten me up.*

"Hey, where's your roommate, Kathy?" *Damn! I did it again...too soon to ask that, too soon.*

"She's in Toronto on a business trip. She left yesterday and probably won't be back until Wednesday or Thursday. Why?" Lisa thought the 'why' part was artful. She liked to watch Ray scramble for words. "*Why?" Hell, Ray, no mystery there.*

"Uhh, I was just wondering if I might get the chance to meet her tonight."

"Nope, sorry. Maybe some other night." *Good one Ray, good one.*

"Maybe you'd like to double some night, Kathy and her boyfriend, and you and me."

"Sounds good to me. Although, I've never met her boyfriend, so I can't tell you what he's like...but she likes him, and I like her, so he's probably alive enough to join us. I'll talk to her when I see her. The glasses are in the cabinet, you pour, and I'll get the music."

A moment later, a soft Latin beat flooded the room and Lisa returned. Two half glasses were at the edge of the counter. Lisa reached for hers but was intercepted by Ray who stepped forward, slid his arm under hers and brought her close. His hand, behind her neck, pulled her face close to his and he kissed her, gentle at first and then harder and longer...the kind of kissing that left them both breathing harder.

"Mr. Oliver, you do kiss well," Lisa whispered.

Lisa's skin was warm and smooth on his cheek. Her faint jasmine scent was the glimmer of a golden promise to his senses for more Lisa—just for the taking, and Ray was consumed with that promise. He kissed her neck and Lisa held him tighter, feeling his chest pushing against her breasts, his thigh pressing between her legs. Lisa wanted more of him; she led him to the couch.

Eyes closed, minds wrapped in communion, lips on lips, and hands exploring each other's bodies. They lay together, fondling, unrestrained in their desires. Ray unbuttoned her blouse and unfastened her bra. Lisa removed it, settled back alongside of him, and unzipped him. She slid a hand into his underwear and gently groped. She expected him to be erect, restrained by his shorts, but it wasn't in the place where it was supposed to be. She was surprised when she didn't feel him at all. Was something not right with Ray? *Oh, no, Ray please don't tell me there's something wrong*...but then she felt its root and its direction, it was down his right pant leg. She pushed her hand down his pant leg, feeling him—further, and even a few inches further yet. Unbelieving, she removed her hand and felt him on the outside of his pants.

Ray gave a little grin, and skinnied his pants off, kicking them away from the couch.

"Oh, my goodness."

And, indeed, it was an oh-my-goodness sized appendage. Lisa reached out, felt it, admired it, stroked it and couldn't believe her good luck.

"Lisa, tell me if you're uncomfort... "Uhuh," Lisa said, but his words were lost in her wonderment of Ray's gift.

"We can be more comfortable in the bed," she said.

Ray didn't need to be told twice. The rest of their clothes fell to the floor four seconds later.

In bed, Ray pulled her gently over on top of him. She was eager and foreplay was unnecessary. She sat on him, feeling his hardness between her legs and began sliding back and forth, long slides, pleasuring herself with each. Lifting her hips, she reached behind herself, caught several inches of him, and guided him into her, starting him on the way to an experience she only dreamed about. She moved down on him slowly, feeling herself stretching wider, a pleasurable hurting, as he moved deeper into her.

Again, Lisa was lost in a swirl of her own theater of the mind and hardly heard him. Her needs became rhythmical. Little strokes, deeper each time. Up and down again, and over again, and further inside her with each stroke. It was wonderful and several times the words "good…good…good…" sometimes softly, and sometimes in grunts, escaped unbidden from her lips. They rolled over and Ray moved on top of her. She thought for a moment that when he climaxed and pushed harder it might hurt, so she clutched his root nearest his body and held her hand as a buffer between him and herself.

But it was unnecessary, as he reached climax, Lisa relaxed her grip and slid her hands out and around his back; she let him settle in and could feel his throbs inside of her; he fit her perfectly.

Their lovemaking was a lusty marathon, lasting for hours until both, exhausted, fell asleep. Just before dawn, Lisa awoke with a cramp in her left thigh. Both thighs made her feel like she had been doing leg lifts, her back ached slightly and her muzzy felt deliciously sore. She stood and rubbed the leg cramp out. Ray was still asleep, the outline of his wonderful tool showed under the sheets. Lisa sat on the edge of the bed and squeezed it gently. It began a slow rise, coming awake even before Ray. And it was twice more before sunrise.

Chapter 19

It was almost noon when they rolled out of bed, had a playful shower together, and began sorting out the day ahead of them, but lunch seemed the most compelling of any of their thoughts. Lisa remembered she turned off her cell phone last night and knew that Mike at times could get squirrelly. If he called a couple of times and didn't get an answer, he might call the police to come by and check on her wellbeing—that wouldn't do. She powered on the phone. Ray opened the door and Lisa grabbed her purse as her cell phone rang. She reflected that when juggling boyfriends, it was a good idea to be mindful and keep all the illusions intact. It was Mike.

"Mike, good to hear your voice."

Ray gritted his teeth and swore inwardly, but knew enough to keep his mouth shut this time. *Good to hear your voice? Hell, she'd been with him over the weekend just a week ago... lonesome for him already? And after last night? Crap.* Caveman thoughts scrambled his brains for a minute before he settled them down.

"Yeah, that'd be great. At nine-thirty then...good...I'll be there. See you then."

"What's up?" Ray asked, dreading the answer.

"Mike needs a pickup at the airport tonight."

A barely audible "Oh," dropped from Ray's mouth.

She came to him, hugged him and kissed his lips. "Cheer up sunshine, Mike and I do more talking than anything else." and she gave his length a little squeeze. "We're old friends, but the fire dimmed, so we just end up talking about what we want in life. And, that's where Mike and I are at. Leave it alone, it'll work itself out. You'll see."

Ray and Lisa ate a leisurely lunch and while Ray was able to temporarily crowd thoughts of Mike from his mind, Lisa's mind flipped between Ray and creating mental checkboxes of things she had to do so that Mike's homecoming wouldn't turn into a disaster.

Lisa dropped Ray off at the law quad, finished her class and hurried home…she had a lot of moving to do. First, Mike's clothes and books back into her bedroom, launder the sheets, dump the wine bottles and Ray's flowers, wash the wine glasses, wash the tub—Ray's hairs would be hard to explain—Mike's shaving equipment into the medicine cabinet, slippers under the bed, vacuum, and in general tidy up the place. Actually, the flowers were pretty nice; maybe she'd keep them and tell Mike she bought them for him. She jumped into the work and was done in a couple of hours. Ray knew enough not to call for a couple of days, but Robert didn't. She wondered how she going to avoid that?

Mike's flight was on time and she picked him out of the crowd—he was the one waving a cosmetic bag over his head. They made their way to the car and whipped down the highway, Mike talking as fast as he was driving, some business but mainly about how much he had missed her. Mike's confession of longings made Lisa uncomfortable and her "me toos" sounded lame.

The apartment was exactly as Mike left it. It was reassuring, and it was easy for him to believe that Lisa was unchanged as well. For Mike, it was time for bed and Lisa. And Lisa, whose fire had been lit by Ray, was happy to oblige.

Mike made love like a man possessed and she met his passion with her own desire. Occasionally thoughts of Ray or Robert would ghost through her mind but they weren't disconcerting. Lisa admired her lovers, especially Ray, and switching thoughts of them pounding away on her was a secret and vicarious thrill. Mike was insatiable and the love making, more lust than anything else, was a marathon by any standards. Mike's pent-up energy gradually dissipated, one relaxed moment replaced by another until he was gently snoring. Lisa hugged him and kissed him gently, knowing that she had to deliver a message to him that he didn't want to hear, and she didn't want to give.

Mike was up early and going over his presentation for the fourth time. Lisa showered and dressed. They grabbed a quickie burrito at Mickey D's and she dropped him off at work. Mike would be finished around noon and would be having lunch with the board. Afterward, she'd pick him up and he'd drop her off at school. Mike had the evening planned.

They stopped at Robino's, a working-class Italian family restaurant with old fashioned red and white checkered table clothes. One glass of Chianti later, the waiter took their order of spaghetti and meatballs. Mike ordered another round of drinks, and although the basket was only half empty, Mike ordered another basket of bread sticks and butter. The food was good and plentiful and as Mike ate, between mouthfuls, he told Lisa how well his presentation went. But how afterward, the CEO told him, in a serious voice that they 'wouldn't be needing him here anymore.' Lisa heard the excitement in Mike's voice as he related the story, his words tumbled out and his hands moved in the air in emphasis, as if they were helping to extract the words he used.

"I stammered something about 'you're letting me go?' and set my glass down hard; half the drink sloshed out. I think my face went white, and then probably red…my heart pounded and I stood up. My chair rocked back and fell on the floor. I'm glad they stopped me before I started finger pointing and swearing. It was their idea of a joke…a joke that went badly. It's like they say about jokes, everything's in the timing. It took a few seconds—long seconds to my mind—before they emphasized the words "needing him here" and then again, almost in unison, when they saw my distress. It was their way of offering me the job in Seattle—it was mine, the salary, the expense account…everything. Mine! They hoped I would take it. They were being cute; the offer was intended to be a surprise. By then I was hyperventilating…they were over-talking each other, trying to calm me, and their words were a babble…I couldn't get focused…I thought I was going to have a heart attack. It was one of the worst moments I've ever experienced."

"If anyone did that to me, I'd tell them to get screwed...I would quit. I'm glad you got the job, but what a terrible price to pay. Is everything patched up?"

"Yeah, it took me a little while so I could hold my drink without spilling it...and we laughed about it awhile later, but it was a brief and horrible, sinking feeling. I will never, never, never do that to any of my employees. Not ever."

Lisa was proud of Mike's accomplishment and genuinely had hoped for the best for him. But now that Mike's life was secure, she knew what was coming, and again dreaded it. *Today is Friday, and we'll have a good time of it; Saturday too. Sunday afternoon, just before he leaves in the afternoon, that's when I'll have to do it. There was no easy way to do it. Happy endings are for kid's books. Adults usually have their hearts wrung out at the end of a story, and this story can't end differently.* Lisa's masked her misgivings well, submerging the inevitable conflict, knowing that like impending doom, there never was a "best time," or a "right time," just recognition that "it's time."

Their conversation drifted back and forth, trading stories of their days of intensity and boredom. It was apparent that Mike had submersed himself in his work, and believed that Lisa had done the same. He had called Lisa at least once a week and pretty much knew about Lisa's life in general, but it was a pleasure to him to hear her say it all again. He was interested in anything and everything Lisa...but Lisa couldn't tell everything. She looked him in the eye and spun stories for him...out with the girls, an occasional barbeque with friends, cramming for exams, and an occasional flaming out on the couch with a couple glasses of wine blurring her thoughts. And Mike, of course, bought it.

Dinner wore on and the conversation slowed; dessert, another drink, and eventually handholding and reminiscing. The candles had burned down about half way. It was a busy night, and the waiter began nudging them along, asking them three times if there might be anything else they might want. They noticed a few people standing in line and got the idea.

"It's getting late, maybe we should be going?" Lisa nodded.

Mike checked the bill, calculated the tip with the waiter's pen on the bill, tallied it up and flipped his plastic onto the table. The waiter was back soon enough. Although he looked like a red headed Irishman, he said, *"Gratzi,"* and gave Mike the boxed-up breadsticks. Lisa couldn't help herself. A picture of Robert walking out of a restaurant with a box of anything flashed through her mind and a half smile crept across her face.

The warm wind ripped through the car as it purred down the highway. Mike was elated and rambled on about whatever crossed his mind, and was focused on how he was changing the Seattle office when he pulled into his parking space, the lot was almost empty. When Lisa opened her door, she saw the double black, short body Cadillac parked two spaces away; the driver's window down. Mike, by then, had walked around to meet her. Lisa's eyes made brief contact with Robert's and her breath sucked in. *Please God, don't let him make a scene.* She walked quickly away from him.

Robert's car started and rolled backward, into the street, its wheels squawking as it jumped forward and out of the complex.

"Damn," said Mike, "check that out...must be some kid...but driving a Cadillac...if his dad knew that'd be the last time he drove it, I'll bet." Lisa didn't say anything. She was already working on the next step—what if the phone begins to ring? After a half hour, she began to relax...Robert hadn't returned and pounded on the door, and the phone didn't ring. So far, so good.

The evening moved on to the familiar—music, a couple of drinks, and to bed. Mike couldn't quiet his mind, even after lovemaking, he began another conversation which petered out only because Lisa fell asleep.

Saturday morning, the phone rang. Lisa's heart jumped when she thought it could be Robert. But it was Mike's buddy Frank who invited him over to watch a football game with a couple of other friends. Mike readily accepted and while he was gone, Lisa caught up on her studying. It was late afternoon when Mike came back.

Chapter 20

Sunday, midafternoon, was worse than Lisa ever could have imagined. Mike maneuvered her to the couch, and sat her down. A nervous grin flickered across his lips as he knelt before her and shakily presented a large diamond engagement ring. His voice a little shakier than his hands as he asked her to marry him.

"Ohhh, Mike.... Ohhh...." Her voice quivered, and that was all that she could muster.

"Please say yes." His eyes already beginning to well up...her hesitation could only mean no. His heart was pounding so hard it felt like it was about to rupture; his throat and lips became dry, and he felt slightly faint.

"Lisa...please..., will you be my wife?"

She watched his face melt, becoming a dreadful mask.

"Mike...I just can't." Her answer was as soft as his plea as she reached out and covered his hands and the ring. And it was done. Her next words were as difficult for her, but perhaps because there was an end in sight, she didn't have to search for perfect words—her voice found the hurting but necessary words she knew that Mike would understand.

"You want a wife who'll make babies, care for them, cook, clean house, do the laundry, shop, and grow old with you. That's not my life...I don't want that. Please understand...you're asking for my life and I can't give it to you...it's not in me to do those things."

Mike let her words sink in, slowly rose, and sat heavily down on the couch beside her, pursing his lips and giving out a long exhale. His elbows found his knees, his palms cradled his face and covered his slow, silent tears. His voice was constricted with emotion but he managed to say, "I always hoped that you might have a feel for those things...that you'd not be so...oh, maybe career minded is the phrase.

You're right, it's those things that I want. I thought all women wanted marriage, a home and family, they did where I come from, anyway. I prayed you might want those things too…maybe in time you will." And after a long pause, he asked, "Do you think that you'll ever get married?"

The apartment was now so quiet they could hear each other's breathing.

"Probably not," she said, not really convinced if that was true. But she saw the need to end their relationship, and knew what Mike had to hear.

"I sometimes think I'd like the security and companionship, but in a couple of years I know it'd be a disaster—with kids, a terrible disaster. We'd probably end up hating each other…and kids…what then? I don't want babies. I don't want the responsibility. I don't want the obligation. What I really want is to be independent."

A half hour passed, each minute seemingly longer than its allotted sixty seconds. Mike cleared his throat and asked, "So, what are your plans?"

"Graduate, return to Minnesota and Deloit Touche, eventually specialize, and work my way into management—maybe work in one of their European agencies for a couple of years. You?"

"It's back to Seattle. If I don't screw up, I'll probably have a life time job with Mycroft Purcell Inc. And, like you, I'll work my way up and probably retire comfortably."

"Well, yeah, that's good…I'm not looking for a retirement. I want my own accounting business. If I gain seniority, and position—and get some money together—in time, I'll have that. My plan is to be successful and croak at an old age in my office."

"You can always come to Seattle and work with me," he said, but he already knew the answer.

"Probably not the best thing to do—our memories would haunt us, and we'd never get anything done."

And there they sat waiting for time to pass and their departure to the airport. Mike was crushed, but there were practical things to consider and had to be said.

"I have a company car in Seattle, so I don't need the Benz. I love it, but the company will pay for only one garaged car…so, I'm going to sell it as soon as I can. Frank always admired it and always said when the time came, he'd like the first option. Looks like its time. If he wants it, I can probably sign the title over to him whenever he gets his money together. When I get rich, I'll buy another. You're close to the semester's end, so maybe you could get a ride from one of your friends till it's over?"

"Yeah, I can do that."

Mike continued while staring at the wall, "the lease on this apartment will expire…I won't be renewing it, but you can stay here until the last day. And, you don't have to pay me back for anything…the few bucks I left you are yours. They'll come in handy until you get your first paycheck."

"Thanks…I owe you big time. I'm sorry that this isn't turning out."

And, after a long pause, she added, "think you'll get married?"

Mike paused, took a deep breath and said, "I'm going to be sick for a long time, but, yeah, eventually I'll probably meet a girl and…" his breath suddenly left him and his voice cracked falsetto. He took a deep breath. He was trying to hold it together, but his emotions were roiling and threatening to overcome him. Before he could stop it, he said, a little louder than necessary, "Lisa, I'm always going to love you…if you ever… have a change of heart, please let me know." And he let out a heart rendering sigh.

"Thanks…I love you too, but marriage is…." and her voice trailed off and the sentence was never finished, but Mike knew the words. He just couldn't understand how you could say you love a person and not want to be with them forever.

Just as Mike's feelings were squeezing his heart, a lot of thoughts were also rocketing through his head. One in particular made him feel particularly guilty; he hadn't said anything about the birth control pills. Despite her decision, it was still possible with all the lovemaking they had done, that she might be pregnant. It was a long shot, a desperate hope, but maybe being pregnant might give her a reason to reconsider, even a little, enough to give him a second chance. He held that ace close to his chest and inwardly prayed. Abortion? He didn't think so; Lisa wasn't that kind of girl.

It was late afternoon, and the sunlight was taking on a golden glow. Soon, it would be time to leave. Like an otherwise happy couple in the aftermath of an argument, they moved through the rooms for the next hour, not talking, but making themselves busy and avoiding each other. Mike packed and repacked his bags several times, she straightening up the rooms. Ultimately, it was time. He took a last look around the apartment. Memories…even simple ones, previously unremarkable, now swam before him like a collage of photographic stills, flooding his mind with a bittersweet pang of happiness and regretful loss. This place had always been his refuge. For him, now, it held only a growing, gut wrenching sadness. For Lisa, it was a sad but inevitable end. She felt sorry for Mike. How could he not have seen it coming?

"Ready?"

Lisa nodded her head and picked up one of his bags and made for the door. Mike glanced around one last time and shut the door on what had been his happy life.

The car's radio had been turned up a little louder than necessary so they wouldn't have to force a conversation. Mike was wrapped in his disappointment. Lisa felt sorry for Mike, but that compassion was mixed with an ongoing review of her resources—which would run out first, her money or the lease?

At curbside, the porter took the bags from the car. Mike and Lisa kissed for probably the last time. Even Lisa had a lump in her throat.

"Call me…please," Mike managed to squeak out, "and often." He added with an attempted smile, but it came off a little crooked. She said she would. Lisa couldn't understand it, but a tear rolled down her cheek. And that prompted a few more from Mike. He turned and walked quickly away.

Chapter 21

Lisa took the long way back home. This time, the apartment not only felt empty, but it had a kind of coldness about it. She thought it was probably her imagination, but the fact that Mike was not coming back underscored the finality of it all and gave her a little shiver. She was relieved that it was over and knew in her heart that in time their phone calls and the emails would become fewer and farther apart. For Mike's sake, she hoped that Mike would find another girl. He was a good guy, but just not the one for her.

At times, she wondered if there ever was one…maybe all that she said to Mike was the truth…maybe she didn't need anyone, what then? A series of boyfriends to keep her company, and when her good looks faded and no man would be interested, what then? A childless spinster, alone, for the rest of her life? Bringing up children by herself was not an alternative. Did she even want children? Her own childhood seemed to answer that question.

Love? Lisa wasn't sure what that was. It seemed as though there were no other options except to make a difficult choice with difficult consequences, and that frightened her. Were those the only two alternatives to a woman's life? Lisa searched her soul for the thousandth time…what was being Lisa truly about?

Chapter 22

It was almost two weeks since she and Mike broke up. Ray and Robert called often. She enjoyed their conversations, but invented excuses to avoid seeing them. She had a sympathy for Mike that was inexplicable, and it welled up as often as Ray and Robert's calls and often in between, and would make hollow any liaison with either. If she could define her feelings, it would probably be along the lines of a haunting and remorseful disloyalty. She needed a little more time to ease her conscious. Tonight, Lisa decided was going to be an evening of solitude, wine, and music.

The phone rang and Lisa looked away from the annoying noise and stared out across the darkening court yard. This evening wasn't a good time for phone calls; she wasn't home for anyone. The message recorder kicked on; it was Ray…another message on top of Robert's. Maybe tomorrow guys, maybe. She found her "Blue Bastard" accounting book and tried to lose herself in it and in a small way did. By 10:00 p.m., the book rested on her nose and cheek, and she was snoring. Lisa didn't wake up until mid-morning, but only because of the ringing phone. It was Karen. Lisa let it ring, not eager to speak with anyone.

Chapter 23

Ray was out for a morning jog. The sun light had cleared the building roof tops and leaf shadows patterned the sidewalk; the air was refreshing. The Sports Coliseum was about a mile from the Law Quad, and he jogged it at least three times a week; he'd be loosened up by the time he got there. His usual work out was a half hour on the heavy bag, and a half hour on the speed bag, more if he felt particularly frustrated. Today, it'd be more. Lisa was etching her presence onto his soul.

He slammed the bag and rocked it with a series of straight lefts and rights, hooks, and then he shouldered the bag and released a flurry of combination punches as it swung back; and then again. His breathing was faster, punctuated by snorts of air when he threw and landed his punches. In a fight, blows were usually a matter of opportunity and calculated precision. But he wasn't fighting. His blows were more like an angry woodsman using his ax against a reluctant tree. The bag became Lisa's boyfriend, sometimes maybe even Lisa; anywhere his punches landed was good. *Lisa's been with her boyfriend for three days, three freakin' days!* And each word was punctuated by a smash of his fist into the bag. He pounded the bag until his breathing burned his lungs, and his arms and fists were tired. He stepped back, sweat streaming from his forehead and his body, and unbeknownst to him, a snarl on his lips. The bag swinging slowly.

"Damn! Sure'd hate it if you were angry with me."

Ray looked over to see a college kid, probably a member of the university boxing club, standing there with a grin on his face.

Ray managed a smile, and out of breath, closed his eyes and nodded…an acknowledgement of what he considered to be a compliment. Ray thought to tell him the secret…*all you need to be like this is to have a taste of someone you're in love with and know she's screwing another guy*...but the kid was young, in time he'd probably learn the secret himself.

Ray regained his breath, moved over to the speed bag, and began its rhythmic pounding. That was an art that took a beginner a little time to perfect. The bag's rebounds were quick, too quick to follow with the eye, but with experience you could hear the steady bam, bam, bam and could anticipate the bag swinging back. Ray's mind was flooded with thoughts of Lisa and his fists continued the tattoo until fatigued. He began missing and knew it was time to quit. He was exhausted. What he needed was a shower...a cold shower.

The walk back to the dorm was uneventful, except once when a red car passed and Ray, snatched from his thoughts, momentarily thought it might be Lisa. He would take a shower and call her when he got back. He needed to see her.

Ray pushed his door open and stepped inside. The cell phone on his desk was ringing.

"Lisa! Hey, how are you? I missed you."

"Yeah? Good, it's nice to be missed. I've got some errands to do. Want to keep me company?"

It was "Fanfare for the Common Man" time. Copland's cymbals clashed, kettle drums sounded, trumpets blared, and Ray's breath swelled his chest and stuck there for a couple of heartbeats. She had asked him over once before when he least expected an invitation. And now, again...kind of...an accompaniment wasn't the same thing as an overnighter. Confusing? Yes, and unsettling as well. Ray would be more comfortable if he could figure her out; black and white was much more preferable than whimsy.

Lisa didn't wait for his answer. She overrode his thoughts, answering for him, "Good, I'll pick you up in a half hour, see you then," and clicked off the phone.

Ray, cut short, was left holding a dead phone to his ear. He had been advised and given leave. *Was he that transparent? What made her so cocksure of herself? Things were supposed to be the other way around; he was supposed to be leading this dance. That's gotta change.* But at present, he was willing to eat anything, even minor slights.

Ray's spirits picked up and he was delighted when the red Benz pulled to the curb. Ray jumped in and the Benz purred forward.

"Lisa, you look beautiful. I really missed you."

"Yeah, you told me...except not the beautiful part." She shot him a quick smile.

To Lisa, errands and shopping were the same. Ray was thinking maybe a post office, or a cleaners, even a bakery or a fast food pick up. Wrong. Grocery shopping, and a new blouse and shoes were what she had in mind. Ray gritted his teeth and smiled throughout the next couple of hours. There was no place to enter into a serious conversation. It wasn't what he had in mind, but he was with Lisa and that made it all worthwhile. Eventually, she would have to stop shopping. He'd find a quiet place and tell her what he hoped for.

His plan was good as far as it went, but Lisa hadn't read the program. Ray found a quiet, mall sandwich shop. He was bubbly with excitement and told her again how much he missed her and wanted to see her, then felt stupid for repeating himself so often. About halfway through the meal, he suggested as tactfully as he could that she and her boyfriend might not be the best pairing. And, since their night together, maybe she was thinking that as well? He was certainly available.

Lisa's jaw dropped. "What! How dare you!" and she rose, tilting her chair back at an almost sure to crash angle. "You are one of the most presumptuous people I've ever met. Yeah, we had a night together, but so what? You think because of that I've fallen in love with you, or something like that? Not so." Her voice was loud enough to startle people at the next three tables. Women pretended not to hear, but little smiles flickered across their faces. Male companions shifted their heads slightly and gave sheepish grins, wanting to get a glimpse of Lisa and thankful it wasn't them in the soap opera unfolding before them.

Ray's face reddened, and his mouth opened and almost closed twice. This is not what he intended that was for sure. His hands went up and made small just above the table, up and down "quiet-down" patting motions. All he could say was, "Please," his eyes darting left and right.

Lisa looked around her and saw that her outburst had caused a stir. She sat back down, fuming and staring a hole in Ray. Ray began backpedaling as well as he could.

Ultimately, in a blather of apologies and invented explanations, Lisa's anger began to cool. Ray was vastly uncomfortable.

"It's none of your business but I'm going to tell you what happened this weekend." Ray wasn't sure he could stand any more anxiety, but leaned forward to share the confidence, thankful that she was quieter.

"Mike and I broke up. It was painful for both of us. I'm not interested in another relationship."

Ray, despite a feeling of having been whipped, was elated. He also knew about what would happen if he said so. That would have been really bad form. His thoughts raced and he said, quietly and sincerely, the truth.

"You are the most wonderful girl I've ever met. You're in my thoughts all of the time, and I've got to think you like me as well. When I'm not with you, I'm miserable. I just couldn't help saying to you what I said. I want to be part of you and your life."

There, he said it, and a lot better than the first attempt. He watched her face, trying to read her, maybe anticipate an objection, ready to create a defense or a retreat.

"We had a great night together. I like you and that's all I can say for now."

"Hey, okay. I'll settle for that. It's a start." He hoped that his smile covered his lie; his insides were shrinking.

"There's plenty of time, take it easier. I'm still working things out in my life."

Ray felt awkward and bumbling. This was the second time since he'd known her that he managed to create disaster from an otherwise promising time.

Both were quiet during the ride back. Lisa dropped Ray at the Lawyer's Club. Each looked at one another for a long moment. Ray said, "Sorry." Lisa nodded her head, and said the same.

"Give you a call tomorrow?"

Lisa nodded her head, "Yeah, that'd be okay. Less serious next time though, eh?"

It was Ray's turn to nod and say goodbye. He watched her car until it turned and was lost in the traffic. Ashley's Pub wasn't a far walk. Ten minutes later he was slamming down a succession of beers, trying to blank his mind.

Chapter 24

The next couple of days were a real push for all students. Midterm exams were taking place and the heavier course load they carried, the more they had to answer for. They had two days off from classes for final preparation, and then two days of exams. Karen and Lisa exchanged calls, usually to compare notes. They were tethered to their work and vowed to celebrate or commiserate soon afterward. Robert and Ray called as well, but the calls were only to remind Lisa that they were thinking about her. In a week it was all over. Most of the student body, including those whom just barely passed, breathed a sigh of relief when their scores were posted. For some it was a sign they had to buckle down harder, for the others a sign that they should consider finding a job. For Lisa and her friends their green light go-ahead was a breath of fresh air.

It was the first weekend that almost anyone had to themselves. Karen, not missing a beat, called.

"Hi, it's a beautiful day out there, ya wanna do something?"

"What did you have in mind?"

"Well, the mids are behind us, so why don't you come over for a cookout?"

"What, lunch? I just got up."

"Naw, later on, dinner."

"Party?"

"Nope. Just us."

"Hmmm, sometimes you're not to be trusted. 'Us" as in exactly who? I'm not up for anything special…what'd'ya have, a physicist you'd like me to meet?"

"Ha, nope. All out of physicists, but we have one neurosurgeon left."

"Oh, Jesus …you mean Robert?"

"Uh, yeah...the one and only."

"Did he put you up to this?"

"Nope. Brad and I just thought a 'que would be a good idea."

"You're timing is impeccable. So, here ya go No else knows, you're the first except for Mike. Mike and I broke up yesterday. He's back in Seattle."

"Holy crap! You did it! Good for you. That took some guts. But you know you had to; it was eating at both of you. My guess is that Mike didn't take it too well...probably same for yourself as well."

"Yep. I don't even want to think about it yet."

"Okay, no pressure. You want to come over and schmooze?"

"With whom? Robert? I'm not anxious that he knows about Mike and me."

"Well, just come on over. It'll be good for you...and Robert too, he's been wasting away thinking of you. We can keep it general."

"Thanks for the invite, but almost any other time would be better. Being social at the moment isn't one of the things I feel like doing. I'd truly be not much fun for anyone to be around. I'm going to have to pass."

"Okay, I understand...but you won't feel this way forever. Maybe next weekend?"

"Thanks, I'll see. It'd definitely be a whole lot better than today. Thanks anyway, sorry."

Lisa was glad to have ducked that one. Karen was glad to hear the news, and she knew that Robert would be as well.

Lisa could have partied with Karen and Brad, but she needed something a little more personal and dialed without putting the phone down.

"Hello, Ray...thumbs up or down...you passed I bet."

"Yeah, did very well...you?"

"Same. We should celebrate tonight."

Ray's pulse double clutched. "Love to. I'll stop over around eight...okay with you?"

"Yeah, you have a ride?

"Yeah, one of the lawyer chicks in my class will be happy to give me a ride."

Lisa laughed. "That's good. I'm happy for you…how come she can say yes so soon? You just found out about it now."

"Well, she's standing right here next to me."

"Ah, I see…well, bring the "chick" too; it'll be a fun evening."

Ray chuckled. "Yeah, that's for sure…actually, a classmate is visiting and we're going to have a quick bite and a couple of beers. He can drop me off. You want me to bring something?"

"No, just you."

There was no mistaking the implication. Ray really didn't have a ride. But he also didn't like feeling indebted to Lisa for accommodating him so often. He realized a need to start demonstrating a little more of a self-reliant Ray Oliver. The ride was a trivial matter, but somehow accepting favors made him feel slightly uncomfortable. And he didn't like the humble feeling that came with it. He'd find a way there even if he had to walk.

Ray didn't have a car, but Tom Berlin did. Tom was a first-year law student who lived next door. Ray could hear the stereo and knew that Tom was in his room. He would have offered Tom ten bucks, but thought better of it and started at five. They settled on seven and Tom dropped him off at eight o'clock. It was the essence of a good deal; they both thought they had come out ahead.

As the car door slammed, the apartment door opened. Lisa, waved. Tom gave Lisa a long look, and shot a lopsided lucky-dog grin at Ray. He drove slowly off, looking over his shoulder at Lisa.

Lisa greeted Ray with a warm lingering kiss, smothering his hello. A low, mellow saxophone rode effortlessly over its notes in the background. It was a wonderfully familiar scene to Ray. Lisa had set out a cheese plate and a bottle of red. Less than a half hour later, they shared a passionate kiss in an awkward two step to the bedroom.

Ray couldn't contain himself and was off in a couple of strokes but outside of the pleasure, it had no effect on his randiness. His equipment was jammed better than any aphrodisiac ever could have produced. He loved Lisa and loved making love to her. Lisa had an immense pent up desire for Ray and indulged herself, at times almost unmindful of Ray beneath her. Intense feelings overwhelmed her and she floated in and out of an orgasmic grip so often that it was practically a sustained climax. Ray was enraptured by Lisa and the sight of her breasts swinging up and down while she hammered away thrilled him. Yet, a sudden insight flashed though his mind: the love making wasn't romance or even love, it was lust…as much for him as her, but with a difference, he loved her…would she love him? His thoughts lasted only two seconds before they were melted into nothingness by the soft, throaty sounds Lisa was making. Awhile later they both crashed back to earth and waited for their breath to return. Lisa wobbled a bit on her way to the bathroom.

She rolled out a couple of towels on the couch and Ray joined her. They poured wine, cuddled, and talked. Being naked on the couch was novel. The bedroom was dark and although they knew each other well by brail, it was also very exciting to see and touch each other in the lamplight. The touching grew and their conversation slowed to a stop, leaving their tongues free for other use. Ray carried Lisa into the bedroom. They rolled onto the bed and into each other. It was going to be a long night.

Chapter 25

Robert, Karen and Brad were on the deck sucking down a couple of beers. It was noon and they were celebrating the hurdle they had just cleared. In a few months, Robert and Brad would be wearing the titles of doctor of neurosurgery, interns for sure, but nonetheless doctors. And Karen would get her star as well in an advanced accounting degree. If they came this far, they knew they could go the distance.

"Hey, what'd'ya think of a barbecue later this afternoon—a celebration of past good things, and good things to come."

Karen looked at Brad and told him it's a great idea and he should call her when it was ready.

"Hmm, Doctor Lawrence...how do you feel about that?"

"Well, Doctor Temple, I believe that it is an excellent idea...however, I require a nurse...Ms. Lisa Marnen would be perfect."

"Ah, yes...done. Mrs. Temple call the woman and invite her."

"Actually, not a bad idea. I'll let you know," and she went in to get her cell.

"Robert, you're still pretty much stuck on Lisa, eh?"

"Yeah, she's the one."

"Whoa, Robert...that's pretty serious...you mean the one you'd like to date for a time, right?"

"Nope. That one could be a lifelong partner for me. I'd like to make that work."

"Crap, Rob...we're just about graduated...there's a whole flock of ladies out there for you. Kind of an early choice, don't you think?

"Nope, she's what I want." Robert delivered the last few words a little more intense than he intended.

"Ya, know, what you need is a couple more beers and maybe a cold shower or two. Relax, man you are totally overboard. Here, catch." Robert caught the cold can of beer Brad threw to him.

Karen hung up the phone, and came back to the deck.

"Well, we can have the barbecue, but Lisa won't be able to make it."

A picture of Lisa and her boyfriend entering the apartment a few nights ago flashed through Robert's mind and he thought *How could Lisa be screwing her boyfriend and him? It wasn't right.* It was nothing he could talk about, or even wanted to.

Robert could guess that Karen must have told Lisa that he was there. If she wouldn't come, then it meant that she wasn't that interested in him. He winced inwardly as if a cold breeze had just blown slowly across his soul.

"But" Karen continued, "*the reason* that she isn't feeling too well...." Karen loved prolonging the end of the story, so she drew the information out, dangling the reason with the inflection in her voice and a long pause. She could guess at the effect it would have on Robert.

"Hmm," Brad said, "not feeling well...then it's just the thing for Dr. Lawrence to treat."

"No, you big silly, the reason she's not feeling well is that..." she said tracing a slight downward arc with her jaw, and widening eyes focusing on Robert, "she and her boyfriend, Mike, broke up and he's gone back to Seattle. It's final!"

Robert felt like cheering, but restrained himself; there was another essential part. "Was it her idea to break up, or was it his?"

"It was a long time in coming, but it was her idea. She just didn't have the guts to broach the subject before."

Robert's smile went almost around his head. His thoughts were racing...*maybe that night with her head tilted in my direction...maybe I'm the cause...maybe she's in love with me...and then his mind settled down. Robert don't get carried away. Maybe it had nothing to do with you and you're just lucky. Go with that. Go slowly, Robert, go slowly.*

He finished his beer.

"Well, I didn't believe it was anatomically possible," Brad said, "for a guy to down a beer with a smile on his face. But you did it. Amazing!"

Robert's only reply was, "Thank you. I'll have another, please."

Chapter 26

Several days passed and Robert called Lisa every one of them. This morning, he was fantasizing, wondering what his parents would think of Lisa when the phone rang. It was practically a telepathic event.

"Robert, this call isn't too early for you is it dear? You didn't call me yesterday…is everything alright?"

"Yes, mother. Everything's fine, just celebrating a successful midterm." The weekly calls had become ritual. Robert couldn't remember when it started, but somehow or other it had become an established routine.

"We're thrilled. Ohhh, you're going to be a doctor…." her voice rose when she pronounced "doctor" and it quivered in a rising and eerie sound trailing off in a high-pitched soprano. Robert hated that. She had done that to him a couple of times in front of different groups of her friends. It was the kind of emphasis that some people used when talking to children. But he would never correct her. And her excited thought was almost always completed with an obligatory, "We're so happy for you," or sometimes "proud" and a hug. This time, she concluded her thought with "proud," and had he been within arm's reach he'd surely have gotten the hug as well.

"Robert, your father was saying to me just the other day—we haven't seen you in a month—that maybe we should get together…a nice dinner somewhere. What do you think? Can you come up on the weekend? We'd love to see you."

"Well, to tell you the truth," he said, as he quickly conjured up a reason why he couldn't."

It was unlikely his father's idea but something his father would gladly support. In all likelihood, however, his father wasn't even aware of the suggestion. Robert knew his father to be a standup kind of guy, except when it came to "mother" and then he was definitely a stand-down type of guy. Whatever the issue was, he would grouse a little, but inevitably succumb only after convincing himself that he had salvaged something of his male dignity. Robert saw that he and his father were alike in that respect. His fear was that psychologically there might not be an end of it. Mother called the shots in the family and you knuckled under or you paid the price.

The price? Well, Robert knew that instead of driving around in a late model Cadillac that he could well be driving an old clunker, or perhaps no car at all. Tuition? Mother. Spending money? Clothes? Mother. It all seemed to come down to the great levers of obligation and money. For his father, the price had already been paid it in his early years by assuming the yoke. For Robert, finishing his internship and becoming a full-fledged neurosurgeon, with an appropriate salary, meant that he might be able to discover some breathing room. He looked forward with pleasure to that day. He loved his parents and would do nothing to displease them, but he also knew he needed his soul back.

"Tell you what, I might be able to squeeze a weekend in a little while. I might even have a surprise for you."

"Surprise?" and she hung on to the word for a three count. "What kind of a surprise?"

"I've been dating a girl and I kind of like her."

"Oh, Robert…how nice. Is she from a good family?"

What a crappy question. Good family: translation: does she come from money? "Nice enough, I suppose, I didn't get down to questioning her about her background. I just think she's nice and we get along." *Yeah, mother, I'm banging her regularly. She's kinky and she loves it as much as I do.*

"What's her major? What does she plan on doing when she graduates?"

Gee, you never skip a beat do you? "She's getting an advanced degree in accounting."

"Accounting? Hmm, I was kind of hoping to hear that she was a med student."

"She plans on working for an international corporation, probably in Europe."

"Oh, well I guess that's something now, isn't it?"

"Yes, it is...." And he said that with a slightly detectable note of finality that ended the inquisition. Part of being successfully in charge was knowing how far to go. She dropped it.

"I'll tell your father and I'm sure he'll be surprised and pleased. Maybe you could bring her with you when you come up for the weekend?"

"Be happy to if she'll come. I'll let you know ahead of time...and if we do, let's just keep it private okay...no party, please."

"Of course, dear," and then she launched into an immediate segue as though the previous conversational bomb was just an oh-by-the-way of no real consequence. "Did I tell you about the Park Crest Women's League and what we're going to do this winter?"

He would like to have said he could care less, but realistically that wasn't an option. He said no, and Mrs. Lawrence, unrestrained, began a half hour monologue of the charitable and good things the "League" was going to accomplish, with Robert giving an occasional uh-huh, and even an umm here and there. Most of the time, he was daydreaming about Lisa. The one sided dialogue dragged on until she received an incoming call on her phone and dumped him for the new caller.

"I'll call. Love you mother," were his last words...the last of which was choked by the click of his mother's phone.

And while this early morning conversation was going on, Lisa was in her bathroom, and not feeling too special. She felt as though she had the flu. Her knees pressed on the cold tiles and she had a good grip on the toilet bowl, upchucking her guts out.

Chapter 27

Lisa at first suspected but now believed that she was pregnant. Her mind raced, trying to capture her situation and the consequences of pregnancy. Her options now were to have the baby, or abort it. To have it meant that her return to Touche wouldn't be as smoothly received at it could or should have been…at least not what she envisioned for herself.

Could it be done…yeah, but many of the options that might be available to her might be quietly closed; she would never know of them. Single, childless people were more mobile; able to take jobs others would not. Children meant potential downtime, and were baggage the company could do without. The corporation wasn't heartless when it came to their employees, but managers were bottom-line people when it came to what was best for the company. The corporate goal, not individual workers and their problems, was their focus. Finding an apartment that took kids, day care, doctor's appointments—all that took money and time. She hadn't a lot of either. It was not the start she hoped for. Additionally, she owed Touche several thousands of dollars. She would probably end up in a job with fewer advantages.

Abortion? The thought tugged at her soul and thoughts of her mother crowded her mind and overwhelmed her with an upheaval of emotions she always managed to suppress. Lisa remembered telling Ray that her mother dumped her and disappeared. If she'd told him the truth, she would have ended up crying. She couldn't stand the thought of what she had seen. So, she lied. Her mother hadn't dumped her. Neither had she dumped her as a baby. Lisa had been eight years old. Her mother struggled as a single parent to care for Lisa and fight a growing cancer; she did the best she could.

The part that was true was that her surrogate parents were orphans themselves. They told her about her mother, and took her to the hospital for a last visit. She watched her die. Lisa longed to have more than that last touch and hug, but her mother's cheek lay heavier into the pillow and she passed away. Lisa didn't cry, but she felt as though her soul had been wiped away and she went dead inside. But the touch and hug remained as vivid now, as it had been then—a forever lasting remembrance. Her surrogate parents would have honored her mother's request to raise her. They loved her too and would have gladly have done so, had they not died. Did she owe her mother anything? How about the family that loved her for as long as they did? Did any of that have any claim on her decision to have the child or not? Questions on top of questions, and no one to help. She felt trapped, unable to make a clear decision. Her control over her life vanished, and her world was crumbling.

It took a lot of soul searching but eventually she was forced to find the courage to do something she never wanted to do. The decision to keep the baby arose out of her deep longing for her mother—suppressed for most of her lifetime—a bond born of loyalty and mourning. Consciously unacknowledged, but gnawing away at her insides throughout her adult life. The second decision was not at all to her liking, but it was practical. Yet, even so, it might, in time, still offer a way out. Not nice, but a way nonetheless. It was the best she could do.

Chapter 28

Things were beginning to happen fast. Finals and graduation were a couple of weeks off. Mike's friend Frank had come by to pick up the car he bought from Mike, and also, agreeable to Mike, took Mike's clothes and belongings as well. The apartment was now wholly hers and outside of its furnishings, bare except for her luggage, clothing, a few books, laptop and stuff in the refrigerator; Mike let her keep the stereo speakers. Being without a car was a pain. In a week, Mike would be in town to retrieve his belongings from Frank. Lisa knew he'd want to see her. Odd, she'd wanted to see him too. Robert and Ray called frequently, and the landlord wanted to schedule a walkthrough damage assessment.

Tonight was a Robert night. She had gone out with Ray three times over the last couple of weeks and had fooled around only once. Both Ray and Robert were rushing her. Before she was flattered, now their attentions were frustrating, each demanding her attention and she, knowing she couldn't keep both, didn't want to pronounce her decision.

Robert was the chosen one, so she began spending more time with him, slowly distancing herself from Ray. Ray's calls increased. She was polite and conversational, but whenever he suggested getting together, she turned him down. Eventually, Ray with anger and hurt clearly in his voice, asked her if there was anyone else. She denied that there was, saying that it was nothing more than a personal choice; she was still feeling badly about Mike. She just wasn't dating anyone right now, and would rather be alone to think about her future. Ray almost bought it, but not quite. He stopped over once unannounced; she didn't answer the door. The distancing was going poorly. Ray was angry and couldn't understand the arm's length treatment from her. Lisa, liking him as much as Robert, couldn't bring herself to tell him—it was the same dilemma she had with Mike. How can you say "I like you, but I'm going out with another guy. Goodbye." That, however, was the truth. On the other hand, the truth was never Lisa's strong suit.

Tonight, she would tell Robert she was pregnant. A lot depended on how he took the news.

Robert, now a frequent visitor to Lisa's apartment, felt at home. He clicked the door shut behind him and gave her a hug, warmly returned.

"I didn't see your car outside?" Robert said. "Thieves in the neighborhood?"

"Nope, I had to let it go. It was a lease vehicle. I'm so near graduation I didn't want to extend the lease for another month. So, I turned it in. Sure miss it though." She made the lie up on the spot, Grinch like.

"So how are you getting around?"

"Karen's been picking me up. Her hours are the same as mine and it's just a couple miles between her and me. I kick in for the gas. It works."

Robert nodded. "Nervous about graduating?"

"Yeah, who wouldn't be?"

"Yeah, me too. I'll be interning right here though, at the University Hospital so it won't be much of a change in scenery for me. Still dead set on returning to Minnesota?"

Lisa nodded.

"The reason I ask is that I took the time to check...hope you don't mind, but Touche has a large branch right here, just outside of Ann Arbor."

"Yep, I'm aware of that," she said, but didn't elaborate.

"Well, then, why can't you just transfer here. We don't have to say goodbye. We can keep on seeing each other."

"Well, for one thing Touche in Minnesota has been grooming me for a particular job...that's why they sent me here for the advanced degree. The job is mine when I graduate...there's no comparable job in Ann Arbor. And, that job will be a springboard for an international position. In addition, I owe Touche several thousand dollars for my support and tuition they spent on me. If I don't go back, they'll demand payment in full. So, yeah, back to Minnesota...why don't you do your internship in some Minnesota hospital? You could see me there."

"Good point, similar reason. My father sits on the Beaumont hospital's board of directorship, and several other boards, and has membership in several professional societies in Michigan as well. He's got a lot of influential contacts. He'll support and promote me in my career, at least in the beginning, and that's the most important part. Without him, I'm just another med grad; with him I have some leverage."

"Ah, Robert...too serious. Let's get out of here and go for a walk. The weather's kind of nice."

The weather was nice. They walked arm in arm down to the main road and back again, twice around the pool, threw small sticks at the ducks in the pond and watched while they dived for the "food."

Their conversation was general but eventually reached a point of nothing new to be said...there was a long period of quiet, and it was then that Robert, with a small gulp in his throat, suggested they have dinner with his parents. Lisa felt her heart thud in her chest, and fought off a "No, thanks." She knew she had to meet his parents, and it was a "do it now, or do it later" but do it she would have to. They didn't know it yet, but they were going to be *one big, maybe happy*, family. "Yeah, I'd like that," she said, and Robert gave her a relief inspired hug. Up to that point he wasn't sure that she was up to meeting his parents. He himself, even felt a little uncomfortable bringing a girl home to meet his parents; he had never done that before.

"Okay next Saturday, we'll have dinner there and come back before midnight. We can double up on our studies Sunday. Great! I'll call mother and let her know."

Lisa hated it when grown men referred to their mother as "mother," sounding more title than a simple noun. "I'll call my mom," sounded so much better; Mother, so miserably formal, so little boyish. *And, oh, yeah, don't we share the same wine-through-our-nostrils trick? Damn, some things stick in your mind forever.* "Good, I was hoping to meet your parents." And she gave Robert a reassuring smile.

Lisa decided against announcing her pregnancy that evening. Robert would be so flustered he probably wouldn't eat for a week. His mother would sense something different and be on him like another skin. She'd probably bombard both of them with questions, and that wouldn't work too well for a first meeting. So she said nothing, walked back to the apartment, and ended up in bed with Robert.

Chapter 29

The Lawrence residence was pretty much what Lisa expected. A huge structure, mansion like, no doubt built by Mrs. Lawrence to her specifications on the most excellent piece of property in the neighborhood. The landscaping was beautiful and probably tended by a full-time gardener. Inside, Lisa took in the plush carpeting, polished wood floors, two huge crystal chandeliers, hand tooled oak paneling with a scattering of oil paintings, and a spiral staircase with ornate carvings. How many rooms? Lisa couldn't even guess…pantries, studies, a music room and probably even servant's quarters?

    A large linen table cloth was draped over a long dining table whose elaborately carved legs stood below it like ornate tree trunks. On the tabletop were crystal and sterling silverware—the real stuff. She guessed that dinner would probably be announced by someone other than Mrs. Lawrence. Intuitively, Lisa knew the dinner would be catered…she just couldn't see Robert's mother working in the kitchen other than making a light lunch for her husband—maybe. They sat in the front room and made small talk. Lisa was uncomfortable because Mrs. Lawrence was a commanding figure, a role she had grown used to through the years of her affluent life style. "Mother" took charge of the conversation. A maid, no small surprise to Lisa, brought them drinks, a Manhattan and a martini for the Lawrences, and red wine for Robert. Lisa opted for a Coke with ice.

    "Well, Mrs. Lawrence, that's a question I've never been able to fully answer even for myself." Lisa was ready for this one. "My parents were killed in an auto wreck when I was five and I lived with an uncle and aunt in Wyoming. I have no brothers or sisters. My father, from what I was told, was involved in some kind of government work for NASA. My mother was an engineer on the same project and they were killed on their way to work. And now, both my uncle and aunt are dead as well and they didn't have any children. And that is all I really know of my family."

Mrs. Lawrence pegged Lisa, the product of government workers, as strictly middle, middle class. Because of her parents terrible deaths, she wasn't inclined to dig any deeper, unwilling to unnecessarily offend her. Lisa had counted on her story to do exactly that. Robert sat still, kind of transfixed with the new information. But Mrs. Lawrence did inquire, gently, as to the relatives.

"I was a child at the time and uninterested in what they did…but I do remember horseback riding on their properties, and visiting some kind of oil pumping stations. Anyway, they had a large home and lived well. I had a knack for numbers and they sent me to the University of Wyoming in Laramie, and I've been working away at success ever since."

Mrs. Lawrence had been defensive her whole life and while outwardly pleasant, inwardly she was wary. To her, Lisa's story had enough holes and negatives in it to make the red flags in her mind show through her eyes. *University of Wyoming, Laramie—how provincial, how parochial, how zero, Family? None. Another zero.* Mrs. Lawrence's basic survival skills were heavy on the quid pro quo. What was Lisa bringing to the table? *An accountant? How zero.* But all the while these, and other negative thoughts flowed through her mind, she nodded as though interested in Lisa's story, but thought that Lisa's idea of "success" really amounted to landing a young man from a good family like Robert.

It only took Mrs. Lawrence about fifteen minutes to size Lisa up and know she wasn't the girl for Robert.

Mr. Lawrence, however, saw a beautiful young woman. She sparkled when she spoke, and seemed warm and friendly; and she had a great body. Robert, he surmised, got a terrific girlfriend. Unlike his wife, he hadn't projected her as a future daughter in law and neither did he weigh her in terms of money. She was simply Lisa, a girl Robert liked and that was good enough for him.

Dinner was announced, as predicted by Lisa. The maid even did a little curtsey which made Lisa smile; it was like something from an old-time movie. Lisa didn't have to worry about snorting the Champagne, there was none. Ice cubes and water filled the crystal. Lisa was wrong, it wasn't catered. Mrs. Lawrence hired a chef for the evening. The dinner began with French onion soup. Afterward two roast maple glazed ducks were carved at the table by the chef, who then introduced the accompaniments she had made: creamy garlic mashed potatoes, artichokes with mustard-aioli, cider roasted acorn squash, and a gingered cranberry-pear chutney. The chef, a large woman, wore a bright flowery smock instead of a chef's coat—probably not the best for a large woman, but her appearance lent a light touch to an otherwise formal event. Chef Suzanne gave her reasons for the inclusion of each creation, and why it was necessary to balance the sweet, sour, and savory flavors to enhance their appeal. She was delightful. The dinner was better than any Lisa had ever experienced in any restaurant.

The rest of the evening went well—brief, but well. Another round of drinks and then polite goodbyes. Mrs. Lawrence said how lovely Lisa was and wished that Robert would bring her back soon. The sentiment was echoed by Mr. Lawrence. Lisa and Robert thanked the Lawrences for the dinner and their hospitality. And out into the cool air they went, wondering how the evening really went for the Lawrences.

After a couple of miles, driven in relative silence, Robert turned to Lisa and said, "NASA? Engineer? Oil well pumps?"

Lisa laughed. "Yeah, I just felt like it, that's all. How impressed do you think your mother would have been with the truth?"

It was Robert's turn to laugh. He didn't care.

Chapter 30

The table had been cleared and the dishes were done. The maid and chef were paid and gone. Mr. and Mrs. Lawrence mixed their own drinks, a bit stronger than the correct mix the maid prepared. Mrs. Lawrence began the post-mortem.

"She's a nice girl, but a bit classless, don't you think?"

"Classless?" How so?"

"Well, did you watch her eat? She rested the fork and knife on her plate as though, as the saying goes, oars on a boat. That was terrible."

"I didn't notice. I was busy eating and talking."

"And, another thing...did you notice how she piled her food onto her fork...she used her thumb! For Christ's sake, if she did that at any of the Park Crest Woman's League luncheons or dinners, I would have had a nosebleed."

"Nope, didn't notice." Mr. Lawrence was more interested in his Manhattan than his wife's observations of fault. *Who cares*, he thought and idly began wondering about how many sips it took to finish a fresh Manhattan.

Mrs. Lawrence, running a close review in her mind's eye, continued.

"And another thing, did you notice her napkin?"

"Nope."

"Well, it was on the table as often as her elbows. Did you see how she lowered her head when spooning her soup...and from the wrong side of the rim at that."

Mr. Lawrence, controlling his annoyance, said, "Well, dear...sometimes you have to make allowances. Did you notice for instance, that Robert adores her? That he could hardly take his eyes off of her...and, I'm thinking that he might have even been sliding his foot up and down her leg while we ate."

"Dear God! Robert! You say the most outlandish—no, shittiest—things imaginable. He didn't really do that, did he?"

"No, maybe not—they were sitting side by side—but I'm trying to remember…maybe it was his hand on her thigh."

"Robert! That's our son you're talking about."

"Yeah, a great guy and lucky to have a girl like that."

"Did you know that whenever you drink, your conversation goes off color? I think you've had one too many Manhattans. I'm going to bed…you coming up?"

"In a little while, it's too early. I might catch the last period of the Red Wings game. I think they're playing New Jersey…the Devils are an awesome team…should be a good one."

Mrs. Lawrence hated sports in general, and hockey in particular. She couldn't understand why her husband liked it. Mr. Lawrence thought he might have heard something like 'to each his own' as she walked away. He smiled and clicked on the TV.

Mrs. Lawrence laid in bed thinking about her son… the usual thoughts of what his life should be like…somehow, she had to subtly introduce Robert to another girl…one from a family with means and a more professional degree than "accountant". She had already been shopping for candidates over the last year through the Park Crest Women's League. Several of the ladies had eligible daughters, all with acceptable credentials. Mrs. Lawrence drifted off to sleep comfortable with the thought that Lisa had to go.

Chapter 31

Two weeks later, Robert's graduation party hosted by Mrs. Lawrence was a huge social success within the circle of the Park Crest Women's League. Robert's black wavy hair, perfect white teeth, blue eyes, and comfortable manner charmed the ladies. Lisa wore a white short dress. Her long blond hair spilled in loose curls over her bare, tanned shoulders. Her shapely body and green eyes drew cautious stares and quick grins from the men and wives' elbows in their side when they were less cautious.

The party was held in the Lawrence's garden patio adjacent to the house. Lawn and shrubs had been trimmed to perfection and bug-bombed two consecutive days prior to ensure a perfect late afternoon affair; and the catering was, of course, exquisite. The only thing Mrs. Lawrence couldn't control was the weather and whom her son invited. The heat of the day carried over into the evening. Among the guests were several young girls, all of which were single and recent college graduates from "good families". Mrs. Lawrence's guest list was carefully constructed and she took the time to introduce each and every one of the young ladies to Robert—the homelier ones when he was with Lisa, and the more attractive ones when she could get him alone.

Lisa was aware of "mother's" game, but could care less. She had a secret that trumped any competition.

Chapter 32

Ray's mind was in turmoil. His best time for studying was usually after a long, hard workout at the gym where he could exorcise his bitter feelings. But towards evening his sense of loss began to settle in again. He knew it was over. Lisa didn't have to say the exact words, but he knew it just the same. And suppose he did find another guy at Lisa's doorstep…what then? Beat him up? That would prove nothing. She would hate him for doing that and how would that change her mind anyway? What was the profit in that? He forced himself to concentrate on the positives.

He'd be a graduate lawyer in couple of weeks. If he were really smart, he'd cling to that, work doubly hard, and get on with his life. Lisa was wonderful, but sometimes blessings come in disguises—maybe she wasn't the one for him, although at the present time he sure thought so. He was young, strong, relatively handsome, and articulate. He had the promise of a professional career and would eventually have an admirable income. Must be some woman out there at least similar to Lisa…and that's where he began stumbling…the word "similar"…he still wanted a Lisa no matter whom the woman would be.

He called Lisa once, on graduation day, but she never answered the phone, or called him back. And that was the last time he tried to contact her.

Chapter 33

It had been almost two years since Ray Oliver left Vincent Sardi and the Sardi Construction Company. Sardi hadn't yet made his "big score" of money in either business or a champion boxer. In many respects his business had taken a downturn. Because of a slump in the economy, the home building business was tanking. He had opened up a home re-modeling sideline and that, and a few other odd jobs, were keeping him from sinking. He was watching his dream of an Italian retirement begin to fade

Charles Sanders listened to his friend Sardi complain about the same things many times before. The quid pro quo, however, was that Sardi would listen to Sander's own version of personal inequity with the same patience. They were a pair.

Sanders owned a trucking company. He did odd hauling jobs, and had a city contract which was his bread and butter. When things were going well, he was up. When not, he was down. The roller coaster of financial obligations gave him headaches and indigestion.

Sanders and Sardi struck up a casual acquaintance at the gym about a year after Ray had left. It began as they watched a sparring match with an intense interest and both loudly and excitedly urged the boxers several times to *jab, jab, right hook, follow it up, follow it up.* Both were offering the same advice at the same time. And both let out an exasperated breath of disappointment when the fighters didn't pick up on their advice. If they were at the finish line at a horse race they would have been beating their programs into their palms in frustration. Sardi and Sanders, of course, overheard each other's excited encouragements. They had seen the fighters in the same light and shouted advice from a similar pool of expertise. This sameness of boxing strategy led to a conversation. They learned that each had an intense interest in boxing and both had been boxers. From a few casual words at ringside, and then a couple of drinks at a local bar, and then a few dinners and more drinks through the intervening months, they became friends—kindred spirits. They learned that each owned a business. They each had worked hard, and believed they deserved more than they had accumulated so far in life. The trick was how to get it. Charles Sanders and Sardi's view of opportunity was identical. Like Sardi, and many of his dealings, Sander's, as well, were often over the legal border. Both schemed, lamented their losses and tried to figure out the road to riches. Sanders wanted wealth to travel the world in comfort and style. Sardi wanted wealth for a comfortable retirement in Italy. How to achieve those goals was the topic ever present on their minds and the one topic they were most fond of discussing.

Sardi was going through another sleepless night. It was almost 2 a.m. Escape from the tethers of his life captured his thoughts and made sleep impossible. He had been lying in bed for hours. From nowhere, an idea occurred to him. As he rolled it around in his mind and tweaked it, the idea took form and began to please him…eventually he began to think it brilliant. It just might work. But he needed help to swing it. What would Sanders think? If Sanders thought it good as well, then maybe between the both of them, they could get what they wanted. It was certainly worth discussing.

In the morning, Sardi invited Sanders to a late lunch at Crispino's, one of their favorite restaurants. Crispino's was a small, once successful Italian neighborhood restaurant opened fifty years ago, by Grandpa Crispino, and ran to the ground over the ensuing decades by a succession of sons and their cousins. Although, in truth, the business was into hard times because the neighborhood had gone down. The better businesses had been replaced by second and then third tier businesses. Appliance and resale shops, and a couple of hair salons didn't do much for the area, neither the decrepit neighborhood houses a block off the business drag…nor did the shabby winos hanging around for a handout, or the occasional stolen or burglarized car in the Crispino parking lot or curbside do much to insure patronage. But

Crispino's had been there in the majority of the clientele's mind practically forever. It was pure nostalgia that kept the place going. Particularly on the weekends, the middle-aged Italian parents brought their families in from the suburbs and played "remember when." The food was plentiful and the wine, for the regulars, was homemade and came from underneath the bar. The price was right.

Vincent Sardi and Charles Sanders huddled at a darkened corner table, finishing off their spaghetti. The topic of their conversation was usually business. Each took turns commiserating and philosophizing about their businesses, their gains and losses, but mainly their losses. Each said pretty much the same, and their responses were usually an affirmative grunt or a single word. "Yeah, uh-huh, naw, and fuck it" about summed up the full range of commentary regarding each other's business woes.

Sardi's idea buzzed around inside his head like bees in a jar. He was waiting for the best time to present it. As the meal wound down, their stomachs were comfortably full, and a couple of drinks completed the setting. It was time for the idea.

"We should come up with a better idea to make some money," Sardi began.

"Yeah, like what?"

"Well, look at who's successful…banks, classy restaurants, franchised food chains…."

"Yeah, but they got their problems too…high overhead, rising costs…when the prices get too high, people stop coming. I can't hardly wait for the day grocery stores start asking a cover charge if you wannna shop there."

"I'm thinking narcotics is a lucrative trade," Sardi said. It was such an unexpected statement that it hung in the air for long seconds before Saunders replied.

"Trade? You have money for a while and then you get killed. What kind of business is that? Not for me."

"Yeah, narcotics can be that way, but what I'm thinking is something different. I've been thinking of this for a long time. You know my cousin Sal? You met him a couple of times at the gym. Well, he's into all kind of shit…union stuff, and for a price fixing someone who needs fixing. He's also into dealing—probably for the last two years. He's got a shitload of money, but he keeps looking over his shoulder whenever we go out. Kind of creeps me out, but that's Sal."

"So?"

Sardi leaned forward, his voice considerably lower.

"So, I'm thinking like a legitimate business man. Know who has a lot of money? Insurance companies do. Look at all the TV advertisements and the junk mail. AARP, Blue Cross, AAA, State Farm–even small-time dime store insurance companies that advertise in the want ads or TV guide. They're always hustling and they make the big green. Insurance companies don't go broke."

"And what's that got to do with us???"

"Well, I've been thinking…usually when I lay down to sleep worrying about how I'm going to meet payroll."

"Okay, yeah…so tell me," Sanders said in commiseration.

"It's really simple…just like an insurance company works. You got something and you want to protect it…you insure yourself against its loss."

"Yeah, so I'm listening."

"So, the dope guys ship big loads for big bucks. Sometimes they get busted. The cops arrest the dopers and confiscate the money and the dope, and shut the operation down. The dopers lose big time. Let's say, for instance, that you and me guarantee a shipment. If it goes through without hitches, we get to keep their insurance money. If it doesn't, we lose; they keep ours. They're out nothing and they're still in business."

"That's stupid. You've always been a pretty smart guy, Vinnie, but I'm not getting this at all. Are you saying that if they get their dope they have to pay us for that? How's that work? If the dopes worth a hundred thousand and they give us a hundred thousand, where's their profit? That's doesn't make any sense. It's stupid."

"No, it's not. Listen, those guys will step on it maybe ten times. That hundred grand of dope actually represents maybe a million bucks or more. That's our edge. That's where we can make money."

Saunders leaned back again. His eyes were sharply on Sardi; behind them his mind was busy looking for holes in the concept.

Sander's skepticism began fading into interest; the questions began to flow.

"We do the delivery? How's that work without exposing us to risk?"

"Yeah, we'll deliver, that's part of the selling package. We buy an old piece of shit delivery truck from a newspaper ad. We give the guy cash, he hands us the title, but we don't register it; we steal a plate the night before the deal goes down."

"And how are we to know that the stuff was safely delivered—no cops?"

"The doper guys will be wary so they'll want one of their own in the deal. The doper guy will give the locations to the driver and help his guys load and unload. We hire our driver off the street; he won't know what he's carrying. We'll pay him enough to keep him shut up; no questions. The truck will be followed from the deliver site by one of our guys. When our truck driver is away free and returns the truck to the parking lot, our guy will call and tell us the delivery is complete; the same with the dopers who received the stuff—a double check. If there's no call from my guy, we'll know something went wrong."

"And what's to keep the dopers from calling you and saying that the delivery didn't happen?"

Two things: One, the call that we get from our guy following the truck will confirm or deny that, and two, if this works, this insurance business will be a big benefit to the doper. He has a vested interest in being *honest*. He deals in millions, a couple hundred thousand won't mean that much to him…although, I got to say, if we kite this project up to several millions, he might just pull a shitty. For the time being, I think we're safe."

"And where will we be to get the good word and split the dough?"

"Anywhere we want."

Sanders looked deep in thought.

Sardi continued. "That's the risk—that's where the money is. It's the same thing with all insurance companies. They take the risk hoping that they won't have to pay out. They're successful because the paying out part is minimal. If we win a couple of times, we can afford to take a hit."

Sanders took a gulp of wine, leaned back, stared at Sardi for a moment, and then leaned forward, pressing his forearms on the edge of the table as he craned his neck forward.

"And how do we get the money to cover a big shipment? You got an extra hundred grand? I don't."

"No problem, just a little gamble."

"Gamble? So's Russian Roulette. Being broke is one thing, being dead is another; dope guys don't fuck around. What happens if they don't like our face? What happens if the first time out we lose? We're out big bucks. Where's that going to come from, eh?"

"So, you mortgage your business and I mortgage mine—we pay it back. Sardi broke out into a deep laugh, "Charles—nothing ventured, nothing gained."

Charles Saunders didn't mind doing the unethical, even the criminal but he needed the reassurance of a clean escape in case the plan failed. And while Sardi explained, Sander's mind was steadily building defenses.

"And how do you propose to contract a drug shipment?"

"The head doper is going to be cautious. He doesn't know me, only what my cousin will tell him. I'll lean on Sal, and explain that if this works—without telling him the whole deal—he can make some big bucks without risk. He'll like that idea and maybe be able to open the door for a meeting with the big guy. That guy probably won't like the plan at first, but he's a businessman and I think I can convince him to see the wisdom behind it. He'll either go for it or he won't. Initially, he's not going out on a limb with a big shipment. But we might do a few small deals at first…50 thou or so as a test, and then maybe a hundred thousand. If he feels secure, he'll probably step up the deliveries. Like all businesses in the beginning, it's a matter of trust. Like I said, nothing ventured, nothing gained."

Sanders had larceny in his heart, but he never had ventured into the big time where he could get seriously hurt. This scheme was daring, and so bizarre that it just might work. The influx of sudden money was a powerful attraction, but his cautious side kept throwing up red flags.

Skepticism crept back into Sander's face. He had leaned, but he wasn't won over.

"Charlie, look, at first it's just you and me. We dip into our savings, mortgage our businesses, whatever, and cover a first shipment, maybe a hundred grand. We make some bucks. We do it again, and again, until we're up a couple hundred grand each. Each time, the doper guy begins to trust us more and more. Then we show the money to three "investors" and sell them on the plan. They'll want in on it; we'll form an association. The first time they make an easy hundred grand they'll be sucked into another project like a thirsty man wants water. And, if they get lucky a couple of times, they'll have money to play with. With two hundred thousand of investment money each, and the investor's money—we can cover a million dollar deal and double our money each time; we can even take a hit from time to time. It's a self-perpetuating business. Dope, like money, ain't never going to go out of style."

Sanders wasn't convinced. Sardi saw Sanders' wavering and made a closing, and what he hoped to be, a convincing and final argument.

"A few good deals and we'd be set for life."

Sanders reflected on that until he said, "And where do the guys with the couple hundred grand each come from? I don't think I know that many guys well enough to talk about a deal like this. I don't know, it's a lot of money to risk. If the first deal fails, we're wiped out and in debt, maybe worse. It's a lot to think about. I think we need another round," and he waved to the waitress, circled a finger above the rims of their empty glasses and a minute later two drinks appeared.

They sat in silence, considering the plan. Two gulps of wine each, and more silence.

"I don't know, Vinnie. I just don't know. Let me chew on it for a day or two. Maybe. I'm not saying yes, just maybe. I'm tired of the hauling business and arguing contracts, and bitching over bills. Maybe this would be a way out…I gotta think."

Sardi nodded his head. "Hey, ya know, I ain't even hit Sal with it…maybe it won't go anywhere and we're worrying about nothing."

The men finished their drinks. Sardi signaled for the bill and left a generous tip on the table. Outside, the men looked at one another. Sanders nodded his head as being deep in thought, "I'll call," he said and both made their way to their cars.

Chapter 34

Ray spent Saturday morning and afternoon moving into the Renaissance City Center Apartments, part of a high-rise complex at Brush and E. Larned, two blocks away from Woodward Avenue, Detroit's main drag. It didn't take much to settle in; he didn't have much. By Saturday evening, everything that was his was contained in the apartment.

His one-bedroom apartment was on the twentieth floor and had bay windows affording a nice view of the city's downtown which started at the river and disappeared northward from view. The hotel was three blocks from the law offices of Wentworth, Solomon & Hughes, his new employer.

Early Monday morning was typical of most cities shaking the sleep from its eyes. Most of the downtown restaurants within walking distance were closed until eleven. What Ray wanted most, anyway, was a black coffee. He took the elevator down to the lobby, and walked through the skyway tube which bridged the street traffic to the Renaissance Center building—the RenCen—seven tall towers, interconnected and jammed with offices, shops and restaurants. It was also the World Headquarters of General Motors. Now that was a city contract he would be interested in...the tax inducement was initially forgiveness by the city, but there were other lucrative considerations.

He found a coffee shop and ordered a large black coffee, eased himself into one of their cheap plastic seats, and watched the parade of people getting their morning started.

It was Monday morning, cloudy and threatening to rain. He sipped away at his coffee until it became cold, dumped the cup, and walked the three blocks to the law offices before the first raindrops began falling.

Ray had walked through the doors WS&H for three summers while interning and the building never ceased to impress him. It occupied an expensively rehabbed 1910 office building on Jefferson. Inside, it showcased luxury: a huge crystal chandelier hanging from its domed center once marked the middle of the old, smaller lobby; now it marked the middle of the lobby's busy and modern reception area. Gilt mirrors and oil paintings were interspersed on the walls behind the two semi-circles of columns surrounding the lobby's reception area, thick carpeting, smaller mahogany and cherry desks flanked by elegant black and dark green leather chairs in four islands which functioned as meeting areas, accommodating six people, eight if they were small. The décor proclaimed importance and means. Through this large anteroom, lawyers clutching their briefcases walked briskly past the reception area and disappeared into elevators, while others huddled off to the sides, leaning against the buildings columns, or gathered in the meeting areas. It didn't take a lot of imagination to feel the pulse of business and fortune; Ray was home.

The thirty-first-floor penthouse office of Mr. William Wentworth was guarded by a receptionist. Ray identified himself, was announced, and told to wait. Fifteen minutes and two buzzes later, he stood before the desk of the law firm's managing partner. Wentworth greeted him warmly and welcomed him back, coming around his desk to shake Ray's hand. He wore a dark blue courtroom suit with a red striped tie, he was about sixty years old, apple shaped, and wore thick glasses which magnified his eyes giving him an owlish appearance. His thick, white hair curled tightly against his scalp, looked almost knotted. Ray remembered the first time he met Wentworth. It was three years ago and he was present, with other interns, to hear an introductory to the law firm. For the first full minute into the speech, he couldn't help but wonder if Wentworth could get a comb through that mess of hair. He recalled that Wentworth noticed his staring, paused, looked at him and said, "Yes, I do comb my hair from time to time, but it doesn't seem to do any good...does it?" It was a question that Ray dare not answer. As Ray's face reddened, Wentworth smiled and said, "Don't worry, I'm aware of that...but try to focus on what I'm talking about." That made Ray redden even more and Wentworth laughed. A low and husky laugh, but he did laugh and that was a great relief to Ray. For almost three full years he had passed him in the hallways, but he never before had exchanged anything more with him than "Good morning."

Just before Ray returned to school, he met with two senior partners of the law firm, Mr. Clive Bertram, and Mr. Aaron Rosen. They discussed in general terms of what hiring on at WS&H would entail. Today, they had gathered again in William Wentworth's office, congratulated him on his graduation, and took seats on either side of the table, adjacent to Wentworth. Despite having done so before, they once again discussed his employment, what they expected of him, and what he could expect in the way of work, and his benefits and his pay. Ray once again affirmed all that they had previously discussed and that he felt comfortable with the conditions and salary. This time, however, it was a not just an informal discussion. They presented him with a contract of employment. Ray read the contract, as any lawyer would do...it wasn't a lengthy document. After a few minutes, satisfied with its content, Ray grabbed the pen that lay on the desk and signed. All three smiled and congratulated him once more, welcoming him to WS&H. Wentworth expressed his personal satisfaction with Ray's scholarly accomplishment, and the work he had done for WS&H over the past three summers. And, surprising to Ray, he handed him a "signing bonus" check of five thousand dollars.

As Ray was expressing his thanks, Wentworth buzzed the receptionist and asked her to send up Rodney. Ray was handed off to the subordinate who gave him an unneeded orientation of the building. The only change since Ray's summer stint was the office assigned to him. The room looked like a revamped storage room—which in fact, it was. The lobby's décor of plush leather chairs, brass, chrome, and fine wood desks didn't make it up from the lobby. An oak desk, a worn swivel chair, computer, some beat up filing cabinets and a coffee maker completed this new domain. The items were sufficient, but decidedly an example of mid-80s décor. His desk, by the door, matched the other two desks in his room, which were fenced off from each other by room dividers. Those other two desk chairs were occupied by two young lawyers pounding away at keyboards, both men looking in a sweat. Each looked up for a moment, waved, mumbled a hello, and stuck their nose back into what they were writing. There were other offices on the floor, but none like this one.

Rodney, his tour guide, told him to grab a coffee. A girl would be up soon enough with a stack of legal files. He explained that Post-it notes, as to what was needed, would be attached to each case, also a deadline which Rodney advised, "Be sure to make the deadline even if it means working after closing. In fact, there is no such thing as a closing time. You just work until you're finished. The money is excellent, the work is brutal. Good luck. And, by the way, don't be too concerned with this office. Your office is being readied and should be useable in a short while—theirs too," he jerked a thumb over his left shoulder. And with that, Rodney disappeared.

Twenty minutes later, an office girl named Sonja wheeled a cart full of briefs, reviews, and new appellate decisions into the office and dumped them on his desk. She told him her name was Sonja—with a "J". She was a plain looking brunette, nicely dressed except for the tennis shoes. Which, she was quick to explain when his gaze dropped to the floor, were for office use only. She said that when she went out for lunch, she wore heels. She wondered aloud if he would like to see the entire outfit sometime? And not waiting for a reply, disappeared just like Rodney.

Ray felt an uncomfortable tingle as though he had just undergone a brief, light sand blasting. He shook his head and headed for the coffee pot; he'd figure Sonja out later. The remaining liquid in the pot was becoming thick; he made another pot. A few minutes later, the guys in the chairs came out of their cubbyholes to fill their cups; neither one of them said thanks.

Ray was looking at a one-foot tall stack of yellow paper and folders. He picked up each case and read the Post-its, checking their deadlines first. Bad news, two of them were due in the morning. Their jackets were thick. Ray swore softly under his breath, grabbed the first one and shoved the stack to the back of his desk. It was a simple property dispute and the response was straightforward. He jumped on the computer, brought up the pertinent legal sites, printed them and proceeded with his argument and enumerated the step by step reasoning which should ensure closure and client satisfaction. The brief was finished in two hours.

The second case dealt with the near drowning death of a child in an unprotected, unattended swimming pool on private property. The owner was clearly at fault because he had failed to fence the pool. It was an "attractive nuisance" and the cause of the unfortunate occurrence. The child was found floating face down in the pool by the mother, who lived next door. The child hadn't died, but suffered irreparable brain damage and would require lifelong care. Ray could only guess at the anguish and hostility, but that wasn't his job. Now, almost three years later, the judgment had been rendered and was being challenged by the defendant. Because of his failure to safeguard the pool, let alone not notifying the insurance company that he had a pool, his home owner's insurance refused to indemnify him. His contention was that if he had to pay the amount proscribed, he would become a pauper and unable to support his family. He didn't object to paying some, just not all—even half was far beyond his reach. He appealed. WS&H had delivered the plaintiff a verdict of $750,000 and lifelong medical expenses. Ray's research supported that verdict and it would be forcefully argued in the ensuing appeal; becoming a pauper was irrelevant. The complainant's recourse? Sue the insurance company, not WS&H.

It was evening when Ray finished up. He passed several offices on his way out and could hear the tickety-tack of keyboards. Outside, it was cool. He sucked in the evening air to clear his mind and lungs and thoroughly enjoyed the walk back to the hotel.

Ray's apartment was dark. He walked over to the window and watched the traffic cruise Woodward. The city's nightlife was beginning to show itself.

Ray, on the other hand, felt that he had been on a fast track for the last couple of weeks and wanted to crash. He grabbed a beer out of the refrigerator, kicked off his shoes, and lay back into the couch and reviewed his day. Completed response to two cases and a five thousand-dollar check. Not too bad, Mr. Oliver. He gulped down another beer, showered, set the alarm, and rolled into bed.

Chapter 35

Sardi's lifelong focus was always what was in his best interests. He sized up people in two ways—the daring who knew profit could be found on both sides of legality, and all others whom he only thought of as useful. His past "business associates" were partnerships of acquaintances that fit his standard—willing wheels and cogs in money making opportunities who like sharks in bloodied water, rose to the occasion and sank back into the depths afterward until they got another sniff of opportunity.

When Sanders told him in the restaurant that he didn't know anyone who had a hundred grand to invest, Sardi could have said, he did...but he didn't say that. Truth was that he did, but only if he could promote the project. That was the catch. He wasn't about to tell Sanders that he had connections. That would have been easy on Sanders. Sanders had to sweat a little and he could use the money later as leverage to inspire Sanders to greater investment. For now, he didn't have to know. It wasn't a sure thing anyway. The guys with the money were pretty hardnosed. Each was different but what they all had in common was that they wanted the "investment opportunity" laid out in black and white, no ifs, maybes, probably or could be. That made perfect sense to him. If he could sell them the idea, then yeah, the deal would be on. Even more so, the first time they scored, others would be anxious for part of the action. Then the project would be an easy sell. He needed only to sell a couple.

Sardi didn't beg. But he was forceful and persuasive enough to make the simple plan palatable. But not to all. He spoke to seven associates. Two laughed and told him to call them some other time, and two just shook their heads and said they had a meeting elsewhere. With the other three, there was some rolling of eyes, but the doubling of their money with each shipment caught their attention big time. Could it be done?

Sardi called Sal and impressed on him the necessity of a trial run...maybe a two hundred and fifty thousand dollar drop. He had five investors that would front two hundred and fifty grand. Would he float that to his boss? Sardi believed that Sal's boss dealt in million-dollar deals. The problem was that he didn't have a million and certainly not a million to risk. If he had enough time he could kite his earnings from a couple of deals, include a couple more associates, and cover a large contract, but not now. He needed a couple small deals to raise money and interest other investors.

"Sal, I'm thinking that this could be big. But like everything new, a trial run would be a good test."

"Vinnie, I'm thinking the guys aren't going to like that. They don't do small deals."

"So, whats to lose? It's a test. Either it works or it doesn't. Your guys aren't out a dime." Sardi didn't like sales, and he could feel it slipping away. "Think, if this one time works, next time it'll be bigger, much bigger. My guys don't want to go any higher because the arrangement is unproven. If it works, then more later. Your guys wouldn't mind going into it if they were secure. What the hell, they aren't sticking their necks out. We are."

"Ah, I don't know...."

"Sal, do it for me...just this once. I'll make it good for you."

"Yeah, like what?"

"I, uhh...I'll give you a quarter of my share. What'd'ya think about that. A quarter...that's twelve and a half grand...no, I'll round it up. Thirteen grand. Yours. Just make it happen."

Sal thought about it for a few seconds and said, "Make it an even twenty and we'll see."

Vinnie almost exploded. *Twenty fuckin' thousand dollars? You thief, you bastard, my own brother-in-law...*but, he only thought those words, fought down his anger, and choked out, "Man, that's a pretty heavy price."

"Yeah, but if it's a go, then we'll be okay for the next time, hey?"

"Okay, but there won't be any splitting next time. Your boss gets the deal—the insurance money. That's it."

Sal was disappointed that this wouldn't be a continuing stream of money for him and said so.

"You're breaking my ass. Look, just get the ball rolling. I'll take you out for lunch one day and we'll talk. At the moment, I'm straining my ass to get the cash. How can I give you what I don't have. You think I'm gonna keep my share? Naw, I gotta pay back the guy that fronted me the cash. You know what I'm making on this deal? Practically nothing. I'm giving you the lion's share as a favor. Give me a break, meet me half way."

Sal told him that he'd give it a try and hung up.

Vincent Sardi breathed heavily, almost snorting. He was thoroughly pissed. But he needed the deal. Sal, he thought, was worse than the sharks he had for partners. Fuck him.

Chapter 36

It was a hot, Sunday mid-afternoon. The small red and blue neon sign in the dirty front window of the Peerless Truck Trailer Company indicated "Closed" and the same was written on a rusting metal sign which hung from the chain barrier blocking the side drive to the loading dock in the rear. It was an industrial area. Sunday mid-afternoon traffic was almost non-existent. Just past the barrier and around the corner of the building, was a dirty car containing two big, ugly men. Their concern was the large truck being unloaded at the middle bay. Their job was to keep nosy people away and lean on the horn if the cops showed up.

Two guys were unloading the truck. Large, tightly wrapped, bales of marijuana were kicked out of their stacking order in the truck and bounced out onto the dock. Their momentum was quickly caught by two other men and redirected, skidding and rolling them onto a pallet set against the dock wall. Each bale that hit the dock was accompanied by a cheer and inexplicable laughter. The men had been sampling the bales and were high. When the Hi-Lo driver picked up a pallet they each had a rest. Every now and then one of the men would begin singing in Spanish…mostly short, bawdy songs that were just sounds to Sal except for a few words which were similar to his Italian. It wasn't much to translate the occasional puta into *putana*, and he could guess at *tetas*. The men were enjoying their work. Sal sat on a bench with Reuben overseeing the work…Reuben the Cuban was in charge, but no one called him that.

Reuben was tall, muscular, about forty-five, with grey streaked, wavy black hair. He had a deep voice which commanded attention. While he could muster a hardy laugh and a friendly demeanor socially, underneath it all Reuben was a serious, fearsome person. He once beat a man senseless for calling him Reuben the Cuban…it would have been OK if the guy would have called him Cuban Reuben, but how was he to know? Even Reuben didn't know why he didn't like the nametag; he just didn't like it. Afterward, everyone knew that he could be called Cuban Reuben, but no one did, they just referred to him as Reuben and looked down when they uttered his name. He liked that. He also carried a knife and it was known that he'd turn a person into fish bait if he were really pissed. So when he shouted in Spanish, "Quit fuckin' around and get the job done," each man understood that it was to him, personally, that Reuben was talking and they ceased their casual air and bent to the work.

Another hour and it was done. The unloaded truck was driven off by the dock crew. The two ugly guys backed their car against the yard's back fence, parked, grabbed their automatic rifles, and came into the building. They would remain for the night, guarding the merchandise and be on hand for the four morning pickups—the distribution that meant money. They nodded to Reuben and Sal in passing, and the overhead bay door creaked and squealed as it rolled down and was locked. Sardi's brother in law, Sal, got into Reuben's car. Before Reuben started the car, Sal asked him to wait a minute, he had something to talk to him about.

"Not here. I drive and you can talk—get the chains." Reuben pulled forward and waited for Sal to hook the chains with the "closed" sign behind them. They pulled out onto Dix Highway and headed east, towards Detroit.

Reuben cranked up the air conditioning. Derelict buildings that flanked both sides of the street slid past them. A stray dog walked through a parking lot, tail down, beaten by the sun.

"Ya wanna talk about something. So, what'd'ya got?"

Sal felt a little hesitant about promoting Vinnie's idea, but it did have merit and maybe it might work. If it did, then it was a gold star for him. He took a breath and said, "Okay, so here it is. My brother-in-law, Vinnie, got an idea. I think you might be interested. It wouldn't cost us a thing and might be good business for us. He wants to talk to you and the boss and explain the deal. You guys might want to take twenty minutes and talk to him."

Reuben turned in his seat and gave a quizzical look at Sal, before exploding. "Your brother-in-law got a plan? Everybody's got a plan. I got a plan, mine works, I don't need no bullshit, half-assed craphole plan… your brother-in-law…who the hell is he? Is he a big deal? I don't have time for little stuff. A twenty minutes explanation…what's that…it can't be worth much if that's all it takes."

"No, no…hey, Reuben, I'm thinking it sounds pretty good. Might work. We might end up with a lot more money."

Reuben pulled the car to the curb and studied Sal's face for a full minute. "So, you think he's got something, hey?"

"I think so, but I don't really know how it'll set with you guys…I take care of the little stuff, you make the big decisions…but, I'm thinking this sounds pretty good, and maybe you might be interested."

Sal gave Reuben a brief overview…he didn't have all of the specifics, but he understood enough to promote the plan.

Reuben looked at Sal with a comical look of disbelief on his face. He began to smile, grinned, and then laughed out loud. "You gotta be shittin' me. Insurance?" Then he started pounding his palms on the steering wheel, punctuating each laugh. "Man, but this ain't gonna fly," he said, but I'll tell the boss…for you, I'll tell him. But I don't believe that this one will get off the ground." They drove in silence for a half hour. Every now and then Reuben would snort and laugh to himself. Sal, cringing inside, thinking all the while that he was looking stupid in Reuben's eyes. Reuben dropped Sal off at the restaurant where his car was parked. He looked at him, nodded, and said once more, "Insurance!" Sal could hear him laughing as he left the curb.

It was almost evening when Sal called Vinnie. "Hey, Vinnie…" and that's as far as he got before Sardi cut him off with an anxious "how'd it go?"

"Not so good, he laughed me off. I felt like a chump. So, I want you to know I did my part, I went to bat for you. Sorry, I couldn't make it happen. I delivered the message and that's all there is to it. He said he'd pass it on, but from his reaction I'm thinking the idea is pretty much dead."

"Hey, okay. Thanks…I was just trying to make a buck…if it worked, it worked. Back to the drawing boards, eh?" You eat?"

"Yeah, I just had dinner. Sorry about the deal. Call me for lunch next week—you owe me one." Each worked up a friendly but hollow laugh, and hung up. Sal was thinking he looked bad in the eyes of the organization, not something he wanted to happen ever again. He swore to himself, no more deals with Vinnie.

Chapter 37

It was noon, two days later, and Vinnie was soaking up the sun in Hart Plaza. He was seated on a park bench and cramming a Coney Island hot dog into his mouth when his cell phone went off.

"Mr. Sardi?"

He washed a chunk of hot dog down with a swig of Coke. "Yeah?"

"This is a friend of you brother-in-law—we had a discussion the other day …"

"And…?"

"We got to thinking about it and would like to have a meeting with you. We're interested in the details of your plan. Tomorrow at two, at the Zocalo restaurant would be good. Ask for the Hudson table. See you there. Reuben hung up; it was more of a summons that a request. Sardi didn't like that, but he was used to assholes.

Zocalo's, a Mexican restaurant in the heart of Detroit's Mexican town, was pretty much empty for 2pm on Wednesday afternoon, which was perfect for the business that Sardi and his two new acquaintances were engaged.

Sardi was led to the Hudson table and introduced himself. The two men seated at the table were into their meal and gave him a quick up and down look and returned to their next bite. *Okay, so these guys are assholes. They didn't even wait for me to order. Just as well.*

He took a seat, ordered a beer from the waitress and declined lunch, saying he just finished an hour ago and wasn't hungry. He began the outline of his insurance plan. The men nodded…they asked a lot of questions, particularly about delivery and verification, means of delivery, how delivery was to be verified, and how the money changed hands. At different times they said the scheme was one of the dumbest they ever heard of…but agreed, that in a bizarre way it made sense and might prove valuable. Sardi asked them about the frequency of the deals, and what could he expect regarding how much of a product was being moved. Lead times were important because large amounts required "partners" and investments. The two men balked a bit at the mention of partners, but since they were only involved in the payoff and wouldn't be interfering in the delivery, they wound back down.

Eventually, the whole plan was clear; no more questions on either side. The one that deferred to the other in the questioning received a nod. He told Sardi that the meeting was at its end and he would have to leave and if they agreed to a deal, they'd call him. Sardi stood up and said, "Thanks for the beer," turned and left. He was thinking *definitely assholes* as he left the restaurant.

Chapter 38

Lisa graduated two weeks prior to Robert graduating. Mike's car was already sold and the apartment's lease was expiring. She talked to the apartment complex manager and outlined a sad story, convincing him that it would be a godsend to her and she would be grateful if he could extend the lease for one more month; she'd pay in cash. He was hypnotized by Lisa's eyes and the word "grateful" went banging around inside his head He crumbled and took the next month's rent from her hand and stuffed it in his pocket. He asked if maybe one day he could drop over for a coffee. Lisa smiled, and said, "I have a boyfriend, and he probably wouldn't like that." The implications of "grateful" in the manager's mind evaporated. The month's extension of Lisa's apartment was never recorded, but the apartment's vacancy was. Robert moved in with her the following weekend.

Chapter 39

Lisa and Robert were both glad to get back to their apartment, both relieved that the dinner with his parents went as well as it did, and both relieved that it was over. Robert set two glasses on the counter and poured out a red wine.
"Wait...I don't think I want a drink. Thanks anyway...but you'll want one," the last she added with a slight emphasis.
"I thought a little celebration was in order after having faced the Lawrence family dragons."
Lisa smiled at him, stepped to him and gave him a loving hug and kiss. She had made her choice. Robert returned the affection.
"I'm going to tell you why I don't want a drink. Okay? Ready for this or not, here ya go...."
Robert could sense a slight strangeness in Lisa, and he gave her a quizzical look. Something was up.
"I'm pregnant."
Robert's eyes opened wide and his lips wrinkled. A slight rush of breath preceded his first word, which was cancelled half way through its pronunciation. He stared at her and swallowed hard.
"Yep. Pregnant, that's me."
Robert managed to say "Wow." And then, "Wow" again, a little higher pitched.
"Any further thoughts beyond 'Wow'?"
"Uhhh, yeah...lets...uhhh, sit...I...we need to think."
"Hmm, not quite what I expected, but so far so good."
Robert gulped half of his wine and filled the glass up again. They sat. Robert's thoughts were like tires spinning on ice, engine racing, but he couldn't hang on to an idea long enough for it to gain traction. Finally, he said, "When did you find out...how long ago?"
"Last week. Near as I can guess, I'm about five or six weeks gone."

"God...."

"Well, yeah, maybe, but I'm thinking it probably had a lot more to do with you and sex. Now what?"

An "Uhhh" sound came out of his mouth but he drew a blank and nothing further proceeded it.

"Yeah, that's about as far as I got too."

"I'm thinking the options are having the baby or getting an abortion. What do you think?"

"Abortion is out of the question." She pressed her fingertips against his lips…"you haven't had as much time to think about this as I have."

Although Lisa would have an abortion, she knew it would haunt her for the rest of her life; for her it was a true dilemma. If she had the baby, she wouldn't be able to take care of it on her own and have a career too. Everything depended on what Robert would do.

"I'll marry you Lisa. It'll all work out. I will be the most excellent father and I'll love you forever. You'll be happy. I promise you that."

That was the escape that she knew was both the salvation and ruination of Lisa Marnen. Unknown to Robert, it was an offer given to a person between a rock and a hard place. She closed her eyes for a moment and took a deep breath, letting it out slowly.

"That's very cavalier of you Robert."

Her words were a bit more of an observation than he thought the occasion engendered. "Did I say something wrong?"

"No, not at all, but usually the man presents a ring and asks if the woman will marry him. Is this your idea of a proposal?" Lisa intended a humorous remark, but Robert was slightly embarrassed.

He stammered, "No, no…of course not," caught his breath, and said, "I apologize. I just was overcome with the idea. The truth is that I was going to ask you to marry me; this just speeds it up a little. As beautiful as you are, as intelligent as you are, I believe you've had many opportunities to marry if you chose to. I feel a little vain in presuming that there might be something in me that would make you choose me above all of the others…but, I love you from the center of my soul and would gladly spend the rest of my life with you. I pray that you see enough in me to say yes…will you marry me?"

Lisa couldn't help but think of Mike on his knees before her just a month or two ago asking the same question. If it had been Robert, the answer would have been the same. But *then* and *now* were worlds apart. Was Robert the father? Lisa didn't know, didn't really care, she knew she had to make a good choice; she needed someone to care for her and the baby. In time, Ray would, Mike would…but Robert and his family had the means for a very comfortable life now, not sometime in the future. And, hovering in the back of her mind like a pre-nuptial agreement, what if there was a divorce? Who would deliver a better settlement…an insurance guy, a lawyer just starting out, or a neurosurgeon from a wealthy family? Her decision was made before Robert asked. *Would* he ask? That was the only real question in her mind.

"Better," she said, "and yes, I will marry you." Lisa was actually satisfied with the thought, but she also saw a part of her world ripped away from her. Lisa genuinely liked Mike…Ray…and Robert and could be happy with any one of them. But marriage meant yoking her life to another, something she would not willingly have done. That desire for independence is what made Lisa, Lisa. Now she had to compromise.

Robert, almost a little giddy said, "Mother is going to have a…" but before he could finish, Lisa's hand shot out and her fingers pressed against his lips. "No, 'mother.' It's just you and me. What we decide is what we decide."

"Ah, yeah…you're right. But mother"—Lisa's hand was in the air again, but he caught her wrist. "Wait, please, I have to explain. My mother controls our family—my father, and me to a large extent—and, yes, she does get a little overbearing, but she pays the bills. I'm their only son and they have certain expectations. Our wedding, in her mind, will be the social event of the year…one that requires months of planning…and you know she'd glory in that. There will be halls to consider, musicians, flower arrangements, caterers, garden parties, name brand guests—probably the governor and other politicians for all I know—it'll be a circus and one that she's practically lived for. I know because she's been kind of casually hinting, outlining it for me for the past three years. She's a planner! And, that's going to be a big, big problem."

Lisa figured as much, but she needed to get "ringed" before she went to work on Robert. So, she said, "We're just going to have to work things out for ourselves and try not to offend anyone. I don't know exactly how to do that, but where there's a will there's a way. We'll do all right. Trust me; trust in us." And she gave him a warm kiss, toppling him over onto the cushions; they mixed well into each other like a sweet fragrance on a warm breeze.

Robert received regular, considerable cash gifts from his mother throughout his life, and larger ones during his college years. He, consequently, wasn't without resource. He accepted the money gratefully; his acknowledgement of each gift lent a warm glow to his mother's heart—and through the years these wisps of largess were slowly woven into tie cords, as she intended them to be. From birth, and each year afterward, a considerable amount of money was deposited into a trust created for baby Robert. The sum increased each year as he got older. When he reached eighteen years of age, his trust received ten thousand dollars and he received a car. It was then that he first became aware of the trust. When he reached 20, twenty thousand and another new car; and at age 25, twenty-five thousand and the black Cadillac he was now driving. And the ever-growing trust was in addition to his tuition and living expenses. Robert had a comfortable amount of money at his disposal independent of his mother's fortune, although pitifully small in comparison. Robert was frugal, but where Lisa was concerned he would have given her everything and more if he could get it. So, it never crossed his mind as extravagant when he withdrew twenty-five thousand dollars from his account and bought her a diamond engagement ring.

Chapter 40

Two days later, Lisa wore a four-carat ring on her left ring finger; sadly, on her part, more adornment than promise. Robert, however, was thrilled. Breaking it to his parents would be another matter. He believed the engagement announcement would be well received. He could foresee nothing that would displease his parents; they would be happy. But he also knew that setting the wedding date within a few months would meet with a stiff objection and unavoidably lead to telling them that Lisa's was pregnant. That would be a horse of a different hue. Robert could see the ugly look on his mother's face, a thought which was displaced by an even uglier, bizarre thought that flashed through his mind: maybe she'd have a cardiac and die—problem solved. "God! He rocked his head, "What thoughts! This is going to be awful!" There was no way around it.

Less than a week was too soon to return to the Lawrence's and announce their engagement, but under the circumstances it couldn't be helped. It had to be done soon enough and after what Robert told her about his mother's wedding plans for him, she knew Mrs. Lawrence would feel she had been cheated, blindsided. She would blame Lisa as a scheming opportunist that seduced Robert and intentionally became pregnant. Lisa knew it. The collision couldn't be avoided.

Those thoughts didn't occur to Robert. At worst, all he could see is that a hurried wedding would certainly raise eyebrows in his mother's social circles. He could already hear her: 'What will the ladies in the Park Crest Women's League say?' The whisperings would mortify her; she wouldn't be able to sleep. Her social standing was everything to her. And his father…Robert guessed it would be similar to any other confrontation he had with his mother; he'd support her. But later, he'd work on moving her to acceptance, although he wasn't always successful. Robert and Lisa looked at each other and smiled weakly in anticipation of the coming storm. Lisa forced the question.

"I'm thinking that we should just tell them," Lisa said, "whatever is going to flap, is going to flap. Get it all out in the open and begin putting some plans together."

Robert gave a slight negative shake with his head.

"I know my parents well. If we do that, mother will dig her heels in, hard. Dad won't be able to move her. We'll have no further chance at moving them to our viewpoint. It's a matter of love and life, and has happened to people since time immemorial. They'll eventually see that, but we don't have time. The biggest obstacle for mother is the old-fashioned social view. She'll consider it a disgrace she won't be able to swallow. To her mind, this is not only *not* supposed to happen in the family, but actually *can't* happen. It's forbidden." That last remark made Robert chuckle.

"Let's go at it slowly and carefully. They've only met you twice. Several more times over the next couple of weeks will make it easier. That'll be easy. When we're engaged, she'll want to show us off to everyone so several get-togethers will be a natural thing. And once everyone sees that we're engaged, it'll be that much harder to balk at a wedding. They don't really know you yet and they'll need time to warm up. We'll announce our engagement next week, and we'll tell them a few weeks afterward why the wedding has to be so soon."

Chapter 41

It was a quiet Sunday afternoon when they drove up the driveway of the Lawrence household, each with queasy stomachs. Robert rang the bell and Mr. Lawrence opened the door which widened at the same rate as his smile. "Ha! Robert and Lisa. Greetings, good to see you both…come on in…hey, Roberta, guess who's here?"

Mrs. Lawrence disliked interruptions during her reading hour; especially if the characters' romance was heating up—"bodice rippers" were her favorite genre. She snapped the book shut and put it under the chair's cushion.

"Robert, Lisa…what a nice surprise," she said from the study's doorway and hurried to them, giving Robert a hug and a kiss on the cheek and Lisa a handshake. "We were just talking about you two and wondering when we would be seeing you next."

They stood in the foyer, smiling at one another for an awkward moment: the Lawrences wondering why they were there, and Robert and Lisa about to tell them.

"Mother—"

"Holy Smokes!" Mr. Lawrence said, grabbing Lisa by her left hand and held it up. Mrs. Lawrence's eyes bugged out a little and she said, "Oh, my God" and then again, a lot louder, and then she gulped an "Ohhh, Robert!" as her hand slid onto her stomach and pressed inward.

"We're engaged," said Robert, a superfluous understatement that went unnoticed.

Mr. Lawrence hugged Lisa and shook his son's hand wildly. He seemed sincerely happy for them. Mrs. Lawrence smiled graciously, took Lisa's hand and said, "That's a beautiful ring, and what a large a diamond. I'm happy for both of you." She managed a socially correct hug for Lisa. The phrase "My God" in Mrs. Lawrence's thoughts was actually a screaming stream of MyGawd, MyGawd, MyGawd! Please tell me this isn't so. Robert what have you done? I've got to stop this, Her distress was almost audible. But Lisa didn't have to hear Mrs. Lawrence's thoughts, she could read her face right through the smile and knew exactly what she was thinking. *So, not good enough for your son, eh? We'll see!* The battle lines that began taking shape at the graduation party were now hard drawn. The men were oblivious to the undercurrent.

Mrs. Lawrence's arrogant dislike of Lisa led her to form quick, unreasonable opinions from the start. She judged that Lisa was a hick farm girl lacking in social graces and having an intellect commensurate with what was expected from the no-name schools she attended—an advanced degree? —she's beautiful, how easy it would have been for her to trade favors for a degree. Mrs. Lawrence further construed Lisa's charming and engaging manner as more ingratiating than genuine. And, from that viewpoint, it wasn't a long jump to see her as a timid spirited young woman hoping to better herself through marriage. No, she could not allow this marriage. Lawrence family name and status would not be conferred on Lisa. Roberta Lawrence's mission was to make sure it didn't happen. However, there were a couple of serious flaws in her thinking. One was that she didn't believe Lisa could read masks; and the other, that Lisa was a timorous soul and could be intimidated.

Never one to miss an opportunity, Mrs. Lawrence plunged in. "Oh, Lisa. This is wonderful news. The Parkcrest Women's League ladies are having a luncheon on Tuesday, can you make it. Please say yes, some of them couldn't make the graduation party and I know they'll want to meet you…and the others had so many nice things to say about you. I know they'll want to see you again. Engaged! How thrilling!" And, of course, Lisa stared into the mask and agreed to the luncheon.

Robert and his father were excited and talked rapidly, clapping each other on the back several times, sometimes laughing, sometimes snickering at some long-ago event in Mr. Lawrence's own engagement and wedding. Probably not the things to say aloud in front of Mrs. Lawrence, or Lisa, but each pair were so immersed in their conversations that neither paid attention to the other. Mrs. Lawrence was explaining to Lisa about the importance of the Park Crest Women's League and named several well-known, wealthy and influential members, hinting that such a club would be a perfect place for her to meet people that might be able to do her some good.

They had been standing in the foyer for about five minutes when Mr. Lawrence suggested a Champagne toast. Mrs. Lawrence seconded the idea and Robert and Lisa couldn't refuse. They sat in the study, holding crystal flutes that materialized from a large collection of cut crystal housed in the study's leaded glass wall display cabinets.

Both Mr. and Mrs. Lawrence made toasts; Mr. Lawrence meant his. When Lisa saw the opportunity, she switched glasses with Robert; his was empty. Robert grinned a little and proposed another toast, finishing the remainder of his glass. Lisa faked a sip. At an opportune time, they invented a reason to leave. At the door, Mrs. Lawrence said she'd call with the time and Robert and Mr. Lawrence would have an excellent afternoon while they were at the luncheon.

As they drove off, Mr. Lawrence said, "Well, how about that. Engaged!" Mrs. Lawrence muttered softly, "Shit!" and then followed it up with "How grand," loud enough for her husband to hear. She filled her glass with Champagne, moved the bottle to the table next to her chair, and grabbed the book from under the cushion.

Chapter 42

What started out to be a nice summer day quickly devolved into an angry scene as Robert and Lisa broke the news to the Lawrences. Mrs. Lawrence took the news badly. She alternated between rage and fitful crying, during which for several long minutes she paced the floor, sometimes in a circle unconsciously duplicating her inner turmoil. *Pregnant, pregnant, pregnant—damn, damn, damn*—the recurrent thoughts drummed against her consciousness. She felt ill, almost faint, and hands to her temples, slumped into a chair. Mr. Lawrence just looked out the window.

In a few minutes Roberta Lawrence was back on her feet. Rejecting the water proffered by Robert and began to wail.

"All of my plans," yelled Mrs. Lawrence. "You did this animal thing without any regard for me or the family name. You have shamed us." Mr. Lawrence continued to look out the window, but noted her objections went from "my" and "me" to "us." She was looking for support. His nature was philosophical. In his mind's eye, he could see it all. *What is, is what it is. They will get married, have the baby, and probably live happily ever after. Maybe even have a few more. What's the shame in that? Marriage, yeah, once upon a time that was a prerequisite. Nowadays, it seems to be a fading convention.* He didn't understand or share the concept of social shame that his wife expressed. Robert went to get her a glass of water. Lisa ran after him, not wanting to be left alone with Mrs. Lawrence's big scene.

"What will the League think? They will guess—they will know. And then, quickly, "How far along are you?"

Lisa was dumbstruck at Mrs. Lawrence's reaction. An occasion of joy trashed forever by her rude, self-centeredness. "About five weeks," she answered with a flatness of emotion and a matching stare.

"Oh, my God…I have no time to spare…oh, Robert, there are doctors that might—"

"No mother, no. Never!" His face was twisted in an ugly anger she had never seen before.

"Oh, of course not…I'm just upset…please forgive the remark." But she did intend "the remark" and wished they would make the baby go away.

"Oh, but this makes a mess of everything." She was actually wringing her hands.

"What mess are you talking about, Mother?"

"Why I planned a huge wedding, the best of everything, the best people, the best—"

"This is, in fact, my wedding," Lisa said. "Why do you take it on yourself to plan my wedding?"

Although highly angered, Mrs. Lawrence saw the need for a quick and humble retreat. She hastily adopted a conciliatory face, conjured a plausible explanation, and answered in an apologetic tone.

"We have only one child and want it to be the best for him…and you as well. This was to be our wedding gift to you both. Lisa, please believe me. I had no intention of leaving you out of the planning. Of course, it is your wedding. I would love to have your support and would be honored to work alongside of you. I believe I've gotten a little carried away with it. If I've offended you I am truly sorry and apologize. Please. I value your input and know the event wouldn't be the same without it. I regret the intrusion. It's just that it's such a sudden surprise. I am happy for you both. Surely you won't refuse our gift."

Humbleness and apology went down hard for Mrs. Lawrence, but she was a veteran of many battles and instinctively knew when to disengage.

Both Robert and his father's face showed open surprise. Their thoughts stopped abruptly. They had never seen, much less thought Mrs. Lawrence capable of such a backpedaling apology.

But Lisa's expression never softened. She had a very good idea as to Mrs. Lawrence's soul and disbelieved her twisting and turning. Underneath everything said, Lisa didn't have to guess. She knew exactly what this wedding was going to be. Mrs. Lawrence will have her picture splashed across every high society magazine and newspapers in the state—further if possible—rubbing shoulders with the famous and influential. She and Robert, despite being bride and groom, would be relegated to a lesser prominence. Lisa considered Mrs. Lawrence the consummate socialite, a woman whom unconsciously presumed a mantle of royalty, but in fact the only similarity to a royal title was that she was a soul sucking matriarchal queen.

"Roberta," Mr. Lawrence said, "You might want to re-think the loss of plans. You've been thinking about a weeding for years. All of those caterers, bakeries, dress makers, decorators, and wedding halls are still in existence—and some may have improved during the years. You still have their addresses and phone numbers, I'm sure, and an agenda, and an invitation list. Nothing lost there. It'd be easy to update. They were all patiently selected by yourself in the first place. Merely share the data with Lisa and see if she approves of the choices. She'll probably want to change or add a few things herself. That would be a rightful thing to do. Everything will work out. Think about it."

Mrs. Lawrence mellowed a bit. William's observation was wise and still gave her some wiggle room to influence Lisa. *Half a loaf.*

"Mother, I know it will be short notice and probably raise a few eyebrows. We can't help that. Let's do the best we can to get the event off the ground and get along with each other while doing that."

Mrs. Lawrence could see the wisdom in that too. It had to be done. However, she could never come to terms with the untimely pregnancy. It was disgraceful. She already felt the embarrassment that tongue wagers would cause—and she was sure that would happen. Her cheeks grew pink when she envisioned the awkwardness in announcing that Lisa had a "premature" baby. Only the charitable would believe her.

Robert suggested a walk in the garden. The present turmoil slowly receded. Twice around the garden without a mention of the wedding or pregnancy was a relief. Tensions lessened to the point where Robert and Lisa judged it to be an appropriate time to say goodbye.

After they left, Mrs. Lawrence had another crying fit. Despite it being mid-afternoon, Mr. Lawrence poured them both a drink. It was going to be a long, uncomfortable day and night.

Chapter 43

The wedding was held at St. John's Episcopal Church in Detroit. The Lawrences were themselves married there. They were supportive members of the church for forty years, although they now seldom attended. Mrs. Lawrence's parents, the Piersons, were staunch Episcopalians and very active in the church when she was growing up, as were her grandparents. To be a member of a prominent church was an important aspect of Detroit's elite upper class. But to be also from an "old" and moneyed Episcopalian church family was even more well regarded.

Just so, Roberta Pierson, was born into status. Her marriage, encouraged by her mother, to a prominent physician, William Lawrence, anchored her station.

The church was beautifully decorated. Its vaulted ceilings, stained glass, and overall outward architecture were both beautiful and imposing. It was, therefore, the perfect place for Robert to be married, and a place for friends of the Lawrences to see and be seen.

It was an evening wedding. Each row of pews, on both sides, were lit with a candle at either end. An abundance of flowers pressed against the rail, overfilling the front; some vases being set down a scant two feet in front of the first pews. The invited began filing in at 5 p.m. A choir set the celebratory tone while ushers led the people to their seats. Lisa's friends from school and work didn't fill up as much as Mrs. Lawrence would have liked so she instructed the ushers to seat Robert's friends and co-workers on the bride's side as well.

When the late arrivals trickled down to the last few, and then none, an usher gave the signal, and the French horns followed by the trumpets, coronets, and trombones filled the nave with a swelling music for a full fifteen minutes until a pause was signaled. An audible, subdued rustling of bridesmaid and groomsmen queueing up at the foyer could be heard, and then to the classic strains of "Here Comes the Bride" the processional began. Lisa's wedding gown was stunningly beautiful and brought out an audible "ohhh" in admiration as she passed the women. The guys just stared and thought Robert was a lucky guy.

Mr. and Mrs. Lawrence sat proudly in the front smiling at Robert who, more than a little nervous, avoided looking at them after the first time.

The proper words were said, vows and rings exchanged, and Mr. and Mrs. Robert Lawrence were introduced to the world. The photographers took their pictures, and the brass began a joyful recessional joined by the voices of the choir. Photographers were busy snapping pictures down the aisle and outside. Friends, relatives, and well-wishers filed out of the church and gathered about in small talkative groups.

And it was done.

Gradually the cars left the church parking lot, headed to the reception at the Grosse Pointe Yacht Club. Four hundred people. A band pounded out the old and the new, the sentimental and the romantic. The lighting, open bar, food, and service were impeccable. Amongst the attendees was Governor Timmons, State Representative Renee Hanks, Detroit Mayor McGraw, a couple of film makers, and two successful and well-known authors, and many, many doctor friends and acquaintances of both Dr. Robert and Dr. William Lawrence. True to form, Mrs. Lawrence, or if she could drag her husband into it, had pictures taken with them all. And, of course, why not. In a manner of speaking, it was her party. Lisa's realized her foreboding was misplaced, everything did turn out well and she and Robert were honored as befitting the newly married. The last dance of the evening had both Mr. and Mrs. Lawrence tearing up. It was a wonderful event and Mrs. Lawrence congratulated herself on a job well done. It was time to go home.

Chapter 44

Robert and Lisa, sporting Aruba honeymoon tans, settled on a, five-bedroom, 5,000 square foot two story Tudor just up from Lakeshore drive along Lake St. Clair. The house was immaculate and the landscaping superb. They both liked it the first time through, but thought it was pricey at $850,000. When they showed it to Mr. and Mrs. Lawrence, though, both thought it was just the right home for them and offered to provide half of the price as an additional wedding gift. They couldn't say no to that and within three weeks after closing they moved from their apartment into the house.

"Robert, this house is so big. What're we going to do with all this room? The furnishings will cost about as much as the house."

"Yeah, but it was on the market for forty days and they dropped the price twenty thousand when we offered to pay cash for a quick sale. So, there's some furniture money right there."

"Okay, that'll cover a room or two," she said glibly. "What about the rest of the house?"

"Hmm, don't know, one dragon at a time. I think we did a smart thing by keeping the yard maintenance and landscaping crew. We'll keep the contract to the end of the season and we'll go from there."

"Surely you don't think of doing the lawn by yourself...look at the front, I'll bet its a hundred feet from here to the road."

"Actually, 125 feet. And, no, I don't intend to do the lawn. I was thinking it would give you something to do."

"What!"

"Just kidding. "Let's take a look at the nursery."

"We don't have one."

"Yep, we do. I've been thinking. The bedroom across from ours will do just fine. Just need some painting and decoration. I don't understand the previous owners' penchant for purple, but that color has gotta go. Heck, we have enough bedrooms for several babies."

Lisa thought about babies. One, she thought, would be enough. She wasn't trying to re-populate the earth. Why did anyone want more than one…why did anyone want one in the first place? Her pregnancy had been an accident, but she was determined to see it through. She and Robert had talked about a large family, more his view than hers. But she needed to get married and didn't want to disturb the momentum. So, whenever the subject came up, she was noncommittal and simply segued into their lives after their firstborn. Robert rolled right along with it and seemed not to notice; but he did. He just didn't want to push it and have a disagreement which, after the first baby, might not materialize at all.

Since Lisa and Robert announced the pregnancy, their lives had been a whirl of activity. The engagement party, planning the wedding, the wedding, honeymoon, and buying the house. All had taken place within three months. Now, at five months she was trying her best to adjust to the newness of everything in between while retching and feeling like she had the flu. The discomfort eventually passed, but the impending delivery was ever on her mind and frightened her into sleeplessness.

Their dinner conversations were typical of expecting couples and one in particular, naming the baby.

"So, if it's a girl, what's the name?" said Lisa.

"I think that maybe Roberta for the first name would really please my mother."

"How about Lisa," Lisa said.

"I don't know, which sounds better, Lisa Roberta or Roberta Lisa."

Roberta made Lisa's colon clench. How could she tell Robert? She didn't want to push it. If one name was allowed, then the other would be as well. She'd be damned it the baby would ever bear the name Roberta, neither the first, nor the second name. She needed time to work on Robert. So, she segued.

"And if it's a boy?"

"I was thinking Robert for the first name would be really good. And for the second name, what do you suggest?"

Lisa hesitated, despite already having made up her mind earlier, "I'm thinking of Raymond."

"Where does that come from?"

"That was my father's first name," she flashed a deceitful smile. "Nice ring to the names, don't you think?"

"Oh, okay, well that makes sense—so there it is, Robert Raymond Lawrence. Sounds impressive—lawyer or doctor you think?"

"Oh, perhaps..." she tilted her head, pretending to give it some thought, "...yes, a lawyer would be good." Lisa experienced a flash of reminiscence and an accompanying twinge of guilt. Did she love her husband? Yes. Did she still love Ray? Yes. There was a dualism in Lisa which she was unable to explain. But love wasn't a matter of definition, certainly not logic. Her life view was probably closest to the Stephen Stills lyric that said something about loving who you're with if you have to be away from who you really love. But she was also a practical woman, and her choice of either man was based on comfort and security. Who could blame her?

Into the sixth month, they were told that it was going to be a boy. In the middle of the eighth month, Lisa experienced a couple of contractions, and thought it was time. A half hour later she was wheeled through the doors of Grosse Pointe's Beaumont hospital, and upstairs to the maternity ward. Despite more contractions over the next three hours, she wasn't dilating sufficiently and labor was induced. Fourteen hours later she went into labor, was wheeled into the delivery room, and her boy was delivered. She had vague memories of yelling, "I don't want to do this. Take it out." And, "Get it out of me." None of which were particularly original birthing expressions. Doctors and nurses seldom hear anything new.

Afterward, although Lisa was in pain despite the sedatives, she knew it was over and was joyous. Robert was at her side for the most of it. She was exhausted and sleep was welcome.

Marriage for the first year was good. Baby sitters allowed space for entertainment. Domestics—the housemaids that took care of the cleaning, laundry, cooking and shopping—were the norm in Lisa's new life. During their second year, despite Robert's earnings and finances, he slowly became more frugal, often balking at the household expenses. That never happened before. First the entertainment dropped off, movies, plays and expensive dining were now special occasions and had to be planned instead of impulsive whims.

Laundry—at best, disagreeable...the same with cooking. Lisa hated to cook, but outside of ordering a carryout, there was no other way to make food appear on the table. Robert kept encouraging her to take a more active role in housekeeping.

And his new passion, golf, seemed to be slowly displacing his ardor for Lisa. He spent more of his off duty hospital hours at the Lochmoor Country Club. He and his hospital buddies would play a round of two of golf, and often afterward eat and drank there late into the evening. Didn't they have wives? Well, for the most part the answer would be yes, once. Robert would come home from the club sometimes a bit inebriated, play a little with Robbie, and give Lisa a cursory peck on the cheek on his way up to bed. For Lisa, married life had become a series of joyless routines draining her spirit and soul. Romance, appreciation, and intimacy would have helped, but Robert was oblivious to Lisa's every day, grinding responsibilities. His was a checkbox mind. Wife? Check. Baby? Check. Home? Check. Profession? Check. He had done his job, what more was there to do? From his viewpoint, Lisa had a beautiful home, some hired help, a baby, and now it was up to Lisa to do what a homemaker does. He expected it. He had his job, she had hers. He saw no conflict or any reason why she would not be happy.

That was where he went wrong.

Some of the domestic help had been given reduced hours. Lisa had to take up the slack. She hated housekeeping and often reflected on her simple apartment, a quick vac, maybe a dusting and she was done.

Cooking—carry outs. Dishes for one? A snap. Laundry—some underwear, a couple pair of Levis, and some tops. She had no need for linens, crystal, hardwood floors, expensive party wear, or society put-on manners. What she realized is what she missed most was her own personal time. Lisa time, is what she called it then. But now, in between changing diapers, cleaning the house more often, and cooking a meal that was often eaten alone, there was no Lisa time. The house was huge and to her mind had a lonesome, hollowness to it. That, combined with her lack of friendships wore at her. Her best friends from college had married and moved; some lived in other states. There was no one close to confide in, joke with, visit, or share some measure of enjoyment. Her life had become Robbie and the house. She had worked hard for a profession and now it was pitched on the trash heap of wasted dreams. But Lisa had an ambition in her that burned and refused to be ignored.

She grew restless and needed out. Away from the house, away from Robbie, and maybe even away from Robert.

It was mid-afternoon. Robbie would be asleep for two hours. Lisa called Grace Accounting. She had been given leave for the wedding, and once again when Robbie was born. But now, she was desperately ready to return to her kind of work, what she had been trained to do. What she loved.

The phone rang twice. Grace answered. "Hello, Grace, Lisa here."

"So good to hear from you. I'm sorry I missed your wedding, I got bogged down at work. One of the girls quit and I've been working double time, Saturdays and Sundays. When're you coming back? I need you."

Perfect, just what I wanted to hear. "Well, Grace, I've been thinking about it and my husband and I have been discussing it. I would love very much coming back. Thank you for asking. I can let you know in a couple of days."

"Great. When you come back, we'll have a lot of catching up to do. Okay. I'm with a client now and have to go. But be sure to call, please." And, it was as simple as that.

Chapter 45

Ray entered the lobby of WS&H and wedged his way into a full elevator. He got off on the fourth floor and g'morning'd the receptionist. She nodded as he entered his "office" and dumped his empty briefcase on his desk. A few minutes later his two office associates arrived; one made coffee. They introduced themselves as Dave Humboldt and Jeremy White, and apologized for their abruptness the previous day—they had been pushing deadlines. One was a tax lawyer, the other dealt in maritime. Ray could understand tax, but not maritime—an archaic practice, he thought. Yet, on second thought, Detroit was on a river and saw a lot of private craft, large ore carriers, and foreign shipping. The Detroit Harbor Terminals was a bustling port, so accidents, damaged goods, storage and spoilage must be issues; clearly there must be a need for that expertise. Nonetheless maritime seemed to Ray an obscure field. How could any money be made in that small niche? He'd never given it a thought, maybe he'd missed something. In all of his contract studies he had only been presented with two examples of maritime cases. He'd have to learn more. In the meantime, he was looking for the first contract case to cross his desk. He was still a rookie and would have to grind out anything that was dropped on his plate. He was three months off from taking the bar exam…even then, he wouldn't be a full-fledged attorney until WS&H allowed him to handle his own cases. Up to that point, he would be assigned to a handler…a senior firm lawyer who would guide him and ultimately announce when he was ready. Until then it was grunt duty, smile, and say give me more.

The firm furnished bar exam study materials and he could discuss any concept with his mentor, Sandy Levine. If it wasn't within his guide's sphere of knowledge, then another would be contacted and Ray would find himself with another tutor. That way he got to know several of the shooters in the firm. He blew though his case load as fast as possible, and spent the rest of every evening studying. Weekends? More of the same. Getting lost in his studies and work was almost therapy. It was the one way he could squelch the thoughts of Lisa which still banged like firecrackers through his mind …little memory explosions of their time together, followed by feelings of regretful loss.

***

Several months had passed since Ray signed on to WS&H. He was now inured to the work and kicked it out like an assembly line product. After taking the bar exam, he was finally able to have some Ray Oliver time. He felt confident that his several sections of written bar exam responses were not only adequate, but probably borderline brilliant. The rest of the testing, he thought went as well. He refused to consider failure.

It was the beginning of another week. Ray exited the elevator and nodded to the receptionist, who by now was saying, "Good morning, Mr. Oliver." He gave her a wide smile.

Inside the office there had been a change. Now, there were only two desks, his and Humboldt's.

"Where's White?" he asked. Humboldt told him that apparently White's office was ready and they moved him out.

"Yeah, I remember when I heard that the first time…when was it—two or three months ago? You know, when our "offices" were supposedly being readied? Which reminds me, have you seen Rodney lately? I'd like to mention my disappointment."

"Ha…yeah. Well I don't want to injure your sensitivities, but I was here two weeks before you came through the door, and I heard the same thing. No telling how long White was here before me."

Both gave a half-hearted chuckle. Two days later, White popped his head through their door and told them work was going so well that if he stopped paddling for ten minutes he'd probably drown. Which to them meant that he was extremely busy and presumably happy with the load entrusted to him.

They wished him well, and after he left they wondered to each other what had he done that they failed to do. That question was answered a week later.

Ray Oliver was summoned to an office on the tenth floor. When he entered, he saw several senior firm partners were present, and semi-circled about Mr. Wentworth. Wentworth spoke first, he extended his hand and loudly congratulated Ray on passing the bar; fourth from the top of all tested. He was excited for Ray, and for having him at the firm. The others smiled their approval and said so as well, some just nodded their head but that was enough of an acknowledgement for Ray. His guts were churning. Although he was confident, there was always a "what if" component in everything. He passed the bar; the "what if" failed to materialize; his insides were almost spastic with relief. Wentworth then presented him with a check. Nine thousand dollars: one thousand for each year of college and law school, high scholastic achievement, and three thousand symbolic of each year of internship. Ray accepted the check, thanked them, and told them how he was grateful and very pleased to be a WS&H associate.

The men began filing out of the room. A couple of workers stood aside the door to let them pass. Wentworth stood outside the door and crooked a finger at Ray. Ray stepped out and Wentworth said, "I hope you like your new office." Ray sucked in a deep breath of air, breathed out slowly, and looked quickly back into the room. He watched the workmen wheel their handcarts into the room and begin setting up filing cabinets and bookshelves. A beautiful desk moved past them and then two dark green leather covered chairs. A fish tank completed the installation,

"Mr. Wentworth," I am truly grateful. Thank you ever so much."

Wentworth just smiled. "Work hard, Ray…work hard." He shook Ray's hand again, and said, "…now for Mr. Humboldt," and walked away.

Within a half hour, Sonja with a J, arrived with a cart full of files.

Chapter 46

After three years, Mrs. Roberta Lawrence still considered her son's marriage to Lisa a dreadful mistake. Lisa's family name was neither listed in the Fortune 500 nor mentioned in the Social Register. To her, Lisa was an outcast, a woman without social credentials, a product of inferior schools and one whom simply lacked the sophistication of people like herself and her friends. Lisa just didn't fit. Robert gave her social standing, Lisa returned little else. The grandson? Mrs. Lawrence didn't trust Lisa. To Mrs. Lawrence's mind, the child was always the "hook" and only proof of the child's paternity would satisfy her. She was surprised that it took her so long to think of it. If Robert was proven the father, then she would resign herself to her great unhappiness, but if the DNA proved negative, then it would offer an opportunity to possibly bring about an end of their marriage. She was resolved: the test was the key to undermining the marriage.

Mrs. Lawrence steadily badgered her husband for the better part of a year to have the boy's DNA tested. Didn't Mr. Lawrence work in a hospital? Didn't he have friends that could perform such tests? Why then, would he not want to do it? It was almost a daily commercial, and Mr. Lawrence was tiring of it.

The simple truth was that Mr. Lawrence could arrange for a DNA test. However, he didn't want to. He liked the boy. The boy called him Grandpa. He sat on his knee. Grandpa read him stories, played with him, bought him ice cream and toys. Robert seemed happy; Lisa was a good wife; he liked her almost as well as his own son. And while it was true that the boy didn't resemble Robert, he thought that sometimes they take after the mother—and there was a slight resemblance. The boy was young. Who could tell at his age who he'd favor? Why would he want to "prove" his son wasn't the father? If he wasn't, so what…they get along. Christ, they've been married for three years. Why now? Why the interference? His wife offered nebulous and bizarre answers, usually bordering on family status, dilution of their aristocratic blood, and inheritance, but usually the arguments were only thin screens for a selfish concern for her own social status and comfort. Prime, amongst her concerns, was what would the women of the Parkcrest Woman's League think if they found out? It was a question that must be resolved and if need be, the answer quietly disposed of.

Mr. Lawrence was not moved by her arguments, but also sensed their usually happy life was being displaced by impatience and irritability over common place things that never mattered before. And, he noted that he and his wife needed more than a couple of martinis in the evenings, often which resulted in things said that were better left unsaid. He reasoned that Robert could very well be the father…then, why not a test? On the other hand, what if…. And, he didn't really want to know that answer. But the continual pestering had its effect and Mr. Lawrence eventually caved.

Dr. William Lawrence viewed Monday mornings only as the beginning of a long wait until the weekend. The revolving doors swooshed behind him and he crossed the floor to the elevators. The hospital hallways were busy as usual. Nurses, doctors, med students, and an occasional clergyman, all avoiding gurneys being wheeled as fast as their accompanying IV poles could be safely moved by nurses or nurse aids; most of whom were working on the last couple hours of a twelve-hour stretch.

Mid-morning, Dr. William Lawrence and Dr. Randle Carlisle met in the physician's lounge; steaming hot coffees in front of them. Their coffee meetings were a ritual they shared since longer than either could remember. They stared at the circles of black coffee reflecting the ceiling's florescent lighting. Both men, successful, but having reached a point in their careers where both were thinking retirement might be better than morning rounds. William cleared his throat, and spoke, "Randy, can you do me a favor. Dr. Carlisle raised his eyebrows, "For you, of course…name it."

William Lawrence took a deep breath and exhaled slowly. "Well, the details are personal and a bit embarrassing. My wife and I...and well, uh...oh, hell, there is no other way. He leaned forward and in a quieter voice said bluntly, "Can you perform an anonymous subject DNA test for me?"

What would cause his friend to ask such a question? His tone was so serious and almost conspiratorial. Dr. Randy tried not to be too inquisitive and, to test the water, said lightly, in the same quietness of voice, "You haven't been named in a paternity suit, have you?"

"No, nothing like that." And actually chuckled at that thought, much to the relief of Randle Carlisle, who hoped it wasn't as serious as William initially sounded.

Randy answered, "Depends. What kind of test are you looking for—evidentiary, forensic, paternal, maternal, prenatal or otherwise? There are many kinds of tests—some are complex in their detail, and might entail some legal or medical forms, and others are simple enough and give a quick *match/no match* result."

"When I said embarrassing, I was referring to my wife's overly sensitive concern for our grandchild—practically obsessive. The concern, however, actually stems from her own ego—her personal social image. Just between you and me then—I would really hate for this to get out—but my wife isn't convinced that our grandson is our son's child. She believes that our daughter in law was already pregnant by another, and then seduced and lied to him. She believes that Robert married beneath his station out of honor. I have no idea as to what she's planning following the results of a DNA test.

Are you asking me to perform a test and skew the results towards the family, or away from it? I'd feel very uncomfortable professionally—ethically—to fabricate or misrepresent a result."

"No, nothing of that sort. I'm not asking for anything like that...I just want to know for sure, one way or the other. Actually, I'm all right with it either way, he's a great grandson and the parents get along well. They're happy and that makes me happy. I'm old enough to not really care. Besides, if he wasn't my son's then it would be like an adoption, and that would be okay with me as well. Also, there's always a chance for a second child and at that point the matter would be insignificant. But it's gnawing away at my wife and it's become a chronic, focal point in our conversations. I'm simply worn out."

"Ok, William, I'll do it for you. I'm going to give you a home test kit—a couple of swabs, sealable containers, and directions. Your DNA is the same as your son's, no problem there. Get a sample from the grandchild and return the kit back to me in a day or two. I'll have the results for you the next day. By the way, the test is called the DNA Grandparentage Test just in case you think you're asking for something unique. It happens often enough." His smile was reassuring and greatly reduced William's uneasiness.

A week later, Dr. William met Dr. Randy for coffee, usual time, usual place. This time, however, Randy said he had a consultation and left the DNA test result envelope with William. As he stepped away from the table, he looked aside and said, "Sorry." Consultation or not, Randy's "sorry" was weighty enough to foreshadow the DNA test result. Now, without looking, he knew the truth in the envelope. He wanted the boy to be a Lawrence and was disappointed…but, he also thought of the loving child, and he loved him as well. What now? He finished his much too hot coffee and reached for the envelope. It was as he had expected: no match. He left work an hour early.

"Hi, Roberta, I'm going to have dinner with Dr. Carlisle tonight. Sorry. A medical case just came up and we have to talk. He was tied up and suggested a dinner later tonight and I agreed."

Roberta Lawrence was used to late calls and ordering from the local deli. "No problem. Thanks for calling. Will it be a late night?"

"No, don't think so. Just a dinner and a few drinks."

"Shall I wait up for you?"

William Lawrence actually wanted to avoid his wife, especially this night. The paternity was one topic which he did not want to discuss, and he knew that his wife would be on it in the middle of their first drink.

"No, not really unless you want to?" he said, as diplomatic in tone as possible.

"No problem, I'll see you then."

"Great," he said and ended the call. "Shit, he said through compressed lips. Forget dinner. Dr. Randy won't be available, but I know that Dr. Martini will be."

The Gin Room was a quiet, piano bar about a half mile from his home. *Not a bad drive, especially after a couple of martinis—less chance of a traffic stop.* He made his way down the row of bar stools to his favorite table in the back and ordered. The second martini went down as smooth as the first, and the third was the smoothest of all three.

When he arrived home, Roberta was on the couch and sipping away at her martini. The remnants of a deli order on the coffee table. A book in her hand.

"So, how'd it go today?" she asked.

"Very good not counting a malfunctioning x-ray unit, a woman who fell out of bed, and one child with a broken ankle whom a sedative didn't help—had to put her out; don't like to do that. Otherwise, just peachy."

"Did you talk to Dr. Carlisle about the DNA test?"

Damn, that didn't take long,

"Nope. Didn't get a chance to…he was very busy today."

"Well, you had dinner with him, didn't you?"

"Yes, but the topic never came up."

"Hmm, it was yours to bring up, now wasn't it?

"Well, now that you mention it, but it is also something we can wait on."

"Really now, William, after all this time you think you would be interested in knowing the result."

Not as much as you, but he didn't want the fireworks to start so he kept quiet. He poured himself another martini. She continued with her needing to know mantra, her voice rising slightly at the end of her delivery.

William Lawrence knew where this was going to end—where it always did. In an argument. "I'm tired dear. I'm going to bed. Good night." And he made it to the stairs quite soberly, but weaved a bit on the staircase out of his wife's view.

Mrs. Lawrence poured a fourth martini, and tried to read her book but she was angry and the words just flowed past her eyes without making an impression. And then, an idea.

"Dear," she called up the stairs. It isn't late…do you mind if I call Dr. Carlisle?

William's eyes popped open. *Do I mind? Hell, yes, I mind. Talk about generating a storm, well, that would certainly do it if she found out.*

"Uh, not a good thing to do, dear. I don't think he had a chance to do the test yesterday, he was very busy—probably why he didn't mention it at dinner. I'll get the results in the morning."

Roberta Lawrence considered the information and it sounded plausible. So, rather than skewer her husband's friend with a push, she settled down and went back to her book and drink.

Mr. Lawrence heard no reply, so he presumed that his answer sufficed. A few minutes later, however, he lifted the bedroom phone to make sure she didn't ignore him and made the call anyway; dial tone; no voices. Good. "*Keep it simple, and she'd understand. It was best that way.*

But William couldn't drop the underlying question as to what his wife would do with the information that their son, Robert, was not the father. It was a question that broke into his thoughts a couple of times a day. He never asked Roberta before. Now that they both had their martini truth serum, perhaps he should ask.

Mr. Lawrence put on a robe and went downstairs.

Mrs. Lawrence lay on the couch, her book across her chest, and half of the martini balanced on the edge of the book.

"Roberta, you've been extremely insistent on learning about the boys' paternity. As much as you want to know about young Robbie, I want to know too what you intend to do if we discover that our son is not the father."

"Why I thought you knew. I intend to cause a divorce. Afterward, I will introduce him to some other young women that is more acceptable to our social status, and we will live happily ever after."

William was speechless. He sat back in his chair, stunned. His face turned red as he stood. He pointed his finger at her, exasperated, his lips tight. He finally stammered, "You…you…." But he was too angry to answer without a non-threatening response. He never finished, but turned abruptly and went upstairs.

Roberta smiled faintly. *Keep it simple; he'd understand. It was best that way.*

It was almost midnight when Mrs. Lawrence went up to bed. William was asleep on his back. She hated that because he always snored on his back…and true to form, he was snoring big time.

She disrobed and sat on the edge of her bed. William was sloppy, she thought, noting his pants on the end of his bed, shirt on the floor, suit jacket loosely draped over the chair…very loosely, the inside of its left front panel gaping open displayed a large white envelope in its pocket with Dr. Carlisle's name embossed in its upper left hand corner. Irresistible. She took the envelope and read the letter. The bottom line: no match.

Ha! He lied. He had the results. No match! Robert is not the father. She took the letter downstairs to the den and ran it through their copier. With shaking hands, she replaced the envelope and carefully hung the jacket on the back of the chair.

Despite the four drinks, Roberta wasn't sleepy any longer. Her wide smile and occasional chuckling kept her awake. Well, so William lied; no matter. He is forgiven.

***

The next morning Dr. Lawrence decided on his best course of action. He would lie to Roberta, telling her that the DNA matched and Robert was the father. He shredded Dr. Carlisle's letter.

That evening he told his wife. She nodded her head in understanding and said it was such a relief to know for sure and thanked him for having the test done. There was no more conversation about it. It was a pleasant three martini evening which ended with both of them being in one bed, happy in their thoughts.

Chapter 47

Several days later, Mrs. Lawrence called Lisa.

"Hello, Lisa, so nice to hear your voice."

Lisa replied, "and yours too." Both lies washed each other's away and died in a moment of silence.

"We haven't seen much of each other for a couple of weeks. I was thinking that it'd be nice if you dropped over for lunch, maybe this afternoon or tomorrow."

"Um...good, tomorrow would be good. Robbie will be in preschool for a couple of hours. Thanks for the invite." They passed small talk for the next five minutes before saying goodbye.

Lisa, wary, was thinking that Mrs. Lawrence's call was unusual. Her tone seemed overly friendly. *I wonder what's going on in her stuffy, little mind, but, timely anyway since I've got a few things to say to her.*

Two trains rode this track, both headed directly at the other.

***

Thursday afternoon Lisa stuffed Robbie into his car seat and struggled with the straps. The parking lot of the Hillsdale Preschool was beginning to fill. Lisa was lucky, she got a spot near the door. She undid the reluctant straps from Robbie, wondering why for probably the thousandth time that the seat makers couldn't come up with a better idea instead of straps, buckles, oversized button catches and all the rest of their restraints. Couldn't they just Velcro him into the seat? Sometimes she pinched Robbie in a buckle. He didn't like it, neither did she. Try to explain some of his innocent red marks and maybe a bruise to some inquisitive and overzealous teacher—next thing she'd be visited by Child Protective Services.

At the door she did what Robbie liked a lot: she pointed to her eye, then her heart, and then at him. He giggled and said, "I love you too, mommy," hugged her and was handed over to his teacher who met them in the lobby.

Goodbye for three hours. Lisa felt free again…except for the impending meeting with Mrs. Lawrence. Almost three years into their association and Lisa still thought of her mother-in-law as Mrs. Lawrence— never Roberta or any other sort of fondness. Hugs and a kiss on the cheek? Never. However, neither Mrs. Lawrence nor Lisa were interested in familiarity. They simply couldn't stand each other, but in front of others did remarkably well in keeping their feelings buried where no one could see.

"Hello, Lisa, nice of you to come." Proper manners demanded that. And, if anything, Mrs. Lawrence was proper.

"Thank you for the invitation."

"I've had Sarah set the table in the sunroom." She turned and led Lisa from the door.

The sun room was bright, shaddowless. The interior was painted white, the spotless windows invited views of a perfect flower garden. Green plants and flowers nicely set off the room's dimensions and oil paintings added the perfect touch of color. In the middle was a white rattan table set with a bright blue tablecloth, silverware, and smoked turkey/orange/cranberry tea sandwiches, Danish open-faced sandwiches, a cheese plate, a pitcher of iced tea, and thermal carafes of tea and coffee.

"Your table is gorgeous," said Lisa. "There's a ton of food; are you expecting anyone else?"

"No, just you and me. I hope you're hungry. A few of the ladies from the Parkcrest Woman's League might stop by later this afternoon. But that will be much later and all of this will keep.

It would have been nice if Mrs. Lawrence let her know it was only for her, but she didn't. Lisa saw that she had been "worked in." They filled their plates and glasses.

"So, how are things going at work?" Mrs. Lawrence said

"Great, I've been working for Grace Accounting for two years now. Grace, the owner, likes my work. She has two others ladies working in the same office, but she defers the more complex accounts—spread sheets, legal, and cross references to me. I view that as a compliment."

"And how does your working—being away from home—affect Robbie."

"He does well. We can afford a full-time baby sitter so Robbie's never alone and when I come home, he's there to greet me. Our sitter loves him and he's treated well. She usually takes him to pre-school. Since I was coming here, I took the day off and drove him myself. It's good to take a day off every now and then. You agree?"

"I wouldn't know. I don't work at a regular "job." She smiled; the word "job" had a slight haughty ring to it.

Lisa began thinking that it hadn't taken Mrs. Lawrence long to begin prying. She hadn't even finished her first sandwich. Where was this going?

Mrs. Lawrence began pressing. "How are things between you and my son?"

What a thing to ask, some nerve. "Things? Like what sort of things are you interested in…entertainment, political, our eating habits, or maybe our sex life?"

Mrs. Lawrence shot her a deprecating, superior look. "No need to be so touchy dear."

"No need? Nosing into my family life like that, what did you expect?"

"Nosing! Well aren't you the one to talk about nosing into family lives?

"Okay, let's have it. You didn't invite me here for a pleasant luncheon and a girl to girl talk. What do you want?"

"Fine. You're right. There are many other people that I would rather be having lunch with. You are the least! What this is about is that I don't like you, never have."

"Well, no surprises there. I feel the same about you. But we both already know that. So, what's it about?"

"It's about you and Robert. I never felt you were well suited to each other. I think you should go."

"You feel I should go? Go where? What are you talking about?"

"I think you two should divorce."

"And just who the hell do you think you are...have you ever asked Robert about our marriage?" Lisa was pissed, but she knew it wasn't over. Roberta had more to say and to start yelling at her now and it wouldn't do any good until all of Roberta's cards were on the table.

Roberta began a slow smile—an unusual reaction thought Lisa.

"I have proof that he isn't Robbie's father. I think he might consider a divorce after I show him the DNA report which says that Robbie isn't his."

"What? You had a DNA test done without my knowledge?"

She nodded her head up and down. "Yes."

"Have you told Robert yet?"

"Not yet, but I will." Mrs. Lawrence was practically gloating.

"Have you told your husband yet?"

"Didn't have to, he had the test done." Now she was gloating.

"So, you are both in agreement that I should divorce Robert, and you believe that Robert will agree to it. Is that it?"

"Yes, dear—have one of the Danish sandwiches. They are really good." Trivializing a concern was always done from a position of authority to one of no standing. Her remark was intentionally insulting. If Lisa exploded in anger, she would be elated that she had hit a nerve.

"Lisa, dear, I will offer you one hundred thousand dollars, no strings attached, if you divorce Robert as soon as possible."

"Gee, and a car too?" Lisa laughed in her face.

Not quite the response Mrs. Lawrence expected. She had convinced herself that Lisa's background was strictly lower class. A hundred thousand dollars should strike her as huge, too much to turn down. "You think a hundred thousand is not enough?"

"Not enough?" Lisa howled with laughter. "Listen, dear Mrs. Lawrence, you are filthy rich, wealthy, old money. A hundred thousand is a pittance to you. You can tell Robert if you want. That's okay with me. Our marriage, since you wanted to know, was downhill after the second year. Sex…yeah, about as much as you and your husband get it on—how old are you anyway? Sixty? Sixty-five? And your husband probably nearing 70? Uh huh. Robert spends more time at the hospital than home, and thinks more of his golf club, golfing, and professional parties in his free time than his home life. He used to be a real hot number, but his fire's burned out. Have you looked at him lately? He's forty pounds overweight. He comes home and drinks himself to bed. I'm his housekeeper, not his wife. A married life like this is not what I had in mind."

Mrs. Lawrence, at that, recovered a bit and said, "Then you are not opposed to a divorce?"

"Nope, but by my terms, not yours."

"That's not possible, you forget who's in charge here…I have the DNA report."

"Yeah, sweetie, but listen to this. Think back as to when I was first introduced to your snobby Parkcrest Ladies Club."

"That's the Parkcrest Woman's League."

Lisa smiled, "Yes, yes, of course. Do you remember telling me to avoid saying anything personal to Ruth, Amanda, and Kathryn because they were gossips and anything said would soon get around to the rest of the membership?

Mrs. Lawrence said nothing, but it was obvious she didn't like where Lisa was going.

"Well, dear, picture this. I am going to call those ladies and invite them to lunch. We will have martinis in your honor. After the first one, I will slur my words and giggle a bit. They will like that. I will work into my conversation stories about the Lawrence household."

Mrs. Lawrence became tense and apprehensive.

"Eventually after my second martini, I will let it drop that Mr. Lawrence several times groped me on the staircase of their home and made lewd remarks. I will tell them about the sex toys you keep in your dresser drawer, about the porn movies you and your husband enjoy, your excessive drinking bouts, arguments, and other weird habits, or any other thing I can think of. Also, I may accompany Robert to a golf outing at his club and have lunch with some of its members while Robert is out on the course…it will be a repeat performance of lunch with the ladies, except it'll be personal vignettes of our life, disgraceful but maybe less vulgar, but maybe not. When Robert gets back, I will probably be drunk."

Mrs. Lawrence was horrified, and almost speechless. No one had ever dared to talk to her in that manner or ever made demands of her—or threatened her. It was always the other way around. She stammered, crestfallen and finally said, "Please don't do that. What do you want? Money?"

"Yes, of course. But not the way you think of it. You aren't just going to write me a check and expect me to disappear. So, this is what I want, and I believe it to be equitable. The owner of my workplace, Grace Accounting, is older and wants to retire. She will sell me the business if the offer is sufficient. I think two hundred thousand might do it, but I'll start at one hundred and fifty. Robert can keep the "mansion" we live in—it's too big anyway. I need a place to live. I want a nice paid for condo in Riverview, downtown Detroit. I'll keep the car. Robert takes care of our life insurance, all phases of our medical care, auto and home insurance. I want that to continue. I want a continuing yearly salary of seventy-five thousand a year. And all my divorce lawyers' fees and costs paid in full, all school tuitions and costs, and a full time baby sitter. And, a last condition, I would like a lump sum of one hundred and fifty thousand dollars just in case things don't work out.

Mrs. Lawrence said, "You're dreaming. I have enough money to hire the best of lawyers, and you'll be lucky to leave with the barest of minimums."

"Well, I can see you're upset." *It was Lisa's turn to smirk.* "But I haven't finished. First. those expensive lawyers you're talking about will be working for me and you will be paying them. One slip up, as in if they look like they're deviating from the plan and I will do what I say about your precious ladies' club. I would enjoy doing it. But I also told you that my offer is equitable."

Mrs. Lawrence, noticeably shaken, took a deep breath and said, "And so how does your idea of equity work?"

"Very simple. Since I will have my own business, I will be making money. Not a lot at first, but eventually I'll build up to a comfortable net. So, in three years I will refund half of the one hundred and fifty thousand, and reduce the seventy-five thousand dollar a year salary to fifty thousand for a set number of years. Divorces in Michigan are generous to women when it comes to dividing property—and Robert is a well-paid neurosurgeon, we own our home, and he has extensive financial resources. I am sure that I will do very well. And, above all don't forget that child support is expensive and will continue until Robbie is eighteen years old. How much do you figure that will cost? If you oppose me at the proceedings, or anytime afterward, I'll do as I say."

Lisa's delivery was fierce and her threat convincing.

"In time Robert will marry again, and you all will be much happier. I will become just an unpleasant memory, just as you all will become to me. It's just a matter of time when this ugliness will be past history. I'm offering you the deal of a lifetime. Look at it this way, you're gaining a son and losing a daughter-in-law and her baggage. I know that's worth the world to you."

Mrs. Lawrence, expressionless, just stared at her, her mind a whirl.

Lisa smiled and said, "Why don't you have one of those open faced Danish sandwiches. I'm told they are delicious."

Chapter 48

1995 Mercedes SL 500-AMG Roadster, convertible/hardtop in perfect condition. Beautiful.

Pristine condition in and out; mechanically excellent; low mileage. $18,000; not negotiable. 7 to 8p. Alex: 555.248.0101." The posting bore the current date and Ray guessed it hadn't been up for too long. None of the several tear strips bearing the phone number was missing. Ray grabbed the note and stuffed it in his shirt pocket.

He turned the ad over in his mind throughout the remainder of the day. A Mercedes 500 SL. Perfect! Eighteen-grand for a classy sports car with 32K miles, not too bad …everything depends on the condition. Not negotiable…maybe—the actual price depends on how much the owner exaggerated. We'll see. At seven, Ray dialed and said, "I'm calling in regard to the 500 SL for sale …Alex there?"

A feminine voice said "Yeah, my car's for sale."

The quality of her voice and pointed response surprised Ray as much as Alex being a woman.

"Great. I'd like to take a look at it. When can we get together?"

"Eight-thirty tonight is good for me. You?"

"Nope. I'll have to see it in daylight. What's good for you?"

"Lunchtime tomorrow?"

"Yeah, good, where are you at?"

"You know the Renaissance City Apartments?"

"Yeah, downtown, Larned and Brush."

"Right, good for you. Meet me in the lobby at noon. I'll be wearing a pink dress. See you then, bye." And the dial tone hummed in Ray's ear.

Ray was instantly reminded of Lisa. "Alex" hadn't bothered to ask his name. It didn't matter to her; she knew he'd find her.

Ray was in the lobby just before noon. No lady in pink. Ten minutes after twelve, she walked in: pretty, blond, thin, and long legs. She was beautiful. The sunlight bathed the lobby in bright light and heightened the gold luster of her hair. It caught in her earrings, and necklace, and played off the faint white pastel patterns subtly woven into her clinging pink dress. For a moment, Ray forgot why he was there. He admired her for a full minute before approaching.

"Hi, I'm Ray Oliver," and stretched out his hand, although protocol was for him to wait until she offered her hand. Alexis knew the difference, he didn't.

"Yes. I'm Alexis. Sorry I'm late. She hung onto his hand a second longer than necessary—a subtle apology much appreciated by Ray, at least he imagined it to be. He appreciated the gesture, but she was pretty enough for any man not to expect it.

"Follow me." She turned and walked to the elevator bank. Ray was behind her like a pull toy.

They took the elevator down to the parking garage and a short walk later they were at her car.

Its deep almost luminescent red shinned like it had been polished hours before. It looked new and beautiful.

"Pop the hood and start it up, please."

Alexis slid behind the wheel, her dress riding up mid-thigh. Both pretended not to notice. He walked to the front of the car and raised the hood. The engine caught immediately and its soft, satisfying rumble echoed off the garage's concrete walls. In Ray's mind its sleek, sporty appearance was persuasive. He wanted a car that made its owner look successful and appealed to the ladies. This was it.

"Take it for a ride?"

"Maybe not. I'm half way through my lunch time...besides, you'll probably want to let it out and noontime, downtown, isn't the best time. How about 8:30 tonight?"

"Fine. It's a date."

"Business!" she said.

"Uh, yeah...that's what I meant."

Alexis switched off the engine and swung out of the bucket seat. The door clicked shut and both walked back to the lobby. Alexis fielded ownership questions about repairs, insurance, the hotel's monthly parking costs, mileage and why she was selling it. In the lobby, Alexis stopped abruptly and faced him with just a hint of a smile, "I see that you are really concerned with costs. You know, maybe you might want to reconsider buying this car. Maybe it'd be too much for you."

Ray didn't think his questions were out of the ordinary for a buyer. He wondered if she zinged him, trying to force a commitment. He didn't like the technique, if that's what it was. But he swallowed it without a trace of annoyance and said just as quickly, "I just sold my Porsche and thought I'd downsize to a cheaper car and pocket the difference ... yeah, costs are always a wise thing to consider. Have you ever sold a car before?"

Her smile widened, and she nodded slightly. It was as they had shared a quiet, private joke and both were appreciative of the others talent in telling it. "Touche," she said, slightly lifting her chin. "Tonight at 8:30. I got to go," and off she went.

Ray watched her walk away. Her gait was kind of a modified runway model's. Her pelvis almost forward, her steps smoothly placed almost one before the other, her hips swaying rhythmically. It was a bearing of poise and confidence. A difficult walk to master, but once accomplished, a pleasure to see.

At 8:40 p.m. they rolled out of the hotel's garage. The traffic had cleared. As Ray moved through the gears the warm air rushed through the car, its humidity unnoticed. At the light, Ray punched it. Alexis was right, he was going to let it out. She leaned back in the seat and felt the thrill of the acceleration. At ninety, he let it coast, breezing through the next three successions of traffic lights at fifty. Ray was pleased with its power and sound. A few miles more down the road and he said he'd buy it for the 18 K. Alexis laughed and said she knew he would from the first.

"How could you tell that?"

"Because you called exactly at 7 p.m. Because when I didn't get any more calls on the car, I guessed that you ripped off the entire ad. Because you didn't balk when I suggested it might be too expensive for you, and because you showed up exactly on time this evening. I could see you were very interested and I'm not surprised you want it. It's a beautiful car and I felt the same when I bought it…and that's why!"

"How about I needed a car and the price was about right, I'm a bit aggressive, most of the time punctual, and because …because…." And he let the thought drop, but a beautiful car and a beautiful woman next to him excited him and if he told her that, she might think he was getting a little too familiar.

"And because… what?"

"And…because I love it."

"Well then, Mr. Oliver, we have a deal. When can I expect to be paid?"

Ray Oliver was back to earth quickly, any latent romantic thoughts were shelved.

"Today's Thursday…I think I can make that happen tomorrow. I'll call you and let you know."

"Great. Make it happen then."

"Do you have time for a drink?"

"I'm sorry. I'm meeting someone later."

Ray's ingratiating smile faltered momentarily, but he rolled with the punch. "Okay, if I didn't try, I'd never forgive myself."

Alexis purred a soft, "Uh huh," and let him hang. She leaned back, her hair flowing over the headrest, eyes closed, her right hand rising and falling at will in the air stream outside the window. Adele's *Rollin in the Deep* floated out of the stereo and Alexis moved subtly to the beat. The test drive was enough to satisfy Ray and they had an agreement, but Ray was so captured by Alexis that he continued driving, enjoying the moment. He was feeling the same kind of magic that he once felt with Lisa.

After another soft and rolling song, Alexis turned to him, right eye open, and whispered, "Hotel?" And Ray said, "E-yeah...sorry, I was just enjoying the ride."

Twenty minutes later they were in the Renaissance City Apartments' garage and parked. Alexis popped her door, pivoted on the seat, planted her feet on the concrete and stood. When standing, with heels, she was on eye level with Ray. He reached for the door and for a moment they were very close; she didn't move. Lisa had a boyfriend and cheated. Would Alexis? Before he could assemble a second thought, Alexis stepped aside.

Ray put his hope in check and dismissed the event as a wistful invention; Alexis was a very close Lisa. They walked through the lobby and to the elevator bank"Hey, Mr. Oliver, I'm not inviting you up."

"Yeah, I figured that but, maybe I should have told you before, I live in this building too, twentieth floor."

"Ahh.... I see... thanks for the update... I'm on the fifteenth." The doors opened and they stepped in.

At fifteen, Alexis said goodnight and stepped off. Ray nodded and leaned against a rail as the elevator doors began to close. Alexis turned her head and looked back—she was smiling; a good sign. Ray felt complimented. Alexis was thinking she just sold her car for 18,000 thousand dollars.

Chapter 49

Friday morning Ray picked up a cashier's check for 18 K. By the end of the evening he would trade it for the car's title. At 7 p.m., Ray's soft knock was answered by Alexis. Her apartment was twice the size of his. Its furnishings were comfortable and expensive looking. Two large oil paintings—scenes of Mediterranean harbors viewed from the balcony of a hilltop villa—took up several square feet of two front room walls, their warm colors nicely balanced by the décor. A great downtown view filled the dining nook window. Ray was impressed with her apartment, except for the large chair in the front room. There sat a man about his age, handsome, tanned and well dressed.

"Ray, this is my friend, Nicolo. The man stood and was about two inches taller than Ray, looked trim, and smiled down on him with very white teeth, made whiter by his tan. His handshake was soft. Ray disliked him and his handshake almost instantaneously; he thought he could take him in two rounds or less. Alexis brought out the title. Nicolo sat down while Ray and Alexis conferred at the kitchen counter. There were no liens on the title. Ray tendered the check and she signed the title over to him.

"Won't you stay for a drink?" she said.

Ray declined for good reason.

Nicolo, eagerly stood up and thrust out his hand, saying "Well, nice meeting you," in a moderately accented voice.

Ray said, "Yes." There was nothing more to add. It was time for Ray to go and leave Alexis to "Nicolo."

The message was clear and Ray headed for the door with Alexis a few steps behind him. At the open door, "Nicolo" stood behind her with his hands at either side of her waist. Ray thanked her, said it was nice seeing her again, and told again how much he liked the car. Alexis, looked intently into his eyes and mouthed the words "Call me tomorrow;" and winked at him. Nicolo, unaware of the silent communication, was showing his teeth in a smirky "I win, you lose" smile communication of his own. Ray had good reason to smile back; he beat him in round one. Ray practically floated down the hallway and up to his apartment.

Chapter 50

Friday was busy. Sonja "with-a-j" was in and out of his office several times; new cases, old cases, cases with questions--sticky notes asking for clarification or advice. Ray bore down on his work like a fox after a hound. Thoughts of Alexis made his heart sing. In his state of mind, there was nothing he wouldn't tackle or couldn't accomplish. All dragons welcome—and off with their heads. Ray was so excited about calling Alexis that evening that an occasional daydream captured his thoughts. For a few seconds he stared over his desk at the wall, and imagined Alexis being attracted to him. He had become so used to Sonja's comings and goings that he didn't notice that this time, she wasn't going…she remained standing next to his desk, and then moved into the path of his trance-like gaze. Ray blinked, and looked up as if seeing her for the first time.

"Yes. Something you need?" he asked.

"Nope, got everything I want so far."

"Then?"

"Well, I've been in and out all day and you haven't noticed."

"Yes, I see you."

"Nope, this…." and she held out her hand with a diamond engagement ring on her finger.

Instantly, Ray was up from this chair and around his desk, both apologetic and congratulatory.

"I should have noticed, I'm sorry." And holding her hand and admiring her ring, he said, "That's wonderful. I'm happy for you…must have just happened…."

"Yeah, last night. I'm still shaking. I'm so happy I could cry every time I think of it. He was so gallant. He…"

Ray could see it coming. He was truly happy for her, but he didn't have time for a blow by blow, so he interrupted hoping to shorten the story up.

"Who's the lucky guy, anyone I know?"

"Yeah, he used to work with you in the old office—Jeremy White."

"Holy Cow! Jeremy—the Maritime lawyer. Well, good for the both of you. I don't' see him too much anymore, but when you do offer him my heartiest of congratulations as well."

"Oh, I will. Thank you so much."

"How soon do you return to school?"

"Oh, I'm not a student."

"You're a law clerk then, right?"

"Nope. I just work for the company. Nothing special," and she backed toward the doorway, eager to be off down the aisle showing her ring to anyone she missed.

Ray went back to work, forcing himself to focus on case issues instead of Alexis.

He completed his work agenda and the weekend was his. On the way out, in the lobby, he saw Dave Humboldt—the other lawyer in their first "office." He saw Humboldt almost every day and today was no different, except for Humboldt standing at the revolving entrance door and waving his arm off at him. Ray walked over to him.

"Hey, what'd'ya think of Sonja getting engaged to White." He obviously assumed it was common knowledge…among their stable of lawyers anyway.

"I think it's great, I'm happy for both of them."

"Sonja Grayson," remember?"

"Yeah, Sonja Grayson. So what?"

"Well, my boy, here's the zinger. Her last name's not Grayson…it just says so on her nametag."

"Okay, so…."

"Well," Humboldt paused and looked around…he had some information that was definitely not common knowledge.

"And?" Ray said, bordering on impatience.

Humboldt's eyes widened. He leaned forward to pass on his great "secret."

"Her last name is really Wentworth!"

"Wentworth, as in the CEO of this law firm?"

"Yep. That's the one. And his only child."

They nodded at each other. In their minds they could hear the collective slap on the forehead of thirty junior lawyers who, if anyone of them had learned to consider a "plain" girl, would be partner well before the others—not to mention board member and beyond in due time.

"Ah, well, it's hard to keep a good man down," Humboldt said.

"Yeah…my guess is that they'll live happily ever after."

"What we need, my friend is a little luck."

Ray Oliver was a conventional man, maybe even a bit old fashioned for his age. To his mind marrying for money might be a practical consideration, but it certainly wasn't love; it was right up there with a pre-nup. Who could say if it was head-over-heals love for White, or a pragmatic conclusion to a wisp of a rumor—someone must have known of Sonja's connection to Wentworth. If that's what White wanted, then good for him—Sonja was certainly happy—good for her too. But maybe White didn't know. Not a real concern to Ray, but as far a pure luck went, in any matter, Ray nodded in agreement with Humboldt. That is exactly what he needed tonight. He wasn't sure what Alexis wanted, but hoped her long term plans included him.

The lawyers g'bye'd each other and shuffled through the revolving doors and out onto the street. Sonja being Wentworth's daughter was a real surprise. He thought of Lisa and the gradual withdrawal of her affection. That was a surprise to him too…but maybe it would turn out well after all; maybe his heartache was needless baggage—a self-imposed grief he should never have carried. *Let it go Ray, let it go.* It was 6:30 p.m. and still warm. Twenty minutes later, Ray was in his shower.

Chapter 51

The phone rang twice before Alexis answered it.

"You have dinner yet? No, okay that's good. Thrown on your tennies and jeans, toss on a casual shirt, and meet me in the lobby. I'm in the mood for a pizza and a walk around downtown."

"Splendid idea," she said, "see you in fifteen minutes."

"Good, he said, and hung up, hoping to be first this time. *Ray, he thought, you're being childish*--and he chuckled at the brief insight. But it was simultaneous and neither heard the other's phone being hung up.

She bounced out of the elevator quite a different woman. Ball cap, a bright T-shirt, jeans and sandals. Ray loved the evening look as much as he did the afternoon look. An Indian Summer wrapped Detroit in its warmth and was like a gift to both of them.

"Pizza Papilas okay with you," he said.

"Good. Want to take the people mover?"

"No, it's a great night, let's walk; it's only a couple of blocks. I need to stretch out."

It was just about 8 p.m. and the restaurant was full, but there was no line. Ray and Alexis stood near the staircase, taking in the loud noises and crowded tables. After a ten minutes wait, an upstairs waiter yelled to one of the downstairs waiters: "Table for two." The downstairs waiter, a master of sign language, pointed at them and then upstairs. The upstairs guy took over and seated them.

"Drink?"

"Give us a minute, okay."

The waiter cocked his head and gave them a half a "look," missing only a clucking of his tongue, and started to leave.

Alexis quickly said, "Beer," which halted the waiter in mid-turn.

"A pitcher of beer—Miller Lite okay with you," in a quick aside to Ray, and received a nod.

"Okay…I come back." And the waiter was gone, not to return for ten minutes. Food at Pizza Papilas was usually good; service a flip of the coin, but a noisy carnival of sound and motion was ever present. Even though both Ray and Alexis had to speak a little louder than usual, it was more fun than annoying; they felt like they were part of a lively party. If either was feeling the slightest apprehensive of their "first date" the ambiance suspended any awkwardness they may have felt.

They ordered when the second pitcher arrived, and finished their pizza an hour later—a half hour wait for a pizza was about the norm for Pizza Papalis.

Outside, the night had settled in and the bright lights from the businesses on Monroe and the partying crowd brushing passing them on the sidewalk served to continue the lightness of their combined spirits.

Ray's face lit up. "Hey, I know, let's go to the Greektown Casino—it's at the other end of the block." Simultaneously hooking her arm and redirecting their walk. She put her hand on his arm, and kept it there while they walked and talked. It was an unconscious act on her part, but Ray felt particularly warmed by it.

They stepped through the Greektown Casino doors and into a tumult of sound like coins being tumbled in a washing machine accompanied by an almost interminable "binging" of slots paying out to their lucky players.

"What'd'ya like, slots? Poker? Blackjack?"

"I don't know much about any of the games. I'm a slot player."

"I'm kind of a blackjack guy, but the slots are good to me too. Let's take twenty bucks each. If we double it we leave; if we lose it we leave."

"Deal."

Alexis found empty seats at two quarter "Blazing Sevens" machines. Ray sat next to her and both slid in a twenty. The credits jumped up and they began playing. Alexis played a quarter on each button push; Ray maxed his--75¢ a roll, about twelve rolls a minute—nearly $540 an hour, but what player ever stops to think about that?

Down a few dollars, Ray stopped and watched her play. "Why so timid? You can't make any money that way. Why don't you increase your bet, or step it up a quarter on each roll—max it out and then start all over?"

"I don't know…this way my money lasts longer…does your method work?"

Ray laughed, "Heck, I don't know…give it a try."

Alexis was having a great time, and she was up for almost anything. *Okay*, she thought. Four pushes of the button and Alexis, on a max bet, hit a $300 double jackpot. She was delighted and gave Ray a hug as her machine "binged" away. She started to talk, but ended up laughing and pointing at the machine. Ray was happy for her and waited for the "binging" to stop before he made another bet. Two rolls later he hit for seventy dollars.

"Okay," he said, "goal! We have to leave or otherwise our luck will leave us."

"Ahhh, Ray, things are going so well…I'm thinking a little longer can't hurt. What'd'ya say? You know that three hundred bucks is all right—I'm happy with that—but I've never won anything before. Winning is more exciting than the money."

Ray had to laugh. Alexis was practically hyper.

"Actually, I'm kind of partial to the money. Winning is nice, I hope we do it often. But…yeah, sure. Let's do it. Do you want to blow it all, or save some?"

Alexis grinned, her eyes were wide, her spirit in sync with the happy beat of the moment. She didn't answer Ray at first, but after a few moments she said, "Okay, this time, though, we do it on a time basis. After one half hour we leave, win or lose. Okay?"

Ray said, "Lead the way," and they attacked the machines with the intention of breaking the casino.

One half hour later, Ray was down fifty bucks and Alexis about a hundred.

Ray put his hand on her shoulder, and said, "Time. And now…" but Alexis finished his thought, "…it's time to leave." The gambling had been fun, but the casino noises were beginning to crash into them.

They found a redemption machine. It sucked in their vouchers and cranked out the bills. Ray folded his and put the wad in his pocket. Alexis fisted hers, said, "Ha!" and plunged them down into her purse.

"Drink?" Ray asked.

"Nope, got enough…Ray, I'm having a great time, but I'm thinking we need to sit and talk. Maybe we should walk back toward our hotel."

"Okay, but I have a better idea, let's ride."

"The People Mover?"

"Yeah, we can catch it here in the casino, and take it back to the Renaissance Apartments, or just walk around the RenCenter."

They meandered through the casino to Level 3 and hopped aboard the first string of cars that came along. It rocked its way through the Bricktown station and then into the Renaissance Center. The next stop would have been their hotel, but truly neither Alexis nor Ray really wanted the evening to end. Alexis grabbed Ray's arm and stood up.

"Let's get off here…we can walk."

"Walk? Our hotel's the next stop…?"

"No, walk" as in let's amble over to Hart Plaza, grab a bench, and watch the boats…the fountain's going—or maybe we'll just walk aimlessly and enjoy the riverfront."

Anything to prolong his time with Alexis was certainly okay with Ray. They walked around the Dodge fountain. The lights were ever changing, in sync with the water jets. They avoided the spray on the downwind side, found a bench, and watched the river reflect sparkles of light and wavy colored lines on its black onyx surface. An occasional ship's horn would sound its presence and passage up or down the river. It was romantic. Ray held her hand. She placed her other hand on top of his and snuggled closer.

It was quiet...all except for what was bounding about in Ray's head: *What's this all about; where is this going; why me?*

And almost as if she was reading his mind, she said, "Yesterday, you met Nicolo, and now you must be wondering why it's you and me here instead of Nicolo and me."

"Uh, yeah...that crossed my mind," said Ray, giving a weak voice to what had been screaming through this mind since the beginning of the evening.

"Well, it's not too long of a story and to give you the reason Nicolo will never be a regret, I'll tell it to you. Nicolo and I have been out to dinner twice. I really don't know him too well. I met him at a New York fashion convention and he's here now, as then, on a business trip. He comes from wealth—his father owns vineyards and textile mills in Italy. Nicolo's fortune is actually his family's. He hasn't sweated for a dime, ever. One day he'll inherit it all...that's his selling point...one, I'm sure, he pitches to every woman that pleases him. What I see is a mid-thirties playboy who is used to having things come his way. He's handsome, educated, glib, and irrevocably spoiled. He's also married with children."

Ray liked the "married with children" part.

"How'd you know that?"

"He told me. Not directly, of course, but he took a call in my apartment and spoke with his wife."

Ray turned to face her; his curious look begged the question.

"My last name is Lombard, a family name taken from the Lombardy district in North Italy where my parents were born. I know my blond hair doesn't make me look Italian, but I am. Both my father and mother have blond hair, common enough in the population there. A common joke there is that the blond-haired Austrians slip over the border at night and make love to the Italian women because they don't like their own. Sounds crude in English, but it's pretty funny in Italian. Anyway, my parents came to America and worked in the fashion industry. I was born here and we spoke Italian at home. My Italian isn't the same dialect as Nicolo's, but close enough. Nicolo and his wife spoke in Italian. He didn't think that I spoke anything but English…Europeans are used to that."

"They traded 'I love you's' and stories about their kids…he asked if the kids missed him, and finished off with a 'can't wait to come home and see you again.' He later told me that it was a business call. I was about to burn him to the ground, but it was almost seven and you're kind of punctual. I bit my tongue and a few minutes later, you knocked."

"Did you burn him?" Ray said, not trying to conceal his delight.

"Yeah, and in Italian. You should have seen his face."

"Well, he lied and deserved it. I'm happy you didn't get involved."

"Nope, nothing would have happened anyway. I thought he was attractive, but too cocky…he was full of himself. He didn't know it but last night was going to be our last date anyway…he just made it easy. So, there. That's it."

"Nope, not all."

"Like what more?"

"Me. Why me?"

Her answer was thoughtful, and slow in coming.

"You know when you decided to buy my car?"

"Yeah."

"You saw it and liked it right away, right? Well, it was something like that. You should have seen the look on your face when you met me for the first time in the lobby. I liked your eyes; I liked what I saw. I wanted to know more about you. I also knew that I was going to be in Montreal for the next three days…you had my number; I didn't have yours. I felt I had to take a chance. I'm glad you weren't busy."

Montreal…three days" the words ricocheted around the inside of his head. *Damn!* Ray swallowed his disappointment along with any bright ideas he was trying to gin up for the next evening.

The evening breeze began to pick up. It was becoming cool. Ray put his arm around her and she moved closer, resting her head on his shoulder.

Ray gave Alexis' wanting to know more about him a thoughtful minute before he began an abbreviated version of his life.

"Well…about me…there's not really too much to know. My father abandoned my Mom and me when I was a kid, my Mom died a few years later. I don't have any sibs. I graduated UofM law school, and now work at Wentworth, Solomon, and Hughes, a law firm just down the block from our hotel. It's pretty much what I thought it would be: hard work. Winning is expected, but even experienced lawyers run the risk of losing. Do that a couple of times and you're gone. My future? Hard to say. If successful, I'll be rewarded with greater challenges and greater compensation. At this point, what's really important to me is to excel and arrive at a point where I never have to worry about money. I'm twenty-eight—be twenty-nine in February. I've never been married and I don't have any children. You?"

"Children?"

"Nope, but good. I meant it's your turn."

"All right…" She took a deep breath and let her answer out as slowly as her breath, "well, I'm twenty-seven. I don't have any children. I make a good living as a fashion designer and consultant. I have excellent business connections, at first through my parents and later others I developed on my own. I employ three ladies that acquire the latest in working materials and translate my sketches into reality. Lately, I travel a lot—usually to New York, Montreal, Rome, sometimes Paris. I've never been married. I've had one serious relationship five years ago which I ruined in favor of my career and two others afterward that were not so serious—I'm not counting Nicolo." She chuckled quietly at that and nestled her cheek into Ray's shoulder. Ray imagined her in his arms.

A young man and young woman strolled along the river walkway. They stopped to kiss, their embrace silhouetted against the lights of the far Canadian shore. Waves from a passing ship lapped the walkway's pilings, lending a rhythmic cadence to the scene—like heartbeats of the couple's intimacy. They kissed again and moved on. Ray rolled his cheek against Alexis, the fragrance of her hair—of her, was like breathing beautiful music. It was Lisa all over again, except different—maybe better, slower paced, somehow more comfortable. They had been together for only several hours, but Ray already knew that Alexis mattered to him.

Ray leaned over to kiss her, but she gave his lips a playful push with her cheek. "Hey, there's a time for that...." Remember, I said I want to get to know you. Can't talk and kiss at the same time, right?"

"I was thinking that maybe we could talk between kisses."

"Hmmm, spoken like a lawyer. You know that wouldn't happen."

"I look forward to the future. Thanks for the encouragement."

"Okay, Mr. Oliver, just friends for now...let's walk."

The riverfront was deserted except for a few strolling couples, and two small groups of revelers from the local taverns. They were boisterous, but not mood wreckers. The night held lovers safely in a soft grasp, oblivious to distraction.

Ray and Alexis wandered and traded stories of their lives, what they thought was good, bad, or didn't matter. It was a little after one o'clock when they entered the Renaissance City Apartment's elevator. Ray rode with her to the fifteenth floor and walked her to her apartment...the hallway was quiet. She unlocked her door and turned to him, and they kissed. Long. And wonderful. She brushed the door back. Ray leaned forward, but she put her hand on his chest. She gave him a smile that would warm his heart for the rest of the night, and said, "Goodnight, Mr. Oliver. I'll be back from Montreal in a couple of days. I want to see you again."

Ray nodded goodnight, his heart pounding— "want to" was so much better than "hope to."

Chapter 52

Tomorrow, Alexis! Ray was pumped at the thought. He felt like a kid waiting for Christmas. She'd be home sometime tonight; he'd call her tomorrow. Just the thought of hearing her voice made the world right for him. At five, he called.
"Ray, just thinking of you."
"That is a real compliment. Thank you. How'd it go?"
"Montreal? Well, like the fashion world says, it's one of the best kept secrets in the industry. Actually, I did very well, although for some reason Montreal usually gets only honorable mention in the fashion world. But it's coming into its own and starting to arch eyebrows. I believe that making an inroad there is tantamount to making a good investment in a lesser appreciated company. The way I look at it, it's poised for a takeoff and I'm on the runway. My designs received great interest from the UK, and the Russians and I expect that I'm going to be busy. Translation: I'm going to make some good money. Other than that, the food is great and the hotel was excellent. And how'd it go for you?"
"If it hadn't been for work, I'd've been bored out of my mind. Have time for dinner tonight?" Ray had hoped to be smoother, but he was eager to see her and the question leaped out of mouth.
"I'd like that, but sorry, can't…I brought home a lot of baggage. I've got sketches I'm sorting, memos to make to myself and staff, business replies, thank you's, and quotes for a couple of smaller boutiques and larger, high-end businesses that seemed really interested in my work. That's the other side to my "glamorous" life. I won't be able to settle down for about three more days. Designing, contacts, and pricing are pretty much the cogs of this business…this is where I make money or lose it. And after that, maybe even one more day to get myself together."

"Okay, but when you get tired and hungry, please remember me."

"Remember you...hey, I came back didn't I."

"Good to hear. If that were the only reason, I'd be vibrating with boundless joy. But I'll dwell on that thought and hold it as a close second. Just so I don't interrupt a stream of thought, give me a call when you're ready." Alexis was as disappointed as Ray, but business is business, and a friendly "goodnight, I'll call," was the most reasonable thing to say and she tactfully segued into it.

Ray found a beer in the fridge, snapped a cap, and sucked away at it. The second one tasted better. It was only 5 p.m. TV was mind deadening...not even a hockey game later that night. *What to do, Ray?*

Ray looked out over Woodward Avenue...street lights, slow moving cars, and the neon advertisements of all of the comforts, food, drink, and entertainment. He considered the advertisements and called two lawyer co-workers...one who was more of a friend, and the other, in his desperation, an occasional associate. Neither was home. *C'mon Ray...think of something...* An hour passed during which he had two more beers. And then a small weakness crept over him and he reached for the phone again.

"Hello," said Alexis.

"Hi, this is a pizza delivery guy who wants to deliver a large, with everything, pizza to your address. Can you possibly make room for it? I could be there in about a half hour."

Alexis laughed. "Hello, Ray. I'm touched. Maybe I answered too quickly. I've been at my work since about 9 this morning ...and I'm tired, and hungry too. Tell you what...the pizza sounds good, but right afterward—you have to promise—that you'll go home and leave me to my work."

Ray's smile spread his lips so thin that his words came out almost without their aid, ventriloquist like. "OK, promise...in about a half hour then. See you." And he hung up, before she had a chance to change her mind.

Papa Roma's was two blocks away. He could have had it delivered, but he thought she might better appreciate the personal touch. He called and picked up the pizza about twenty minutes later; and in exactly one-half hour he was knocking on Alexis's apartment door.

"Hello, pizza guy," she said and took the pizza box out of his hands. She sat it on the kitchen counter, flipped its lid, and grabbed a piece. She closed her eyes at the first bite, and "ummed."

"Yeah, I'm hungry too." Ray folded his slice and took a mouthful.

Alexis took two more bites before saying, "I been so into my stuff I haven't paid any attention…I've had about ten cups of coffee today and little else…maybe a couple of crackers. I'm famished."

"Glad to save your life then." He looked around the apartment and saw several boxes, bundles of material swaths, a large folio of drawings, three of which were spread out on the floor, and two suitcases.

Alexis just nodded and reached for another piece.

There were two pieces left when they were done gorging.

"Ray…great…thanks for being so thoughtful."

"To tell you the truth, I was being more thoughtful of myself. I really wanted to see you."

"And me too…but, when I'm doing my job, I'm really into it. Like, I believe you are with yours. It's just not something where a casual approach will do. You are either on top, or reaching for it…or you'll never make it."

Ray nodded in agreement and finished off his Coke.

In a nonchalant tone he said, "Now that we're full and maybe comfortable…did you really mean it about that half hour time limit thing?"

"Ray, you promised."

"Yeah, I know, but I thought I'd just test the waters."

"Well, *the waters* say stick to the agreement. But so you don't go away totally disappointed, I am inviting you, four days hence—this Saturday—to a home cooked meal, courtesy of myself."

Ray's anticipation soared. "Great…just you and me?" And, instantly knew that was a dumb question. It was not only dumb, but by inference it also made him sound as if he might be thinking of a passionate liaison as dessert. Of course, it wasn't far from his mind, but he knew the question was inappropriate and it left him feeling awkward. *Red flags all the way Ray; kind of stupid don't ya think?* Embarrassment comes in different degrees, and Ray experienced a light shade of it and its attending warmth. He inwardly cursed himself for appearing so obvious. He glanced at the counter in answer to her sudden stare.

Alexis had taken it all in and was most femininely aware of what had just raced through Ray's mind. "Well, actually no," she said slowly, letting Ray feel the full measure of his indiscretion for a moment.

Ray forced a little foolish smile and said…nothing.

"My parents are in town and I've told them about you. I want you to meet them; they want to meet you."

Ray slowly sucked in a lung full of air. He was totally surprised. Meeting the parents was a serious step forward; to his mind it was practically the same as saying he was the chosen one. He was thrilled, and counted it as being amongst the best news that he had ever had in his life. But it didn't erase his feeling of awkwardness.

"I'm surprised and honored, and look forward to meeting your parents, and having dinner. Thank you very much."

They rose from the table and made their way to the door. Standing there, for a quiet moment, Ray slipped his arm around her waist and bent forward for a kiss. She smiled, avoided his lips, and kissed him softly and neatly on his cheek, and they both grinned.

"Good night, Mr. Oliver."

"Good night, Ms. Lombard," he said, and with similar passion and precision kissed her on the forehead.

Chapter 53

"Dad, Mom, this is my friend, Ray Oliver."

"Ray, my parents, Americo and Assunta."

Dad and Mom were seated on a couch. Dad stood and shook hands with Ray. They exchanged smiles, pronounced the other's name, and agreed it was nice to meet each other. Mom, offered a smile. Ray returned the smile and took the hand she offered, bending slightly at his waist in a modified bow. Mindful of their Italian roots, it struck him as a European mannerism, but then she was seated and he couldn't do otherwise. He felt a moment of awkwardness when her smile widened, and she framed a heightened regard of himself with her eyes. She was sizing him up—a mother's concern for her daughter.

"So very nice to meet you, Mrs. Lombard." He was grateful to recall the family name. She inclined her head with an ever so slight turn in a slow and graceful, elegant movement. It was a return of the compliment, and since she was still smiling, he hoped it also meant approval. He nodded politely and took a seat next to the coffee table, across from them.

Before the moment passed and became a search for conversation by either, Alexis said, "Mom and Dad just returned from Italy, they vacation there every year." Ray was thankful for the bridge.

Americo pleased with the memory, said, "We have a home just outside of Parma—near Milano—and vacation there often. We rent to students for most of the year. They typically attend the University of Milano, and want to backpack throughout Europe during the summer break. That matches us perfectly. It is what we used to do. They leave, we move back until they return in the fall. This time, we probably stayed too long…it was difficult to leave." And then, reflecting, "I met my Assunta in Parma. We attended the university there and …"

Alexis nodded to her mother, "I'm going to make a couple of drinks, want to help"?

And, of course, Mom was eager to help…more so to be alone with her daughter. There were questions that had to be asked.

As they walked into the kitchen, "Ah, what a wonderful aroma."

Alexis was focused on the drinks and bypassed the comment saying, "I thought we'd start with a couple glasses of Negroni."

"That's your father's favorite aperitif, but it's too bitter for me. A glass of wine would be better."

Alexis poured her mother and herself a glass of wine. "Too bitter for me as well," she said as she assembled the liquors needed for the aperitif. "I have an antipasto in the refrigerator," and nodded her head in that direction.

Assunta removed the large plate containing an artful arrangement of different cheeses, olives, prosciutto, veggies and chunks of ciabatta bread, and placed it on the counter.

"So…?" Assunta began with a quizzical tone and upraised eyebrows.

Alexis took a deep breath…she knew what was coming.

"Yes?"

"Is he the one?" Mom flashed a teasing smile just as pointed as her question.

"The one? Why, whatever do you mean?" Alexis said, in an obvious, half-hearted pretense of not understanding. She hoped her mother would drop the subject.

"Hmm, let me see…he's very handsome, he has great hair and nice teeth. He's mannered, educated, and has a great…uh…form—he looks very strong."

"Form? Mamma!" she said, pretending to scold, "You're a married woman! If dad knew how closely you examined another man, he'd probably think that he's not doing his job. Besides, he's mine and those qualities are for me to notice and decide."

"Ha, I thought so!

"Ah, ah, ah…don't go reading anything into that."

"Yes, of course not." She swirled her wine and appeared pleased.

"Okay, enough of that. Let's get these Negronies on the road."

Alexis poured equal amounts of red vermouth, gin, and Campari into two Manhattan glasses, added a twist of orange peel and a couple ice cubes.

"Alexis, that wonderful aroma... *oss bus*?"

"Probably the wine."

"No. That's oss bus...I've made it hundreds of times for your father."

"Yes, it is...but Ray might know it as *osso buco*—a menu item he's probably seen before but not *oss bus* because that's our word for it. So, if he asks, I'll say it's osso buco."

"Of course," she said, with barely a thought to what her daughter just said. Instead she asked what was unrelated but foremost on her mind: "How do you feel about him?"

Alexis's cheeks pinked.

"Smettere...quit," she said in a soft, but pleasant enough tone. *God help us get through this night.*"

Alexis and Assunta brought the drinks to the two men and returned to the kitchen to bring out the antipasto, tableware, and their own wine glasses.

Americo was past the *meeting Assunta* part of his conversation and into a question Ray asked about retirement.

"Thanks for the compliment, you suggest that I'm too young to retire. But becoming a little philosophical, Ray, you are born and for the first ten or fifteen years you are too young to do anything. And when you are at the end of your time you are too old do anything. So, you only have the middle years to do anything. Your time is limited. So, you should enjoy every hour you have, every minute of every hour. Work, create, and enjoy your life. My wife and I are always happy, more especially when we are in Parma. Friends, family, and good food; the countryside is beautiful. That's what is so appealing and may influence our decision to retire early. We believe we could be happy there for the rest of our lives."

"That sounds wonderful. I wish I had deep feelings for someplace in particular— some longing in my heart like you do…but, I haven't. Retirement for me is a long way off. I was raised in a middle-class neighborhood. We lived there until the neighborhood began to decline. We moved to my aunt's home on the other side of town, and I lived there until I left for college. My aunt, and the old neighborhood are gone. I've never had any desire to re-visit the old neighborhood. I've never returned there. Truly there is nothing that I could go back to."

Their conversation was interrupted by the arrival of the antipasto and drinks.

They picked at the antipasto for an hour and complimented Alexis on its excellence. Ray, both hungry and a bit nervous, picked more often, but more so to cover the taste of the Negronies. He didn't like them, but when Americo said he'd have another, Ray felt obliged to follow suit. The conversation was lively and seldom wavered. Soon Ray felt in a subtle way that he was not just meeting her parents, but he was being welcomed into the family.

Alexis exited the kitchen and announced that dinner was ready. Americo and Ray sat at the dining room table, while Alexis and her mother—despite Alexis' mild protests—helped serve. Assunta poured glasses of cabernet, Alexis ladled out the soup—minestrone, which was later replaced by the main course: osso buco with a gremolata garnish.

Ray asked. Alexis answered: "osso buco are cross-cut, braised veal shanks. When the marrow leaves the bone during braising it creates a hole—and that is what osso buco means in Italian—a bone with a hole in it.

Ray nodded his understanding. Inside, he was thinking *"bone marrow, good God, who eats that?* Apparently, he was going to. Ray was a steak and baked potato guy. Maybe another negroni would overcome what he imagined bone marrow to taste like.

"And," continued Alexis for Ray's benefit, "although the traditional accompaniment is Risotto alla Milanese, this time I made creamy baked mushroom risotto." Her parents weren't north Italian purists—a creamy mushroom risotto would be welcome. The idea of a traditional risotto was lost on Ray.

Dinner was leisurely and pleasant. They loved Alexis' cooking and ate enthusiastically. Ray was to discover that an Italian dinner consisted of several courses and that he should have taken it a bit easier on the antipasto. He could feel his belt.

After dinner was probably the most stressful part of the evening for Alexis. They all had a few wines with dinner, and her mother and father were feeling quite comfortable and talkative. She, on the other hand, was ever watchful for a drift in the conversation which might lead to discussions of engagements, marriage, and babies… which would probably start with how much they loved their grandchildren. None of that subtle and deeper meaning, she knew, would be lost on Ray. She was ready to deflect any such diversions from general conversation. No need to rush "family" onto Ray at this point.

But that's exactly how it went.

It started with Assunta's reference to Alexis' brother and sister. "They live in Milano and have two children."

Good grief, thought Alexis, *I know where this is going.*

"Ah, before the family history," she said, "Sorry, no espresso, but we have coffee and dessert. A minute later she brought out a large carafe of coffee, and a silver tray of mascarpone/pistachio filled cannoli and almond flower cookies.

Assunta loved desserts and the appearance of her favorites slowed her down as she whisked a few, politely, from the tray. Americo moved on to the type of law that Ray practiced and that sealed the conversation for a while as Ray explained the differences between civil and criminal law and being convicted criminally, yet still be sued civilly. The coffee and desserts steadily diminished. The conversation stretched out and to the relief of Alexis, there was no more mention of family or anything involving matrimony that might possibly make Ray, especially herself, uncomfortable. It was well into the evening when Alexis brought out the final course—a bottle of Bellini Vin Santo and filled their glasses.

The conversation wound down until it was appropriate for Ray to say goodnight.

Americo and Assunta both said they were very pleased to meet him and hoped to see him again. He thanked them and returned the compliment. Alexis walked him to the door. He thanked her for a wonderful evening, her wonderful dinner, and for making him an honorary Italian for the evening. This time the kiss lingered. Alexis walked back to her parents with a crooked smile, a sudden warmth, and rosy cheeks.

Assunta, ever aware of her daughter's subtle nuances, whispered to herself, "Thank God, she's in love."

Chapter 54

A week after Ray met her parents Alexis called her mother and broke the news of their engagement. She was as delighted as Alexis.

"Dad there?"

"No, but he'll be back soon enough."

Excitedly, Assunta asked "Have you set a date"?

"No, mamma, it's only been a week, we need to talk about it."

"Have you decided where the wedding will be"?

"No, mamma, it's only been a week, we need to talk about it."

"Have you told your brother and sister"?

"Nope, but I will right after we're done talking."

Assunta was radiant with the news, and being first told—although such notice was an unexpressed protocol that most women share. She told her that she was so excited for her, that she needed to pee …which was true and not an old Italian expression.

"Americo," she called, "Americo, here, take the phone."

"What's wrong," he said slightly alarmed, as he came indoors.

"Nothing. Everything is wonderful!"

At that, Americo guessed that his daughter or daughter-in-law in Italy was pregnant again, or that Alexis was engaged. He couldn't go wrong and would be pleased with both of his guesses.

"Engaged," he said aloud and cheerily. He told her that he and her mother, despite the short time they spent together with Ray, liked him very much. It would be a good match—hopefully as good as his own marriage. And in a few words of loving acceptance, "You have our blessings."

Right after this call, Alexis called her sister in Italy. Before she got beyond, "Hello," Adriana said, "Ahhh, Alexis. You're engaged! How wonderful. Is he the guy you told me about last month, yes?…Ohhh, yes." And then a batch of questions followed.

"Let me guess, mamma just called you with the news."

"Yes, she couldn't wait."

"She was probably dialing on the other phone before we hung up."

"I'm so happy for you." And their conversation moved slowly forward, sharing memories and family stories, not only like sisters, but maybe more importantly, like good friends. And then a segue into wedding plans; it was a long call.

The same affinity and affection was repeated when speaking with her brother, Dominic.

Alexis was as excited to deliver the news as they were to hear it. Despite coming close to an engagement once, she never made such an announcement. She felt butterflies in her stomach and, like her mother, a need for a bathroom.

Later that evening, in Alexis' apartment, looking out over the downtown traffic and lights, they snuggled together on the couch, and she casually asked, "Have you given any thought to our wedding?"

Typically male, Ray answered, "Uhhh, not too much. I guess a church somewhere or a Justice of the Peace…or go on a cruise somewhere and have the captain of the ship marry us."

"I was hoping for a little more comprehensive answer, as in setting a date, choosing a hall, music, catering, making deposits, printing and sending invitations, a wedding gown, tux, flowers, limo, honeymoon …you know, all of the things that a wedding involves or might involve. They just don't occur; they have to be planned."

"Yeah, some of that would have occurred to me, but I thought that you ladies knew how to do those things and I'd just be there to take directions and help out, and be there at the proper time."

"Those are the exciting and fun things…are you sure you want to get married?"

"Yes. I'm sure!"

"How many people would you invite to the wedding?"

"Hmmm, never thought about it. I don't have any living relatives…a couple of guys from the law firm, but maybe not. The guys at the firm are working sixty-hour weeks so I doubt that any of them would take, or want to take time off. There's always the company pressure to bill more, and time off would not be looked at as compatible with its goals. There is a tremendous amount of competition. All the rookie lawyers want to shine in the company's eyes. I'm thinking I don't really have any close friends. Maybe my boxing mentor, Vinnie. And, Vinnie travels to Italy often enough—he might come, but he's usually absorbed with his business interests and his stable of boxers. A week off for a wedding is probably not a high priority with him. He'd think, 'Okay, so get married, and bring the bride to see me later.' So, I'm thinking the only person coming to the wedding would be me."

"So how come you get to take time off"?

"Because married lawyers are more stable and would benefit the company in the long run. Young singles are usually bed hopping or are prone to the throes of a disastrous relationship either of which may cause problems in their private lives and eventually affect their work and ultimately impact the company. The company views marriage as long term and divorce as a detriment that may result in some downtime. They actually encourage marriage."

"Well, if you're not so particular about the details…I kind of saved this one for the last… mamma and papa were married in a church just outside of Parma, the same church that my sister and brother were married in, the same church that their kids were baptized in, the same …."

Before she could say more, Ray leaned forward and kissed her. He surmised that the idea originated as a slight hint from her mother; a cherished, motherly wish and nothing more. And it was all right with him. In fact, he was thankful for the suggestion as he had no ideas of his own. He could see that it would be a plus to both Alexis and her family, and himself. Why not?

Ray said, "You think we should go to Italy and get married there? Right?"

"Yes, it would be like getting married and going to Italy for a honeymoon. Except, we would already be in Italy."

How can you beat logic like that?

"It's a wonderful idea." The load of arrangements, to his mind, just disappeared. Getting married now seemed effortless. All that was left was to choose a date—how difficult could that be? Just choose a date…throw a dart at a calendar. One date is as good as another, right? Of course, he was wrong.

"The wedding looks simple enough from where we sit. But my family needs to arrange all of the things I mentioned and do it without us there to shepherd them. I know they'll do a good job of it, but just the same they will be doing the lion's share of putting it together. We need to offer whatever help we can. And, my wedding dress…it may need alteration. My mom made it for her wedding and my sister wore it for hers. I'm next. I need to be there a week ahead of time. And, there's the matter of arranging the flight and rooms."

"Rooms?"

"Yeah, I had another idea I was saving. We can go straight to Parma and get married probably a week later. And then, afterward, instead of flying back home, we can visit Venice and maybe squeeze in Pisa and then on to Rome.

"Sounds good to me. I never gave any thought to anything outside of Parma and the wedding. How much time do you think we'll need?"

"I think we might do Venice or Pisa in four days, but that's kinda pushing it. I think we need five or six days in Rome.

Ray 'hmmd' and smiled, "I see you've already been thinking about this."

"Yep. Marriage is a serious thing. We're going to have a good time."

"So, what do you figure…two or three weeks?"

"Probably. You ever do much plane travel?" she asked.

"Nope."

"Well, often there's scheduling conflict and departure dates are sometimes unavailable. And that's not to mention departure times—I don't think having to be at an airport at 3:20 in the morning is too wonderful."

"Well, it'll be a new experience for me. But I'm thinking if I unload the details on a travel agent, the agent will make it all happen. Piece of cake. I'll take care of those details."

"I wasn't sure if you'd balk at any this."

"To travel the world with my wife? Maybe we could do that every year. What could be a more pleasant dream"?

Alexis wore her happiness like a halo. She knew the answer to that, but she would save it for later.

Chapter 55

Ray was excited about his engagement and forthcoming marriage. He loved Alexis with all of his heart and soul. When he broke the news to Wentworth and company they were delighted. They reminded him about tying up loose ends at the firm. He was ahead of them on that. Choosing a date presented a number of problems. It wasn't an easy dart throw. Yet, despite a few conflicts in time, he arranged his cases to allow a free block of time and he had prevailed upon his clients, and whatever co-counsel he may have teamed with, to agree to extensions. He had an open door.

The account manager handling his cases approved, but his staff was already in overload, especially since Ray was taking a block of time off. And since Ray presumed himself to be a partial cause of the overload, it wasn't difficult to persuade him to meet with just one more client and secure the case. He could delay the case as long as necessary. Just secure the case. It didn't seem that it would interfere with his time table. It sounded reasonable to Ray and he agreed.

Ray read the initial complaint. The name of the potential new client was Charles Sanders. He owns a trash hauling company. The gist of his complaint was that the City of Detroit wouldn't pay him for services rendered and threatened, if he pursued the matter legally, to tie up the payment in prolonged litigation for years, and the discontinuance of this contract and any future contracts. They did not deny the debt, they just indicated that the money wasn't in their budget. He argued that when they signed the contract, the money was there, otherwise they wouldn't have committed themselves. He needed the money now.

Ray met with Mr. Sanders that afternoon. Sanders explained how his meeting with Corp Counsel went, the argument, and him telling the Corp Counsel to get stuffed. It was an angry meeting with nothing getting resolved and ended with resentment on both sides.

"I'd like you to smooth over our disagreement, apologize on my behalf if it's necessary, and get them to get off their dollars."

"Well, Mr. Sanders, we've had similar cases and have always been able to arrange a satisfactory ending to the dispute. I understand you need the money, but nonetheless it will take some time to wear them down without becoming involved in a courtroom drama. If you are willing, we can go for a settlement…you have to figure out what kind of a loss you are willing to take, and we will get this behind us."

"Loss? What the fuck are you talking about? I want everything that is due to me. They owe me, make them pay!"

"Okay, I understand. I was just suggesting an option."

Ray used the words "us" and "we" similar to wrapping his arms around the potential client and saying he was not alone, that he had a friend, and they would work together to solve the problem: a team. That usually helped persuade a potential client to become a client. In fact being a good lawyer also included being a good salesman.

"I can force them to comply with the terms of the contract. However, it's going to take some time. That's why I suggested a compromise—a settlement to get your money quicker. If you are willing to wait, which you've indicated you would rather not, then it will take some time."

"How long?"

"The city is having budgetary problems bordering on insolvency. It's not unusual for any corporation to delay payments. If I understand what you told me correctly, they didn't deny the debt, only that they couldn't pay it at this time. Is that right?"

"Well, not in so many words…but, yeah, they said it was a budget problem."

"So, while the money may have been there, they apparently robbed the fund for other uses and will, after a delay, probably make you whole."

"Again, how long before I get paid? And 'probably'—what does that mean"?

"Don't know how long before the case gets resolved. But I do know that the matter of a receivership would be in the hands of the governor. If it goes that far, and if he doesn't want the city to go under, he'll bail it out. You will then be paid, but often after the regulators are done it amounts to only pennies on the dollar. My guess is that after all of the paperwork is finished and the final decision has been made, the wheels of the city will begin to turn and you will be paid something."

"And what about future contracts. He threatened to blacklist me."

"A moot point. It depends on their resources…how were they able to do the job without contractors before…do they need to outsource the job? Can they deny you a contract? Yes, certainly. But negotiation and bargaining usually start out harsh…they mellow when the bottom line receives mutual accord. You'll have to wait and see what you and they are willing to agree on."

"Shit! So, if I hire you, I'll have to wait. If I don't hire you, I'll have to wait. And all the while I can end up with a lot less that I'm owed. Is that it?"

"In a nutshell, yeah. But there's another thing…you may not be first in line to be paid. If you have a lawyer, he can push for you, if not then you are on your own and probably won't get too far."

"If I go for a settlement, how much can I recover?"

"They'll stick at anywhere from 10% to 30%, maybe less for a while, but I feel confident we can negotiate somewhere between 50% and 70%. How much are you owed?"

"About a hundred grand. How much on lower side of 70% are you considering?"

"Ray didn't answer the question, but continued, "If the City goes into receivership all of their lawsuits will be put on hold. There is no telling when they will get around to hearing your case. I will file a continuance if such a thing takes place, and it is possible that your case will go forward."

Sanders thought about if for a few seconds, and then said, "Okay, then go for a settlement."

Ray opened his briefcase and handed Saunders a legal form. Saunders glanced at it. He had a general idea as to what it said and that was sufficient for him, he didn't need a blow by blow. He signed it. Ray told him he'd be in touch within the next couple of weeks.

"Make it as soon as you can, eh"

Ray shook his hand and promised to do whatever he could.

The firm was always eager to do business, no matter how lucrative—much like drips in a bucket, all contracts affected the bottom line. Wentworth lawyers were expensive. A breach of contract was a piece of cake and wouldn't cost them much time, but was still worth an appreciable amount. The name of the game was settlement. The client would be charged a percentage of what they settled for. They thanked Ray for bringing in the business. The manager and available associates congratulated him and wished him well on his wedding.

A few minutes later Ray stepped through the revolving doors and out into the brisk air. True, he would return to the grind in several weeks, but for now he felt as though a great weight was lifted from his back.

He would be seeing Alexis soon; all other thoughts vanished.

Chapter 56

Ray arranged his case load to allow him three weeks absence from Wentworth and company. Crunch time in the fashion business, for Alexis, was particularly manifest in spring. But she had worked hard on the launch of her spring design collection. She was ready, and immediately soon afterward there would be a window for their trip to Italy. Fall fashion was already decided and in the hands of her second in charge. With a little help, her designs would be packed and ready to go soon after she returned from her wedding. The optimum time for their wedding, they agreed, would be mid-September; and by then the weather in Italy would be in the mid-70s; perfect. They would arrive in Parma on September 2, and get married on Saturday, ten days later. By then her parents and relatives would have had three months to put the wedding together, and she would be present for any last-minute needs. Afterward, they would travel through Italy and depart Rome on the 19th.

The travel agent cobbled together an itinerary as close to what they wanted as could be done. No direct flight to Parma was possible with their desired scheduling. That leg of their passage would have to be from Heathrow, UK to Parma. But even at that, it was only a couple hours delay, including the layover. And they would hit their Parma target date on time. After that it was Parma to Venice by car, a stop in Pizza, another maybe in Florence, and a flight to Rome and then home. All settled, and locked in. Nice job Ray; nice job travel agent.

The church was on the outskirts of Parma. An old timer, constructed mainly of heavy wooden beams and sheathing, and bearing a slate roof. It had been repaired many times in its two-hundred-year history. Held together not just with nails and spikes, but its existence owed more to its several generations of congregants' memories and village tradition.

The church was packed with family and friends. The priest took his place, the crowd quieted, and he gave the sign of the cross and a blessing to all gathered. Ray was escorted to the altar by Alexis' brother Dominic, the best man. Alexis was brought to the altar by Americo and given over to Ray. The priest began the wedding ritual. And, as a surprise to Ray, after saying each part, he repeated it in English for Ray's benefit. Alexis' mother thought of that and insisted it be done. She might have thought there was a greater likelihood of Ray being bound by the vows, if he understood the ceremony. It was a beautiful ceremony and tears of happiness ran down Assunta's cheeks as well as Alexis's sister's...and as well as most of the women, married and single, that were there. Marriage was highly desired amongst the women of the village. The married vicariously relived the experience, those that were single were enthralled with the idea that their day would come. Americo was joyful, both because he was happy for Alexis, and that he could now quit worrying about her.

Afterward everyone was invited back to Alexis's parent's home for the reception. It was a grand event held in the garden. It started in late afternoon and carried over into late evening. The variety of food was overwhelming, all brought in by family, neighbors, and well-wishers. Ray ate his fill, and more because relatives and their friends kept offering him morsels and small plates, saying *mangiare, mangiare,* eat, eat, especially the heavy-set ladies and men. And, wine—no end of wine. Some of the young men wanted to toast him and Alexis. Alexis was familiar with this aspect of an Italian wedding. She cautioned him to be careful, because one of their major goals was to get the groom drunk. They several times offered him Grappa. He accepted the first couple of shots to be sociable, but declined having more as diplomatically as possible. To him grappa went down like gargling broken razor blades and then swallowing the pieces. He thought that if he could have washed a shot of grappa down with a Negroni— definitely not his favorite drink—he would have.

The band was loud and energetic. People danced, drank, and ate...a repetitive sequence pursued by all. Ray danced with Assunta, and all of the female family members, including several other ladies, friends of the family he thought, who grabbed him and forced him into a dance. Alexis danced with her father, all of her relatives, neighbors and any well-wisher who grabbed her hand. She got Ray on his feet and enjoying the tarantella so much, that it was he that got her up and dancing the next one. Round and round, faster and faster. The fun lasted until everyone was stuffed, surfeited with food and drink, and beginning to tire. Ray and Alexis had a romantic last dance, and the party slowly melted away.

Alexis had a list of everyone that contributed anything to their wedding, thoughtfully prepared by Assunta at Alexis' request. Some lived close by, some a distant drive. They thanked everyone profusely, missing no one. Ray suggested reimbursement to Americo, but he wouldn't hear of it…the wedding was his and Assunta's gift to them. He and Alexis graciously accepted their gift.

Ray rented a car and they said their final goodbyes. Alexis, in an aside, asked her sister, Adriana, to take good care of the wedding dress. "Who knows maybe you or I might need it for one of ours in twenty years." They hugged and said goodbye again.

They drove off: Venice, Pisa, Florence and Rome—all of Italy was ahead of them.

Chapter 57

The rumble of the plane's tires reverberated throughout the fuselage as the Delta Airbus 319 airliner slowed from 160 mph landing speed to a slow crawl as it taxied toward its designated parking. The plane's air pressure normalized and the a/c cut off. A stewardess announced in Italian, German, and then in English "Welcome to Fiumicino Airport, Rome, Italy. Thank you for flying Delta airlines today. The outside temperature is 19.4° C; 72° F. The time is 1400 hours; 2 p.m." The murmur of the passengers gradually rose. The first-class passengers deplaned. Ray and Alexis made their way through the crowded terminal, grabbed their luggage from the carousel, and hailed a taxi. *The driver told them €65. When Alexis argued with him in Italian, he dropped the price to €55. A short while later they were headed to Rome, about twenty miles away.*

Hotel D'Novona was a first-class hotel in the heart of Rome. The brochures available at the desk indicated it was within a walking distance to most attractions, named them, gave a brief description of each, offered several tours, and the bottom of brochure noted that it was a €50, *prix fixe*, ride to the airport.

Ray noted the cost of the airport fare and pointed it out to Alexis, saying "shouldn't it be the same both ways?"

"Ahhh, she said, and sighed, "that's the Italian way—kind of like our renowned sculptors—a little chiseling here, a little chiseling there, and soon you have enough to pay the rent. But 5 Euros is 5 Euros; look at it this way, somewhere down the line we'll negotiate a charge for 5 Euros less than the asked price and we'll be even."

"Can't argue with that. Makes perfect sense, kind of."

Their room was apartment sized, spacious, airy, indeed first class, and beautifully decorated. A king-sized bed with a double row of pillows, a comfortable couch, table, padded chairs, direct and mood lighting, a small refrigerator fully stocked with soft and alcoholic drinks, a TV, coffee pot, and especially for the women, a hairdryer in the bathroom. That particular inclusion, Alexis knew, is common enough in America, but a noteworthy item in Europe. They were high enough that the traffic noise was minimal. There's was a rooftop and street view, store fronts with shrubs and flowers up and down the street. And, the ultimate. Ray couldn't help but smirk when he saw that the fully glass paneled shower was located in the bedroom, close to the bed.

Alexis saw his grin, matched it, raised her eyebrows and nodded her head slowly as she read his mind. "European, you know."

They would be there for three days—enough for Ray to get a quick look at Rome. Alexis had been there many times and was pleased to be his tour guide.

They popped open their luggage, hung and ordered their clothing, shoes and slippers, and stashed their luggage in the closet.

Ray reached into his carry-on bag and removed a fifth of scotch and a bottle of soda, and poured out two drinks.

As they sipped their drinks, Alexis said, "Ray, it's closing in on 5 o'clock. I'm thinking it's kind of late for sightseeing. We could go for a walk, have a drink at an osteria. Find a store, buy two bottles of wine, come back here around 7, call room service and order dinner. What d'ya think?"

Ray didn't have to give it a second thought, "Perfect, let's go."

The osteria was an unpretentious opening in a wall with five tables on the sidewalk and three inside. Small, pleasant, quick service, and good Chianti. They ordered a bruschetta appetizer...tomatoes, mozzarella, tomatoes, chives, a touch of garlic and a sprinkling of balsamic vinegar. The bruschetta and wine were so good, they considered ordering seconds and forgetting their original plan. The only reason they didn't was because the osteria was closing in twenty minutes.

Around the corner was a grocery store which sold the basics. It didn't have a large inventory, but adequate to supply the simple needs of the local hotel and apartment dwellers. They bought two bottles of Chianti and walked back to the hotel. Alexis poured the first glass while Ray called room service and ordered. The dinner was excellent. Two more glasses of wine and each felt mellow and romantic. Alexis said, "I think I'll take a shower and jump in bed."

Ray said he thought he might just like to lay in bed until she was out of the shower.

"I think, that you might be a voyeur. Let's see."

Ray said nothing, just grinned.

Alexis wrapped a towel around her and stepped from the bathroom and into the warm shower. She squirted shampoo on a sponge, soaped the glass, dropped the towel and pressed herself against the bubble covered glass, rubbing it clear in spots, giving Ray a few different views. A minute later, Ray was in the shower with her, and several minutes later they were in bed.

Ray said, "That was exciting. *I saw you looking at me as much I looked at you.* I think we're both voyeurs. What d'ya think?"

Alexis said, "Come closer voyeur and I'll show you."

Three days later, after seeing some of the sights of Rome, it was Arrivederci Roma; goodbye Italy.

Chapter 58

Ray had terminated his apartment lease and moved into Alexis' apartment just before they left for Italy. Moving was simple enough, his furnishings were all rented. He didn't own much: clothes, books, and a computer.

The first couple of weeks home were taken with settling in and catching up on the work that awaited them. For both, it was a marathon of phone calls; for Alexis it was design modification, suppliers, planning, and discovery of an intrusion on one of her designs.

For Ray it was both legal work and paperwork — not the least of which was registering their Italian marriage and updating their new status on all their personal records. A snap for a competent lawyer like Ray, but nonetheless time consuming and completing and hand filing forms at the various civil bureaus was a legal bother, but necessary. He could have had it done by the Wentworth clerks, but it was personal and he didn't need other eyes looking at his documents. Not that there was anything strange, but he preferred to keep his personal life private. By slaying at least one dragon at a time, as often as possible, at the end of one month they had settled in to a manageable stream of challenges.

After grabbing a couple of days of moving in and relative leisure, Alexis announced her return to her associates and conferred with them regarding their fall line of fashion designs, their markets, and their competitors. Kelly, who was charged with securing their time slots and order of modeling on the runways; Sarah who was in charge of previewing the work, order of dress and arrangement, and introduction of the styles; and Beth who was the liaison between the entire staff.

"Alexis," Sarah said, with a tone of concern in her voice.

"Yes."

"Cuffs...there's a problem."

"What kind of problem?"

"Well, your idea of a three-inch fur trouser cuff is wonderful. It's beautiful and classy. But Salon Veronique has a very similar motif, and that's not good. Not only did they almost replicate your trouser fur treatment, but they also duplicated it on their waist length jacket, another aspect of your design."

"How do you know this?"

"Our seamstress called and said our last drop-off was ready. Bonnie scheduled me for a 2 p.m. pickup. We went into one of the several private side rooms and she showed me what she'd done. Everything was correct and beautifully done. A few minutes later, the work was pressed, securely wrapped, and ready to go. For me, it was a simple in and out.

Alexis, I don't have to tell you that Bonnie has her reputation to worry about. You know, she would die before allowing one designer to see another's work... or warn one of a comparable design. And posted warnings are abundant: *Keep your designs to yourself. When trying on, keep the dressing room door closed and locked.*

But as I was walking past one of the dressing rooms, the door was partly open...it should have been closed, but it wasn't. I recognized a model that worked for Salon Veronique. I caught her reflection in the dressing room mirror. She was showing herself off to another model and they were, uhh, oblivious of anything else except each other...and the ensemble, which was being tucked in place by the dresser. Anyway, it was just a glance and no one noticed me; but that's all it took. The model was wearing a long black slack outfit with a dark fur cuff, maybe three inches wide just above her ankle. Pretty much the same as ours. I also noted the waist length jacket she wore also had a fur cuff, maybe two inches wide. I think it was a black, sequined jacket. Very smart looking. I took it all in at a single glance...it wasn't as if I were spying. But if they were indiscrete enough to leave the door open, then why not look? This is a competitive business and you've taught me to be extremely cautious with designs; they should have been. The warnings practically scream secrecy."

Ouch, it's a sure thing they aren't going to change their designs. So do I do create a new design, modify what I already have, just tough it out, or just dump it and come up with another design. Gotta think about this. Not too much time left.... A thought flashed through her mind.

She called Kelly. "Has the runway order been set?"

"Yeah, about a week ago."

"Can you tell me if Salon Veronique is ahead of us?"

"Let me check...uh, yeah, they're two slots ahead of us."

"Crap...uh, thanks Kelly."

"Anything wrong?"

"Nope, everything is just peachy. Thanks for your hard work. We'll talk later."

Kelly knew when Alexis said "peachy" that it was better not to ask exactly how "peachy" things were, and she offered as pleasant a goodbye as possible.

For a couple of minutes Alexis' hopes had jumped. If she could show her designs before Veronique, then she would have first exposure and that would bode well for the showing. It was always a plus. But her hope just crashed.

Alexis returned her attention to Sarah. "My head is swimming with the number of designs we put together. I can't recall; how many variations of that design did we make?"

"Two."

"Their color?"

"Well, one black—very similar to theirs—*and one gold, stitched pleating to mid-thigh,* and a little wide at the cuff."

"How many are we showing?"

"It's in the *evening wear* category and there are only two submissions for each design studio. And we have the slots, so two it is."

"Well, that's some help. It won't be a super major undertaking to tweak it in time …just a major undertaking. Any suggestions?"

Sarah had a ready answer. "With the black, maybe a red lining for the jacket which would give it a little flash, three large black glass buttons on the jacket and three smaller ones in rows, parallel to each other, on the front panel of the slacks, starting about three inches down from each hip so they show just below the jacket. And, for the gold, use a white faux Artic fox fur with the same button and fur treatment and only a two-inch wide cuff."

"Give me a little time to think about this. Thanks for the information. I'll get back to you soon." *I think I'm going to throw up.*

"Hello, is Bonnie there?" asked Alexis.

"Yes, please hold."

"Bonnie here…."

"This is Alexis…."

"Hi, glad to hear from you. Did you like my work on the last two?"

"Uh, yes, very much…but I've been gone for two weeks and just got back two days ago. I haven't had much time to get a look at all you've done. The reason for this call is that I have a problem. I've learned that another studio has produced pretty much the same as one of my designs and I've got to do something with it or miss the slots. Can we meet?"

"Uh…sure, this is actually a super good time for change…there's only one design on my cutting table at the moment. I think we can work something out…come on down. There are several shows…how much time do we have before yours?"

"The showing is in three weeks."

"Yes, you're short. The reason I have only one on the cutting table is that most of the studios have their stuff completed. Trust me, I'm not insulting you. I just have a real good feel for the industry and its ebbs and flows. In the beginning of a new season, I'm swamped. Always. But Yeah, piece of cake—a change that is; little tweaks definitely, An entirely new design, hmmm, well, I could give up sleeping and get it done. Come on down and we'll see. We'll be using Room 223. Three o'clock good with you?"

"Thanks, I'll be there. You'll be saving my keester."

Alexis bundled up both the gold and the black, evening ware outfits and at 3 she was at the door of Room 223. They met as old friends, more than just business associates. They hugged each other and when Alexis showed Bonnie her wedding ring, Bonnie squealed like a teen rather than her sixty-five years, and moved in for another hug. Alexis told her about her Italian wedding and travels and Bonnie seemingly couldn't get enough. But in time, they slowed to the point of the business that was before them.

"You've done a beautiful job on my evening ware designs, and I wouldn't change a stitch, except for discovering that a competitor will be introducing practically the same design. So, despite all of your good work, I've got to have it undone."

"Okay, so how much un-doing are you thinking about?"

"Well, I've just had a little time to think about it, but I have a couple of ideas." She shook out the creations onto the cutting table. "The black one…I'd like you to remove the fur cuffs on the pant legs and cut the fur into one-inch wide strips, two inches long, and space them an inch apart vertically, as many as needed to surround the pants cuffs. And two vertical rows of smaller black, faceted, kissing stacked buttons, on the front panel, parallel and about ten inches apart.

And, as for the jacket, I'd like a bright red lining, three large black, faceted glass buttons down the front, and the same fur treatment on the sleeve cuffs as on the slack cuffs, but one inch shorter. The sleeves I'd like them shortened so they extend about three inches beyond the elbows. And, that's it."

"And the gold…?"

"It's pretty much good to go, except I'm thinking a faux Artic Fox fur trim on the sleeve cuffs and slacks, just like the black outfit. Maybe a white jacket lining. And the same fur across the top of a gold lame short sleeved blouse, maybe something with a straight across neckline. I have no design for the blouse, I'm entirely in your hands…some adjustable model-sized blouse probably—maybe just bibs—no, no not bibs, the model has to off-shoulder the jacket to display the lining's contrast. I don't know. I'll leave that up to you. And, the same style blouse, maybe in white, for the black number as well. You make them, I'll buy them."

"Okay, sounds like a winner. But I'm thinking if you use the four smaller faceted buttons on the black slacks, they'll look a bit odd in contrast to the large buttons on the jacket. So, would you consider for the sake of balance using two rows of three, large buttons, but just slightly smaller in diameter than the jacket buttons? And instead of "kissing stacked" sew them on conventionally. A little space will avoid a cluttered look. Also, since the "gold" is pleated, I'd eliminate the front panel buttons entirely, and also the buttons on the jacket—just let it hang loose and casual."

"Crap. I forgot the pleats," said Alexis as she considered the advice for a moment and the wealth of experience Bonnie had. She was pinched for time and actually thankful for the advice despite it chafing against her own designer's ego. She really had no choice, and quickly enough said, "Yep, good. Go ahead and do that. Now, the big question—is it all doable? Can it be done soon enough? The showing is in three weeks and I need packing time."

"Yeah, I believe I can do it. If I run into trouble, I'll call you within a couple of days."

Alexis thanked her twice more and left the sewing studio breathing a lot easier; her headache much relieved. Ray would be home in couple of hours and the world would be right.

Chapter 59

Ray made dinner reservations at The Royal Hilton. Tonight was to be a romantic celebration. Both were elated over Alexis' recently announced pregnancy, and it was her birthday. So, the very best of foods would be the order of the evening.

They ordered a filet mignon Beef Wellington, with sides of fresh green beans sautéed in garlic and white wine, herb roasted potatoes, glazed carrots, and a mixed green salad with balsamic vinaigrette. The entrée was done to perfection. Its taste was superb and well matched by the succulent flavors of the side dishes.

Alexis was savoring a mouthful of filet mignon when Ray began telling her of how his college classmates once plastic wrapped the bathroom's toilet seat and he discovered it in the middle of the night the hard way.

Alexis laughed out loud. But in the midst of her next intake of breath, she made an ugly gagging sound and her chin jutted upward, her hands went to her throat.

Ray yelled, "What's wrong!" Alexis made no response. She couldn't speak, her eyes grew wide with terror and panic distorted her face; one hand on top of the other clutching her throat. She reached out to Ray with one trembling hand. Heart attack flashed through Ray mind, and he was immediately out of his chair and at her side, his chair toppling backward and alarming other patrons. He shouted, "Quick, call emergency, my wife…" but there wasn't time for more.

Everyone could see her distress. Ray, thoroughly unfamiliar with emergency assistance, held her hand and then thought of something he had seen in a movie. He lay her on the floor and pumped her chest with his hands in a CPR movement several times over her heart. There was no improvement. She quickly grew worse. A woman came from nowhere and knelt beside Alexis.

Alexis face was turning from blue to grey; her lips still bluish. Her eyes stared at the ceiling, opened so wide they were practically round. She was soundless. Her arms hung limp to her sides.

The kneeling lady yelled to him, "I'm a nurse. She's not having a heart attack—she's choking. She checked Alexis' mouth for an obstruction and found none. She and Ray got Alexis to a slumped standing position and the lady performed the Heimlich manoeuver. Once, twice, three times and twice more. Ray was panic stricken as well as he watched Alexis turn grey, and the life drain out of her. The woman told him to try. "The manoeuver needs to be forceful" she said, "you're stronger. Ray grabbed Alexis from behind, formed the fist the woman told him to and placed it on Alexis' diaphragm. Up and in, she said, as hard as you can. Don't be afraid of breaking ribs. The ribs will heal. Do it!" she yelled. And Ray did.

Alexis couldn't breathe, she couldn't talk. Someone in the background said EMS was on the way.

How long would it be, thought Ray. Alexis needed help minutes ago. *God, get them here now.* Alexis by now had been out for about two very long minutes. He could see her vitality fading, slipping away. Things happened way too fast; his mind was frozen with those thoughts, his helplessness overwhelming. He was useless and he knew it. His heart pounded; his legs spaghetti. He was beginning to hyperventilate. *Ray, for God's sake don't lose it, and fought his own pounding heart for control.*

EMS arrived, checked her mouth, Heimlich-ed her quickly one more time before rushing her out of the dining room on a gurney. One of them yelled out over his shoulder, St. John's Hospital.

Screw that, Ray said to himself. He bolted after them and demanded room in the vehicle for himself. They shook their head, but didn't have time to argue with a madman. He squeezed into the crowded compartment and the driver sped off. The medic performed a tracheotomy on Alexis; tried oxygen, tried probing, but were fearful of pushing the obstruction further down her windpipe or lung; she needed a lung x-ray. All Ray could do was watch, mind numbed. She didn't stir. He said, "She's pregnant," as if that would make a difference. It didn't, but the medics noted it and would pass that on to the doctors for whatever it was worth. The medic inserted his finger into the hole created by the tracheotomy and searched for an obstruction; none; he intubated her and applied suction.

In the emergency, members of the hospital staff, already alerted to incoming by the ambulance driver, waited for them. The doors of the emergency vehicle burst open, and Ray jumped to the side as her gurney was hauled out. She was rushed from the vehicle to the operating room. He ran after the gurney, trailing just a few feet away. An OR nurse stopped him by blocking his way and, with a hand on his chest, said, "Let the doctors do their job." Ray was in a panic, and would have fought her, but the logic got through to his panicked mind. He obeyed. The nurse led him to an adjacent waiting room. Sit, stand, pace the floor. Sit, stand, pace. Ray was wild with fear for Alexis' life. Alternately, crying silently and praying, he finally sat on the edge of his seat with his face in his hands and rocked his head slowly from side to side.

And there, Ray experienced the cruelest passage of time anyone could be expected to endure. Each second seemed longer that the last. The minutes lengthened and refused to pass. *Too long. Should have heard something by now. What's wrong?* But deep inside a chill was creeping over his heart. He knew what was wrong. At first he was anxious for the doctor's report, but now he dreaded it.

About a half hour later, two surgeons appeared. They approached and both put a hand on his shoulders. One said, "I'm sorry. We tried everything we knew. She gone; probably died enroute. It was just too long without oxygen. The obstruction was lodged deep in her lung and…." The doctors' voices became an unintelligible droning, he tuned them out and stared at the floor. *This is crazy. People die by being shot, in car accidents, airplane crashes…all sorts of things…but not by choking at dinner. That was absurd. This can't happen. It's too stupid.* His head bent downward and he puked on the floor and his shoes.

The intake desk nurse approached Ray and wanted the basic information regarding Alexis. Ray was in no mood to provide her the bureaucratic bullshit. He felt like punching her face in. *Alexis just died, she's still warm, and you want fucking information for your records so you know where to send the bill? You heartless bastards, so you ... I'm dying here myself, and you want to...Christ!* He wanted to die, but the thoughts poured in. *Alexis's body—what's to be done with her? He couldn't stand it.* The nurse stood silently by, saying no more. Ray bolted for the door, Alexis' purse in his hand.

Alexis' identification was in limbo as far as the hospital was concerned. The procedure then was for an unidentified patient to be shipped to the morgue, and that's what they did. Although Ray had no idea of what occurred in the aftermath of a hospital patient's death, he was to find out soon enough.

Ray had decisions to make—ugly decisions that he didn't want to make, didn't want to face. But he was the only one who could make them...Alexis had to be taken care of. He and Alexis were young. Thoughts of death never occurred to either. Funeral plans? None. Burial or cremation? No idea. Cost? No idea. Where? No idea. When? No idea. The mere thoughts of these choices sent Ray into a horrible downward spiral of wretched emotional collapse. He could barely think. His friends? Only acquaintances at the office. Her friends? He didn't know any of them...had to find her address book. Her belongings? He couldn't bear to think that far ahead. And Alexis's body...what is to be done with her?

Eventually, he pulled himself together and did, tearfully, what had to be done. The funeral home, he chose at random on his computer from a list of local homes. The home representative was gracious and consoling, and asked the needed questions gently. Ray responded woodenly, his voice seeming to him to come from elsewhere, outside his body maybe...another person, a surrogate standing in for the real Ray Oliver.

Ray's mind was whirling. He had to call her parents...father or mother, brother or sister. He had to man up and do it...the father, he thought, might be able to handle it better than her mother—not much better, but maybe just more able—Ray had to choose someone. He dreaded breaking the news to the family.

It took two calls to Alexis' father. The first to advise him of her death; the second to get his view of burial vs cremation. Ultimately, Americo, gained his voice and said that cremation was acceptable. It was, in fact, the means that he and his wife had chosen years ago. Both calls choked the vitality out of each and they were barely able to say goodbye.

Since Alexis just conceived, there was no autopsy and the fetus, not being viable, was not removed. She and her non-birthed were cremated together.

The funeral and burial were attended by Alexis' family. They returned to Italy the day after the memorial service.

Ray had never felt so alone.

Chapter 60

Ray was three cups of coffee into the Monday morning when his cell ring tone went off. The text read: "conference in ten minutes, room 2018; important that you be there."

Damn, 20th floor, just down the hall from Wentworth's office. What now?

Jerry Silverton from HR's legal division and Oliver's own case manager, Robert Yearling, were already seated and motioned for Ray to take the chair opposite them when he entered. A yellow legal pad was in front of Silverton; a company personnel file was in front of Yearling, and between them was a voice recorder.

Does not look good, thought Ray as he sat in the chair. "Any coffee," he asked more to break the stony silence than having a need for coffee.

"No. This won't take long. We won't be here long enough to have coffee."

His gut feeling was a sense of foreboding which crept across his chest and tapped at his heart.

"Mr. Oliver," Yearling began, "I have before me a few notes governing your performance and demeanor over the last couple of months which has necessitated this meeting. I will read them to you."

Oliver sat up straighter in his chair. If there ever was a time for a belt of straight whiskey, this was it.

"First, however, before I begin this summary, I wish to express our deeply felt condolences for the loss of your wife. It was tragic and we, Wentworth and company—anyone here who knows you--knows it was a gut-wrenching blow to you. That is, by way of saying that we can understand to the degree possible, what such a loss means to you."

There was an awkward moment of silence and then Mr. Yearling said, "Now, to the point. You processed and litigated several cases since your return from your honeymoon. They were done with your usual expertise. All were resolved to the immense gratification of your clients and, of course, our company. You sir, have caught the eye of Mr. Wentworth and he and others of the board began considering you for preferment. You just didn't plod through cases, you finessed them. We have read your briefs and spoke to your colleagues who have nothing but respect and the highest of esteem for your lawyering ability. You are to be congratulated for your thoroughness and preparation in each and every case.

You have continued in this excellence of expertise until around mid-January, following the unfortunate demise of your wife.

After your return to the company, your performance was—oh, well let's just say lackluster. And that was understandable with the emotional burden you were carrying. However, the company is a business—its reputation is paramount. Winning, as you already know, is the absolute goal. And you are expected to cope with your loss and move on.

In early February, the Jefferson case—you weren't prepared and it had to be handed off to Mr. Alsop. The Priebie case, you came close to losing it and by the grace of Mr. Jessup's intervention and his good standing with the judge, it was adjourned for two months while we could mount a better defense. The Rasmussen case—a car accident involving a fatality—once again, not ready for trial. There are other instances. Here's one that maybe you can explain…in the mornings, on the elevator, there have been reports of a definite smell of alcohol surrounding your person."

"Who said that?"

"Doesn't matter. The allegation is disturbing."

"Okay, probably my mouthwash. I always brush my teeth in the morning and use mouthwash."

"Mr. Oliver, again, at the end of February, you have been twice observed sleeping at your desk."

"I've been having my emotional ups and downs, that's no secret, and I've been taking medication to keep the swings under control.

They make me sleepy. I've been off of them for a couple of weeks now, I don't believe that will happen again."

"In March, you missed three days of work. You said that you were sick. Did you see a doctor? Which one? May we have the doctor's name?"

That question almost made Ray blow up. *How dare they interfere in his personal life...*and then he understood, or thought he did, why the legal eagle was there. *Was his job in jeopardy? Was this "meeting" the documentation stage and first step to termination of employment.* He choked down his fear and anger, and willed himself to cool down. He had to be respectful and at least appear cooperative

"Well, yes of course, but I didn't see a doctor. I understand your concerns. The meds I took belonged to my wife. She felt nauseous and experienced some anxiety because of her pregnancy. I took them because, as you suggest, I wanted to deal with her loss and at times I was overwhelmed with remorse and a general ill temperament."

"Okay, we don't really need to follow up that closely. I just wanted you to know that, added up, these things are frightening to an employer, especially of an employee as talented as yourself and a valuable asset to our company."

"I was actually reluctant to read you these notes, but they needed clarification. The one that I must bring before you now—really a difficult question, and better introduced by Mr. Silverton."

Mr. Jerry Silverton did a brief throat clearing, glanced at his legal pad, turned on the voice recorder and said "Initial interview of Mr. Ray Oliver, lawyer for Wentworth and Company re SBA complaint number 13640-18." He began: "Do you know a Mrs. Alison Cooper?"

"Yes, I do. She was my mother's best friend and I've known her since I was a little boy. Why do you ask?"

"Mrs. Cooper's son, Conrad Cooper, or rather his lawyer, Mr. Bracken of Keller, Smith, and Feinstein, filed a complaint against you in behalf of Mr. Cooper. I want you to know that this is only an interview, not an investigation, and you do not have to respond if you do not want to. However, the purpose of this interview is to determine how we, Wentworth and company, should respond to the complaint. This complaint comes to us by way of the *MI State Bar Association*, and must be answered. Therefore, it behooves you to provide us with as much information in this regard as you can.

Mr. Cooper contends that you swindled his mother, Alison Cooper, out of twenty-five thousand dollars. Mrs. Cooper's check for twenty-five thousand dollars was deposited in your account. There is no reason as far as Conrad Cooper is concerned that she would willingly give you a check for that amount. He believes that you, as a confidant, unduly influenced her, and coerced her into giving you that money. Can you give us an insight as to what occurred?"

Ray composed himself and answered. "Yes. I've known Mrs. Cooper my entire life. She is a close friend and I would never do anything to harm her. A couple of years ago, she learned that I became a lawyer. She was delighted. *'If your mother was alive, she would be very proud of you,'* she said often enough. So, when she asked me to construct a will for her, I complied. I didn't charge her—she was a family friend. I suppose you could say she was a "client" of mine, but I never looked at it that way. She was like my second mother.

She and her son, Conrad, had not gotten along too well for the last ten years, probably longer. He didn't visit her often enough, balked at doing things for her, and usually dropped by only when he needed money, and once asked her if he couldn't have his inheritance prior to her death so he could invest in some property he had in mind. She did, in fact, leave everything she had to him in the will, but she didn't want him to have it all at one time. She thought he'd go 'hog wild' in her words, and spend it all in a short time. So, she proposed that I put together a trust for him of twenty-five thousand dollars and he would get that first, the bulk of the will would be disbursed to him five years after her death. She was convinced that he would be reckless with the money and hoped that at least he would have something left, if he learned anything from his squandering. And, that is what she wanted.

About a week ago, it was on a Friday, she gave me a check for 25K made out to me, to create the trust. She trusted me implicitly. I told her that I would. She also gave me fifty dollars, cash, for my troubles. I had to smile at that.

Anyway, I took the check and the cash—she actually said she felt better having given me some money for myself. So, for her, I did good. I put the cash in my pocket, and the check in a clasp envelope containing several other checks—some from Wentworth, a federal tax refund, and a stock sale.

Around noon, I stopped for lunch at Bailey's. I had a few beers and a sandwich. I got to talking with a couple of lawyers there that I knew, and before I was aware of it, it was close to 4:30. I needed to get to the bank before 5, so I left in a hurry. Got to the bank just before closing time and slid the envelope to the teller. She counted it, gave me a receipt and deposited all of the checks in my account. The bank was closed for the weekend, so I intended to create the trust as soon as I could find the time."

"And so, what did you do with the money?"

"For the next couple of days, I just let it sit in my account. I spent my time on the Rasmussen case and several court appearances. I figured I had a couple of days to create the trust.

On Thursday, I discovered that Mrs. Conrad had died in the evening of the day I received her check."

"That would be on the previous Friday?" questioned Silverton.

"Yes, that's correct."

"On that day, Wednesday, I discovered that Mr. Conrad was in a hurry to gain his inheritance and had his lawyer file a death certificate. That effectively froze her account. I was unable to create a trust or deposit any monies into her account. Since I had already created a will for her, I had all the pertinent information regarding her account. It would have been no trouble to return the money into her account, but at that point it wasn't possible.

It occurred to me that I could have given Mr. Conrad my personal check for the amount, which would have satisfied her intentions. But that transaction wouldn't appear in the summary of her will, and the necessary accounting would easily disclose the unexplained expenditure in her checking account. Conrad was the executor of the will, but following probate, discovery regarding the check would easily put it on my doorstep. I did not want any personal connection with Mr. Conrad. I dislike him intensely. I was already short of time and didn't want to get into a legal wrangle of a nuisance lawsuit regarding my alleged misbehavior despite the fact that I did nothing wrong."

"I understand. Thank you for your cooperation and candid explanations.

I want you to understand, though, the seriousness of this allegation and its consequences. If an investigation is warranted, and it is established that you acted in a fiduciary capacity for Mrs. Conrad, and have violated that trust, then ultimately you will be charged with professional malpractice as a result of a breach of trust, which also assumes personal liability. The way the law reads is that it doesn't matter if the violation was willful, fraudulent, negligent, or inadvertent.

The usual outcomes are admonishment, reprimand, suspension, and disbarment.

If you are found guilty of professional malpractice the end result will be disbarment.

Ray now knew why the Legal Eagle was present. Ray's stomach twisted and he felt like throwing up.

However, there are exceptions, Mr. Silverton continued, such as Mrs. Conrad was a family friend and is now dead. It may be difficult to establish a fiduciary relationship. And that is the crux of our argument and the direction our reply will rely on. If we fail, however, and negligence or an inadvertency can be proven, then you are back in the hot seat. Both are bad.

If you are disbarred, you will not be able to practice law…or give legal advice to another. You will then be out of a job. However, in Michigan, after five years you can apply for reinstatement, but you will have to re-take the bar exam."

Some consolation. Five years. Re-take the bar. His professional life would be over. If he had to wait five years for reinstatement, there is no guarantee that any firm, even Wentworth, would want him given his notoriety. His contemporaries would be five years up the ladder of success even if he were fortunate and could start again. And there would always be the stigma of his disbarment.

"Do you have any questions?"

"How long will it be before I receive the results from the Michigan State Bar Association if it has been referred for investigation?"

"Don't really know, I would guess that it'd be a month or less. It's up to them."

"And, in the meanwhile…?" Ray let the inferred question hang in the air.

"Okay. Mr. Oliver: meanwhile. We think it is possible that you have a drinking problem. Do you?"

"No, I do not," replied Ray, maybe a bit too forceful.

"We would suggest that you avail yourself of a clinic—at our expense—and see if there is, in fact, a problem that can be resolved. Attendance is entirely of your own volition. It is not mandatory or predicated on any threat. We don't talk about it, but there are several of our lawyers, men and women, that have had similar problems. You would not be the first. They have all returned to full capacity, without injury to their career, and are full-fledged members of the Wentworth team. We want that for you."

"Anything else I should know about?" said Ray, hoping it didn't sound dismissive.

"No, that about covers it. We'll let you know…and the clinic?"

"I'll chew on it. For now, I have to do some soul searching. Thank you for the heads-up, the offer of help, and your support."

"You're welcome. One other thing, though, you can finish the cases you started and are working on now, but only in the capacity of clerking. You will prepare the cases and they will be handed off to your colleagues until you have decided whether or not on entering a clinic."

Mr. Silverton, at this last minute, also suggested that if Ray was willing, he could write a check for the 25K and they would forward it under the Wentworth company letterhead with an explanation to Mr. Conrad's attorney. That might forestall further inquiry if Mr. Conrad was willing to withdraw his complaint. Since money seemed to be his only objective, they didn't see why he would pursue it. This was tricky, he said, because it would look like Ray was trying to buy his way out of a complaint rather than to make Mr. Conrad whole. If it was perceived in that light, then the complaint could possibly receive continuance despite Ray's intention. Mr. Silverton told Ray he would take the step under advisement and consult with the other attorneys in his division before letting him know.

Actually, this meant that Silverton would speak with Mr. Bracken, Mr. Conrad's attorney, and feel him out. Mr. Bracken, in turn, would speak with Mr. Conrad. If all was well with the exchange, then that would be the end of it. If not, and Mr. Conrad wanted a pound of flesh and felt that Ray needed punishment, then he would not drop the charge. And Ray would feel the grind of the legal machinery.

Messrs. Silverton and Yearling stood, nodded at Ray, shook his hand, and left the room. Ray took a deep breath and followed them. He went downstairs to his office and worked on his cases for a couple of hours. But Silverton's and Yearling's words and warnings constantly interrupted his thoughts. At home, in the refrigerator, was a bottle of Johnnie Walker Black. It called to him; he left early.

The walk home was invigorating, except when he got to his apartment, it was the same—noticeably cold and cheerless. He headed straight for the refrigerator, opened the bottle of JW Black, and took a couple of swigs from it. His thoughts, generally always the same, were of how happy he and Alexis had been there. As evening approached, he thought playing some slots at the Greektown Casino, and maybe a walk along the riverfront might rekindle pleasant memories. A short while later he entered the Greektown Casino…but went to the bar for a quick one. It was not his best move.

Chapter 61

Lisa began her search for Ray at Wentworth, Solomon, & Hughes.

She spoke with the receptionist: "I know he doesn't work here anymore, but can you tell me of someone who might have been his friend while he worked here?"

"What's this all about?"

"He's being offered a job, and the offer won't last long. I need to get in touch with him. I was hoping that a friend of his might know where he is."

"Yes, Mr. Oliver...I remember him. Just a minute..." and she punched in the number to the stable of lawyers on the fourth floor.

The ringing stopped and Lisa could hear the person on the other end making a general announcement to those on the floor— "anyone know where Ray Oliver is?" The consensus was a silence that meant no...but one of the guys in the background said aloud that if anyone might know it'd be Cahalan—John Cahalan. They went to lunch often enough. John's not here, he left a few minutes ago. The receptionist thanked him and checked the in/out board, "Sorry, he's out on a case...doesn't give a return time."

"Can I have his card?"

"Don't have one, but I can give you his office number." She wrote it on the back of a general WS&H business card and gave it to Lisa.

Lisa gave her a "thank you" nod, stuffed the card into her purse and left.

***

Cahalan's phone began ringing at 8:30 and interrupted his morning coffee ritual. But business was business and he picked up after two sips and three rings.

"Mr. Cahalan, my name is Lisa Marnen and I'm a friend of Ray Oliver's, and I need to get in touch with him. One of your fellow lawyers at Wentworth said you might be able to help me."

"Hmmm, maybe…are you a process server?"

"No, old girlfriend."

"Pregnant?"

"No."

"Paternity suit? I can help you with that." She imagined him smiling.

Some friend.

"No, nothing like that."

"How about you give me your number and when I see him I'll give it to him."

"Yeah, that'd work. But no telling when you'd run into him. I need to see him right away. I really can't wait. It means work for him…I understand he's not lawyering anymore."

"Yeah, that's a shame. He's really an excellent lawyer…and a general all around good guy. Tell you what…I have no idea where he could be, but when I used to drink with him a couple months ago, it was in a sleaze bar on Gratiot—Barney's, near Beaubien—because we knew we would probably get shit faced and didn't want to be seen by anyone we knew—it was that kind of a dump. And later, when I went off the rails, I knew I was in trouble and started attending Alcoholic Anonymous meetings. I gradually got myself together and would often meet Ray at the bar and tried to get him to go to the meetings. He insisted that he wasn't that far gone. Yeah, well…finally, I just gave up. Man is a creature of habit; he might still be going there. Other than that, I haven't a clue."

Lisa thanked him and said she'd check it out."

"Okay, but be careful. There's a lot of low-life's hanging out there…trust me, I know."

Chapter 62

Lisa stopped in Barney's three times that week and had a soft drink by herself, despite being zoomed, each time, by at least one derelict who thought that she might want some company. She gave each a hot, piercing stare, and told them to "fuck off"; and they melted away. On her third visit, she sat at the front end of the bar as usual. It was just noon when the back door opened, its frame briefly filled with sunlight before it shut behind Ray. Ray had made the rounds of other bars and now he was here. She watched him stagger to the end of the bar, sit heavily onto a barstool, and order a drink.

"The usual?"

He nodded. And the bar tender sat a scotch and water in front of him. Should he be serving a drunk? He had been snatching nickels, dimes and quarters off the bar and short changing drunks for forty years—he didn't give a shit.

It had been about three years since she saw Ray. She watched from a distance of several bar stools as he knocked down the first drink, ordered another, and stared at the glass. He was disheveled and blended neatly with the bar's clientele; he belonged. But she remembered a better Ray...this wasn't the Ray she knew. What had happened to him? *You are so much better than what I'm seeing.* She slid off her barstool and walked over to him. He was oblivious, unaware of her presence, as he was of everything else. It was just him, the bar in front of him, and the glass in his hand. He felt the subtle touch on his shoulder and turned. A soft voice said, "Hello, Ray. Let's talk." If he had been sober, he would have discovered a pair of striking green eyes looking deep into his very essence. "Uhhh, uh..." he stammered while he blinked his eyes trying to think and trying to focus. The green eyes continued to penetrate while he tried to recognize the face. With effort, he slowly brought her face into focus. He knew her. "Lee-sha?"

"Yeah, sweetness," she said in a soothing tone, "it's me. Been awhile…we should do some catching up. Let's say we go home together…like old times. You want to come home with me? Just you and me…come on Ray, let's get out of here." She said these last words as though she were convincing a child. He pieced the words together and had a general understanding of what she was saying. He nodded agreement. Lisa glanced at the nearby bartender and asked what he owed. He waved at her as to say the bill had been paid. She added a couple of bills from her purse to Ray's change as a tip and steadied him as he slid from the stool.

He leaned on her as she led him toward the front door. She, straining under his weight, and he staggering, lumbered out of the bar. The late afternoon sunlight was stunning. He leaned heavily on Lisa. She propped him up against the wall of the bar and managed to keep him upright until she flagged a cab and got him in it.

It had been difficult and clumsy, but Lisa finally got Ray up the condo staircase, through the door, and onto the bed. She looked at him. He was totally out of it. He hadn't moved from the time his head hit the pillow. She sat on the edge of the bed, and gently brushed strands of hair from his face. It was only three years since they were lovers. What a turn of events since.

Sardi called her again around noon, inquiring again about Ray. And now she had an answer for him. He invited her to lunch at Pernelli's. She was famished and readily accepted.

First, Ray had to stay put. It wouldn't do for him to go wandering while she was out…he looked and smelled like a derelict. The solution was immediate. He was out cold so it didn't matter if she pushed, pulled, or rolled him around. It took all those efforts to get his clothes off—right down to the skinny. He was still well muscled. She glanced at his equipment. *You're really gifted… too bad we couldn't have lasted, but I had to do what I had to do.*

But memories were just old stories. She stuffed his clothes in a laundry bag and would drop them off at the one-hour cleaners; they'd be ready when she returned after lunch with Sardi, and picking up Robbie. Ray wasn't going anywhere.

Lisa checked Ray once more as she prepared to leave. He was snoring loudly as she left the apartment, locked the door and made her way to the lobby. The doorman seemed to click his heels as she nodded to him while he held the door open. Then he dutifully signaled for a cab. "Pernelli's," she said as she slid into the back seat. The driver made a noise of approval as though it was his favorite restaurant. She shot him a cool glance that said it all—there was nothing they could ever have possibly shared in common. The cabbie soured at her reaction. Sticking to his driving, he made no attempt at small talk and didn't thank her for the generous tip.

The Pernelli valet opened the cab door as though Lisa was expected. He then ushered her into the lobby, made chilly by a large water fountain that sprayed a fine mist into the air. The restaurant's Italian background music, obligatory statuary and attractive red, green and white motif meant little to Lisa. She had Sardi on her mind as she approached the Maître d' at his little podium.

"Is madam expecting company?" he asked.

"Mr. Sardi's table please," she answered, and was led to Sardi's personal corner table where she took a seat. The Maître d' signaled for a waitress and said "Mr. Sardi will be here at 1:30." He nodded once and moved back to his station.

"I'll have a Beefeater martini, straight up; use the pimento olives." The waitress disappeared.

Half way through the martini Lisa saw Sardi walking toward her. He flashed her an easy smile.

"I can't but help remember the last time we—you, me and Ray—had dinner together. Seems like Ray should be here," he said in a friendly voice.

"Well that's an interesting thought, but so much has happened between Ray and me that wouldn't be enjoyable. Since we didn't part on the best of terms, the conversation would probably be more than a little strained."

Sardi didn't know what transpired but he could guess. Breakups never went smoothly.

He looked up as his usual glass of Chianti was set on the table before him. He stared at it momentarily, pinched its stem and lifted it. He looked through the wine; noted its clarity, smelled its bouquet, swished a sip in his mouth, savored it and then downed it like it was beer. "Sally," he said, "bring me the bottle and another martini for the lady." Lisa had half of the first martini left and declined the offer. Sally was back in a minute, and Sardi poured another glass of wine, except this time he used his empty water glass.

When the wine in Sardi's glass reached the half-way point, Sally returned to the table. "Can I take your orders?"

Sardi skipped the antipasti and salads and went right for the entrée. "Gimme the Bistecca Alla Fiorentina—the 22 oz Angus porterhouse steak, rare, that's all I need. Lisa, her hunger enhanced a bit by the martini, opted for the sautéed chicken breast—the Piccata Di Pollo Al Limone and the Insalata Mista with the house dressing. She was hungry and Sardi was buying.

"Another martini?" the waitress asked. "No, just bring a glass and I'll have some of Mr. Sardi's Chianti." Sally gave Lisa a smile and was gone.

They talked about a variety of things but avoided the subject of Ray and Lisa's break-up. Sardi was in the midst of telling her about the wonders of Italy when they saw the waitress balancing a tray, making her way toward their table.

The dinner plates clattered slightly as Sally whisked them from the tray and set them down with an expert flourish, filled their glasses with Chianti, and then uttered the one word which all waitresses learn at waitress school: "Enjoy." She then did a three-quarter pirouette and walked off with the grace of a ballerina—one who had been to waitress school.

They ate leisurely and enjoyed a casual conversation, but eventually it turned to Ray and why Sardi wanted to see him.

"I don't want to go into detail, but I have a job for Ray. I understand that he was fired from the law firm where he worked. I don't know the circumstances, but I'm thinking he must be in need. I like Ray very much and want to help him. I have an unusual opportunity for him and hope that he'll be interested. But I need to see him sometime in the next couple of days. I hoped that you are still in contact with him and would be able to arrange a meeting. Can you?"

"Yeah, I can do that. He'll probably want to know what kind of job."

"I'll have to tell him when I see him. Nowadays, I spend most of my time at the gym. Tell him he can meet me there."

A short while after lunch, Lisa glanced at her watch and told Sardi she had to go. "Thanks for lunch. I'll tell Ray what you said." And her heels clicked on the tiled floor as she made her way to the door. Sardi finished the bottle of Chianti.

Chapter 63

Lisa had slept, showered and was gone long before Ray Oliver cautiously opened an eye. The other half of his face lay buried in the pillow. If he hadn't had such a foul taste in his mouth and if his nose wasn't still full of alcohol laden breath, he would have noticed the sweet perfume borne by Lisa's bedding...and that would have been his first clue as to where he was. He lay there exploring the room with one eye, looking for something familiar. The room's brightness made him squint. He attempted to recall the previous day but the hammering in his head wasn't helpful and his bladder felt like it was about to explode; he would think later.

He rolled to the edge of the bed and sat up. Huge mistake. He dug his elbows into his thighs and lowered his face into both palms, and sat hunched over, coming close to pitching forward onto his head. Thunder rolled inside his skull and the sunlight streaming in through the windows stabbed into his eyes when he peeked through his fingers; he felt like puking but fought the urge. Standing was going to be an event, but like many other mornings he would master it. Crouching at first, he held on the edge of the bed until he gained his feet and unsteadily made his way to the bathroom. He saw a couple of pictures on the dresser—Lisa with different guys, and one of him and Lisa; bits and pieces of old memories began trickling in.

The warm shower was a godsend. By the time the water became cool his mind had become much clearer. He wondered about meeting Lisa and how he had gotten to her apartment, but all he could recall for sure was starting the day early at one of the local gin mills. He had no idea of yesterday's events and that realization sent a slight tremor of fear through him. Instinctively he knew that willpower and strength made the difference between the user and the used. He had always been the user—he forced issues and made things happen, but he knew that yesterday he had shown neither will nor strength—and as his awareness grew, he knew, as well, that there had been many such "yesterdays." What was happening to him? Vignettes flashed through his mind like a kaleidoscope of disjointed pictures—each a view of himself as though through another's eyes—weak, defenseless, and mindless—naked to everyone, prey to anyone. He was powerless to stop this punishing, soulful flood of self-recrimination. The water turned cold and its jets seemed intensified, but he stood, transfixed by his thoughts, oblivious to the punishment. Ray Oliver was thoroughly focused. *What am I doing to myself*? Then *Alexis is gone—nothing I can do about that.* And as tough as he was, the truths stung him sharply and repeatedly.

In the end, he couldn't decide which he hated more, the cold water or the cold answers. He turned off the torrent of cold water and stepped from the shower. In the medicine cabinet he found an aspirin bottle and quickly swallowed four tablets. Two would usually do but this morning he wasn't taking any chances.

Ray toweled and began looking for his clothes. After a search, he discovered that he didn't have any. The closet held several dresses and small sized slacks. The only wearable item that would almost fit him was a yellow robe…hell, that didn't matter; he put it on. Somewhere in the kitchen, he knew, there would be coffee. He rummaged about in the cupboards but all he could find was tea. In a tall kitchen cabinet, however, he found what he was looking for and nuked a cup of instant in the micro. The world wasn't quite right yet, but it would get there…a cup at a time.

The first cup went down, hot…the second cup was savored in the living room; Ray leaning back in a basket chair with his feet up on an ottoman. The sunlight was tolerable and he no longer felt like throwing up. The floor had stopped leaning and the ache in his head was bearable. He had been sitting there for about a minute when he saw the wet bar in the corner of the room. In a knee-jerk moment, he had set the coffee cup on the table and was standing before the bar, opening its ornate cabinet doors. Inside were several bottles of the best...smiling and reflexive, he picked up a tumbler and began pouring the Scotch. But he tilted his hand back and the flow stopped. He looked very hard at the glass and the bottle, and then into the mirror behind the bar where he saw a shameful, naked and haggard middle-aged man with no future or direction. Months ago, he remembered seeing a well-dressed lawyer on his way to the office or a courtroom. Those days all gone with the first and last drink in a bottle.

He found the basket chair, flumped into it, and resumed his coffee. His downfall, of course, started with his drinking—an attempt to blot the hurt of Alexis from his mind. The sweet remembrances of Alexis were punishing. But now, in his heart, he could feel her disapproval as though she were speaking to him.

It was so strong, perhaps she was. He was floundering in self-pity.
Enough!

And that realization and moment was his first step back to his world.

Thank you, Alexis.

Chapter 64

Sanders invited Sardi for lunch at Crispino's. By the time Sardi got there, Sanders was on his second beer. Sardi ordered a wine and waited for Sanders to get to the reason for their meeting.

"Ya know, it's a beautiful day and I shouldn't be feeling like this, but...."

"What's wrong? We both made a couple of hundred thousand already. I think you'd be dancin' with happiness."

"Yeah, our business is good. But my business isn't."

"Meaning what?"

Sanders stared at the table cloth for a moment. "Ya know," he began slowly, "a good part of my money comes from city contracts. And, one kind of hinges on the other...like, if they like my service, then it goes a long way to getting another contract...under the table or over, it works both ways. So, I have to kiss their ass a lot."

"Yeah, okay, so..."

"So, long story short, what happened a couple of months ago really screwed things big time. I have this great contract for garbage hauling...actually it's the only one that's keeping me afloat. The only problem is that the city is slow in paying. I need the money now; they tell me they'll get to it. That's not doing me any good. So, I go to the Corporation Council and talk to a city lawyer. I tell him my problem; he tells me the city's problems. They don't have it in their budget at the present time, and I'll have to wait. "Budget," I said, "if it was in the budget when we signed the contract, you should have enough to see you through to the end of the contract." He agrees, tells me it was last year's budget, and doesn't budge. I tell him, I think I'm going to stop my trucks. He says—and I'm still trying to believe this happened—he says, 'go ahead. We'll fill in with the trucks we used to do it with, and hire another company to pick up the slack. If you sue, okay, but we'll stretch it out and it'll be years before you see a penny...and don't ever even think of getting another contract.'

So, I'm pissed and I tell him to get fucked. He leans back in his chair and says, 'thank you, Mr. Sanders, that'll be enough. The door is right behind you.' I stormed out of his office and wanted a piece of his ass. I needed a lawyer to sue the bastards. I was hot...and maybe not thinking too well. Ya know that guy you introduced me to last year? ...that lawyer friend of yours...I have his number on my calendar."

"Ray Oliver?"

"Yeah, that's him. So, I give him a call and explain the situation. He tells me that he works for a big firm downtown Detroit...Wentworth and something or other. Well, he tells me that he can't do any independent representations...that he receives assignments through this company. So, I can't get him.

"I'm still pissed, so I knock on the Wentworth door and tell the *greeter* I need to talk to this Oliver guy. When I get to his office, he says I have a case. Can they do this to me? Maybe, he says, but they've handled cases like this before. So, I'm liking this approach and tell him to go ahead. Only this Oliver guy I'm talking to says he isn't the one that's going to represent me, but another lawyer will be appointed. I'm liking this Oliver guy and thinking maybe he'd do me some good, but they assign another lawyer.

I don't want to do too much explaining about my relationship with the city to this lawyer guy they sent me to. I tell him no insult intended, but I would like to work with Oliver. The lawyer asks me if I've ever had any legal work done by Oliver, and I say, yeah, sure. Well this lawyer says Oliver doesn't do any independent work outside the company.

"So, I tell this company guy to get on with it and he does. And it goes exactly the way the city lawyer told me. They send me a letter that says because of the impending litigation, they are suspending the contract; no monies will be forthcoming. And that, essentially, they'll see me in court at a date to be determined. Okay, I figured that was coming. My lawyer guy says not to worry. After a couple of months, nothing's happening. He's my champion, I need him to press them and do the "negotiation" thing that the first lawyer mentioned up front. Well, ain't nothing happened so far. The lawyer guys says they're in discussions, but I'm being ruined.

"So, what do you want from Ray Oliver?" asked Sardi.

"I want to drop the other guy and get Oliver to make something happen with the city lawyers. Is there a chance to settle up? Yeah, I think so…but then Oliver gets falling-down drunk and punches out a guy at a casino, musta been a hundred people around to see it, now, he's in trouble. This other lawyer started the legal shit with the city—yeah, okay, I started it—but I think Oliver can make some kind of connection with the Corp Counsel lawyer. I need him if I want to get my operation back on the track. I want to make nice with the city and get my contract back and any additional contracts he might come up with…I think he can do it. I didn't like him at first, but we talked, and I'm thinking he's pretty sharp after all and might just do the trick. I need him and I want him out of the jackpot.

"Can you do anything for me? You know some cops; you have connections. I need some help."

Sardi looked at Sanders while his mind mulled over Sander's words. *"Yeah, I know some cops, but not on a personal basis.* In most of his police contacts, they were the ones who arrested him. His other police contacts, he couldn't be seen with in public—they were those that gave him information or did "favors" for a price, and they constituted the difference between "some" and "most" of his police contacts. But Sardi did have other resources. If Sander's business was in the dumper then how would it affect the *insurance* business? Every investor was important. Sanders was a partner, at least a fourth of the business.

"Charlie, we're starting to make some big money in our enterprise. I'm thinking it won't be too long when we can both quit the day jobs and retire, and you won't have to sweat the city's money. I know you're concerned with your business as I am with mine. But the deals are getting bigger each time. A few more deals, and we won't have these worries.

But to ease your mind a little, yeah, Charlie, I'll take care of Oliver for you."

Chapter 65

Partlow and Kearse hammered on Mr. Thomas O. Stephens' front door. Tom looked through the peep and cracked the door. He was looking at two rugged men, one of which wore his nose on the side of his face. Both looked mean.

"Mr. Stevens?"

"Yes?"

Partlow flashed a small silver badge. Stevens was more interested in their faces than the badge. "We're First Precinct Detectives Randall and Williams. We'd like to talk to you about your Assault and Battery at the hands of..." Partlow paused and consulted a small spiral tablet he withdrew from his jacket pocket, "Mr. Ray Oliver."

"Oh, yeah, come on in." Steven's unchained the door and Partlow and Kearse stepped inside, shutting the door behind them; Kearse softly slid the lock in place while Partlow followed Stevens into the front room.

Stevens limped over to the couch and sat down with apparent great difficulty.

"I can't begin to tell you how much my back hurts and the headaches I've had." He groaned a little in emphasis.

"Well, Mr. Stephens we certainly hope you are feeling better soon." Despite the rough look of their faces, they seemed sympathetic and polite enough. Mr. Thomas O. Stephens leaned back into the cushions and relaxed.

"What can I do for you?"

"Well, actually a couple of things," Kearse said...and almost as an afterthought, "that picture on the TV...is that your wife and kids?

"Yeah, my son's eight and my daughter is ten."

"Nice looking kids...in school now?"

"Yeah, they won't be home for a couple of hours. Why?"

"Ah, just idle curiosity…your wife…out shopping? Mine makes it an afternoon ritual…almost every day. I suppose she's believes she's helping the economy, but on a policeman's salary…hey…" And he gave a kind of hopeless smile.

Stephens nodded, "Yeah, a little food shopping and pick up the kids. She just left. She'd probably like to have met you. You're the first officers that have ever been to our house."

"Well, what we have to do won't take long…ya know, your wife looks like a pretty hot number. Any good in bed?"

"Wha…what? What do you mean? Steven jumped to his feet, apparently recovered in full. "There's something wrong here…" and then the realization, "you're not cops." But it was too late. They had jumped up and were at his sides. They grabbed him by his arms, shook him like a stuffed toy, and manhandled him into the kitchen. Kearse grabbed Stephens by the left elbow and plunged his hand down the disposal, holding it there. Partlow reached over and put his finger on the switch. Stephens began screaming and Kearse cuffed him across the face.

"Shut up, you fuck'n idiot.

Steven's head shook up and down like a Bobblehead doll, tears began rolling down his cheeks.

"You asked if there was something that you could do for us? Well, there is…and you better get it right the first time or…and Partlow moved his finger like he was going to throw the switch. Steven's high pitched-terror stricken voice gave out a couple of pitiful "pleases" and several "don'ts" and a string of "please, God, Jesus, no, no, nos."

We want you to call Detective Harrison. He's in charge of your case against Mr. Oliver. You will tell him that you no longer want to prosecute and want to drop the case. He'll give you some shit about all the work he's done and probably tell you you're a puke for doing this. But you will do it. You will drop the case. And, if you don't, we'll be back to finish this job. One other thing. You will make it is abundantly clear that this is your own idea and that no one has attempted to sway you in your decision. He will ask, you better make sure you give him the proper answer...that it is your own idea. And one other item...fire your shyster lawyer...there's not going to be any civil suit against Mr. Oliver. Got that?"

Stephens blended his okays with his yes, yeses in a quick stream that made him sound like he was speaking a foreign language.

"Repeat what I told you."

Stephens did, quickly and obediently.

Kearse released Steven's elbow and Stephens jerked his hand out the disposal. They rough housed him back into the front room and shoved him down onto the couch.

Partlow, whose nose lay left of center, gave Sevens additional incentive.

"Your wife looks real good. If we have to come back, we're going to tape you to a chair and give you a front row seat. You're going to watch while I fuck her, and then me and my partner will change places. Then we'll take you into the kitchen and do the job...you're going to need her to dial EMS...know what I mean?" Stephens did.

"Got any whisky in the house?" Stephens was too frightened to answer. Kearse cruised through the kitchen and found a couple of bottles in a kitchen cabinet. He and Partlow took a swig from one, and told Stephens to take a couple of drinks. He did. They spilled about a third of the bottle on him and the couch.

"Stay there for ten minutes. Don't look out the window. Drink some more."

The front door shut. Stephens reached a shaky hand out toward the bottle. He was still sitting on the couch when his family returned. His wife looked at him, smelled the whisky, and said he was disgusting. There was no further conversation.

Chapter 66

Barton: "I gotta name."
Sardi: "Is it good?"
"Hell, yeah. I only give you stuff that's been verified. I need five-grand. That's a lot. I know your friend and his boys got hurt big-time last week, so it's worth a lot—five big ones. What'll it be worth to you the next time?"
"Gimme the name."
"No, you know it don't work that way. I need some hot dogs. Tomorrow around noon, Hart Plaza, near the Dodge fountain." When Sardi said "okay" Barton just clicked off the phone. "

Sardi agreed to the deal, but he didn't like Barton's curt manner or being cut off. Barton was an asshole, but Sardi needed his info so he ate his shit. But there would come a time when he might burn the uppity, crooked cop just because of his insolence.

It was a little after 12 when Barton approached the hot dog stand in the plaza. The sun beat down on the pavers, and the mist from the fountain was carried away by the breeze and settling on the noon time strollers. The heavy-set guy in the stand was taking in the cash and handing out the hotdogs. Barton waited his turn. "I'll have two to go…ya got any Louisiana hot sauce?" The vendor looked at him and shook his head no, saying only ketchup, mustard, onions and relish and pointed to a sideboard where each sat in its own cubbyhole. Didn't matter, the message got through. The vendor took the paper sack with the five-grand package in it and put two hot dogs in foam containers on top. "That'll be eight bucks." Barton handed him the eight bucks. Between the bills was a slip of paper with the name of the guy who ratted them out. It was a death warrant. Two phone calls later the dealer had the name.

Barton knew what was going to happen, he didn't care. It was just another doper. Who gives a shit? It didn't matter to him; it wasn't his informant.

The police precinct station was constructed in 1955. The walls had water spots and stains on them, and the paint was peeling—even in the lobby area which was seen by anyone who waked into the station. The back rooms were the detectives' area and one small room reserved for the precinct narcotics unit. It was a dump of a room and one of the reasons that Barton couldn't wait to retire. The windows didn't seal right and on windy days the shades would move in and out. The floor was worn tile; the desks had drawers—some of them even worked. The file cabinets were banged up and on the side of one cabinet you could see the outline of a footprint belonging to some frustrated officer.

Barton, through the years, eventually came to realize that he was in a dead-end job. Retirement after twenty-five or more years, a small pension dwindling in value, and some medical, dental and vision coverage which lasted only until he would be forced onto Medicare. Not exactly something he looked forward to. He found after some deep thought what he considered "the angle." The name of a snitch was worth a pile of gold to people in the narcotics trade. Every Narc developed snitches from the arrestees; he was no different. It was expected. It was how police business was done. But he couldn't ever give up his snitches. So, he thought it not a bad idea to give up the other crew's snitches. They'd never know, and he could make a few bucks…maybe quite a few.

Getting into the other shift's file cabinet was easy. A long steel bar was placed through each handle of each drawer in their filing cabinet and an ordinary Master lock was passed through the flange on the bar and through an eye bolt at the top which was secured to the cabinet. Picking the lock was easy and he was usually the only cop in the office for hours at a time. He would pop the lock, withdraw the bar, and rifle through their files. He got the names from the narcotics crew's bust records. True, the informant was only identified by a number, but those idiot cops were occasionally a bit lazy and sloppy. Behind the bust records, a few files back, were the interrogation sheets of all the arrestees. The sheets were matched to the cases. In the list of names, following the latest bust a few new numbers popped up. Some were repeats, but several other interrogations were of new clients. Barton figured there was a snitch because the second crew's arrests were up. Sure enough, one of the new arrestees was listed at the scene of the crew's latest bust and was present at three others. Could be that the snitch was an outsider, but probably not. It was more or less a scientific guess…after all, who gives a shit? *Jeeze—they always try to hide in the crowd. They think if they're arrested along with their buddies that no one would ever think they did the tipping.* He knew he could squeeze 5 g's out of this one. Barton hated snitches, but missed the irony in what he was doing.

Barton worked a "dirty" crew. The guys other officers didn't want to work with. Not because they were cowardly but because the other cops noted that things began to come up missing from time to time. They had their suspicions, but never said anything out loud, to anybody. They just dropped out by requesting reassignment. Because of the reassignments, gradually over time, a new crew was formed of likeminded officers. And Barton was in charge.

He couldn't tip Sardi as to when a rip was going to happen, because of two things. He had to report their narcotics arrest efforts to his bosses. If they were to bust a place and no one was there, okay, that happens, but if it happened several times—no money, no weapons, no dope, no people--it wouldn't take long for someone to figure out there was a leak. And, the other big reason was that there wouldn't be any "table money" for him and his partners. But there were big bucks in dropping the name of an informer every now and then and that's the way he wanted to keep it. That was a little secret he shared with no one. Sardi paid well for the information and no doubt knocked a little off for himself when he passed it on.

This was the greatest job on earth. When they ripped a joint there was always a little extra cash on the table…hey, he reasoned, ya didn't need it all for evidence anyway. So if there's a hundred grand on a table, and only sixty shows up in court...who knows, it's more than enough for a conviction and it makes the cops look like honest guys. Beautiful. His crew didn't really need the dope...dope, he concluded in a perverted sense of fairness, was *really* illegal and it and any weapons had to be confiscated...all, that is, except for a handgun or two which he kept for a just-in-case kind of a job. His personal snitch would tip him, he would make the raid, confiscate what had to be confiscated, and later paid off the snitch. On the other hand, if a snitch was a druggie, all the better. He would withhold some of the dope as part of the pay off. He wouldn't have to lay out any cash.

The only hitch with the table money was that you couldn't spend it too well. You can't spend more than you make—including overtime. It was a red flag, it just didn't look right to have a large home, a cottage, a big boat, and a new car on a cop's wages. But the duffle bag in his garage was getting lumpier and lumpier and he believed that in a few years he was going to have a most excellent retirement.

The table money invariably came from the lower echelons of the dope dealers. And those they busted pretty regularly. It was usually some dope house, or maybe what the dopers considered a "safe house" but the word eventually would get out. Barton and company would then go to work. It was always dangerous work, occasionally a shooting. But like the infamous bank robber, Willie Sutton, when asked why he robbed banks is supposed to have answered, "Because that's where the money is." For Barton, dope busts were exactly that. A couple of thousand here, a couple of thousand there, and pretty soon it begins to add up; and he was happy with that. But he knew that the really big money was at the top. He would never see it, unless he stumbled into it by accident. But he always hoped. For him, it was the big bag rolling off the Brinks truck with no one around. That fantasy played in his mind over and over. That's why he took great pains to develop snitches. So far, it was only lower level stuff, but it helped stuff the duffle bag.

Chapter 67

Lisa came home with Robbie from day care and sat him in the middle of the front room floor. She handed a covered hanger to Ray and a bag, his suit, underwear and socks. "You look nice in my robe, but these will fit you better."

She kneeled on the floor next to Robbie. "Robbie, this is a friend of mine. His name is Ray Oliver. Ray, this is Robert Lawrence, Robbie for short."

Robbie just stared at the strange man wearing his mother's yellow bathrobe in their front room. It would have been nice if they readily took to each other, but they didn't. Robbie was hesitant. Ray was uncomfortable, but said, "Nice to meet you, Mr. Lawrence," and offered a handshake. Robbie just looked at him and withdrew a little.

Lisa hugged Robbie and she shook Ray's hand. "See, like this, he wants you to be his friend." Robbie wasn't convinced of any friendly intention. His viewpoint was that there was a tall, unfamiliar man in their front room wearing his mother's bathrobe and "things" just weren't as they should be. Cause for alarm? You bet. And Robbie's face scrunched up and tears began flowing.

Lisa calmed him down shortly and suggested to Ray that he might want to change into his clothes.

Ray found the bedroom and dressed. When he returned to the front room, Robbie was comfortably seated on Lisa's lap, his tears had ceased.

"Here, sit next to us," Lisa said.

Robbie was still a little apprehensive of Ray, but after eyeing each other for a couple of minutes, Ray touched his own nose. Robbie followed suit. Ray touched his ear. Same for Robbie. Neat game. After a few more exchanges, Robbie was smiling. Lisa said, "Looks like everything is going well. I'm going to change—get acquainted with Robbie."

Robbie balked a little when his mother left, but Ray picked up a toy truck nearby and spun its wheels. Robbie liked that and spun the others. He then walked over to a box in the corner and dragged it to Ray's feet, dumped out a load of Duplos and started snapping them together.

Ray slid down to the floor and helped him build a tower, and then a bridge, and then a block house. Robbie was delighted to have someone to play with.

"Do you like school? Nod. Robbie touched Ray's cheek and smiled.

"Hungry?" she asked?"

"Yes, famished. But first can you tell me what happened?"

"You mean how you got here? I got you out of a bar…you were drunk. I brought you here."

"Don't remember. Where's here?"

"My place…you are in a condo complex in Rivertown, alongside the Detroit River."

"A lot has happened since we parted…Ray nodded at Robbie."

"Robbie? He's a wedding gift."

"Still married?"

"No. You?"

"No, … kind of… paperwork pending, haven't the courage yet to pursue it. But no is the correct answer."

Lisa give Ray a questioning look.

"My wife died three months ago."

"I'm very sorry."

"Yeah, me too."

"How old's the boy?"

"Three."

"Does he talk? Yeah, but he's got to warm up to you."

"I don't know much about kids."

A thought of Alexis' pregnancy flashed through his mind, and he immediately stifled it. Any thought of her and their unborn child wrenched at his soul and was pure anguish.

Ray seemed to study the pattern in the carpeting and breathed out, in a subdued tone, "Lisa, I'll tell you straight. I'm done in. My grief has captured me entirely and I can't shake it. Lately, I drink too much; got in trouble at a casino, and believe I am about to lose my job because of that. I feel wretched, and kind of believe that my life is pretty much over. I gave notice and terminated my lease. I checked out from my hotel two days ago. I've been sleeping in my car. I'm hoping that when my contract is settled, probably minus a penalty fee, I might get my security deposit and a few bucks rebate. Right now, I'm pretty much broke. I have no place to go to. I am totally screwed. My present assets are thin. I have a car—it's still parked in the hotel garage. My clothes, computer, books and a couple other assorted belongings are in storage at the hotel. And that's my present status."

Ray's eyes were taking in the floral pattern of her carpeting while he did his confession. And, still in a subdued tone, "I'm curious. Why were you looking for me?"

"Sardi. He wants to see you. His friend, Sanders, told him you're out of the lawyer business. I've been looking for you for days—that's what I've been doing instead of eating lunch. I met one of your lawyer associates, I think his name is Cahalen, who thought he saw you one morning going into Barney's on Gratiot near Beaubien. A real dive. I followed it up and there you were, sloshed, and leaning against the bar. You were a sight. I got you home, dumped you in the bed, and took your clothes. You were out cold, and I didn't want you out wandering around. Your clothes were rumpled, stained with mustard, ketchup, and whatever, and looked very much like you had been sleeping in them. I dropped your clothes at the cleaners when I went to work.

"Thanks. I'm ashamed, and probably should stay ashamed for the rest of my life. Thanks for taking care of me. How'd you ever come across Sardi?

"Think back...remember when you took me to the Gym and afterward to dinner with Sardi?"

"Yeah?"

"Well, remember we were about to graduate and I told him I was getting a degree in accounting. He said I should get in touch with Grace, his accountant. She was looking for help. I called her business, Grace Accounting, and spoke with her. She offered me a job, I took it. After two years she was thinking of retiring, and I bought the business. Sardi, and his friend Sanders as well, are a couple of clients I inherited."

"Why does Sardi want to see me?"

"Don't know, he likes you. When you see him he'll tell you. I can tell you this much, he's into something pretty big. His income has skyrocketed and that's just the assets I know of. If I were you, being in the toilet so to speak, I'd see him as quickly as possible. He might be a help to you. But first take a couple of days. I'll talk to him, tell him we're in contact, and I can arrange a meeting for you—maybe three of four days from now after you re-hab yourself. You don't look too healthy...cleaner, but a tad unhealthy. You can stay here for a few days. We'll pick up your stuff from the hotel; you could change your forwarding address to my place. In the meantime, you can sit for Robbie while I work, drop him off at daycare and pick him up afterward, take a walk in the park and just chill out. Ray, I'm thinking you don't really have another choice. Get yourself together. Here are the house rules: no drinking; no sex.

Thoughts of Alexis and Wentworth and company pounded through his brain— 'get yourself together' was about as compassionate and effective as Robert Yearling, his Wentworth case manager, telling him that he has to cope with his loss and move on. His life was gutted. No drinking...yeah, okay. I've already had my experience. No sex. No problem there, Alexis is ever present on his mind and sex would be dishonorable to her memory.

Robbie said, "Hungry," a statement, not a question.

"Okay, Robbie. I'm bringing dinner pretty soon."

And to Ray, "There's a restaurant in this complex, it has carry-outs and they're good. You have any preference for dinner....?

Ray shook his head no.

"Then, I'll surprise you. She smiled and said, "Robbie likes Chicken McNuggets and French fries. Be right back." And she was gone.

Ray said to Robbie, "You really like Chicken McNuggets?"

Robbie nodded yes.

"Hmmm…well, I guess I like them too."

They built with the Duplos until Lisa got back.

Chapter 68

It was payday for the grunts, the guys that loaded, unloaded, transported, stacked, unstacked and sweated discovery by the cops. Most of them had already been in the slammer several times but there was no social stigma among them attached to that kind of annoyance. What discovery did mean to them, and what hurt, was the inconvenience of jail time and the interruption of the money flow. Money for the dopers meant money for the grunts. It was a never-ending cycle. Money changing hands up and down the ladder. But the grunts would never see the long green being passed amongst the dopers, to the politicians, or to the cops. They could not even conceive of how that was done, their only concern was for their pay. They would only see the "short green" handed out to them on a payday. But that was welcome and worth the chance they took. Some just kept the money, others shared. It let them live, and often spelled the difference of being dirt poor and just poor for the families they left behind in whatever south-of-the-border crap city, town or village they came from. Outwardly, they knew it was illegal. Inwardly they saw nothing wrong with what they did. After all it was money, and wasn't that what the American idea of entrepreneurship and capitalism was all about? The inconvenience of the law never overrode their focus on the money. Neither they nor the dealers focused on American idealism. It was always as it ever has been—just the money.

Sardi, as usual, contacted the investors and advised them of the meeting place where they would discuss their next "project." This time, it was not in the usual restaurant setting where they settled business speaking in cautious, guarded sentences of how much, when, and were they in or out. Easy enough to understand. This time, it was in an old warehouse not open to the public. Overall grey, large, hollow sounding. It was lit by several unshaded lightbulbs hanging on ten-foot wires. No need for hushed tones there. But it was creepy and the tone of their voices were naturally subdued. None of them liked it, especially Sardi who felt a creeping apprehension from the time Sal told him of the place, and almost dread once its steel door clanged shut behind him. The place, however, was designated by his brother-in-law, Sal, at the behest of his doper boss. This time, Sal would be present. Sardi, although apprehensive, could not refuse.

Sardi, Sanders, and each of the investors looked upon their financing of a "project" as merely as an investment, distant from the trade itself. None chose to acknowledge that they were part of the trade and as culpable as those who actually did the hands-on receipt and distribution of the junk.

The investors went readily to the meetings, eager in fact. This time in particular because the last "shipment" went bust. They lost their money and they were angry. At the meetings, they never disclosed their real names, usually referring to each other by the names each chose for themselves: Mr. Black, Mr. White, Mr. Brown or other colors, and that name was written by themselves on one of those stupid party stickers that they then stuck to their shirts like some idiot party hostess. It was easier to remember colors than Christian names. None wished to know more of the other. Except Sardi, he knew them all. He introduced Sal as Mr. Green, appropriate for the focus of their business.

The unspoken question common to all, after the first and recent fiasco, was exactly how "safe" was their money. Sal, as representative of his boss' enterprise, told them their money was safe.

Sal sat in the chair at a dusty workbench, facing the semi-circle of investors on his left and a line of five grunts on his right. Four other men were in the background, not readily apparent to any of those sitting in front of Sal. They were a group apart, seemingly disinterested in the meeting, sitting and drinking beer. It was payday for the grunts and they were relaxed. They didn't understand much English. They didn't know the purpose of the meeting. All they wanted was their cash and out the door…just like always before without a meeting.

Sal said, "You are wondering exactly how safe your money is." Most of the investors' heads nodded slightly in agreement. "The key is a no brainer. The answer is to keep our transactions secret. No cops, you win. Cops, you lose. Keeping the exchanges secret is paramount. Occasionally, a hot shot cop might stumble onto our business. Sometimes an informer, even in our own organization, might snitch for some bucks. But the price for that, he semi-smiled eerily, is total."

One of the investors, not understanding, looked at him and said, "Total?" Sal just stared at him until realization of what "total" meant made the investor's eyes widen; no further questions.

The grunts were whispering to each other about what they were going to do later on with their money. The voices of the four men in the background were getting a little louder. Occasionally they tossed their empty beer cans which clanked and rolled along the cement floor.

Sal continued, "The last transaction did not go well. You lost. The reason for the loss is that we have uncovered an informer in our business. The cops were tipped. We have come to understand insurance as a necessity of doing business. In the interest of continued business, we are going to give you a demonstration of security."

"Jose, come here." He motioned for Jose to come forward. No misunderstanding there.

Sal got up, and motioned for Jose to sit." He did. Suddenly, the meeting took on a threatening tone. The grunts all took a deep breath as did the investors, Sardi, and Sanders.

Reuben the Cuban and another man stepped out of the beer can tossing group in the shadows. Reuben's partner had a shotgun. Reuben explained in Spanish that a traitor was within their group—an informer. The grunts didn't take time to look at each other, they all shot a glance at the door and began to stand. Reuben's companion racked his shotgun. The threat was immediately understood. Their eyes returned to Jose as they sat back into their chairs.

Sanders, and the one of the investors stood and began a weakly voiced protest, but quieted down when the man with the shotgun commanded them to "sit down and shut the fuck up." Three other men, one armed with a shotgun, stepped into the light. Everyone froze, no one said anything…except for Jose. He knew what was going to happen. He was shaking and blubbering in Spanish, begging for help.

Reuben, in Spanish, pointed him out as an informer and asked the grunts if they knew what happened to informers. No one said anything. Didn't have to. Death was near.

Two guys grabbed Jose and began to rope him to the chair. He struggled and was struck on the side of the head with the butt of a shotgun. He struggled all the harder. One guy grabbed his throat in a strangle hold and that settled him down. His tie-down was completed. Not only were his arms tied to the arms of the chair, but a rope was looped tightly around his chest and both legs were tied to the legs of the chair.

Reuben sneered and said, "Watch what happens to informers." At that, one of the men grabbed Jose in a headlock and held him steady. Reuben took a hammer and two nails from the workbench behind him. He placed the point of a four-inch nail on top of Jose's head and used a rusty hammer to pound it through Jose's skull and three inches into his brain. Jose was screaming. It wasn't enough to kill Jose, but it was ugly and horrific.

Although the brain doesn't transmit pain, the bone and flesh of his skull did and the sound and feel were terrible. The vibration echoed around and across Jose's head and set him off on a sickening squealing. Reuben then placed a second nail seven inches away from the first and pounded that one in as well. Three strokes.

In the group of grunts sat Diaz, Jose's boyhood friend. They came up from Honduras, through the jungles and desert, endured thieving bandits and hardships. But they made it to the US. They both thought if they could get a job they could send money back home, make a way for their relatives. It was a dream. They found no job. What was available was low paying, back breaking labor and always the threat of arrest. They were illegal…so what. Just words; they were human. They needed to live. When they wandered into the Latino neighborhoods, it didn't take long for them to see where money was to be made. If they worked a little in the drug trade, saved their money, they could get free and live the life they wanted. Diaz, however, didn't want to work for wages. He wanted money now. When he was arrested the first time and the cop suggested he could make a fast buck by telling him when the drugs were moved and where. He agreed. His big mistake. But after the drug bust went down and after his release, he returned a week later as the cop told him and he received a thousand dollars.

Now his friend Jose was about to be killed. He knew that Jose was not the informer. It was he, himself, who was the traitor. Now his friend was in the chair was going to be murdered. But as he watched, he knew that if he stood up and said, "NO! Not Jose. I told the cops. It was me…." he knew that he and Jose would trade places in a heartbeat. So, he sat there, cringing and sorry to the center of his soul and without the courage to speak up.

Jose looked up into the face of his fellow grunts. He was innocent and they were going to kill him. He had no idea that Diaz was responsible. He took a last look at Diaz as if to say good-bye my friend, and closed his eyes; and stopped screaming.

All of the men stood in shock, transfixed by the horror before them. The two other men with shotguns ordered them to sit down. They obeyed. Reuben reached over to the bench and pulled an extension cord from the counter. Its end plug had been cut off and the wiring had been peeled and stripped to expose two, four-inch ends of bare copper wire. Reuben wrapped the copper wire around the nails that protruded from Jose's head. He looked out at the gathered men, smiled, and plugged the extension cord into a bench socket.

Unlike an electric chair, the jolt of electricity went from nail to nail instead of head to ankle. The effect of the shorter distance was as immediate, but uglier and horrifying.

It was almost as if an explosion occurred in Jose's head. Instantly, Jose's eyes bulged outward, one left its socket and lay on his cheek, but flopped backward when his head snapped back. A convulsive shaking tore through his body and his feet clattered on the concrete floor. Blood came from his nose and his tongue jutted out. Jose's head quivered upon his neck a few seconds even after the circuit breaker clicked off. But it didn't matter.

Reuben didn't have to tell Sardi and the investors to leave. They were on their way before Jose quit quivering.

Reuben told the grunts in Spanish that the demo was over, and they should remember it well. "Get your money and get out." One of Reuben's men moved amongst the grunts and passed out cash. Diaz was the last one to be paid. He fisted the money and turned quickly so no one could see his tears.

After everyone was gone, Reuben told Carlos "pull the nails out of Jose's head, get him out of the chair and roll him in a carpet. Then shoot him in the chest a couple of times through the carpet roll and drag the roll over to that far wall." Reuben was the boss of the enforcers because he could think better than most. And he was thinking: *It'll confuse the cops' forensics and make it an arguable problem if for some reason this should ever become a court case. But that'll probably never happen because this warehouse isn't used too much. The body won't be found for a long time. It'll rot in a couple of months, especially when August rolls around, and there won't be much left to discover after the rats get to him.* This, to him, was very funny and he laughed until he almost choked.

Chapter 69

Ray entered the gym by the side door and made his way to the manager's office. Vinnie was sitting in an old, beat up leather swivel chair at the desk reading *Ring* magazine.

"Aaah, Vinnie!"

Vinnie spun around at the sound of Ray's voice and stood to give him a bear hug.

"Good. So good that you're here."

"Lisa said you might want to see me."

"Yeah, let's go into the office—it's more private and we can talk without interruption."

They went to the back of the gym to a dimly lit small room, quiet and perfect for critiquing young boxers out of earshot of others. They settled into a couple of comfortable chairs and began:

"Ray, I remember your Lisa from the first time you came to the gym as though it were yesterday. Now, I only know Lisa as my accountant. I asked her about you, and she told me that you two were no longer together. I was sorry to hear that because I thought you two made a good pair. Anyway, she said she would find you and connect us. I'm grateful for that."

"Yeah, a lot of things happened since then. I don't know how much you know about Lisa and me. I was crazy in love with her and believed she felt the same about me. Then, for some reason just before graduation, she grew distant and our calls became fewer and fewer. After I graduated, she dropped from sight altogether. I learned through a friend of hers that she got married. I was stunned. Couldn't understand it. Still don't, but now that's no more than a distant memory. Probably a good thing she left me though, because later I met a wonderful woman and got married."

Vinnie gave out with a big smile, "Ah, good for you. Is she pretty? Can she cook? Like kids?"

"Oh, Vinnie," Ray felt himself choking up, but fought it with a deep breath and a swallow. He said softly, avoiding Vinnie's eyes, "Yeah, all those things…but she died a few months ago." Vinnie instinctively felt Ray's sorrow. He paused slightly and put his hand on Ray's shoulder. And said, "I'm so sorry," There was nothing more to be said.

"So here's the whole story." Ray shrugged his shoulders, took a deep breath, and continued. "After that I got crazy. Started drinking. Couldn't concentrate on anything, and screwed up most everything I touched. One night, drunk and playing blackjack at the Greektown Casino, I sat next to an obnoxious player. He kept making stupid recommendations, telling me how to play and what to play. We had a couple of words, and I lost it. I punched him twice and he went down, hitting his head on a table. He sued me and that didn't sit well with the company. Lawyers are supposed to be above such things. I had already screwed up at the office once, and this was the second time and decidedly more public. So, this time, a far more serious offence, means that I am going before a board and will in all likelihood be disbarred."

"I can't tell you how truly sorry I am to hear that. Don't know what that means in terms of your employment. So, how long before you're back in the courtrooms."

"I'm afraid it's going to be a long time. If I'm disbarred it'll take years."

"So, how are you going to make a living?"

"Don't know. I'm broke. I need a job. I don't even have a place to stay. I literally have nothing except a change of clothes and some personal items. At present, I'm staying with Lisa. She's helping me. I don't know how long she will be willing to do that. There's no romance left between us. She's just helping an old friend. Vinnie, what'd'ya think, can I get a job at the Sardi Construction Company?"

He hoped to bring a lighter tone to their conversation which on his part was so melancholy.

Vinnie laughed. "Funny you should ask. I'm sure I can find you work there, but that's not for you. I sold the company. I'm now a paid consultant for another couple of months until the new guy can better understand contracts and learn a few ways to cut corners and maximize profits.

I'm in a new business now, and it's the reason I wanted to talk to you. I need someone that I can trust. When I go down the list of my acquaintances and associates, I can't find anyone I'm willing to trust with a large amount of money. I don't have a friends list. I need a new face in the business that no one recognizes. I need a partner who can keep a poker face and project an image of being tough. It's necessary to play the role of a tough guy. I think you have those qualities. The only associate I have that does know you is Sanders…and he will certainly keep his mouth shut about that.

You say you are facing a decision which will prohibit you from practicing law for a couple of years. Simple enough: no job, no money. You need a new start. You're wounded and don't know where to turn. You need a bundle now. I know if you score big bucks, you can make it—you're plenty smart enough."

"I used to think I was smart—not any longer. But yeah, I need a springboard; a bundle of cash would put me back in the game. I don't know exactly how, but I would find something. Maybe I could afford a business of some sort…make payments…I don't know."

"Well, that's up to you. I actually don't need this deal…I have enough money. Sanders does too. But this is easy money, and I just can't pass it up. When I finish this deal, I'm leaving town. Sanders has sold his business and this is his last deal as well. After that, he's headed for Canada—did he ever tell you that he has a dual citizenship? Well, that doesn't matter, he's smart enough to make it on his own."

"But what about Sanders' lawsuit against the city?"

"Screw it. At the time his business was in jeopardy he needed money. We've done so well lately, money is no longer his concern, neither is his business. Let the city go to hell. Sanders doesn't care anymore."

"So, what do I have to do, murder someone?"

"No, nothing as extreme as that. But I want you to know it's particularly high profit, and not without personal danger. How long have we known each other? Ten, fifteen years...maybe more. I trust you as if you were my own son. You know that I cut corners, have always cut corners...complete honesty in business is not my strong suit. There is money to be made if you are bold, observant, and an entrepreneur. You have to have an ability to gather like-minded people around you to bring about deals and finesse their conclusions. I'm going to make one more business deal and then I quit. If you want, you can share my deal.

Ray listened intently. Vinnie was nibbling around the edges of something he wanted to tell him, but wasn't sure how Ray would take it. He was being cautious.

Finally, "Okay, Vinnie...what is it? What are you trying to interest me in? How dangerous is it? Is it illegal?

"Please don't dislike me for what I do. Is it illegal you ask? Yes, very. Is the money good? Yes, very. Dangerous? Yes, very...but manageable to a degree."

"What exactly is this business?"

"It's an insurance business."

"Insurance is kind of cut and dried. It doesn't fit any of those things. What are you leaving out?"

"Yeah...you're right. But this is a special kind of insurance."

Ray's face wore a quizzical expression, but he swallowed his questions.

"My partners and I have in the last two years made about six million dollars each and lost two million each. Not too bad, eh?"

"Okay, you're four million ahead; you've got my interest. What is the business?"

Vinnie explained to him what they do and how it works. Ray was stunned and extremely reluctant to jump into such a racket. But Sardi persisted, and explaining that the system has worked eighteen times.

"We started with a little. The last couple of deals have been in the millions range. As a result of our working together, we have developed a business relationship. Sure, when a million or more dollars from our side is lost, my partners all grumble. But they come back because their wins are always more than their losses. The dopers love it because their initial costs are covered. My partners love it because the deliveries are usually successful. Occasionally there is a tip-off and they lose. That's the risk end of the business. Overall, very successful."

"Gee, Vinnie, I just don't know. Sounds too risky."

"Ray, this is the last go around. It's going to be a little different though."

"How different, what do you mean?"

"Well, the risk will be absolutely minimal."

"Why do you say that?"

"Recall when I said that the dopers and my partners babysit the money until we receive a call. At that time, either the dopers leave with the cash, or we leave with it."

"Yeah, and—"

"Well, this time it'll be different because we are going to fake a delivery. There will be no dopers or narcotics involved. Sanders and myself will front the cash for our share, and your share, and all five associates will bring their bags of cash—I'm thinking 500K each—and in time they will be given the bad news. They will leave, and you, representing the dopers, will take charge of the cash. Later you, me, and Sanders will divide the money and disappear. The partners will never question the transaction. I have already prepped them about a future, even greater deal. They're hungry. And, besides, this isn't their only business. They make a lot on their own enterprises. A million dollars to them is attractive, but not enough of a loss to dissuade them from a second bet given their record of successes.

Ray, racked his brain. He believed he was about to be drummed out of the legal profession; he had no other skills. He was without a plan. He was without money and no hope of being hired into anything resembling a profession. Legal consultant—forbidden. Sales? No, never, no matter how desperate. Real estate? Same thing. Banking? Not with his record. Legal researcher for another lawyer? No money in that. But he had never done anything illegal in his life. How could he go to the dark side, even for Sardi…his life had always been in defense of the right and just, except for a few bad guys who deserved punishment, but legally were entitled to a vigorous defense. So, had he knowingly defended the guilty? Yes, but he hated it. But wasn't that almost like doing something illegal? No, because as a lawyer he was obligated to mount the best defense he could for clients like that. Would he defend a murderer knowing that, in fact, the person had committed the murder? Yes, he would have to. What was the moral sense of that? All of the noble tenets represented by law, became confused when he began considering different viewpoints.

Maybe he could do this thing, one time, one big score, and he'd never do it again. The scheme had merit. As opposed as he was, it seemed to be the solution to his present mess. Like Lisa said, he was in the toilet and he didn't have much of a choice. There were more reasons to do it, than to not do it. He consented by a nod to Vinnie followed by a deep breath and exhalation.

Iacta alea est! The die was cast.

Vinnie had not been totally honest with Ray when it came to the dangers of their business. In the beginning, it was only a couple of thousand dollars transactions. Both sides were a little nervous. But now, having been through many transactions, they were more comfortable with each other, more trusting, and came to view the deals as business as usual. The value of the shipments escalated. Now, they were dealing in millions. Vinnie wondered how long it would be before the dopers decided they were done with the insurance business and would simply rob Vinnie and his partners. Why not? There were millions on the table. If it occurred to him, why not them? If the robbery became a shooting affair, then death was likely. The dopers probably had them outgunned. But Vinny wasn't sure of his partners. Suppose it became a shootout. Not good!

The more he thought about it, the more he wanted out. What good was money if you end up dead? He had enough money to last a lifetime, why push it? Easy money, though, had always been attractive to him. So, he thought heavily. Could we pull off a robbery, without risk, and rob them before they rob us…but how without a confrontation? And, then the epiphany. Vinnie smiled at the thought as the way to do it occurred to him.

And that's when he began thinking about Ray. They could do each other a favor. And, yes, it could be done.

Chapter 70

Sanders and Sardi moved their baggage into their MGM Grand, 8th floor Executive Corner Suite in the early afternoon. They threw their cash filled gym bags on the couch, checked the adjoining room, and set their computer and the two bill counters on the coffee table. Their bags contained 500 K each.

The bill counters were the latest in hi-tech mixed bill discriminators whose hoppers could handle 500 mixed denomination bills at a time, and count them at a top speed of 1,500 bills per minute. The machines each had a UV/Magnetic counterfeit currency detector and would spit bogus bills out into a separate bin. The legitimate bills would be separated into their respective denominations and a tally of the total worth was streamed to a computer whose monitor maintained a split screen. Two counters; two tallies in real time. Each finished stack would be rubber banded. When 500 thousand was counted, the banded bundles would be tossed back into the investor's gym bag and sealed, and the investor would identify it with his mark.

This is not to say that the investors were dishonest and could be a little light in their count, tempting as it was, but it was a means of ensuring to each other that each had an equal risk, and an equal right to their portion of profit. All knew that if the count was light, the dopers would be furious and they would not want to experience their retaliation. However, if the reverse occurred, they had no recourse, but to take the hit. Not fair, but it was a risk inherent in their illicit business that they were willing to take.

Each of the investors was advised that their monies would be re-counted and accuracy was paramount. All agreed and the monies were pre-counted. The investors wanted to be present when the counting was done… just to be sure that those doing the counting were as honest as they were.

If the bills were all new 100s, then a million dollars would take about 17 minutes. But it wasn't that easy. The monies were usually mixed, mostly 100s and 50s, and a lot of 20s. Tens and fives were not allowed. The real pain was when bills were crumpled or folded, or had tape on them. These had to be straightened out before they could be put in the hopper. That took time.

If you can count at the highest speed of 1,500 bills per minute and you had ten thousand one hundred bills it would take a little less than seven minutes to count a million. But because the bills are old, a lesser speed is sensible. And, because they are of mixed denominations, and only 500 thousand is being counted, it might take close to twenty minutes per bag. That's why Sardi and Sanders agreed on using two bill counters.

At two o'clock Sanders, Sardi, and four investors met and sat at a MGM Grand lobby table. There was little conversation, just spurts and sudden starts which trickled off into diminishing responses. Every deal made everyone sweat a little more than usual. Fifteen minutes later Ray joined them wheeling a large duffle bag on a clothing rack. Sardi told the men that Ray represented the other half of the business.

One of the investors looked at Ray and questioned, "What, only one guy?"

Ray leaned forward, putting his face close to the guy, giving him a sharp, menacing look and said in a rough voice, "That's all we need." And that was that. No more questions. Their kind of business didn't require congeniality.

Each had a two-drink maximum—that was all that was allowed; that was the rule. After the first drink, Sardi and Sanders brought two of the investors upstairs and cranked up the counting machines. They ran their own cash through the machines to show the investors their matching cash. Then, Sanders and Sardi ran the investor's cash through the machines. The cash was quickly counted, banded and tossed back into their gym bags which were thrown in a corner next to Sardi's and Sander's bags.

One of the guys snapped on the tv and a kids' cooking show appeared.

Within seconds, "Get that shit off there...ain't they some sports program on there." And that prompted a channel search which eventually produced a football game.

"Ah, better, much better," said the guy with the "clicker" as he settled back in a chair.

There was a bumping sound at the door. Everyone froze...Sardi answered the knock. A voice said, "Ray." The door was opened and Ray horsed the clothing rack with a duffle bag on top through the doorway.

Ray glanced at the counting machines and said loud enough for everyone to hear, "Hmm, those are the same kind of counters we have. They're accurate. It's all here," he said, and leaned the duffle bag on the couch and raked out a pile of money. Three quarters of the bag was stuffed with newspaper, only the top portion was loaded with a half million of Sardi and Sander's money. When it spilled out, it was easy to assume that the bag was filled with money, and it was at least four times the size of the investor's gym bags which lent to the illusion.

The men were startled by another knock at the door. Ray quickly stuffed the money back into the duffle bag and threw it on top of the other gym bags.

"Yes?" Sardi said.

The familiar voices of the other two investors answered. "Getting kind of quiet down there, and we finished our second drink. Thought we'd come up and join the crew. I'd like to get this over, one way or another." And it was seconded by the other investor.

The business by now was so casual that a pile of money on the floor caused little anxiety. Everyone had done this deal before. Several times, to the point that they were so relaxed that the first two investors were fixated on the football game after they saw who was at the door.

The money from the last of the two investors was counted. Their bags had a lot more 20's than 50's and hundreds. Sardi took a break from his counting machine and joined the football watchers. This made the counting by Sanders take a little longer. The last two men watched the money counting machines run through the bills, but were distracted by the football game. Eventually, they left the table and stood in the doorway, watching the game. The counting of Ray's money drifted into the background shouting of a couple of back to back touchdowns and successful kicks for extra points. Ray's money was not counted and his bag joined the two latecomers' bags and tossed on top of all the other bags.

The room Sanders rented was a luxury King accommodation, nice, spacious. In the corner of the room were six gym bags and a large duffle bag. Collectively, six million dollars. Six million dollars sat nearby yet none of the men spoke or commented on the cash. The small talk amongst the investors centered on cars, hot vacations spots, and the football game. They had done this several times before; neither friends nor foes, just tough street businessmen. Each despite their familiarity with one another, knew this was the time of sweat and possible treachery. If something could go wrong, it would go wrong. Sardi and Sanders didn't carry guns, but didn't know if any of the investors did. In less than a minute any of them could be dead. On the other hand, their business was beneficial to both sides and each had an interest in keeping the arrangement. Trust was imperative, although even having been through several deals in their criminal enterprise they were still apprehensive. The small talk tended to bridge their fears. However, the amount of money present was always tempting. Sardi and Sanders and their investors assumed the doper faction had guns. Any armed robbery would probably result in a shootout. But shootouts usually never go as planned. That thought tended to stifle any innovative, independent thinking. Bodies and police were not anything the investors wanted and they felt confident that it was the same for the other side. Sardi and Sanders, and the investors, were present in the warehouse when one of the doper helpers was murdered. Retribution was ugly.

What they were waiting for was the signal—a call or no call—that decided which team would leave with all of the bags. The rule was that Sardi would be called by his driver by 9 o'clock to say that the delivery went as planned. If no call, then the delivery had failed and the men were either dead or in jail. The same call of success or lack thereof would soon be apparent by all. …the thumbs up as to who got the money…or no call, signifying the total loss of their investments.

Nine o'clock came and went; as did 10 and 10:30. No calls. The silence was not well received. The cursing began around 9:10, and each investor added additional cursing of exasperation as time ticked by. All successful delivery calls had always been on time. That was the rule. So, when the calls didn't come, they became a bit edgy. They stayed hoping that there was some unusual occurrence—a flat tire, an accident—something that would account for a missed 9 o'clock call other than a police raid. But there was none.

At 10:30. Ray dialed his own cell number. After a brief pause, he spoke into the phone loud enough for everyone to hear: "Yeah, I know. Send Reuben and another to help load the "stuff". It was a line Sardi scripted for Ray.

At the name Reuben, the investors all had a flash picture of Reuben plugging Jose into the electrical outlet. They wanted no part of him and were ready to leave.

To all appearances, this time, Sardi, Sanders, and their co-investors lost. The shipment had been busted. Each had sweat rings under their armpits. They were angry and grumbling. But they also knew that was the price. Bet 100%, win 100%. This time, lose 100%. But what eased their pain slightly was that they all knew that the money they lost came originally from past successful dope deals.

The men still bitched audibly. They were pissed, but resigned. One of them, out of the blue, said, "Remember the warehouse? I'd hate to be the guy that ratted them out and gets caught." The warehouse murder was vivid in their minds. Better to shut up and leave. At that, the men said nothing more. Sardi and Sanders piled the now covered money counters, computer, and monitor on Ray's clothes rack and following the others, bumped it over the threshold and out into the hallway. No one was likely to say anything to anyone regarding their loss or having been involved in any money deal. A solemn bunch of sweaty guys got on the elevator with a luggage rack loaded only with equipment and down they went. Sardi and Sanders both were glad that none of the investors asked them why they didn't sweat.

They left the investor's gym bags with Ray.

Ray opened the door to the adjoining room, moved the money into it, and locked the door. He was amazed at how well the scheme worked. He was to stay with the money until Sardi and Sanders came back in the morning. The bags had money in them, but those bags also held his future.

The valet brought Sander's car out and loaded their equipment. Sardi got into the passenger's seat; it was Sanders' turn to drive. This was the last time they would be doing this. They congratulated themselves on a clean and final goodbye to the insurance business. Sardi asked, "Do you feel bad about the investors' loss?" Sanders pursed his lips and blew through them: "phhattt!"

"Well said, Charlie, well said!"

Chapter 71

Ray's cell phone rang at 7. It was Sardi, "Me and Sanders are coming up." Minutes later, Ray checked through the peep hole and admitted Sardi and Sanders, carrying four large suitcases. As soon as the door shut, they clapped Ray on his shoulders, grinned, and laughed. "We did it! We did it!" and both, in a final, "You did it!"

"Never knew what hit them," Sanders said, followed by Sardi's "Piece of cake." "Yeah," Ray said, "well, I was sweating plenty. I couldn't guess as to what they would do. No one rolls over that easy."

"They've done enough big dollar deals; they're used to it. No one likes to lose, but if there's another chance to make it back and more, they're all for it. The trick is that we win more often than we lose. "They never complained before and it'll be the same this time. Let's get to the business at hand. I want to be safely gone as soon as possible."

"Ray, we're going to stuff the duffle bag you carried with a third of a million—which is your cut; close enough except for a couple hundred dollars...look at it like you're buying us a very good lunch. The rest of the bags will be going with us. Charles and I will split it later. You can keep the duffle bag, or you can stuff the cash in a couple of these suitcases. I would suggest that you do that—you'll look more like a tourist leaving the hotel. After we leave, neither of us will be seeing each other again."

Ray sucked in a breath. Vinnie was like a father to him. He recalled when his father left and never came back. He understood on a practical level because of the business, but not to see Vinnie again...that hurt.

"What do you mean...ever again?"

"Sorry, but it's got to be that way. We need a clean break from the business. If, for example, some RICO or Narcotics investigative bureau grabs ahold of our dopers, contrives a case, and squeezes them, I'm sure our insurance business will come up. The only connection they will make is between me and my so-called brother-in-law Sal. He knows me, but no one else in our organization. And, to tell the truth, he's not even my brother-in-law, we just called each other that in the beginning and it stuck…he was the first Italian I met here in America. He was fresh off the boat like me and we were like brothers from then on—the in-law part was kind of joke—making it like a legal bond. We stuck together and helped each other since. He saw his opportunity with the dopers, I saw mine in the construction business. We stayed in touch.

We don't need legal problems—especially tax inquiries. So, it's best that we go our separate ways.

In a year or two, I'll learn how the dopers are doing. If they're not bobbing and weaving in a dance with the law, I'll get in touch with you. Until then, we gotta say goodbye.

Ray split the money and filled up two suitcases. He shook hands with Sanders and Vinnie and wished them luck. He faced Vinnie and nodded to him. Thank you for the help and your faith in me. Sorry I wasn't the boxer you wanted. He hugged Vinnie and was hugged back just as earnestly. Each fought back a tear.

Ray carried the suitcases down to the garage, and tipped the valet $5 for bringing up his car. He declined the valet's help in loading the suitcases

Chapter 72

Lisa grabbed the phone on the third ring, "Lisa? Ray."

"You missed dinner."

"Yeah, I know. But I was working with Sardi and didn't know how long it'd take and I couldn't make a call."

"Okay with me, but Robbie missed you. I figured that you and Sardi had some business going and that never runs on a schedule. So, I told Robbie you were at work, and it was me and Robbie for dinner—we're used to it.

"I can tell you that Sardi, and his friend Sanders, are making a bundle. My guess is that it's illegal, but it seems to be working so far. They've been at it for a more than a year. He likes you like a son. If he smiles on you, you'll have a chance to climb out of your hole. He seems to be doing great—let me know his secret."

"You're kidding, right?"

"Yeah. I wouldn't expect him to share. Just kidding. On the other hand, my life is pretty much above board. I don't need any legal complications…and neither do you. Please be careful and don't get sucked into something you can't control."

Yep, good words. I hope you never find out.

"When will you be here?"

"Probably tomorrow, mid-morning."

"Where are you?"

"The MGM casino."

"Isn't that where you got in trouble? No, that was at the Greektown Casino."

"Yeah, but I'm not gambling or drinking."

"So, lemme see, you're at the MGM, not drinking or gambling, and you're going to spend the night. That doesn't leave much—you got lucky?"

She was met with an uncomfortably stony silence."

"In a flash, Lisa remembered that Ray's wife recently died. "Oh, I'm sorry. I was just being a smartass. I am truly sorry for saying that."

After a long pause, Ray said, "No, nothing like that. It's just an… uh, an investor's conference and not everyone can be here tonight. So, I gotta wait until the morning and go over it all again."

"Since when have you become an investment consultant…or whatever you are doing? The "uh" part of what you just said doesn't convince me."

"Well, Sardi had an opening for me on his investment team and I said yes. It's not going to be long term, but it pays well. What I'm doing is more legal advice rather than financial. Everything is going to be all right."

Lisa let out a long breath. "That's good." But she still wasn't convinced that everything Ray told her was truthful. Her radar was up and running. And, mannerisms are something that Lisa excelled at, both affecting and detecting.

"Well," she said, "tomorrow is Saturday and there isn't any child care drop off so we'll be here throughout the morning. If you're going to be later, call. I need to make plans. We have a lot to talk about."

"Yeah, that's for sure—both of us."

Chapter 73

Ray pulled into the parking spot behind Lisa's condo, grabbed his suitcases and lugged them to her door. The doorbell chimed and Lisa appeared.

She looked at him and the suitcases and asked, "You're leaving?"

Ray didn't anticipate Lisa's reaction. But quick as a flash, he said, "No. Sardi is, and he didn't want people to know, so he asked if I'd take his suitcases for him until he was on his way to the airport."

Sounds plausible. Good going. Let's see... you just helped rob four people of two million dollars, and now you're lying through your teeth. Your morality is degrading by the hour. What's next?

"Well, I'm glad to hear you'll be staying for a while. Come on in."

"Hi, Robbie." He smiled at Robbie. The boy looked at him, came forward, and hugged his knees.

"Wow, that's a greeting I didn't expect." He dropped the suitcases and picked the boy up.

"Play?" Robbie asked.

"Uh, no, not right now, but maybe after dinner. I've got to talk to your mother now" Robbie understood that meant "play later" and busied himself with his Duplos.

Lisa poured herself and Ray a coffee.

"Everything okay with you?"

"Yeah. Most excellent."

"So the investors are comfortable with your information?

"Yes. I did a good job...Sardi gave me 500 dollars."

"A good sum for a couple hours of work."

"Yeah, being a lawyer has its advantages. You mentioned that we had some things to talk about?"

"Yeah, and so did you. You first."

"Please, you first or would you rather leave serious conversations to later this evening?"

"Nope, right now is as good a time as any."

"Okay…where to start?" Lisa said. "When I brought you here, I told you that I was glad that you will be staying for a few days. And, that's the truth, but I may not be. I met a man a couple of weeks ago and we've been in touch ever since."

"Romance?"

"Nope. Business. He owns a large accounting corporation. And, at this point in his life, it's maybe more than he'd wants to do. He likes what I do, has examined my books, and has offered me a position—not as an accountant, but as a partner with an option to increase my standing within the corporation if it all works out. I'm going to take the chance. I think he's thinking of retiring. I'm selling my business to the two ladies that work for me. I'll be leaving in a couple of weeks.

This place, this condo, is paid for by my ex-mother-in-law. She pays the yearly lease without question. It's paid up for the next eleven months. She never calls in fact, the further she can stay away from me, and me from her, the better—a mutual agreemen. So, you can stay here for about a year and probably longer.

"Okay, you're turn."

"Well, I'm working for Sardi and it's lucrative. I think my money worries will be over for a long time. As far as being a lawyer goes, It may be possible if I am disbarred in Michigan, I can retest in another state and resume lawyering. It'll take a while, so I'm very thankful of your kind offer."

"Well, that's good news. Here's a big one—especially for you. You know the boy's name, right?"

"Right. Robbie."

"Well, you don't know his full name. The guy I married is named Robert Lawrence. It's usual, probably a male convention, that the newborn's first name is that of his father."

"Yeah, I suppose so."

"Well, Robbie's full name is Robert Raymond Lawrence."

Ray looked puzzled. "And?"

"I wanted the name Raymond as part of his because you are his father and I couldn't tell Robert, so I did the next best thing...I also named him after you."

Ray drew a deep breath and slumped back into his chair, some of his coffee sloshed from his cup and onto the table.

"The boy is mine?"

"Yep, you're his daddy."

Ray set his coffee cup onto the saucer because his hand was trembling slightly.

"You're not joking? He's mine?"

"Yes, there's no mistake about it. The Lawrence's ran a DNA test and they knew he wasn't Robert's. And you are the only other guy I fooled around with." She might have added Mike, but that wouldn't serve any purpose. Ray, she knew, was the father. "And that, and other things, is how we ended up divorced."

Ray's mind whirled with her words.

"And, Ray, you know me from before...I'm kind of a me-first person. That's just the way I am. I tried to deny it when I was younger, but I'm now resigned to that fact. So, as far as Robbie goes-- I'm not the best of mothers, in fact, I'd rather not be a mother. It takes a lot of personal time and dedication. I'm just not that way—not willing to give up my time. So, here's the deal. You adopt Robbie, I'll sign whatever papers you come up with. My ex won't object, in fact he has no grounds on which to object. The DNA test proved he's not the father; he'll be elated."

That Ray was astounded would be an understatement. *Can I agree? If all this is true, yes, of course I will.*

"Also, the boy's day care is paid for...my ex mother-in-law has also agreed to that. She pays by the semester, automatically; she never checks. So, you're in good shape there. I can't think of anything else you should know. I hope your job with Sardi works out, otherwise you're screwed."

Ray, still astounded by the thought of Robbie being his, couldn't think of a response, he just sat still as his mind drifted in his new status as a father. And, finally, "the job with Sardi, isn't long term. I don't know how long it'll last. The main reason is that Sardi has sold his business and is leaving the country.

"For how long?"

"Probably isn't coming back…the same for Sanders."

"Well, I could have guessed it. I told you I didn't think what they were doing was legal, but it generated a lot of money. So much that both guys had established off shore accounts, Cayman Islands I think, and have been pumping money into their accounts for about two years. It was getting increasing difficult to cover their incomes which were often in or close to the million-dollar range. I've covered their monies with accounting miracles, and am kind of glad they've decided to do this. Not good for my business, because they were a great source of income, but I really don't want to be involved any more than I already have been. Good for them. But if Sardi doesn't come back, how are you going to make a steady paycheck?"

"Like I said, if I'm disbarred, I'll retest…maybe in Ohio and see if I can get back into the lawyering business. Ray pictured his two suitcases and said, "Sardi told me he'd help fund me until I can get started. So, how are you going to live? Is your paycheck going to be enough for you?"

"Well, because I've been living rent free for a couple of years—and the car is a freebie as well—and I don't have to pay day care, or health care for myself or Robbie, I've been able to put away a small fortune Additionally, my ex-mother-in-law also agreed to send me 75K a year until I got on my feet. It seems that I'm now on my feet and that'll soon stop. But the money I saved over the last couple of years, and earned, and the sale of my business will put me well into six figures. And with that and what I'm going to make on my new job, I'll be pretty well off.

"When are you leaving?"

"Probably in a couple of weeks, as soon as the business purchase is completed. I'd like you to know although I'm self-centered, I'd still like to know how Robbie is doing. So, if you don't mind, I'll keep in touch."

"Sure, the adoption paperwork and finalization will be quick enough. Since you're willing, I don't foresee any problems." And then, a long quiet interlude. There was nothing more of great importance to be said or discussed, and no words could fill the void.

Ray put his hands out to her and rested them on her hands. What once was, was no more, but replaced with a kind of friendship. There were no more questions or revelations. And just like that, they hugged for the first time in years; the important discussions were had and finished.

"Dinner?"

"Yep, as soon as I put these suitcases in the bedroom, we're off to McDonald's."

Chapter 74

Ray anxiously checked the mailbox every day. Sufficient time had passed, he thought, and he expected to hear from the Attorney Grievance Commission regarding his case. This afternoon, the letter was delivered. Ray held it in his hand, fearful of its content. He took a deep breath, ripped the end of the envelope off, and shook out the letter which read:

The Law Firm of

Wentworth, Solomon and Hughes

Re: Mr. Raymond Oliver, attorney for Wentworth, S & H: Case #1245612

This letter is to apprise you of the decision of the Michigan Attorney Grievance Commission in regard to the grievance of fiduciary negligence, *i.e. professional misconduct,* filed against your employee, Mr. Ray Oliver, by Mr. Conrad Cooper alleging that Mr. Oliver received twenty-five thousand dollars from Mr. Cooper's mother, Mrs. Alison Cooper, and failed to perform her request of creating a trust for her son (himself), but instead retained the money for his own uses.

1. In light of the suddenness of the death of Mrs. Allison Cooper, and consequent inability to be deposed, Mr. Oliver's long term relationship with the deceased, and the timeliness of the deposited monies, the AGC's investigation concluded there was neither a fiduciary bond clearly established nor evidence of any intention by Mr. Oliver to keep Mrs. Cooper's money.

The money has, in fact, been returned to Mr. Cooper and he has no intention to pursue his complaint.

The allegation of Breach of Trust and implied misappropriation of monies, therefore, has failed.

The Michigan Attorney Grievance Committee is also aware of an additional charge against Mr. Oliver, that being a criminal Assault and Battery filed by Mr. Thomas O. Stephens stemming from a conflict between he and Mr. Oliver that occurred at the Greektown Casino earlier this year.

2. The charges of Assault and Battery against Mr. Oliver filed by Mr. Thomas O. Stephens were later dropped by Mr. Stephens. Because the charges were dismissed, there was no prosecution.

Mr. Oliver's record, therefore, is technically clear of inappropriate behavior. And, strictly within the bounds of definition, therefore, satisfies the board's test of character.

3. However, the legal profession does not take lightly the misconduct, or appearance of misconduct of its members. Although the prosecution did not move forward, the board notes that despite the record, the incident did occur. The AGC cannot condone Mr. Oliver's behavior in the alleged assault of Mr. Stephens and is unwilling to overlook the matter.

It is resolved, therefore, that Mr. Oliver be suspended from the practice of law for a period of ninety days from the date of this letter. If another such incident, or similar, should occur within this period of suspension, he will be cited for contempt and risk losing his license subject to the determination of this body.

Michigan Attorney Grievance Committee,

Case #13640-18

AGC Board members,

Attorneys

Ronald Steffens, Michael Hubbard, and James Kovan

And an attached, second letter, from Wentworth, Solomon and Hughes:

Mr. Raymond Oliver, Attorney

We are delighted that you have been exonerated by the AGC regarding Mr. Cooper's allegations.

Following your suspension, in the second matter, the board has decided after due consideration and deliberation, if you desire, you are most welcome to return to Wentworth and company. You may pick up where you left off. We hope that you will consider this offer favorably.

Sincerely,

The Law Firm of Wentworth, Solomon and Hughes

Attorneys

Robert Yearling

Jerry Silverton

Ray Oliver, in disbelief, read the letter twice. Exonerated! Suspension for ninety days? That's it? Even though the suspension was a slap on the wrist, the implied warning was significant. He would behave! He could do the ninety-day suspension standing on his head. Money worries? No problem there. An offer to return to Wentworth? Would he? Certainly.

A heavy weight was off his shoulders and his mind soared with the possibilities of this newly opened door to his future. Robbie was three. He could finish college by twenty-one, and law school by twenty-three. Meanwhile, if he was still working for Wentworth and Company, he'd be somewhere up the ladder of success and more than likely able to secure an internship for Robbie. On the other hand, he could leave and open his own law offices: Oliver and Oliver. In a short while he would be able to hire a staff of lawyers. About the time Robbie graduated, he could step into the business and fulfill the firm's name, making it truly Oliver and Oliver.

He would even teach Robbie to box.

Maybe he could be a champion.

CPSIA information can be obtained
at www.ICGtesting.com
Printed in the USA
BVHW032307150320
575110BV00001B/1